In a Witch's Wardrobe

"A smashingly fabulous tale."
—*New York Times* bestselling author Victoria Laurie

"Funny and thoughtful, *In a Witch's Wardrobe* is an easy read with an enjoyable heroine and a touch of witchy intuition." —The Mystery Reader

"Another engrossing story by an author with marvelous storytelling skills." —Vibrant Nation

"A really entertaining read.... I look forward to the next installment." —Cozy Crimes

"Juliet's writing is creative and wickedly imaginative."
—Once Upon a Romance

"A wonderful paranormal amateur sleuth tale.... Fans will enjoy Lily's magical mystery tour of San Francisco."
—Genre Go Round Reviews

Hexes and Hemlines

"This exciting urban fantasy murder mystery ... is an entertaining paranormal whodunit.... Her familiar, Oscar, half goblin-gargoyle, becomes a cute potbellied pig who adds jocularity to the fast-paced story line as part of the quirky cast (benign, kind, and evil) that helps make this spellbinding tale a fun read." —Genre Go Round Reviews

"*Hexes and Hemlines* carries you along with an unconventional cast, where nothing is out of bounds. Extraordinarily entertaining." —*Suspense Magazine*

"Blending a mystery with all things paranormal and her customary light humor, this title doesn't disappoint. Strong writing, a solid plot, and a spunky, likable heroine add up to this cleverly written, top-notch cozy mystery."—*Romantic Times*

continued ...

"This is a fun and totally engrossing series that hooks you instantly and makes you want more.... I love the mix of vintage clothes, magic, and a lingering possibility of romance combined with mystery."　　—Fang-tastic Books

"Juliet Blackwell has created a series that will appeal to mystery fans as well as paranormal enthusiasts."
　　—Debbie's Book Bag

A Cast-Off Coven

"If you like your mysteries with a side of spell-casting and demon-vanquishing, you'll enjoy the second title in Blackwell's Witchcraft Mysteries."　　—*Romantic Times*

"This awesome paranormal mystery stars a terrific heroine."　　—Genre Go Round Reviews

Secondhand Spirits

"An excellent blend of mystery, paranormal, and light humor, creating a cozy that is a must read for anyone with an interest in literature with paranormal elements."
　　—The Romance Readers Connection

"It's a fun story, with romance possibilities with a couple of hunky men, terrific vintage clothing, and the enchanting Oscar. But there is so much more to this book. It has serious depth."　　—*The Herald News* (MA)

THE HAUNTED HOME RENOVATION MYSTERIES

Dead Bolt

"Juliet Blackwell's writing is like that of a master painter, placing a perfect splash of detail, drama, color, and whimsy in all the right places!"
　　—*New York Times* bestselling author Victoria Laurie

"Cleverly plotted with a terrific sense of the history of the greater Bay Area, Blackwell's series has plenty of ghosts and supernatural happenings to keep readers entertained and off-balance."　　—*Library Journal*

"Smooth, seductive.... Fans will want to see a lot more of the endearing Mel."　　—*Publishers Weekly*

If Walls Could Talk

"A riveting tale with a twisting plot, likeable characters, and an ending that will make you shudder with how easily something small can get totally out of hand ... a good solid read." —The Romance Readers Connection

"Ms. Blackwell's offbeat, humorous book is a fun, light read.... Overall, a terrific blend of suspense and laughter with a dash of the paranormal thrown in make this a great read." —TwoLips Reviews

"Kudos and high fives to Ms. Blackwell for creating a new set of characters for readers to hang around with as well as a new twist on the ghostly paranormal mystery niche." —Once Upon a Romance

THE ART LOVER'S MYSTERIES
BY JULIET BLACKWELL
WRITING AS HAILEY LIND

Brush with Death

"Lind deftly combines a smart and witty sleuth with entertaining characters who are all engaged in a fascinating new adventure." —*Romantic Times*

Shooting Gallery

"If you enjoy Janet Evanovich's Stephanie Plum books, Jonathan Gash's Lovejoy series, or Ian Pears' art history mysteries ... then you will enjoy *Shooting Gallery*." —Gumshoe

"An artfully crafted new mystery series!" —Tim Myers, Agatha Award–nominated author of *Slow-Cooked Murder*

"The art world is murder in this witty and entertaining mystery!" —Cleo Coyle, national bestselling author of *A Brew to a Kill*

Feint of Art

"Annie Kincaid is a wonderful cozy heroine.... It's a rollicking good read." —Mystery Book News

Also by Juliet Blackwell

WITCHCRAFT MYSTERIES
Secondhand Spirits
A Cast-Off Coven
Hexes and Hemlines
In a Witch's Wardrobe

HAUNTED HOME RENOVATION MYSTERIES
If Walls Could Talk
Dead Bolt
Murder on the House

TARNISHED AND TORN

A
Witchcraft
Mystery

Juliet Blackwell

AN OBSIDIAN MYSTERY

OBSIDIAN
Published by the Penguin Group
Penguin Group (USA) Inc., 375 Hudson Street,
New York, New York 10014, USA

USA | Canada | UK | Ireland | Australia | New Zealand | India | South Africa | China

Penguin Books Ltd., Registered Offices: 80 Strand, London WC2R 0RL, England
For more information about the Penguin Group visit penguin.com.

First published by Obsidian, an imprint of New American Library,
a division of Penguin Group (USA) Inc.

First Printing, July 2013

ISBN 978-0-451-24009-5

Printed in the United States of America
10 9 8 7 6 5 4 3 2 1

PUBLISHER'S NOTE
This is a work of fiction. Names, characters, places, and incidents either are the
product of the author's imagination or are used fictitiously, and any resemblance
to actual persons, living or dead, business establishments, events, or locales is
entirely coincidental.
   The publisher does not have any control over and does not assume any respon-
sibility for author or third-party Web sites or their content.

ALWAYS LEARNING   PEARSON

*À Eric
Encore…et toujours*

Acknowledgments

Thanks, as always, to my wonderful editor, Kerry Donovan, and all the other professionals at Penguin who contribute to the editing, copyediting, printing, and art for my beautiful books. . . . I am thankful for all of you. To Kristin Lindstrom for her continuing friendship and support, and to Jim McCarthy for all his wisdom and cheerleading. I don't know how I would survive in this business without you.

My sister Carolyn Lawes has been more than just a supportive source of ideas and edits—she has helped mold my books, scene by scene. You are a true writing partner. Thank you.

To Cathy Romero for her font of knowledge about rural Mexican traditions, and for inspiring Graciela. To Jeremy Reiss for answering my annoying questions about antique jewelry and gemology. To the street fire dancers of Ashland, Oregon, for sharing their beautiful art and a few secrets of their mesmerizing dance! And thanks to Rosa Quinones for her incredible witch's garden.

To the wonderful authors who write with me and inspire me and listen to me complain: Sophie Littlefield, Rachael Herron, Nicole Peeler, Gigi Pandian, Victoria Laurie, Mysti Berry, Adrienne Miller, Cecilia Gray, Lisa Hughey, and LGC Smith. And a special shout-out to Maddee James, whose design sense and smarts are superseded only by her big heart.

To my neighbors and all the members, near and far, of the Mira Vista Social Club—Oaktown *rocks*! Also to J. C. Johnson, Bee Enos, Pamela Groves, Anna Cabrera, Mary Grae, Karen Thompson, Susan Baker, Claudia Escobar, Kendall Moalem, Wanda Klor, Antonio Jimenez, Gomez Gomez, and Bruce Nikolai, all of whom put up with my forgetful writer brain and remind me what friendship is, on a daily basis. And to Muffy Srinavasan and Tim Rood, Jan Strout, Bill Logan, Brian Casey, Shay Demetrius, Suzanne Chan, and the good people of Castillones for helping make my life-in-the-French-countryside fantasy come true!

To my father, who always challenges me and makes me laugh; and to my sister Susan for her ongoing love and support. And thanks to my son, Sergio, for being a constant and wildly interesting inspiration to me, every single day.

And finally, to Oscar. You are welcome in my window anytime, sneezes or no.

Chapter 1

"Let me get this straight: This is a palace ... for cows?" I asked, staring in disbelief at the hulking Cow Palace, which sported a colossal banner that read: GEM FAIRE THIS WEEKEND!

Where I'm from in West Texas, a royal bovine showplace wouldn't have been entirely out of the realm of possibility. Here in the urban outskirts of San Francisco, it seemed rather ... anomalous. In fact, downright preposterous.

"It's not a moo-cow palace," Bronwyn said, adjusting her new-to-her tunic, a rare find from the 1960s. The purple gauze, decorated with rune symbols and pentagrams, matched the violets woven through Bronwyn's frizzy brown hair. "The 'C-O-W' stands for California, Oregon, and Washington. It started out in 1941 as a livestock showcase. They still hold rodeos here sometimes, but they also have concerts and sports events. Anyway, as you'll soon see, the Cow Palace has more in common with an airport hangar than with Versailles."

"And here I had an image of cattle taking tea with the queen," teased our friend and coworker Maya.

"Just wait until we get inside, you cynics. I guarantee you, the Gem Faire will take your breath away," said Bronwyn with a cat-that-swallowed-the-canary grin.

The three of us were standing in a long queue of eager shoppers, waiting for the doors to open. We each had several canvas bags slung over our shoulders in anticipation of acquiring loot for my vintage clothing store, Aunt Cora's Closet. When Bronwyn suggested we close the shop this morning in favor of attending the Gem Faire, I almost balked. After all, my customers had been so good to me — and my store — over the past few months that I hated to disappoint any who might be desperate for vintage clothing this warm, summery Sunday.

But on second thought, I realized, a trade show full of wholesale decorative jewels, stones, and ornaments?

Too tempting to pass up. Way too tempting.

One of many wonderful things about my chosen profession was that I could file "pursuit of objects of beauty and history" under the category of "job-related obligations." And shopping with my closest friends by my side? Even better.

Maya craned her neck to see ahead of us. "I think the doors are opening. All set?"

"Set," Bronwyn confirmed.

"Set for what?" I asked, alarmed. I was unfamiliar with the protocol involved in being a part of such a crowd. Going to concerts, amusement parks, and state fairs had not been a part of my youth.

"Eyes straight ahead, hold on to your purse, and whatever you do, don't trip," Bronwyn said. The Cow Palace's many double doors opened with a series of metallic clangs, and the crowd surged forward.

Carried along by the press of bodies — and smiling at Maya, who was mooing under her breath — we surrendered our tickets, passed through the entryway, and spilled out into the main display area, a gargantuan space undeniably capable of accommodating several herds of cattle. Despite the building's workaday architectural details—massive concrete support beams upheld the domed roof high overhead, crisscrossed by aluminum air ducts and industrial pipes—the structure could indeed have been a royal palace, given the finery on display in the hundreds of booths.

Jiminy Crickets, I thought as I looked around us. A thousand pirates would have had to rob and pillage for centuries to amass such a treasure trove of goodies.

Display boards and folding tables were covered with trays overflowing with sparkling jewels, gleaming pearls, precious stones, glowing amber, fossilized wood, million-year-old ammonites... and then there were the pendants, necklaces, earrings, medallions, rings, anklets, and decorative tchotchkes ranging from bejeweled hairbrushes to tiny curio boxes. Overhead hung massive placards touting everything from investing in antique cameos to the health benefits of copper bracelets. Half a dozen posters solicited the public to INVITE WEALTH INTO YOUR LIFE BY LEARNING TO FIRE DANCE—the scantily clad prima ballerinas shown in the photos were dripping with jewels, coin necklaces, silver and gold chains, and amulets.

"Hey, look," said Maya. "That's the dance troupe I was telling you about. I saw them in Golden Gate Park the other day."

"The what?" Bronwyn shouted over the noise of the crowd.

"Dance troupe!"

"Oh, I though you said 'pants loop.'"

"What's a 'pants loop'?"

"That was my point."

"No, I said 'dance'— Never mind," Maya responded with a smile as she was jostled by a group of young women intent on squeezing in at the front of a table selling discount designer bracelets. "Tell ya later."

All around us was chaos. Glittery, cacophonous bedlam.

"Glad we came?" asked Bronwyn as we started to meander through the aisles of gem-laden tables.

I nodded, dumbstruck.

"I'd say it's worth opening the store a little late on a Sunday," said Maya as she paused to stroke a long strand of polished garnets. The deep wine color of the beads was a perfect match to the ruby highlights in Maya's black locks.

"I wouldn't have missed it for the world," I said a little breathlessly.

I noticed Maya and Bronwyn sharing a smile. Coming here today—playing hooky to go shopping with friends—was an important rite of passage for me. I had never done such a thing, and I was reveling in the experience. The crowd milling around us was mostly female—some appeared to be jewelry makers and wedding planners and artists and dealers like me, but mostly they were shopping just for the fun of it.

"Well, then, we'll have to start doing it more often," Bronwyn murmured. "It's a very important bonding thing. Oooh, look there! Have you ever seen so many pearls?"

We strolled by a dealer with strands of pearls in just about every color imaginable: sky blue, indigo, purple, pink, green, gray. In addition to the rainbow of color possibilities, the oyster-born treasures were offered in myriad different shapes, from the classic gleaming spheres to misshapen, elongated forms that looked like lumpy grains of rice or twisty bits of coral.

The next booth specialized in Venetian glass beads, handmade and swirling with color. Strands of multicolored glass pieces hung from a long fishing line and created the effect of a beaded curtain. The sumptuous glass twinkled beguilingly in the harsh fluorescent lights of the exhibit hall. There were a few dozen finished necklaces and earrings hanging from display racks, but most of the offerings were loose beads in lined baskets.

Maya reached out to caress one piece after another, stroking their slick surfaces, her long fingers rippling the beaded curtain with a pleasant *clickety-clackety* sound.

Although tempted to follow Maya's example, I kept my hands tucked tight into the pockets of my vintage 1960s sundress. The buzzing crowd already felt just a mite overwhelming; I didn't want to add to my overloaded senses by tuning in to an untold number of possible sensations emanating from the jewelry.

Not that I normally picked up much from metal or stone . . . but given my sometimes unpredictable supernatural abilities, it was best to play it safe.

In witchcraft—as in the rest of my life—I'm a misfit. For instance, I'm no good at scrying, or seeing the future in a crystal ball. And when it comes to psychometrics—the ability to feel vibrations from inanimate objects—I am especially out of step. Elemental minerals reflect and hold their owners' energy, so most sensitives are adept at picking up sensations from metal and stone artifacts.

But *I* gather sensations from clothing. The warmth of humanity shows itself to me in the everyday items we wear on our backs. Textiles talk to me. In contrast, metal and stones leave me cold.

"I'm going to go find the vintage stuff," I told Bronwyn and Maya, who were inspecting a series of delicate hand-knotted necklaces made by a woman whose name tag read, appropriately, SAPPHIRE STONE. As for me ... I have a finite supply of shopping energy. I wanted to spend it on items for the store. "How about we meet in an hour? Is there a refreshment stand or food court?"

"Let's check the map," Maya said, studying a brochure that included a map of vendors. Before we left Aunt Cora's Closet this morning she had drawn red circles around a few names. "Okay ... there are a few antique-jewelry dealers in the back right corner, directly in front of the big blue curtain. And the food court's over there, to the side. See you in an hour, then?"

"I'll be there," I said, and headed off.

As I made my way through the venue, I remembered why I generally avoid crowds. The sensations generated by the life forces of so many people together can be overpowering. Outside, in the fresh air, the sensations are dispersed, but in an enclosed space—even a cavernous one like the Cow Palace—I start to feel unnerved, jangly.

Which might have accounted for the annoying, just-out-of-my-grasp conviction that something was wrong. It wasn't anything specific, nothing I could put my finger on; just a vague glimmer, like the here-one-moment, gone-the-next mirage one might encounter on an insufferably long, hot Texas highway.

I pivoted slowly, turning 360 degrees, searching for something out of the ordinary: a practitioner with a pulsing purple-gray aura, for example, or an out-of-control familiar. Or maybe a surprise appearance of Aidan Rhodes, the powerful witch who was self-appointed godfather to the local magical folk.

But all I saw were mothers and daughters enjoying a

day together, sharp-eyed merchants shopping for deals or hawking their wares, artisans and jewelry makers in search of supplies. And mounds of gemstones, trinkets, and baubles decorating every horizontal surface.

Perhaps I was sensing the presence of a practitioner or two in the throng, but that was nothing to worry about. After all, there are many more witches, sorcerers, and psychics walking around than the average person would ever imagine. In such a large crowd as this, it wasn't a stretch to think there might be a handful of powerful folks engaged in nothing more sinister than, say, hunting for the perfect brooch as a birthday present for their mothers-in-law.

Shaking off the vague impressions, I made my way toward the back right corner and stopped to admire a stand featuring jewelry made from antique votive figures called *milagros*. The tiny charms represented body parts: legs, arms, head, heart. Traditionally, the figures were used to pray for health; I had seen chapel walls in Mexico so laden with *milagros*, it was a wonder the aged adobe didn't crumble under the weight. Recently, jewelry makers and artists had discovered the appealing little charms and often incorporated them into their designs. Though tempted, I reminded myself I was in the *vintage* business. The only new items I carried were my own spirit bottles, talismans, and pentacles; I had no intention of turning Aunt Cora's Closet into a spiritual supply store, but I indulged in a tiny witchy sideline.

The next dealer was more up my professional alley: she specialized in Bakelite jewelry. Bakelite is an early form of hard plastic that comes in a rainbow of vivid colors; it is very much in demand by collectors. Plus, the rather bulky, funky design sense of the late '50s and early '60s was hugely popular among Aunt Cora's Closet cli-

entele. This time I let myself give in to temptation. I
spent a good portion of my Gem Faire budget, but
wound up with a satisfying jumble of bangles and earrings tucked into one canvas tote.

Just beyond the Bakelite table I noticed a big sign
that announced GRISELDA'S ANTIQUE JEWELRY AND GEMS.

Behind the horseshoe display counter, I presumed,
stood Griselda. An abundance of frowsy hair had been
dyed an egg-yolk yellow, and hazel eyes were outlined
with dramatic black kohl, like Bronwyn wore. Her bright
teal T-shirt read KISS ME, I'M BAVARIAN, and orange-and-
yellow tie-dyed stretch leggings strained to contain her
voluptuous figure. A pawnshop's worth of gold chains
and tarnished silver medallions hung from her neck,
both wrists were manacled in dozens of broad bracelets
and slim bangles, sparkly rings adorned each finger, and
multiple earrings and cuffs decorated her ears. She was
hard to ignore.

A snippet of an old poem my mother used to repeat
came back to me: *"with rings on her fingers and bells on
her toes, she will have music wherever she goes..."* I
fought the urge to peek behind the counter to see if she
wore anklets and toe rings.

Griselda's brocade-draped tables were loaded with
antique gold lockets, tarnished silver pendants, and
brooches made of bronze and mother of pearl. A large
tray lined with deep purple velvet held dozens of gold
and silver rings, some of which twinkled with semipre-
cious gems and rhinestones.

At the moment the only part of Griselda visible was
the seat of her tie-dyed stretch pants straining across her
backside as she vigorously rooted through a stack of
boxes. Tossing aside crumpled newspapers, she unearthed more decorative items and placed them on the

orange-and-purple paisley tablecloth. She jingled pleas-
antly with each enthusiastic movement.

She glanced up at me, but didn't speak until two teenagers stopped by the display, oohing and aahing over the
fine old pieces. Griselda straightened and gave them a
welcoming, gap-toothed smile.

"This one's a beaut," said Griselda, speaking excellent
English with only a trace of a German accent. She held
up a silver chain with a dented and tarnished but stunning, gem-encrusted silver medallion. "Belonged to a
tavern wench in Madagascar, and it was given to her by
her one true love, a sailor who never returned from the
sea."

The girls seemed rapt, admiring the medallion.

"If you look deep into the blue opal you'll see the
ocean"—Griselda paused dramatically—"and if you believe in true love, you will be able to see flashes of the
lightning from the storm that sent him down to his wa-
tery grave."

The girls giggled and teased each other about what
they saw in the depths of the opal.

"Could I try it on?" asked the younger of the two, a
pretty, petite teenager who looked Latina, with almond
eyes and straight black hair hanging nearly to her waist.

Griselda held the medallion out to her, but the other
teen put out her hand to stop her friend.

"Wait, Marisela. *Don't.* Don't you know opals are bad
luck?" The girl was lovely, exotic-looking, with a glittering nose ring and hair plaited into a multitude of braids.
She had dusky skin, her eyes were a celadon green, and
her hair was the light golden brown of clover honey.

"Seriously?" said Marisela. "I swear, Shawnelle,
you're as bad as my mom with all the superstitions."

"Whatever," Shawnelle replied with a shrug. "But if

your teeth start falling out or your face breaks out with a ton of zits, don't come crying to me."

Marisela hesitated. "Oh, I guess . . . yeah, seems like I've heard something about opals being bad luck before. Never mind."

Griselda snorted loudly, laid the medallion on a silk-covered stand, and—apparently realizing she wasn't going to make the sale—started unpacking more boxes.

"Besides," said the green-eyed Shawnelle as she slipped one ring after another onto her long, slim fingers and held out her hand, admiring each in turn. "We're here on a mission. Remember?"

"Oh, right. 'Scuse me. Do you have any tiaras?" Marisela asked in the general direction of Griselda's backside.

"Tiaras? *Nein*. No tiaras," came the muffled reply. Griselda muttered something about opals and bad luck under her breath.

"Opals aren't necessarily bad luck," I volunteered, unable to contain myself. I'm no gemologist, but opals are a very special kind of stone . . . and I hated it when people misinterpreted old legends. "They're almost alive, and like any living thing they require the proper care and respect."

"Really?" Marisela asked. "You're saying they're, like, *alive*, alive?"

"No way. Stones can't be *alive*; they're minerals," Shawnelle interjected. "My mom told me opals were bad luck unless . . . unless maybe they're your birthstone?"

I started to respond, but the girls' attention was diverted when a buff young man ducked through the massive curtains that separated the staging area behind the booths from the show floor. Tall, large, and extremely fit, he had short blond hair, a prominent nose, and ice blue eyes.

Impressive biceps bulged under the weight of the cardboard boxes he carried in each arm. *"Wo?"*

"Bitte stell'es dorthin." Griselda gestured to a spot on the floor next to the half-unpacked one.

He grunted with the effort of setting his burden down gently.

"Danke, Johannes," she said, and asked him to bring in the rest of the boxes, as it was the last day. My German vocabulary consists of about ten words, but there are enough English cognates that I caught the gist of what they were saying.

The girls fell silent, shy and smiling in the presence of the handsome young man. He nodded in their direction and made a comment in German to Griselda, who waved him off.

"My birthstone's aquamarine," Marisela said, and with a smile in the direction of Johannes she reached out toward the medallion. "But . . . *hey,* Shawnelle, check me out. I'm braving the curse . . ."

"Nein, don't—" said Johannes, reaching out, but a sharp remark from Griselda made him stop abruptly. He ducked back through the parting in the curtains.

Griselda met my gaze and rolled her eyes, in a "What are ya gonna do?" gesture. Then she turned back to the girls. "You two lookin' for something special?" she demanded, apparently trying to encourage the girls to leave. Even though there weren't hordes of customers clamoring to buy Griselda's goods, some merchants hold a special disdain for browsers.

"Like I was saying, I'm looking for a tiara for my sister," repeated Marisela. "It's her *quinceañera.* But mom doesn't want to buy a brand new one; she wants an old one that looks like it got passed down through the family."

"How about a nice pendant?" suggested Griselda, holding out a shallow tray containing a mishmash of tangled chains and medallions. "I got plenty without opals. Or what about a ring?"

"It has to be a *tiara*, for a *quinceañera*."

"Don't even know what that is."

"You don't? Seriously?" asked Marisela. "It's, like, this awesome party when a girl turns *quince*, or fifteen. I had mine last year. It was awesome."

"Way awesome," Shawnelle agreed with a nod.

"Awesome," Griselda echoed. "Still don't got any tiaras."

I had desperately wanted a *quinceañera* when I turned fifteen, but my grandmother Graciela had called the custom "expensive foolishness." Akin to a sweet-sixteen birthday, *quinceañeras* are a rite of passage in many Latino cultures and celebrate a girl's transition to womanhood. Looking back on it now, I suspected Graciela—usually a stickler for observing her native Mexican and Indian traditions—had been trying to save me the embarrassment of having no one show up at my party.

"I have a couple of tiaras at my store," I said to the girls, handing them each a business card.

"Vintage clothes?" Marisela read the card and nodded. "Cool. Hey, do you have any formal dresses that would work for a *quinceañera*? My sister and I still haven't found exactly the right dresses yet, and it's, like, coming up real soon."

"I do, yes." I smiled, thinking of the scads of taffeta, netting, silks, and satins crowding the racks at Aunt Cora's Closet. Depending on a family's economic situation, a *quinceañera* can be a lavish affair on the scale of a wedding. The price tag for costuming alone could run into the thousands. Vintage was a fun, relatively inexpensive alternative.

"Cool. Maybe we'll come check it out."

"I look forward to it."

"Those rings look good on you," Griselda said to Shawnelle. "You have nice hands for rings. Men like that."

"I like this one," said Shawnelle, looking down at a large hunk of turquoise in a setting of tarnished, worked silver. "But . . . I guess I should save my money."

Griselda rolled her eyes and, once again sensing she wasn't going to make a sale, returned to her unpacking.

Now that the object of their admiration had ducked back behind the blue curtains, the girls' enthusiasm waned. They wandered off.

Griselda added several necklaces to the velvet-lined tray, and then set up a little stand that held a jewel-encrusted athame, or sacred ceremonial knife.

Wait just a gol-durned second.

An *athame*? Could Griselda be a witch?

Once upon a time I was confident that I could recognize my own kind. But ever since moving to San Francisco I had met believers of all types, making it difficult to tell who was a self-defined practicing witch, a sorcerer, a Wiccan, a hoodoo, a Feri, or an adherent of the myriad other belief systems and magical traditions. There were so many I lost track.

I had been distracted by Griselda's wild outfit and funny mannerisms—could I have missed the sort of aural presence that might indicate she was a practitioner?

"May I see the opal medallion, please?" I asked, in a bid to keep Griselda talking. I supposed it wasn't really my business whether she was a witch or not—especially if she had taken steps to hide her identity through a cloaking spell or protective charm—but I was always interested in possible kindred spirits.

Besides, that unsettled, *wrong* feeling I had before . . . I still couldn't shake it.

Griselda's kohl-blackened eyes fixed on mine. I waited to feel a flash of recognition or to sense the aura of a practitioner. I felt nothing to indicate supernatural powers . . . but there was *something*. A vague sense of the sinister.

Not coming from Griselda herself, but behind me.

At that moment Griselda's hazel eyes shifted to something over my shoulder and widened ever so slightly.

The back of my neck tingled.

I whirled around.

No one. Nothing. Although thousands of shoppers mobbed the aisles of the Cow Palace, here in the corner we were, for all intents and purposes, alone.

I turned back to Griselda. Without speaking, she picked up the medallion and held it out to me.

I cupped the necklace in both hands, sharing my warmth with it. I waited, concentrated, and felt . . . not much. I really was one sorry excuse for a witch when it came to jewelry. But opals held water within their depths, which was one reason they were so fragile. I wasn't kidding when I said they were alive. So I did sense a slight, tiny shimmer . . . like when I tried to scry by looking into my crystal ball. Almost . . . but not quite.

"You know about opals, do you?"

"It's my grandmother's birthstone. She has several. She wears them every day and treats them with oil, keeps them from the sun."

"Smart woman. They like to be with their owners at all times, and treated with respect, as you said." She nodded, studying me. "Where you from?"

"Texas originally. I've traveled a lot, though. Haven't been back for a while."

"You still talk funny."

"So I've been told." I'd been working on losing my twang, but it was stubborn. Still, given Griselda's own accent it seemed like a pot-calling-the-kettle-black accusation. "You have some lovely items. My shop, Aunt Cora's Closet, specializes in vintage clothing. I'm here hoping to score some nice vintage stuff today. But your prices . . ."

"What's wrong with 'em?"

"Nothing. These are lovely pieces." I gestured to the antique brooches laid out enticingly on the paisley brocade covering cheap card tables. "I was just wondering whether you might consider a wholesale rate—"

"This *is* wholesale."

"Maybe a bulk rate?"

"You're a bargainer, huh?" Her eyes flickered to a point over my shoulder again. "Tell you what. You come back at the end of the day, once the hungry crowds have been through, and maybe I'll make you a deal. Don't like to pack all this stuff back up. If I've got a bunch on my hands at the end of the show, we can talk then."

She looked at me just a mite too intensely. Was she trying to telegraph that she wanted to see me later?

"But I can't guarantee you'll get much at that point," Griselda added. "Just the dregs. You might want to pick out a few choice pieces now."

Who is the bargainer now? I smiled, trying to shake off my suspicions. Surely Griselda was just a businesswoman keeping an eye on the crowd, trying to sell her inventory at the highest possible price.

"Where's this shop of yours?"

I handed her my business card. She returned the favor and passed me a bright purple, shiny one with sparkles.

"Hey, you're on Haight Street? Lily Ivory?" she said, her eyes again shifting slightly. She lowered her voice. "I'm staying at a bed-and-breakfast right over there—the, uh, Morning House. You know this place?"

"I think I've walked past it. The Haight's a great neighborhood, isn't it?"

"Sure. Maybe I should come see your store. I—" She cut herself off when Johannes appeared with two more boxes. One was noticeably battered, and *Mull* had been written in black magic marker on the side.

"Why do you bring this one?" Griselda chastised him. "It's junk, says so right there on the side."

"You want I put it back?"

"*Dummer Junge . . . Ja*, put it—" Griselda stopped midanswer and looked at me out of the corner of her eye. "Unless you'd like to buy it. Give you a good price. Good stuff here."

"You just said it was junk."

"Junk *jewelry*. This not the same as *junk*. There is a place for rhinestones, no?" She flapped my business card in my direction. "Vintage—this means old and used, no?"

"I prefer to think of my inventory as classic."

She gave a dismissive wave. "You say you're looking for inexpensive items for your shop. There are some good pieces here."

Johannes held out the box, tilting it toward me. Griselda opened one of the top flaps so I could take a peek at the contents: a jumble of snarled chains and medallions, rings, and beads. When I reached out to touch, she yanked it back out of reach.

"Fifty dollars for the box, so I don't have to take it home."

"Thirty."

She frowned, then gave me a reluctant, crooked smile.

"Forty, and I'll throw in the piece you were looking at with the opals. I think it likes you."

"Thirty-five." I had learned never to accept the first counteroffer.

"Thirty-seven fifty."

"Deal."

Griselda snatched the bills I held out, and Johannes handed me the box.

It was heavy. Luckily the muscles in my arms and back were toned from the hours I spent every week laundering recently acquired vintage clothing. Nothing like hand washing, twisting, and hanging yards and yards of wet fabric to develop a little upper body strength. Last wash day Maya had suggested we produce a workout DVD: "Launder your way to toned biceps."

Still, though I was sure I could make it out to the car with my burden, I didn't feel like carrying it around the Gem Faire while I shopped. I considered asking Griselda if I could leave it with her, but her attention had already been diverted by a group of older women who were poking through her collection of antique school rings.

Our sale complete, she had no more use for me.

I glanced at my antique Tinker Bell watch; I was supposed to meet Bronwyn and Maya at the refreshment stand in fifteen minutes. Might as well go grab a cup of coffee and take a gander at the contents of my mystery box. As likely as not, it was a bunch of plastic junk not worth five bucks, much less thirty-seven. But one never knew. I slipped the medallion around my neck, gazed into the bright depths of the blue-green opals, and figured I'd made a good enough deal.

As I started down the aisle, I could hear Griselda saying to her new customers:

"Those there are gen-u-ine sweetheart rings, all of 'em given to their girlies when the boys went off to war. . . ."

Dollars to doughnuts Griselda had a romantic tale to tell about every piece of jewelry in her possession. What a character.

Chapter 2

Standing at a tall orange café table, I savored the aroma of a cup of dark French roast coffee and anticipated the energy boost from the caffeine as I looked out over the crowd.

I was already plumb worn out from shopping. How did women *do* this?

I enjoyed shopping under certain circumstances, such as open-air markets in North Africa and beach stands in Mexico. I had once spent an enthralling afternoon—and experienced sensory overload—at a *parfumerie* in Paris. But in general, I quickly grew weary of the crowds, the noise, and the competition for the best deals. Most of my acquisitions for Aunt Cora's Closet came from thrift stores, garage sales, and one-on-one exchanges—low-key, low-pressure bargain hunting.

Several small groups of women were taking coffee breaks, sipping drinks, and oohing and aahing over one another's purchases. A pimply teenage boy looked uncomfortable and out of place accompanying his fifty-something mom, and I wondered what his story was. A couple of gray-haired women sporting neon yellow vendor badges were filling cardboard boxes with multiple cups of coffee, adding cream and sugar.

I noticed Griselda's assistant, Johannes, take a place in the refreshment line next to Shawnelle, who had apparently ditched her tiara-shopping friend to chat him up. She ordered a Diet Coke while Johannes bought three hot dogs, which he proceeded to smother with onions, relish, and great gobs of ketchup, all the while nodding at whatever Shawnelle was saying. I smiled, wondering if he spoke enough English to understand her, or whether her beautiful green eyes said all he needed to hear. They didn't notice me as they passed by with their refreshments.

"Mmm-*mmm-mmm.*"

A man was leaning on the high café table next to mine, sipping a bright red slushy through a striped straw. He gazed into his cup with a frown of concentration, as though lost in the experience. "*Mmmm.* Boy, that's . . . yummy."

He looked up, and our gazes met.

"Good?" I asked.

"*So* good," he answered with a self-conscious smile, his lips stained pink from the slush.

He wore an expensive-looking double-breasted suit, a silk tie, and polished wingtips. His dark hair, receding from his forehead, was slicked into place. *East Coast,* I decided. I didn't see many movies, but I was pretty sure this guy fit the bill for Central Casting's call for a Jersey-based mafioso. He was handsome in a sort of middle-aged, slightly thuggish way, but he looked wildly out of place in San Francisco, where people tended to dress casually, especially for occasions such as the Gem Faire. Still, he was so entranced with his incongruous little-kid slushy I couldn't help but return his smile.

"Jelly Belly?" He extracted a bag of brightly colored jelly beans from his suit pocket.

"Oh, no, thank you." After a youth spent being shunned by virtually everyone in my small West Texas hometown, I was always a little surprised when strangers struck up conversations.

Maya had told me recently that I had to learn to flirt with men, to engage them in "*normal* interactions that don't include witchcraft or murder." It was good advice. She and Bronwyn were trying to get me to stop moping over a certain dark-eyed psychic named Sailor, who had dropped out of my life several weeks ago. Our brief affair had flamed so hot and intense that I feared I had scared him off. Or maybe the problem was that Sailor and I were forever dealing with witchcraft and murder.

"They've got a factory not too far from here," the man in the suit continued, popping a few candies in his mouth. "Went on the tour. Never occurred to me that jelly beans were made in factories. Kind of always assumed there were elves involved somehow."

"I've been meaning to take that tour."

"Highly recommend it. Dropped a few bucks at the retail shop, too, obviously." He held the bag out and shook it as though to entice me. "Go on, help yourself. There's a million flavors in here."

"No, really. I'll be getting lunch soon."

He gave a conciliatory shrug. "You come to these shows before?"

I shook my head. "First timer. It's . . . wonderful."

He looked at me, a questioning half smile on his face.

I shrugged. "Maybe a little bit overwhelming."

"You don't like crowds." It was a statement, not a question. His tone was understanding, his light brown

eyes soft. But there was something about him . . . His
guard was up. He was good at covering up. Like me.

"You from around here?" he continued.

My stubborn Texas twang usually warded off such in-
quiries. "Not originally, but I moved here a while back."

"Like it?"

"Very much."

"Me, I'm not from here," he said unnecessarily. Defi-
nitely an East Coast accent, probably the Bronx. "Makes
me a little nervous, all this"—he made a circular gesture
with his free hand—"artsy whatnot, and everybody's
so . . . healthy. What's with *wheatgrass*? And that whad-
dayacallit? *Gluten*?" he scoffed. "Don't get me started."

I smiled, remembering being taken aback by such
things when I first arrived in California, too. Even here
at the Cow Palace, alongside the typical junk food—like
bright red slushies—the refreshment stand offered several vegetarian options, including one particularly dubious item labeled VEGAN BBQ RIB-ETTES. I was afraid to
ask.

"They do have their own way of doing things. So, what
brings you to San Francisco?"

He hesitated, just a fraction of a second. "Business.
I'm Gene, by the way. I'd shake, but . . ." He held up a
palm stained bright colors from the jelly beans. He gestured with his head to the beat-up cardboard box.
"What's in the box?"

"Junk jewelry. I have a resale shop."

"Yeah? Where'd you find the junk? Thought everything out here was a, whaddayacall? Like a treasure."

"One person's junk is another's treasure, as they say."
I was tiring of our conversation, and figured I had practiced my flirting plenty for one day. I wanted to examine
my new purchases, but hesitated to do so in front of

Gene. Just in case. I don't know what I thought I'd find in the box, but as my mother used to say, *"Don't count your change in front of the poor."* Not that the man looked deprived . . . but figuratively speaking.

A loud gurgle signaled that Gene had finished his slushy.

A woman screamed.

Out on the exhibit-hall floor, people started shouting and jumping. A display of pearls was knocked over, hundreds of the exquisite gems skittering out in all directions. A tablecloth was dragged off of a display table, taking with it necklaces and rings that scattered on the concrete floor. Another scream was nearly drowned out by a babble of shouts and cries.

Finally the cause of the havoc rounded a corner.

Oscar.

Oscar is my witch's familiar. Most witches have *familiar* familiars, like owls or frogs . . . or the proverbial black cat. Not me. Mine is a strange, shape-shifting critter.

At the moment he was in his Vietnamese potbellied-pig form, but as I'd tried to explain to him so many times before—without noticeable effect—this porcine guise was only slightly less disturbing in most crowds than his natural goblin-crossed-with-a-gargoyle appearance. I adore Oscar, but he isn't what you'd call easy.

What in the world was he *doing*? And, most important, why was he doing it *here*?

"Oscar!" I called out, but the shouting of the crowd drowned out my voice.

Bronwyn and Maya joined me at the refreshment stand, their canvas bags bulging with purchases.

"What in the world . . . ?" Bronwyn asked, as Maya looked on, bewildered. "How'd our little Oscaroo get out of the van?"

"I, uh . . ." I trailed off, at a loss for words.

In truth, Oscar was more than capable of letting himself out of the van when he transformed—in his gobgoyle form he had humanlike hands. But neither Bronwyn nor Maya knew that.

It was rare for him to disobey me so blatantly, however. Though we had an unusual witch-familiar relationship, Oscar generally followed my orders . . . unless there was a powerful reason not to.

As I looked on, helpless, Oscar careened through the aisles, wild as a June bug on a string. Onlookers screamed and jumped, laughed and chased, and one or two seemed about to cry. Two security guards, radios crackling, tried to trap him by approaching from opposite ends of an aisle. One guard was noticeably overweight; the other small and very young. They looked determined but clueless.

Oscar evaded the pair by slaloming this way and that, before ducking under a display counter topped with trays of glass and metal beads. In the process he struck one of the supporting legs and the flimsy table folded in on itself, spewing beads every which way. The chubby security guard slipped on the rolling beads and fell flat on his butt, while the younger one, more agile than his partner, tried to cut Oscar off. My familiar ducked under yet another display table, catching the cloth on his little hooves and pulling down racks of necklaces, pearls bouncing thither and yon.

"Oscar! *Stop!*" I stood on my chair and called again, but I doubted he could hear me over the shouts and cacophony.

Over the loudspeaker a crackling voice hailed the security force, calling a Code 571.

"A 571?" Maya murmured. "Suppose that's the code for 'out-of-control porker'?"

Whatever it was code for, it was bad news. The last thing I wanted to deal with was animal control; I wasn't even sure it was strictly legal to keep a pig in the city limits.

"Maya, Bronwyn," I said, "let's triangulate and catch him."

Before we could put our plan into action, Oscar barreled down the wide central aisle, heading straight for the refreshment stand.

"*Hell's bells*, Oscar. *Stop!*"

Oscar stopped.

Ten minutes later four rent-a-cops, one sheepish pig, and one fuming, embarrassed witch sat in the windowless security office, which, despite its formal title, looked a whole lot like a converted utility closet. It was outfitted with half a dozen beige folding chairs, a utilitarian metal desk covered with stacks of papers, and a plastic-topped conference table.

Compared to the law enforcement professionals I had become accustomed to dealing with over the past few months—the San Francisco Police Department—these men were rather hapless. Despite their neat uniforms and shiny badges, I imagined they had been lured into their jobs by the promise of minimum wage plus overtime, the looming threat of a high unemployment rate, and the possibility of one day perhaps qualifying for health insurance. Since presumably they weren't particularly invested in their careers, much less in bringing someone like me to justice, I felt confident in my ability to influence them.

I concentrated, shook their hands one by one, and spoke.

"This was all a simple misunderstanding. My pig and

I are going to go now, and we won't come back. No need to write up a report."

"I guess she's right," said the self-proclaimed chief of security, who looked as though he'd graduated from high school this past June. His chubby cheeks were covered in peach fuzz, and his face was absent the lines and hard planes common to those of us who'd seen a few years. "There's really no need to write this up."

The guards who had chased Oscar around the floor nodded.

One rebel, a pear-shaped man whose plain features were arranged in what appeared to be a permanent sneer, wasn't as easily swayed. He hitched up his pants and said, "Now, hold on there just one minute. I still think we need to—"

The radios on their hips squawked.

"Report to sector 4," came a scratchy voice. *"I mean, sector . . . wait . . . ah hell. That place behind the right rear corner of the show. Behind the partitions. All units. Except—Jimmy, you wait out in front and show the paramedics where to pull up in the rear."*

As though relieved to have something important to do, all four men leaped up and ran out of the room so fast that two of them got stuck briefly when they tried to squeeze through the door at the same time. It was a fair imitation of an old Keystone Kops movie. I was relieved to see them go so that I could join Bronwyn and Maya, who had agreed to haul my heavy box of jewelry out to the car.

The young chief was the last to leave. Upon realizing I was still there, he turned back at the door and said, "Please take your livestock and leave the scene, ma'am."

"Yes, sir," I said, holding tight to the prickly rope one of the officers had tied around Oscar's neck. I yanked him down the fluorescent-lit utilitarian service hallway, his hooves clacking loudly on the worn gray linoleum tiles as he hurried to keep up.

He kept casting me sidelong glances, his pink eyes hangdog and imploring.

"What in *tarnation* did you think you were doing?" I demanded, though I knew full well that in his porcine guise, Oscar had no way of answering me. Which was just as well, since at the moment I was madder than a wet hen and in no mood for his excuses. "Don't you realize what could have happened? You could have been *impounded*. I don't even know if it's *legal* to keep a pig in the city. What if animal control shows up and takes you away from me? What'll we do then, huh?"

Now he looked up and, despite his piggy form, gave me a disgusted look, as if to say, "Are you kidding me?"

Oscar was so much more than an average pig, and he had gotten along just fine without me for centuries. He certainly wasn't worried that the police—much less animal control—could keep a tricky guy like him behind bars.

"Okay, you've got me there," I muttered. "But I'm still furious with you. What were you thinking, coming into the fair like that? You should have known you'd cause a stink."

Unless . . . it dawned on me that Oscar needed to tell me something. Why else would he have disobeyed me, and taken such a chance?

Just ahead of us, a door to a broom closet stood ajar. I ducked in and pulled my pig behind me.

For a few seconds Oscar just stared at me.

"Now transform and tell me what's going on."

He obeyed and assumed his natural form, in which he stood about three feet tall, with greenish gray scaly skin, huge bat ears, and a monkeylike face. But then he folded his thin, scaly arms over his chest and glared, pursing his muzzle.

"Okay, okay," I grumbled. "I'm sorry. You're right. I should have realized you had something important to tell me."

"Uh-*huh*," he said, waggling his head like he'd seen Maya do when she was angry. "Why else would I risk my neck coming into this zoo? Not like there's anything in it for *me*. I didn't even get a lousy order of *French fries*."

"Oscar, I said I was sorry. What is it?"

"Something bad, mistress," he said, then paused like the scaly green drama queen that he was. He glanced over both shoulders, as though worried the mop bucket might be harboring spies. He leaned toward me and continued in a loud whisper, "Something . . . demonic."

"As in . . ."

"A demon."

"Yes, I get that. But what particular *kind* of demon?"

He shrugged.

"I thought I felt something odd, too. But . . . Oscar, you sure you're not just being a bit melodramatic? Because that's a very serious—"

I was cut off as a fire alarm rang out and the overhead sprinklers started spewing water.

"What in the—"

Oscar transformed again as I stuck my head out the door and peered down the corridor. A pair of security officers ran down the hall toward the huge exhibit floor.

"*Get out of here!*" one of them yelled at us, pointing behind them, toward the green glow of an Exit sign. "Fire! This is no drill!"

In general when someone suggests you leave a burning building, you should follow orders. But something told me this wasn't your average fire at your typical Gem Faire. And I, being neither average nor typical, felt compelled to find out what was going on. Instead of exiting, Oscar and I burst through a service door that led into the heart of the massive, hangarlike structure.

Pandemonium.

Small fires were burning in several corners, unaffected by the overhead sprinklers soaking everything below. And yet the flames did not appear to be spreading.

One display table was lit as though a puddle of gasoline was burning right in the center of the tablecloth. Another fire was so hot that the solid gold pieces in a locked display case had melted, the small puddles of molten metal flowing into one another. Still, the flammable tablecloths and posters were not catching fire.

The loudspeaker squawked. *"Do not be alarmed. Please allow the officials through. Move in an orderly fashion toward the exits. Do not panic."*

Soaked visitors streamed out of the exits in a more or less orderly fashion, though a few were crying and clearly on the verge of panicking. More than one paper bag, sodden from the sprinklers, had split open and spilled its contents onto the floor; the items were then kicked and stomped by the shuffling crowd.

Frantic merchants were gathering their valuable wares as frightened security personnel tried to convince them to abandon their items and insisted that everyone leave the building immediately.

I untied the rope around Oscar's neck, telling him to meet me at the van so I wouldn't have to worry about him while I checked things out. Under the circumstances I figured he could take care of himself better than I . . .

and in all this bedlam I doubted anyone would be overly concerned with a free-roaming pig.

I spotted Johannes in the fleeing crowd, ketchup staining his white shirt. All of us were soaked by now; the water made the ketchup run down in streams, like blood. But it was the fearful look in his eyes that worried me.

"Johannes," I grabbed his arm as he rushed by. "What's going on? What's happening?"

"*Ich* ... I don't how to say it in English ... it's *eine Hexenjagd*! Come away!"

I don't speak much German. But I know one word for sure: *Hexen*. As in hex. As in witch.

"Is Griselda all right?" I asked, feeling a tingle of premonition at the back of my neck. "Where is she?"

"Come, now! *Vorsicht*!" He grabbed my upper arm, gallantly trying to persuade me to leave with him. "Come!"

When I pulled away, he hurried toward the exit without a backward glance.

Again I thought that a normal person would be a fool to remain in a burning building, and I'm usually not a fool. But there was something about these fires ... they weren't spreading. Neither were they extinguished by the sprinklers, which by now had rained down so much water that little streams were running on the concrete floor.

Hexen. Witches. And Oscar had sensed something demonic.

I had to see if the security guards needed my help. One thing was for sure: They were trained to deal with things like crowd control, not the kind of havoc demons—and witches—can wreak. Turning toward the back of the hall, I started to fight my way through the throng like a salmon swimming upstream, stroking the medicine bag I wore on a braided belt around my waist and chanting charms of protection.

Griselda's jewelry stand had been abandoned. Its contents appeared to have been tossed, as though someone had rifled through, looking for something. Or perhaps it had merely been ravaged by the water and the rushing crowds, like so many other displays out on the floor.

Among scattered medallions and brooches, I noticed a gold cuff link on the ground. Picking it up and weighing it in my hand, it felt surprisingly heavy, in the way of real gold. I looked for its mate, wondering if it could be part of Griselda's merchandise. But no—the cuff link was slick, with a modern angular design, not an antique. I held it in my hand and concentrated, and thought I felt distinctly modern vibrations. I felt these sensations quite clearly, which shocked me. In fact, there was something so familiar about the sensations, they tugged at the edges of my consciousness.

The massive blue curtains that cordoned off the back from the show floor swayed in toward me, as though blown by a wind from behind.

A lock of egg-yolk yellow hair tumbled from under the curtain to land at my feet.

Unlike everything else in the hall, the hair was dry. I stared down at it for a long moment. The sounds of chaos, the screams and shouts, the sirens faded from my awareness as I stared down at the errant lock of hair. I was afraid to reach down toward it.

Finally, I took a deep breath, reached out slowly, and parted the curtains.

It took me a moment to recognize what I was seeing. Two large plywood boards, one on the ground, the other on top of someone with yellow hair.

Placed on the top board were several cinder blocks and more than a dozen boxes of what I presumed to be heavy jewelry.

Griselda was sandwiched between the boards. Crushed.

Chapter 3

The two security guards who had chased Oscar earlier were standing in an open side door. The plump one was looking outside, as though waiting for something.

The younger one was doubled over, retching.

Convinced the men were too distracted to notice me, I rushed over to Griselda. Grimly, I realized that having been born without fingerprints—a hereditary condition that made basic paperwork, like getting a driver's license, a bureaucratic nightmare—was an asset for things like poking around crime scenes without leaving identifiable traces.

Despite my own revulsion, I reached out a shaky hand and placed it on the arm that was sticking out between the boards, hoping to read Griselda's vibrations.

She was gone. Dead. But the vibrations were strong, not yet completely faded. I felt a wave of overwhelming fear and pain and . . . suffocation.

Griselda had been "pressed." During the European witch hunts, an accused person might be placed beneath a heavy board to secure her confession. Heavy rocks were piled, one by one, on top of the plank to increase the pressure until the victim admitted her knowledge of and complicity in magical practices. Although pressing was intended to be a form of torture, not a method of execution, it was not unusual for it to result in a prisoner's slow, painful death from internal injuries and suffocation.

Griselda's death seemed to have been aided by the athame I had seen at her stand. The ceremonial knife's bejeweled handle stuck out from between the planks, and a thin ribbon of blood had been carried onto the floor by the relentless water raining down.

The scene was horrifying.

I swallowed hard and took a deep, steadying breath. Stroking my medicine bag, I tried to find the calm amid the chaos. But as I knelt beside Griselda, the water from the sprinklers dripping down my face mimicked the tears I could not shed, and black spots danced in front of my eyes. I could feel myself react not only to the immediate, grisly death of this poor woman, but to the link it represented to the persecuted witches, healers, wise women, and outsiders throughout time and across cultures.

As a natural-born witch, I carry that history of violence in my bones.

The far-off sirens grew louder, their shrill whine reaching a deafening crescendo, followed by a screech of brakes. I could see the blue and red flashing of emergency-vehicle lights through the open door.

For a second I considered staying to assist the SFPD. I could even try calling on my sort-of friend, Inspector Carlos Romero, in the homicide department for help. But the truth was that I knew nothing about what had happened and could contribute nothing to a murder investigation.

And besides . . . I was too shaken by what I had seen.

I slipped back through the blue curtain, concentrating on breathing and trying to slow my pounding heart.

Was Griselda's death an isolated, gruesome incident . . . or could it be the beginning of a witch hunt in San Francisco?

I was still shaking by the time I reunited with my friends in the parking lot, so I handed the keys to Maya.

She and Bronwyn had corralled Oscar when he ran out of the Cow Palace. The potbellied pig—who was not nearly as miniature as his breed name would suggest— was now contentedly snuggling in Bronwyn's lap while she petted him and spoke to him in a high-pitched, baby voice, calling him her "widdle bitty Oscaroo."

Oscar adored Bronwyn. It was no wonder: Everyone adored Bronwyn.

Maya drove swiftly through the streets of San Francisco, hopping on the 101 Freeway briefly, then exiting at Octavia and Fell and turning left onto Haight Street.

With each city block we put between us and the Cow Palace, I pulled myself together a bit more. But I was still stunned by what I had seen.

"Well, at least no one was hurt," said Bronwyn. "I know it looked like a stampede, but I think everyone got out okay."

"It'll be a huge mess," said Maya. "Good thing they had a sprinkler system, though. What do you suppose started all those fires?"

My pig and I glanced at each other.

Disparate, small, superhot fires triggering sprinklers, panic, and general pandemonium.

It smacked of a demon at play.

Still . . . the way Griselda was killed didn't seem like

the actions of a demon. Rather, this was the sort of sce-
nario humans came up with when they were frightened,
angry, or greedy enough to be inhuman to each another.

Maya double-parked the purple van in front of Aunt
Cora's Closet, near the corner of Haight and Ashbury.
Known locally as the Haight, the neighborhood had
been the birthplace of the Summer of Love in 1968 and
was still something of a hippie haven. The area had once
housed rock legends like Janis Joplin, Jefferson Airplane,
and the Grateful Dead; more recently, it was experienc-
ing a wave of gentrification as people rediscovered and
renovated the charming old Victorians that sat cheek by
jowl in rows on the side streets. Moneyed yuppies preoc-
cupied with home design now mixed with older hippies
in a strained coexistence with the self-proclaimed "gutter punks," or young people living on the streets, begging
for change.

I adored the idiosyncratic Haight. The moment I arrived, after years of a nomadic existence, I knew I had
found a place where a witch like me might actually fit in,
find friends, and become part of the community. And I
had. It felt great to be home.

If only I could shake that visual of Griselda.

As I walked through the front door of my shop I was
greeted by the scent of fresh laundry mingling with the
sachets of rosemary and sage that I had hung throughout
the store. Humming vibrations reflected the complicated
histories of the clothes on the racks, enveloping me like
whispered hugs. Throughout my years of solitude, the
vibrations of cast-off clothing had kept me connected to
humanity, and I responded to them as you would to a
dear old friend who had seen you through many moments of crazy, yet remained by your side.

Maya, Bronwyn, and I toted in bags of beads and jewelry, my Bakelite bonanza, and the cardboard box from Griselda. Just looking at that box made me queasy.

"Check out these great shell buttons I got for Mom," said Maya as she started unpacking her bag. Maya's mother, Lucille, was a whiz with a needle; she did alterations for our customers, and had recently launched a new venture making reproduction dresses in the style of vintage clothing. Antique details such as buttons, lace, and embroidery made Lucille's modern creations a cut above the competition.

I tried to feign interest in Maya's purchases, but kept seeing Griselda's body in my mind's eye.

"Lily, forgive me for mothering you, but you look like you could use a little lie-down," Bronwyn said. She came over to give me a bear hug, enfolding me in warmth and today's natural herbal scent: tea rose and myrrh.

"She's right," said Maya, looking at me with concern. "Are you okay?"

I noticed Bronwyn appeared a bit bedraggled, and I suspected I wasn't much better. Only Maya looked great, her black locks seemingly impervious to the effects of an indoor rain shower.

I nodded and took a deep breath to steady myself. "Yes, I'm sorry."

"Was it the fire? It scared you?"

I nodded again.

"Witches and fire don't mix," Bronwyn said with a sage nod over my shoulder to Maya. "How about you go upstairs for a bit? Maya and I can handle the mad Sunday crowds."

She was joking. There wasn't a soul in the store but us, which was typical for midday on a Sunday. Customers would start trickling in later this afternoon, but early Sunday was always dead.

I glanced at my watch, which, I was relieved to see, had survived today's dousing. Luckily, a couple of weeks ago I decided to cast a protective spell over it. I figured it could use all the help it could get, considering my life lately.

"I guess I could use a break ... but I think some air would do me more good than a lie-down. I'll go move the van, then take a walk in the sunshine, if you really don't mind."

"You go on along, now," said Bronwyn, unconsciously mimicking my Southern phrasing. I'd noticed my accent was rubbing off on my friends.

I took a moment to fix myself up in the mirror; applied some lipstick, combed my hair and put it up in a neat ponytail, then tied it with a patterned silk scarf.

Oscar wanted to come with me, of course, but I left him at the store. I needed to debrief him further about what he had sensed at the Gem Faire that had motivated him to burst in on us. I couldn't help but wonder what the connection might be to poor Griselda. But that could wait until after the store had closed—I was already off my game, and a discussion about demonic activity wouldn't be conducive to putting up a brave front for my friends and customers.

A stroll in the fresh air and sunshine, on the other hand ... that could cure any number of ills.

After moving the van around the corner and parking it in the driveway I rented for a small fortune, I strolled several blocks down Haight Street, passing by head shops, a brew pub, and several cafés.

I should contact Inspector Romero. We weren't friends, exactly, but we were at least friend*ly*. And, most important, he believed in my powers. Sort of. At the very least he kept an open mind, and wouldn't laugh me out of the Hall of Justice for suggesting that Griselda had been killed by a traditional method of torturing a witch. But still . . . I didn't know what I could add to any official investigation. I kept going over my interaction with Griselda at the fair, but there had been nothing obviously suspicious about it beyond vague sensations and the feeling that she had been looking behind me. I hadn't even recognized her as a practitioner until I made the assumption when I saw the athame. It was possible she wasn't a witch at all; perhaps she had been killed for entirely different reasons.

Absorbed in my thoughts, I turned down a quiet side street lined with the simple but intricately painted Victorians so typical of the neighborhood. With a start, I realized I was only half a block down from where Griselda mentioned she was staying, at the Morning House B and B.

I had noticed the inn on previous walks through the neighborhood. It was painted in many shades of lavender and pink, with touches of gold gilt on the gingerbread trim. The building was larger than the row houses surrounding it, but what made it really stand out was its expansive yard. Set on a double lot, it was surrounded by trees and lawn and ringed with planters full of blossoming flowers and bushes. The garden was well tended, a lush urban oasis surrounded by a white picket fence; the arch over the gate was covered by a fragrant climbing lavender rose. A colorful border boasted orange nasturtiums, blue coral bells, and purple pansies. Fuchsia bougainvillea trailed along the roof over the broad front porch, which held several rocking chairs and a porch swing.

Next to the gate was a white wooden sign that read, MORNING HOUSE. A BED AND BREAKFAST. WELCOME! Below it a sign read No VACANCY.

Had my subconscious brought me here, or was it simple coincidence? Either way, as I walked past I noted the sort of thing the authorities would no doubt overlook: loops of rowan, a magical plant, hung on the spikes of the fence and the little gate. When looped in this fashion, rowan was a traditional protective talisman against witches.

My eyes darted around, looking for other signs meant to fend off my kind. The colorful garden wasn't typical of a witch-repelling palette; traditionally, gardens meant to protect against sorcery were monochromatic, with yellow and white plantings meant to invoke the sun, which was supposedly anathema to magical folk, who were more commonly associated with the moon and nightfall.

The assumption being that witches are aligned with the night and shun the light.

I noticed a line of salt across the threshold and a bundle of stinging nettles on the porch. These were general protection charms; according to custom they were imbued with power by chanting, and could be made *by* witches as easily as against them. But the loops of rowan were something else.

First Griselda was killed by pressing, a traditional way to torture a witch . . . and now loops of rowan were adorning the bed-and-breakfast where she had been staying. Still standing at the gate, I took a deep breath and stroked my medicine bag for strength and calm while I tried to decide what to do.

"Come on in. Don't be shy!" I looked up to see a smiling fellow with a neatly trimmed goatee and mustache, male-pattern baldness, and chubby cheeks. He wore a fuzzy fleece outdoor vest over a plaid shirt and held gardening sheers in one gloved hand. Abandoning the orange trumpet vine he had been trimming, he strode across the small lawn toward me. "I'm Lloyd, the owner. Sorry to tell you, though, we have no rooms available at the moment. We're pretty much full up all the time these days—you have to call weeks ahead of time to secure a reservation."

"I . . ." What should I say?

Surely he wouldn't have heard of Griselda's death yet, and if I started asking questions about her . . . wouldn't it seem suspicious? Still, what with the mode of Griselda's murder and now the antiwitch charms, I couldn't suppress the feeling that there was something seriously scary afoot . . . something akin to a witch hunt. And just as I had recognized the rowan loops, I might notice some other obscure evidence to help with the investigation into her death.

"I'm not looking for a room, actually. But . . . a friend of mine from out of town is staying here, and I believe she might have left something for me."

Normally I might be able to influence this open, eager man to trust me, but I could feel the effects of the rowan. I'm too potent a witch for it to strip me of my abilities, but my power and sensations were dulled by the extra effort. Whoever had cast the protection spell knew what he or she was doing.

Lloyd frowned slightly. "What's your friend's name?"

"Griselda . . ." I trailed off, realizing I didn't know her last name. But this was informal California, after all, so perhaps he wouldn't notice. Or I could pretend that she went by a single name, like Cher. Anyway, Griselda was unusual enough that I couldn't imagine there would be more than one.

"Oh . . . you wouldn't be the one with the pig, by any chance?"

"Excuse me?"

"You have a vintage store down the street? And a pig?"

"Um . . ."

He nodded. "Griselda mentioned your store, said she was a friend of the family. Do you know where she's gotten to? She said she'd be back around lunchtime to settle her bill, but I haven't seen her."

"I, uh . . ." I was digging myself in deeper all the time. "You're saying she's a friend of my family?"

Lloyd looked confused, not that I blamed him. After all, I'd just told him Griselda was a friend, and now I was acting as though I didn't know her.

"I mean, we're not that close . . . I have family in Germany."

He nodded. "That's right. She mentioned that."

"So she was asking about me?"

"I told her where your store was, and she said she would stop by tonight after the jewelry show."

"When was this?"

"This morning, over breakfast." That was long before I'd met Griselda. Was that why she was so intrigued by my business card? Had she been looking for me? But if so, why hadn't she said something when we met?

His eyes fell to my chest. "Pretty necklace."

I was still wearing the worked silver and opal medallion Griselda had sold me along with the box of junk jewelry.

"Thank you, it's new. By any chance, did Griselda leave anything for me?"

"Not that I'm aware of. Was she supposed to?"

"I think . . . she might have had something for me." I held his gaze and concentrated. "Might I take a quick look in her room?"

"Oh, I don't know . . ." Lloyd shook his head, and

started snipping absentmindedly at the thorns on the roses he was arranging in an antique pewter pitcher. "That doesn't seem right . . ."

"I promise I won't touch anything." I was taking a risk, but I wanted to see if there were any other obvious antiwitch signs, things the police would overlook. Or maybe something Griselda had planned to give to me when she came to see me at the shop. I would come up with a way to explain my visit, if and when the authorities found out. "Perhaps you could accompany me to make sure. I just want to check in case she left me a letter, something like that. Out in plain sight?"

After a long beat, he gave a nod.

"I suppose that would be all right." He picked up the pitcher of roses and led the way up the broad porch steps. Lloyd opened the heavy wooden front door, which had a panel of frosted glass etched with a design of the sun rising over the mountains. A symbol of the dawn. Then again, it could also be interpreted as the sun setting over the mountains, a symbol of sunset.

Inside I noted no protective charms other than the salt. The foyer had tall ceilings and red-stained wooden moldings, and the ceiling was decorated with intricate multicolored patterned wallpapers and borders. A faded oriental rug adorned the inlaid wood floor, and a thick red runner marched up the curved stairway. A carved mahogany credenza sat along one wall, and a period bench and hat stand adorned another. I noted an elaborate cuckoo clock, much fancier than one I owned, but with similar overwrought cut-wood details. Painted borders represented traditional California motifs, such as oak leaves and acorns. The only thing that didn't appear historically accurate was the bank of tourist brochures common to hostelries of all types.

"This is stunning," I said. "I'm impressed."

"My great-grandfather built this place. It was once quite fine ... back when you could have a whole staff taking care of it, it must have really shone." Lloyd made a *tsk-tsk* sound. "You should have seen it when I inherited it! It was in bad shape. I've been working on bringing it back to its glory days, but it's mighty slow going, let me tell you."

"It's lovely," I said, and meant it. Morning House was a throwback to a genteel time in San Francisco. It was a bit messier than I expected for a nice bed-and-breakfast, with windows in need of a good scrubbing and cobwebs in the corners, but if Lloyd was running the place by himself I reckoned he didn't have time to get to all the details. "I'm glad to know you're here. I'd be happy to recommend it."

I spoke as though I had scads of friends visiting from out of town. The truth was that I was still relatively new to the city, and before landing here I didn't have any friends. Bronwyn and Maya and a few others in the neighborhood were my first experience with developing sustained relationships.

But if I *were* to need an inn to recommend to out-of-town visitors, this would be the place. One doorway led to what appeared to be an extensive library, complete with a huge globe on a stand; another to a sitting room that featured a fireplace, velvet love seats, and a number of antiques that were so perfect for the space that I thought Lloyd might well have inherited the furniture along with the house.

"Most of the guest rooms are on the second floor," Lloyd said. "This way."

He started up the wainscoted staircase, pointing out

the stained-glass windows that bowed along with the curve of the wall and the original Tiffany lampshades on the pendant lamps.

"Just about everything here is antique, most original to the house."

"I love your cuckoo clock," I said as it chimed, the little wooden bird emerging from a tiny hinged door.

"Okay, I have to admit the clock's not all that old—I brought it back from Europe a few years ago. Just couldn't resist. Still, it looks antique, doesn't it?"

"I've got a similar one. Same story: saw it in a shop in Germany and had to have it."

"Must be nice to have family there. So fun to visit a place when you have a connection to the locals."

"Mmm," I said, not wanting to go into my reasons for being in Germany at that time. In the broadest sense it was true I had been there to visit with family . . . but the reunion with my father hadn't exactly been fun.

"On the third floor are seven rooms, originally the servants' quarters," continued Lloyd. "Can you imagine what this place must have been like back in the day, with a staff of seven working full time? Now it's just me and a part-time assistant."

"You seem to be doing well."

Lloyd beamed. "I do all right, not to toot my own horn."

The old wooden floors creaked slightly under our feet, the sound muted by the plush scarlet runner. Lloyd rapped on a door marked 3, then used a master key to open it.

He gasped as the door swung open. "What the . . . ?"

I stood on my tiptoes and tried to peek over his shoulder. "What is it?"

He huffed again, clapping his hand over his mouth.

I braced myself for something really bad—I half expected another dead body—but when he finally stepped aside to let me see, I felt a wave of relief. Still, it was disconcerting to realize my life had become one in which I was relieved *not* to be confronted with a dead body. When things calmed down a bit, I might want to ponder that.

At least there was no blood.

Nothing gruesome at all, in fact, but the room was in shambles. The doors of a gleaming walnut armoire gaped open, and clothes and shoes had been tossed on the floor. The linens had been stripped from the bed and piled on the mattress in a heap. Cushions from the brocade love seat stood upended, and papers and personal items were strewn everywhere. A small pull-out sofa bed was partially open. Even the ornate brass heating grate had been pulled up and lay on its side on the Turkish carpet.

"This is unacceptable," Lloyd fumed from the doorway. "Unacceptable!"

"Who was in the room?" I asked.

"Just Griselda and her son."

"What son?" The moment it slipped out I realized my error.

"I thought you said she was a family friend?"

"I meant, *which* son. She has four," I fibbed.

"Oh. Well. Johannes." Lloyd was staring at the mess and shaking his head. "Are they drinkers? Looks like they had quite the party in here."

"Lloyd, I don't think this is the result of someone having too much fun. I'm afraid the room looks like it's been ransacked, as if somebody was searching for something."

But what? For the same thing they wanted to interrogate Griselda about? Was someone trying to force her to tell them something? And if so, why didn't she just tell them what they wanted to know? What kind of secret was worth dying for?

"Are you suggesting someone broke in?" Lloyd asked, aghast. "Not possible. Someone is here at all times. Whole place is locked up, tight as a drum, every night. We've never had a problem, not once in ten years. . . ."

"I know it's unpleasant to think about," I said. "But you should really call the police. You may need a police report to file an insurance claim, should something turn up missing."

"But . . . maybe we should wait until Griselda and Johannes get back and ask them what happened." Lloyd's anger seemed to be receding, replaced by fear that his reputation—and that of Morning House—might be compromised. "Maybe there's another explanation. A mother-son spat, perhaps. I'll tell you what: If I had to share a room with my mother—even for a few days—I would probably start throwing things myself."

The police will be knocking on the door of the rising sun soon enough, I thought, *as they investigate Griselda's murder.* Whoever tossed this room had likely killed her—or knew who had.

I really shouldn't have come, as I had now implicated myself one way or the other. But since I was already here . . . In for a penny, in for a pound, as my grandmother used to say.

I edged past Lloyd into the room and placed my hands on the piled bedsheets.

Though my powers were muted due to the rowan hoops, Griselda's vibrations remained strong. I could feel she had been scared. Scared but determined. I felt guardian energy—she was entrusted with something. And she was on a mission.

I cast my eyes around the room again, but saw nothing obvious. No hateful declarations or other obvious antiwitch charms, which might have been present had this been a simple witch hunt. The only thing out of the ordinary was a small ziplock bag on the floor near the vanity that contained snippets of yellow hair. That was a witch move: making sure to dispose of one's hair properly, so that another practitioner could not use it to spell cast. Unless it was someone else's hair, which Griselda had planned to use in a hex. The only jewelry in the room was a pile of gold chains and a single pair of cheap crystal earrings, but there was no way of knowing if other items had been taken.

The lack of jewelry made me wonder: Had Griselda's body been stripped of the pieces I had noticed her wearing when we met? That was something to ask Carlos Romero, if and when I had the opportunity.

Papers were scattered around a small writing desk under the window. It looked as though Griselda was a committed correspondent; there were pages of handwritten notes and letters on thin airmail paper and stationery with hotel logos. A lot of witches are old-fashioned that way; I still wrote on paper to my mother and Graciela, sealing the envelopes with wax and tucking in little items—a dried leaf, a newspaper article, a pressed flower.

I craned my neck to read one of the letters that was partially visible on the table, but it was in German. The last line, however, was written in English: *have a Pleasant Day!* I wondered if Griselda had taken on a typical California send-off as she wrote to folks back home. Somehow the sweet, rather bland phrase made me feel even worse. Had Griselda been composing such a letter this

morning, blissfully unaware of the fate about to befall
her? Might she have had some glimmer of a premonition
were it not for the rowan loops? Or did she even possess
such powers?

"What are you *doing*?" demanded Lloyd, still standing in the doorway and now literally wringing his hands.

I shook my head. "Just . . . pondering."

"Let's ponder downstairs. I think we should leave," he
said, closing and locking the door behind me. "I'll . . . I'll
ask my assistant if he saw anyone this morning when I
was at the farmers' market. It doesn't seem like Griselda
left anything for you, at least nothing out in the open.
Unless someone *was* in here and already took it."

Indeed.

We walked silently down the stairs, through the main
door, and out to the front porch. The heat of the day hit
us as we stepped outside, heavy and redolent of honey-
suckle and pink jasmine.

"Lovely gardens," I said.

"Why, thank you." Lloyd brightened a little. "I do enjoy flowers. Don't you?"

"Yes, very much. What are the hoops for?"

"Hoops?"

"The little circles hanging on the fence."

Lloyd looked puzzled. "They're pretty, aren't they? I
noticed them earlier today—there was also one on the
front doorknob and another on the porch railing."

"You didn't make them?"

"No, and I'm not sure who did. Maybe someone's
just . . . beautifying the city. Like those guerilla knitters?
The ones who knitted pretty little cozies and decorated
the poles of stop signs and whatnot?"

"I wondered about those. What was that about?"

He smiled and shrugged. "This is San Francisco. People do things like that. Sometimes there's a political cause, but a lot of times it's just to improve the world. Cute, huh?"

The knitted cozies on the city's parking meters and stop signs had indeed been very cute.

The loops of rowan? Not so much. Not to someone of my ilk.

"Thank you for showing me your beautiful home," I said, as if this had been a casual social call.

"You're welcome," Lloyd replied. "Do keep us in mind for all your hospitality needs."

As I strolled back to Aunt Cora's Closet, I went over what I knew: Griselda had intended to meet me, yet she hadn't felt free to talk to me when I showed up at her booth at the Gem Faire. Had she been trying to tell me something with all the significant glances? I hadn't picked up any feelings of power from her, yet she was killed in a death specific to witches, and it appeared as though someone had put up hoops of rowan to quell a witch's power at the Morning House B and B. And someone had tossed Griselda's room, looking for ... what?

I put my hand over the opal medallion on my chest. Was there something extraordinary about this necklace? If so, I still couldn't sense a darned thing. And then I remembered that Griselda had first tried to sell it to the teenage girls. So much for that theory.

But right after I handed her my business card, she had offered me that box of mixed jewelry that she insisted was junk.

The interaction had seemed offhand at the time, but perhaps she feared she was being watched. Could there be a treasure in the box of junk she'd sold me? Something she intended me to discover, which might be a clue to the identity of her killer? Something I should find before the SFPD came a-calling?

I picked up my pace as I headed back to the store, then finally broke into a jog.

Chapter 4

I burst in to Aunt Cora's Closet to discover that a couple of magpies had been hard at work.

While I'd been gone, Bronwyn and Maya had entertained themselves by decorating the shop with our new-found Gem Faire treasures. The three mannequins in the window display were draped in rhinestones; the shelves were adorned with strands of imperfect but gleaming pearls woven among the hats and gloves; the display counter was chock-full of sinuous chains and necklaces, lying in wait like so many glittering snakes.

Bronwyn was sitting at the glass display counter, laboriously untangling a heap of chains, knot by filigreed knot. In the display case below her, gleaming glass shelves were covered with strand upon strand of glass beads. On the floor at Bronwyn's feet sat the cardboard box marked *Mull*. Empty.

"Wow, look at all this," I said.

"Like it?" Maya asked, beaming.

"It's amazing, but what did y'all do with the jewelry in the box?"

"It's here, there, and everywhere!" Bronwyn said proudly, then stopped short. "Was that all right?"

"I..." The look on my face must have given her a more eloquent answer.

"Lily, I'm sorry. We didn't realize... I know this was one." Bronwyn handed me a heavy piece made of rough chunks of lapis lazuli and a fringe of tiny bells.

"And this," said Maya, holding up a leather strap with carved brass fittings and green glass beads. Nothing appeared to be worth killing someone over. Then again, I didn't know what I was looking for.

"And here are a couple of pieces similar to the one you've got on, but without the opals. Oh, and I think the crystal chandelier earrings hanging in the front window, too," added Maya as she and Bronwyn hustled about the store, trying to remember which items came from the box. "I'm so sorry. We thought it was all up for grabs. I guess maybe we got a little carried away."

"No, no, it's fine. Really," I said hastily. "I just thought there might be something..."

I reminded myself that my friends didn't know there had been a murder at the jewelry fair and had no way of realizing that anything had occurred besides the smattering of small fires.

I wondered, not for the first time, how much to share with them. As my friends, they had already been through a lot—more than most friendships required. If I was lucky, maybe I could figure out what was happening this time without getting too enmeshed myself, and spare their involvement as well.

I decided to keep Griselda's death to myself for the time being. As my mama used to say, better a blind possum than no possum at all. I didn't actually understand what that meant, but at the moment it seemed appropriate.

Bronwyn and Maya collected several more items they remembered pulling from the tatty cardboard box, but almost everything they showed me appeared to be contemporary ethnic jewelry or just plain junk, like the stacks of cheap, plastic Mardi Gras–style beads. Some of the items, though not particularly valuable, were undeniably pretty, and given our Haight Street clientele I was sure they would sell. But nothing seemed like a secret treasure capable of driving someone to commit violence. Not even anything historic or antique. Maybe Griselda really had just pawned off her extra junk on me. Probably had nothing to do with what had befallen her afterward.

Inspector Carlos always said most murder victims are killed by someone they know. Maybe Griselda had a violent ex-husband or boyfriend, or maybe Johannes had gotten sick of being ordered around like a lackey. Maybe she'd sold someone a fake gem for the price of a real one, and a disgruntled customer wanted payback. Plenty of possibilities.

And after all . . . it's not like every strange murder in San Francisco had to do with yours truly.

Breaking out of my reverie, I realized Maya and Bronwyn were watching me, waiting for a response.

"You know what?" I said lightly. "I'm famished. Maya, would you mind running out and picking up something for lunch? I could really go for a big cup of coffee and a bite to eat. How about you two?"

"I'm starved!" Bronwyn said, sounding relieved.

"Sure thing," Maya said. "What are you in the mood for?"

"Tell you what: You and Bronwyn decide, and surprise me."

"We're on it," Bronwyn said. She took a handful of

take-out menus from the drawer beneath the cash register, and she and Maya settled in to debate the relative merits of sushi versus Thai food versus pizza.

With my friends happily occupied, I focused on the jewelry Maya and Bronwyn identified as coming from Griselda. I held each piece between my palms and concentrated. But as usual I was unable to read any vibrations in the cold of metal and stone. Faint fingers of awareness danced and lingered at the outer reaches of my consciousness, but there was nothing solid to grasp.

It had nothing in common with my natural talent for reading articles of clothing, how easy it was for me to sense what people had been feeling when they wore them.

Giving up, I turned to inspect the cardboard box. It had been used several times; labels in German had been crossed out and written over. The last address, written in a bold black marker, was in Bavaria.

I had been to that part of Germany once, many years ago. I was a teenager searching for my father, who had abandoned my mother and me when I was just an infant. I had encountered a land of storybook cottages, friendly people, hearty food . . . and a few unsavory characters, like my own father.

It occurred to me that I still had an acquaintance in Germany who might know something about what was happening here. It was a long shot, but this fellow . . . well, he made it his business to know people. Supernatural people. And if I was right and Griselda was indeed some kind of witch, she might be on his radar screen. I had no idea where he was after all these years, but as Maya often reminded me, we lived in a high-tech Information Age. Sometimes tracking someone down was as simple as logging on to a social-networking site.

"I'm heading out to pick up lunch," Maya called.

"And coffee?" I said.

"And coffee," Maya confirmed. I handed Maya some money, then looked around for my suspiciously absent familiar. Usually Oscar was piggy-on-the-spot whenever food was being discussed. He had been making himself scarce ever since I wouldn't let him accompany me to the Morning House.

Just as I spotted him snoring under the lacy hems of a rack of 1950s-era negligees, there was a commotion at the front door, and the bell chimed merrily.

Marisela and Shawnelle, the teenagers I'd met at Griselda's jewelry counter, blew into the store. But this time they were traveling with an entourage.

"This really *is* your shop!" exclaimed Marisela. "Wow. *Cool*."

"Hello again. I'm glad you found us," I said, and introduced them to Bronwyn.

"This is Flora and Janelle, and here's my sister Metzli, who's the princess turning fifteen," Marisela said, gesturing to three young teenagers. "It's Metzli's *quinceañera*."

"Congratulations," I said.

"Thanks," the girl said. She and her two friends were already flipping through gowns.

"Metzli is a Nahuatl name, isn't it?" Nahuatl is the language of the Aztecs and of my grandmother, Graciela, who had raised me.

"It means 'goddess of the night,' " a woman in her thirties or forties explained. "I'm Rosa. I'm the mom."

"Nice to meet you."

"And *this* is *mi abuelita*, Carmen." Marisela gestured toward an older version of Rosa. Both women were short and round, with short-cropped and tightly permed hair and broad, smiling faces. "My grandmother, *mi abuelita,* doesn't speak a lot of English."

"*Mucho gusto*," I welcomed them. "*Bienvenidas a* Aunt Cora's Closet."

We had a brief conversation in Spanish that before long defaulted to English. I'm not fluent in Spanish, but because I learned it as a child from my grandmother, my accent is impeccable. As a result, Spanish speakers assume I know more than I actually do, and speak so rapidly that I quickly get lost. Further hampering communication is the fact that most of what I learned from Graciela involved spells and a witchy vocabulary, like the words for "dragon's blood resin" and herbs like eye of newt. A discussion of normal, everyday things usually required a fair amount of sign language and pointing.

Oscar, ever the schmoozer, pranced around and came close to tripping the young women as they giggled and chatted and flipped through the dresses. The girls cooed over him for a few minutes—the typical response when strangers caught sight of my miniature potbellied pig—but once the novelty wore off, they became serious about their fashion hunt. The girls zeroed in on a rack of flouncy formal dresses in the back near the dressing rooms, and seemed partial to those in shades of pink. If this *quinceañera* had anything in common with the others I had witnessed, the dresses would be fluffier and frothier than any wedding ensemble. Nothing like letting an adolescent girl make her own decision about how to dress like a princess for a day.

Marisela held up a blushing-rose-colored, tulip beaded ball gown with a strapless scoop neckline and a skirt made of layers of tulle. Metzli had selected a beaded organza number with a sweetheart neckline and layers of ruffles over another full skirt. Shawnelle found a silky cerise taffeta with a removable single shoulder strap, decorated with silk flowers and beaded gathers throughout the bodice, with a sexy corset-style back.

Not to be outdone, Janelle discovered a burgundy taffeta strapless with feather accents on the scoop neckline and throughout the trailing pickup skirt. It was finished with a ruched waistline that, I thought, would complement her slightly plump, curvy figure.

Maya returned, discreetly set the bags of food in the back room, and, without my having to ask, called her mother, Lucille, to come down to the shop to take measurements. Vintage clothes rarely fit perfectly the first time, and since each piece is unique the only solution is to have a garment altered by a first-rate tailor. Lucille was pure magic with a needle; so much so that at times I wondered if she had a touch of the supernatural about her.

"All right, girls. Follow me," Bronwyn said, and rolled the entire rack of formalwear into the large communal dressing room. "Don't come out until you're gussied up, good and proper."

From behind the drawn curtain we heard the girls chatting and laughing as they tried things on.

"And now for the mamas," I said, turning to Rosa and Carmen. "Are you looking for yourselves as well?"

"Of course . . ." said Rosa. "But I'm sorry to say I have to stick to a pretty tight budget. We've already booked the hall and the band and ordered the cake . . ." She laughed as she idly stroked a strand of pearls hanging on a hook by the door. "I don't know what possessed me to give birth to daughters."

"They're lucky to have you," I said.

She chuckled and waved me off. Her eyes were so friendly, her countenance so smiley, that I imagined she laughed most of the time. And every time she did, her mother nodded and smiled as well.

"One of the great things about buying vintage is that unless you're buying true collectors' items, the pieces are surprisingly affordable." I selected a gown that was perfect for Rosa: a deep sapphire blue with colorful floral embroidery at the yoke. Best of all, its vibrations were warm and calm. "This would look great on you. It's too long, but that's an easy fix."

She held the dress under her chin and looked in the mirror. The silk dragged on the floor, ruining the line, so I knelt and folded it so she could get the full impression. As I leaned over, the medallion fell out of my neckline.

"What a beautiful necklace," said Rosa. She reached down and lifted it up to look at the medallion. "So unusual. Where'd you get it?"

"I, uh . . ." I trailed off, thrown off balance by Rosa's intense gaze. Suddenly I was seeing danger everywhere.

"Oh, hey, that's the one the old lady was showing us at the fair, right?" said Shawnelle, who had emerged from the dressing room in the cerise taffeta and was twirling as she looked at her reflection in the three-way mirror.

"Yes, it is."

"I love opals," said Rosa. "I'm a Libra, so I can wear them. That one in the center is a nice example of a fire opal."

The center stone was a deep, translucent yellow. Most opals are green and blue, or white with flashes of pink and gold.

"What's a fire opal, exactly?"

"They're similar to other opals—they're the same stone in terms of their makeup. But fire opals are a yellow or orange or reddish brown, and come from Mexico instead of Australia, which is where the blue ones come from. There's even an Aztec legend about a fire opal."

"You and your legends, *Mamacita*," said Metzli affectionately to her mother. "You also said the *última muñeca* part of the *quinceañera* ceremony was from an old Mayan tradition."

"It *is*," Rosa insisted with a smile. "I know to you and your friends it's just an excuse for a big party and a pretty new dress, but really the *quince* is a way of holding on to traditions and passing them down through the generations."

Metzli rolled her eyes in my direction, looking for commiseration.

"Don't look at me," I said with a smile. "I have to side with your mom on this one. A *quinceañera* is very special. You're very fortunate."

Metzli gave her mother a bear hug from behind.

"*Gracias, Mami*," she said in a slight singsong.

Rosa squeezed her daughter's arms affectionately. "Anyway, *la última muñeca* means 'the last doll,' and it refers to a girl putting away childish things and becoming a woman. The *quinceañera's* supposed to be the first time a girl wears makeup, though these days . . ."

She looked askance at her daughter, balanced on the cusp of womanhood. Metzli giggled and rolled her eyes again. She was wearing mascara, eyeliner, and blue eye shadow, and had covered her acne with concealer and powder.

Still, it was clear that their teasing and banter was based on a firm mother-daughter bond. I wondered what it would have been like to have that kind of relationship with my mother. I was fortunate Graciela took me in and cared for me after my magical talents emerged and I became too much for my mother, but my grandmother was never one to indulge in foolishness like elaborate parties. She would scoff, telling me the money and energy were better spent on nailing down protection spells. Given how my life had turned out, she had probably been right.

Abandoned by my father, kicked out of my childhood home at the age of eight by my mother . . . no wonder I had issues.

Pushing aside these gloomy thoughts, I realized Marisela's *abuelita* was speaking. Spontaneously, as though she did this often, Marisela started to translate.

"My grandmother says there's a famous story about a magical fire opal. The Aztecs called it *Ojo del Fuego*, which means 'Eye of Fire,' and had the finest jeweler in Tenochtitlán, the Aztec capital city, set the stone in a silver ring after it was discovered in the very depths of the mines. It was considered the stone of Xolotl." In Nahuatl the "x" is pronounced "sh," making Xolotl sound like Sholotal. "Xolotl was the god of fire, disease, and, like, all kinds of bad luck."

Shawnelle snorted as she paraded around the store in the ball gown, loath to take it off. "There's a *god* for bad luck?"

Janelle said, "Hey, want to switch dresses?"

"Sure," said Shawnelle, and they headed back to the dressing room.

"There was a god for just about everything back then," said Marisela in a voice loud enough to carry past the curtains. "It's, like, a Mexican thing. Xolotl is usually depicted with a doglike face, and he could transform himself into an axolotl."

"Okay, I'll bite," said Shawnelle, her voice muffled. "What's an axolotl?"

"I was hoping you'd ask! It's a kind of salamander that lives near Mexico City, which was built in the valley where the Aztecs lived. The salamander's face looks a little like a dog. They're endangered now, so there was a whole public-service campaign to save them. They're really cute."

"Awesome," said Shawnelle as she emerged from the dressing room clad in the pink tulle. Janelle was now wearing the cerise gown, and both girls rocked back and forth to make their skirts sway like bells as they admired themselves in the mirror. "You guys have some pretty wild stories."

"Right?" said Metzli, now wearing an aqua off-the-shoulder gown, complete with crinoline skirts. It was pretty, but far too grown up for her. Rosa held her daughter's gaze, raised her eyebrows, and shook her head. Metzli made a grimace of disappointment, but ducked back into the dressing room to try on another gown.

"*Abuelita* says that when the Spanish invaded, the Aztec priests and *curanderas* conspired to hide the ring containing the *Ojo del Fuego*. It was handed down through the generations. Opals are partly water, so they can carry part of the human spirit, or whatever."

"You said something like that at the fair, right?" Shawnelle asked me.

I nodded. "I heard the stories from my *abuelita*."

"I was wondering . . ." Maya interjected. "I collect stories from local elders. Would you ask your grandmother if she'd be willing to tell me stories and let me record them?"

Marisela spoke with her *abuelita* in Spanish, who nodded, and they made arrangements to get together on Thursday.

Lucille arrived, sewing basket and notepad in hand. After more hemming and hawing and prolonged debate over each gown's relative merits, the girls decided on their dresses. Rosa and her mother also chose their gowns; Rosa selected the sapphire gown I had suggested, and Carmen opted for a loose, classic red-and-gold shift. Lucille would hem both pieces, and take in Rosa's dress a little at the waist. The girls' selections would need additional alterations: a few nips and tucks here and there to make them fit just right, and, in Metzli's case, a panel inserted to expand the bodice.

"The *quinceañera* is a week from Saturday," Rosa said, as I helped Lucille mark the alterations on Metzli's dress.

"*Next* Saturday?"

Lucille, her mouth full of pins, looked at me with wide eyes.

"Um . . . I don't know if all these alterations can be made that soon—" I began.

Metzli spun around, eyes filling with tears. "I knew it was too late! I *knew* it!"

Putting together an elaborate *quinceañera* had much in common with planning a wedding—including the capacity to send normally reasonable people completely around the bend.

"Don't panic, Metzli," said Rosa.

"But, Mom! This is the only dress I *like*. I've tried on so many!"

"It looks *great* on you," said Marisela in a placating, big-sister tone of voice. "Everything'll be fine. You'll see."

By this time Lucille had taken the pins from her mouth. A mother herself, she understood the dynamic.

"No worries, birthday girl," she said soothingly. "Let me make sure I have all these measurements exactly right. I'll pull a couple of the women away from other projects for a few days. We'll get it done. Don't you fret."

Rosa met Lucille's eyes and nodded a silent thank-you. Lucille winked.

"Now, anything else?" Bronwyn asked.

"My tiara!" Metzli said.

Last on the list was what had brought them to Aunt Cora's Closet in the first place: as royalty for a day, no girl could do without a tiara. Fortunately, I had a humdinger of an antique tiara waiting for the right owner.

We polished the rhinestones, wrapped it in tissue, gave the group the name of an informal restaurant down the street that served great pizza, and sent the satisfied *quinceañera* party off with friendly waves and sighs of a job well done.

Lucille went home to get a jump on the alterations, and after putting away the discarded merchandise and straightening the dressing room, Maya, Bronwyn, and I retired to the back room and enjoyed a slightly cold Thai food feast. Sighing contentedly, I sipped a strong cup of French-roast coffee before turning to Maya, my go-to person for anything technical.

"How would I find the phone number of someone in Germany?"

"Depends. You know what part of Germany?"

"No."

"You know her name, though, right?"

"It's a he, and I even know his middle name."

"Piece of cake, then. Follow me," she said, and took a seat at the computer and started clicking. "Sooo, it's a guy, huh?"

"Mmm," I said.

"Would this be an old boyfriend, by any chance?" asked Bronwyn in her oh so innocent voice.

"I wouldn't exactly call him ... I mean ... okay. Yes."

"Good for you! Time really does heal all wounds, doesn't it? Time to put Sailor behind you and move on with your life."

Even just hearing Sailor's name was like a physical slap. Not wanting to engage in this sort of conversation or explain exactly why I was calling a man in Germany, I shrugged and remained silent.

Maya pulled up an Internet directory and tracked down a listing for one Hans Wilhelm Brach. She clicked several times and voilà, up came a bilingual Web page for a psychic who, with the proper monetary motivation, would help you with your love life, your finances, your health, and your career. He would also, the site claimed, contact the dearly departed should one need to "clarify inheritance issues" or "put to rest old demons." Apparently, dropping into the great beyond just to say hi was not the done thing.

I peered at Hans's photo, in which he was posing in front of Tarot cards laid out in an arc on a black silk tablecloth. I would have recognized him anywhere. Same square-jawed face, same blue-green eyes. Same self-satisfied smirk, though he sported a few more wrinkles around the eyes and a thickening of everything, the kind that came with age and overindulgence.

"You want to e-mail him?" Maya asked. "I can just click on this."

"Is there a phone number listed?"

"Right here," Maya said. "I'll bookmark the page for you so you can pull it up anytime."

"Excuse me, Lily, but while it's quiet, would you mind if I quickly run over to Chinatown for supplies?" Bronwyn kept a botanical stand on one side of Aunt Cora's Closet, and recently had been gaining a bit of local fame with her custom tea blends. "Yesterday a customer placed an order for two birthday gift baskets."

"No problem," I said.

"Could I go with you?" Maya asked. "I promised my

mom I'd find out the secret ingredients in your echinacea–rose hip blend. We all done here, Lily?"

"Yes, thank you. You two go ahead. I'm going to finish up a few things here in the back room."

After Bronwyn and Maya left, I glanced at the clock. Germany was eight or nine hours ahead of San Francisco, which meant that since it was two thirty in the afternoon here, it was ten thirty—or eleven thirty—in the evening there. Such a late phone call bordered on rude, but in this case would probably be okay. Unless Hans had changed his habits in the intervening decade, he was a night owl.

I took a deep breath, picked up the phone in the back room, and dialed.

"Lily, what a surprise!" Hans, a psychic, had no need for caller ID. "Well, well. Tell me: How are you? To what do I owe this phone call out of the blue?"

"I need to ask you something. Do you know—"

"*Hey*, you call me up after all this time and I don't get so much as a 'How are you, Hans'?"

I blew out a breath. "How are you, Hans?"

"I am very well, thank you. You know, just the other day I was asked by the German ministry of—"

"I'd love to catch up," I interrupted, remembering Hans's propensity for speaking about his favorite subject: himself. "But right now I need to ask you about a witch from Bavaria named Griselda."

He chuckled. "Half the witches I know are named Griselda."

"She did trade shows, traveled to fairs selling vintage jewelry. Would that ring a bell?"

"Nothing occurs to me, but I could look into it. Why are you asking about her?"

"Listen, Hans . . ." I peeked through the curtains to be

sure I was still alone. "Griselda was killed. Pressed to death."

"Pressed?"

"I don't know the word for it in German." Like many Northern Europeans, Hans spoke excellent English. But witchcraft employed a highly specialized vocabulary, and it was important he comprehend its significance. Although psychics and witches are very different creatures, we were equally vulnerable to the tortures and killings during the purge. As were Jewish sages, healers of all sorts, and the Rom, for that matter. "Pressing is outlined in the *Malleus Malificarum* as a suggested method to extract confessions and information from witches."

"Ah, yes, I have heard of this method. You're saying this woman, this Griselda, was killed this way? Do you have any idea by whom?"

"That's what I'm trying to figure out. I know Germany's a big country, but did your paths ever cross? Do you know of her?"

"No . . . but I will ask around, see what I can find out."

"You might start here," I said, and gave him the return address on the label on the cardboard box Griselda had sold me. "Thank you for looking into this, Hans. I appreciate it."

"Lily, did Griselda . . . give you something? A piece of jewelry—perhaps a ring?"

Chapter 5

An alarm went off in my head.

Could Hans be using his psychic intuition to pick up on my thoughts, or might he know more about Griselda than he was letting on? I trusted Hans, more or less. Or perhaps it would be more accurate to say I didn't *dis*trust Hans any more than anyone else. But given what had happened to Griselda, it seemed wise to be extra cautious. It seemed wise to lie.

"Why would she give me a ring?"

"Amulet rings are used by exorcists to keep demons in check. When such a ring is spun around so the stone is pressed into the palm of one's fist, a skilled practitioner may be powerful enough to go up against even a demonic foe."

"Who said anything about . . . demons?"

"Just a hunch. I'm sensing danger and pandemonium."

I sat back in the chair, impressed. Hans always was a sensitive guy—and not in the New Agey sense of the word.

"Yeah, well . . . that's not much of a stretch for my life lately."

"And I'm sensing a piece of jewelry . . . I think it's a ring."

I glanced down at the opal medallion on my chest. The metal was warm from being in contact with my skin, but otherwise I felt nothing from it. And it wasn't a ring.

"I'm not aware of anything. Why would you think she might have passed me something?"

"Just an idea. Jewelry can be imbued with great power, as I'm sure you know. If this woman had a demon trailing her, perhaps she tried to get the piece to safety."

"Why wouldn't she have used the ring to exorcise the demon herself?"

"Don't be naive. You know as well as I do that even with such an amulet, only highly powerful exorcists could manage to quell a demon. Most would fall under the demon's spell, rather than the other way around. Even just having such a ring in one's possession takes power, much less using it."

"Well, anyway . . . she didn't give me anything," I lied again, just to be on the safe side.

"One more thing: Did you notice a hair amulet?"

I thought about the hair I saw in Griselda's room at the inn. But that hair was "raw"—it hadn't been put into a charm or brew yet. "What would it look like?"

"It doesn't look much like hair, more like twine or silk braided or woven into an intricate, tight design. Women used to make them for their sweethearts, to protect them when they went off to war."

Back in the day people were wildly resourceful and used whatever they had at hand . . . also, in all magical systems, hair was considered to be a powerful memento.

It carried a bit of our personal magic within the strands of DNA.

"I haven't seen anything like that. But why are you asking?"

"Just trying to narrow down what kind of practitioner she might be. A lot of German Rom use hair in their magic, for instance. And such amulets are often used to disguise oneself as powerless, to fly around the radar, I think you say."

I heard a woman's voice in the background, and Hans answered her in a muffled voice.

"I'm sorry. I should let you go," I said, realizing belatedly that it might be awkward for Hans to be receiving calls from ex-girlfriends this late at night, even if he wasn't asleep. Actually, *especially* if he wasn't asleep.

"Let me take your contact information," Hans said. "I'll ask around and I'll let you know what I find out. And Lily? Keep your guard up. It really is great to hear from you . . . once things have settled down a little, I'd love to catch up."

I agreed and hung up, my hand resting on the receiver for a moment while I pondered.

Griselda had several rings on her fingers and dozens in her display. But surely something so valuable—a ring used in demon exorcism—wouldn't have been out in plain sight. I thought back on the Gem Faire, closing my eyes and trying to visualize what I had seen. I couldn't remember anything that might have been a hair amulet, but for all I knew she was wearing it under her T-shirt. And if such an amulet disguised one's power, that would help explain why I hadn't felt the aura of a practitioner.

The more I thought about it, though, the more I realized Griselda had been trying to tell me something while

I stood at her stand. Her long gazes, her suggestion I return to see her after the show or come by the Morning House B and B, or mentioning she might come see me. I wished I had followed my instincts rather than telling myself I was overreacting. She had been scared of something, but unable to say or do anything obvious to ask for help. Had someone been watching us both?

And perhaps most germane: Could I have saved her, had I been more perceptive or on the ball?

The image of Griselda's body again forced its way to the forefront of my thoughts. I stroked my medicine bag and realized that while I had failed to help her, I could at least help find her killer. It was the very least I could do.

I spent the next half hour in a frustrating search for every ring that might have been acquired at the Gem Faire.

The moment Bronwyn and Maya walked in, toting canvas bags full of fragrant herbs and spices, I asked, "Do either of you remember taking any rings out of the cardboard box?"

"Um, yeah. A few, I think," Maya replied.

"Is there a problem?" Bronwyn asked, looking worried.

"No, not really. Just curious."

While Bronwyn put away her packages, Maya scouted out two more rings from our Gem Faire excursion, and then picked a few out of my pile on the counter.

"These were the ones from your box. The others are the ones I bought from the woman who sold the knotted necklaces and the other vendor with the buttons. Bronwyn didn't buy any rings."

There weren't many: two school rings, a fake diamond engagement ring, a plain silver band, a black resin ring with a raven à la Edgar Allen Poe, and a large mock-ivory cameo.

I spread them out on the counter and studied them one by one. I felt a few vague vibrations, but nothing much. The raven—black against a bright yellow background—was by far the most evocative, but it was modern, probably made in the last decade. I slipped it onto the ring finger of my left hand, enjoying the way its bold, large profile made my hand look dainty. It was dramatic and vaguely sinister.

"Hey, now you look like a real witch," said Maya with a smile. "And I mean that in the nicest sense of the word."

As much as I love my friends—and my shop, and my customers—it had been a long and eventful day. As the clock slowly ticked toward the closing hour, I grew anxious to take my pig and head home to the warmth and serenity of our cozy apartment, where I could interrogate my porcine pal in private. Luckily, my commute's pretty short: up a flight of stairs to the apartment above my shop.

So as soon as Bronwyn, Maya, and I flipped the sign to CLOSED, went over the day's receipts, emptied the cash from the register, noted the tally, and straightened the racks, I locked the front door behind them, and followed Oscar into the back room.

I paused briefly to arrange a pile of clothes in front of the jumbo washer and dryer. These clothes were a rarity: new acquisitions that could be tossed right into the machines. Most vintage items had to be dry-cleaned—at a green cleaner, of course, as this was the environmentally conscious Bay Area—or hand washed, or subjected to even more complicated cleaning techniques. I adore the history and feel of vintage clothes, love finding the right outfits for my customers. But the never-ending laundry? Well, let's just say I could use a helper elf.

Speaking of which . . . I looked at my piggy familiar as we climbed the rear stairs. Oscar had his moments, but as he had informed me on more than a few occasions, he was no Igor to do my bidding . . . and he most certainly did *not* do laundry.

A door at the top of the stairs opened onto my apartment, which consists of a bedroom, a bathroom, a checkerboard-tiled kitchen, and a snug living room. By far the best part of the apartment is the beautiful outdoor terrace, where I keep my witch's garden in pots and planters. My grandmother is a kitchen witch and *curandera*, or healer, and raised me in her tradition, which means that botanicals are central to my practice.

I might fail at scrying and divining and intuiting vibrations from jewelry, but when it comes to brewing, I shine.

I breathed a sigh of relief just walking into my apartment; in the tiny foyer was a mirror to repel bad spirits, a consecrated sachet tied with a black ribbon, and a hand-thrown earthen oil pot full of stinging nettles. Throughout the apartment were good-luck symbols and charms to keep me secure and protected . . . especially lately.

I felt safe here, at peace. At home.

"So . . . Oscar, we need to talk more about what you sensed at the Gem Faire."

Oscar usually transformed into his natural self once out of sight of others. But this time he remained in his piggy guise. He trotted over to the sofa, hopped up, faced away from me, and curled onto his side, blowing out a loud sigh.

"Talk to me, Oscar."

He harrumphed.

I was guessing he was still holding a grudge over my reaction to the incident with the security guards. No doubt about it, Oscar was one sensitive gobgoyle.

I sat on the arm of the couch, where I was treated to the sight of his curly little tail.

"I apologized once . . . but I'll say it again: I really am sorry."

One piggy ear twitched.

"I should have known you were there for a good reason. It's just that when I saw the security officers chasing you, I was afraid I could lose you. And I never want to lose you."

Oscar glanced over his piggy shoulder. His standoffishness was starting to melt. When it came right down to it, he was easy.

So I added the crowning touch: "Hmm, I'm feeling a mite peckish. Maybe I'll make a grilled cheese. Would you like one?"

He transformed. "Grilled cheese?"

"Or you could make your own . . ." I teased. Oscar was my first familiar, and once I got over thinking of him as a pet I had to rush home to feed, I taught him how to cook a few simple dishes, such as pancakes or grilled sandwiches. He wasn't bad, though his enthusiasm tended to lead to a kitchen floor liberally dotted with batter and a stovetop spattered with oil. And no matter how I nagged, cajoled, and scolded, he flat-out stank at cleanup.

"But everything tastes so much better when *you* make it, mistress."

I smiled at this blatant flattery. Still, I *was* an excellent cook, if I did say so myself. Blending different ingredients, using the transformational power of heat and fire to create something new . . . cooking is like spell casting in its most elemental form.

I opened the fridge and took out cheese and butter, while Oscar retrieved a fresh loaf of sourdough from the old tin breadbox and laid it on the wooden cutting board.

"Now, tell me: What made you decide to come find me in the Cow Palace?" I asked, slicing the bread for which San Francisco is justifiably famous.

"I felt something, and I figured you needed your Oscar by your side. Even powerful witches need backup sometimes."

"What did it feel like?"

"Something bad. Something . . ." Just as he had in the utility closet earlier today, he looked over both shoulders and dropped his gravelly voice. "Something weird. Maybe even . . . demonic."

"You're sure?"

He rolled his eyes and climbed onto the tiled counter to watch me cook. "I know what I felt, mistress."

"Could it have been a powerful witch instead?" I lit the fire under my old cast-iron skillet.

There was a long pause. "Maybe."

"Can you tell me anything else? It's hard to know what to think when I don't know what, or who, I'm looking for." I started to cut thin slices of the fine, extra-sharp cheddar I had bought at the farmers' market.

Oscar snuck a piece of cheese as he shook his head, his big eyes, as pure and bright as green glass, wide and afraid. He studied my lunar calendar, as though suddenly intrigued by the phases of the moon.

"Oscar?"

"I thought at first . . . I sensed something from a long time ago. Ancient times." Now he began inspecting the pot of basil I kept on the counter for good luck and fresh pesto.

"Who or what?"

"I dunno. When I got inside, all I saw was regular humans. It was a little confusing, all those legs. It's not easy being a pig."

"So, none of the vendors or the guards or anybody like that seemed like an, I don't know . . . an embodied demon—something like that?"

Oscar leaned against the cupboard, waved one oversized hand in the air, and cackled, emitting a rusty sound like an old saw bending. I felt vaguely insulted. Although I was the first to admit my limitations, it annoyed me when my familiar pointed them out. Because I had left Graciela's side before completing my training, I was missing a huge amount of knowledge, especially where demons were concerned.

"Okay, so you came after me because you thought you sensed something ancient, perhaps demonic. But when you got inside the Cow Palace, you didn't see anyone who fit that bill?"

"Isn't that what I just said?"

"I just wanted to make sure I got it right. I'm a little at sea on this one. A woman was killed at the fair, Oscar. She was killed by pressing. I'm pretty sure she was a witch, and someone was trying to force her to tell them something."

He shot me an alarmed look. "That's very bad."

I nodded and blew out a breath.

"I don't want you to be pressed, mistress."

"Thank you, Oscar. I'd just as soon avoid it myself."

I dropped a pat of butter in the iron pan. It sizzled a little.

"That smells good."

"It does, doesn't it?"

"Mistress?"

"Hmm?"

"About the pressing. . . . Demons don't play that way. The fires and all, sure. Demons like fire. And they like to scare people and make them crazy."

"I know."

"But . . . demons are all about having fun in the moment. He might try to play with a witch, but killing one would end the fun. Killing her, especially like that . . . that's the sort of thing cowans do."

I nodded. "Cowan" is a derogatory word for non-witchy humans, and usually I tried to avoid its use. But in this case, the dangerous narrow-mindedness implied by the term seemed apt for the situation.

The pan was heated and ready. I arranged the pieces of bread, placed the cheese on them, and added slices of ripe red tomatoes grown in my garden, reveling in their rich scent. I would sprinkle Parmesan and a little garlic salt on the outside of the bread so it browned on the iron skillet. A gourmet grilled cheese.

My movements were rote, familiar, and evocative of another time in my life. I remembered my mother's kitchen was fragrant with the spices used in recipes handed down through her mother and grandmother. Most of their Cajun customs had been lost after the family relocated from New Orleans to west Texas, but tradition lived on through the food: gumbo and dirty rice, jambalaya and salmon croquettes, red velvet cake and peach cobbler and apple brown Betty. I had a strained relationship with my mother and was rarely nostalgic for her company, but the act of cooking—even something as simple as a grilled-cheese sandwich—bound me to her nonetheless.

As the sandwiches browned, I pondered. It had been months since I'd dealt with a demon, and weeks since I'd been embroiled in a murder investigation. I had been fostering a tiny flame of hope that things might have settled down in this beautiful city by the bay, but the longer I lived in San Francisco the more I realized my decision to move here may not have been entirely my own. It seemed I was needed here. There were crimes in these parts that only a powerful, hereditary witch like me had the skills to address.

After we polished off dinner—I was still full of pad Thai, so I gave Oscar most of my sandwich and made him another after he claimed he was still peckish, despite consuming a large glass of sweet tea, two Pink Lady apples, and three chocolate chip cookies—my familiar groused about helping me wash up, then curled up in his nest of blankets on top of the refrigerator. He was snoring in three seconds flat.

I poured myself a glass of nice Bordeaux and stepped out onto the terrace to enjoy a warm San Francisco night. Unlike in West Texas, where the temperature on a "warm night" might not dip below ninety-five and the humidity remained in the high double digits, here in the city by the bay a tropical evening meant the marine layer remained at sea rather than blanketing the city with nature's version of air-conditioning. It had been unusually hot lately, the temperature hovering in the eighties for days on end. The locals were wilting, accustomed as they were to the traditional foggy San Francisco summer.

But I thought the evening perfect.

And the plants loved it. The flowers and herbs I grew were useful and often essential to my spells: witch's thimbles—also known as foxglove—could be mixed with devil's nettle, yarrow, and fool's parsley to create a po-

tent poultice; cumin and verbena might be ground together for use in love potions; the spiky purple blooms
of monkshood were brewed with cinquefoil and bella-
donna and water parsnips for a concoction that helped
to open oneself to the spirits on the other side.

The garden, the cooking, spending time with new
friends and old clothes . . . all of these things brought
comfort to my life. But tonight I couldn't stop thinking
about what I had seen today.

Poor Griselda. Pressed, then stabbed.

The *Malleus Malificarum*, the handbook for European witch hunters, outlined the method of pressing a
witch. Maybe I should look it up, just in case . . . but I
refused to keep a copy of the vile tome in my apartment.
My neighbor Sandra had one; I could ask to borrow it.
But if I did that, she would have lots of questions, and I
didn't want to have to deal with her. Then I reminded
myself that I lived in the twenty-first century. A copy of
the *Malleus* would no doubt be available online. I would
look it up tomorrow, surrounded by the vibrant shop activity. It would be too much for me tonight, alone.

I picked up my gardening shears and started dead-
heading roses, then pruned the dwarf cherry. Next were
the small containers of herbs and flowers, one for each
astrological sign: chrysanthemums, heather, and pink
rose thorns gave a person temporary influence over a
Scorpio. Historically a lot of folks believed that a witch's
"influence" insinuated an evil plan, but it was often a
method used to cure someone. If an Aquarius took ill, a
brew including foxglove and snowdrops could be especially effective. And the judicious use of henbane helped
with afflictions common to Pisces—though poisonous in
large doses, tiny amounts of henbane used to be added
in the brewing of many traditional German beers.

Germany. I hadn't been lying when I told Lloyd I had family there—as far as I knew, my father still resided in the remote Bavarian village where I had tracked him down when I was seventeen. Could there be a connection between my estranged father and Griselda? Possible, but it wasn't as though all the magical folk in Germany knew one another, any more than we do here. Still, an old friend had called the shop a few weeks ago to tell me my father might be coming to town. For a while I had been on guard, but when nothing came of it I figured she had been mistaken. But maybe there was more to it then I'd thought.

If someone believed Griselda possessed something valuable, ransacked her room, and killed her, but still hadn't found it . . . it seemed to me there were a finite number of places it could have ended up. Either I had that something among the things she had sold me, or it was still with her things from the show, or she had gotten it to someone else or put it into a secret hiding place.

And just where had Johannes gotten to?

I needed some help and advice. One person fit the bill: the local witchy godfather, Aidan Rhodes. I had been livid with Aidan since he banished my—what should I call him? "Boyfriend" sounded adolescent; "lover" seemed an overstatement, considering we'd spent a grand total of one night together. My . . . *friend*, Sailor.

I could also use Sailor right now, in more ways than one. I missed him with a wrenching sense of loss in my gut; his absence—and the lack of news from or about him—made me believe I was an abject failure at romance. But right now I needed him for more practical reasons. With his psychic abilities he would be able read the jewelry I'd acquired from Griselda, I felt sure. Perhaps he would be able to tell me if I had a prized piece, and maybe even figure out what was so special about it that people were willing to kill for it.

I glanced at the stars high overhead. It was late, but I couldn't sleep. Instead I trekked downstairs to the shop to examine the loot from the Gem Faire once more. Perhaps alone at night, when the vibrations were calm, I could sense something.

Spreading all the jewelry we had gathered on the glass display counter, I prepared myself as though I were scrying in my crystal ball—which I still sucked at, despite all my efforts. But I forced such negativity from my mind. I stroked my medicine bag to center myself, blew out a long breath, mumbled an incantation, and slowly opened my eyes. I held my hands out over the mixed necklaces, brooches, and rings, and tried to open myself to any whisper of sensation.

Nothing. Not one darned pulse. No vibrations; no humming.

It was another exercise in frustration, not helped by the fact that I was tired. Feeling defeated, I shoved my hands in the deep pockets of my skirt—only to hit something small and solid.

The cuff link. It was still in my pocket from earlier today.

I shouldn't have left the crime scene; I should have stayed and spoken with the authorities when they arrived to investigate Griselda's death. I had been afraid, though I didn't know of what exactly. Now shame washed over me. How often had I heard Inspector Romero say, *"Tell me anything at all, even if it seems like it's not important."*

I owed Carlos a phone call in the morning. I really didn't know what I could offer, but it was only right to try.

Still, something was holding me back, and I knew what it was: Oscar's words had not been reassuring. Before I talked to Carlos I wished I could be certain whether we were dealing with a demon, some sort of murderous witch, or simply a homicidal human. Though Carlos and I had a decent relationship, it was fragile.

And any murder involving demons—even tangentially— was guaranteed to get tricky fast.

Early the next morning, bleary with the lack of sleep, I grabbed my Brazilian shopping basket to head down Haight Street to Coffee to the People, my favorite neighborhood café. Even at this hour, the weather was warm and unusually muggy, reminding me of Texas.

On the curb outside my store sat a skinny, sleepy-looking young man. Conrad was one of the dozens of street kids who hung out on Haight Street, scrounging for spare change. He spent his nights in nearby Golden Gate Park, but spent most of his days outside my shop. Conrad and I had bonded not long after I opened Aunt Cora's Closet; two social misfits who somehow fit together. He did the occasional odd job for me and watched over Aunt Cora's Closet, and in return I did my best to make sure he had at least one decent meal each day.

"Yo, dudette! How're things?"

I smiled at his use of the feminine form of his favorite word, "dude."

"Hanging in there," I answered, thinking how complicated an honest answer to that simple question would be. "How about you?"

His eyes narrowed. "Keepin' an eye out for strangers."

"I thought there were no strangers in the Haight, only friends you haven't met yet."

"Dude?" Conrad tried to focus, confusion in his red-rimmed eyes.

I longed for the day Conrad would take me up on my offer to help him get off whatever he was on. My concern for his well-being had been solidified not long ago when he'd risked his own safety to protect Aunt Cora's Closet from intruders. He was a good guy, and I was certain he would have a lot to offer once he got himself together. I had been tempted, more than once, to use my powers to force him into rehab, but such a spell would never last. The human will was powerful indeed, capable at times of frustrating even powerful magic. For the transformation from addict to sobriety to last, the subject had to embrace it. Conrad was not there yet, and I could only hope I would be around when that day came.

"Never mind," I said. "I was just joking. Are you worried about strangers?"

"Hey, did you hear about the fire dancing in the park?"

Conversations with Conrad were often a little disjointed. But he was my friend, so I played along. "Actually, I saw some posters about fire dancing just yesterday. And I think Maya mentioned something about dancing in the park. What is it, exactly?"

"It's awesome, is what it is. It's, like, people coming together as brothers and sisters to make *art*, dude. Like the fire is *alive*. Duuuude. You should check it out."

"I will. Shall I get you the usual from the café?"

"Don't look now, but those two guys in the old Ford Scout?" Conrad lifted his chin in the direction of the hat store across the street. "Those are the strangers I was talking about."

I glanced over but saw nothing but a big, mint green truck.

"I said, 'Don't look'!" he whispered.

"Oka-a-ay." I played along. "What about them?"

Conrad frowned.

Despite urging me toward subtlety, Conrad slewed his eyes across the street at the old truck again, and frowned.

"Been there since I arrived. I think those two dudes spent the night there."

I nodded and waited. In this part of town—and given rents in San Francisco—spending the night in a vehicle wasn't all that unusual. After all, Conrad and his friends slept wherever they could—in door fronts, nooks under stairs, or nearby Golden Gate Park.

"Want me to go talk to them?"

"*No*. Dude."

"All righty, then," I said, not sure what Conrad wanted from me. "I'm headed to the café. Unless you tell me different, I'll bring you a bagel and a Flower Power."

Flower Power was a drink that was a proprietary recipe at Coffee to the People and was an homage to the days when the flower children came to the Haight from all over with the dream of building a society of peace, love, and understanding. If only they had succeeded.

"Thanks. I'll keep an eye on 'em. Want me to sweep the sidewalk? Make it less obvious I'm, you know, watchin' 'em."

"You're a born covert operative, Conrad."

"Duuude."

I returned twenty minutes later with breakfast and hot drinks for both of us, plus a jalapeno-avocado-garlic bagel for Oscar.

But Conrad had disappeared, and so had the truck.

Unfortunately, in their place was an SFPD radio car. Double-parked, right in front of Aunt Cora's Closet.

I didn't need the gift of sight to know that this did not bode well.

Chapter 6

In the past when I'd dealt with the San Francisco Police Department, it had been in the form of Inspector Carlos Romero, and he'd always come to interrogate me at my store. Such drop-by visits had seemed rather fraught, but now they seemed downright civilized in comparison.

It was decidedly less friendly to be brought down to the station by a uniformed cop I didn't know. My heart pounded as I followed the young man through a maze of corridors and desks.

Sorry to say this wasn't my first visit to a jailhouse. The first time was years ago, in my hometown of Jarod, where the two-room police department and jail were eerily similar to that of Sheriff Andy Taylor's in the old television series *The Andy Griffith Show*. The second time was not long ago, when I'd been busted for trespassing in Oakland's Paramount Theater. Oakland's jail is the real deal, and I'd spent an unpleasant few hours in custody before Carlos pulled some strings and got me released. (The charges, I am happy to say, were dropped.) Apart from these two experiences, my understanding of the underbelly of law enforcement was based on snatches of TV shows and movies. So when the uniformed officer drove me to the station I rather expected to find myself chained to a table and interrogated in an isolated room outfitted with a two-way mirror.

Instead I had been escorted to a large room jammed with desks, many arranged in pairs facing one another. The desks were occupied by dozens of men—and a few women—dressed in neat pants and shirts, filling out paperwork, flipping through case files, or talking on the phone. The officer who had brought me in led me to one such desk, behind which sat a compact man, physically fit and clad in chinos and a black leather hip-length jacket. Homicide Inspector Carlos Romero, SFPD.

"Thank you for coming in," he said, standing as I approached. Carlos had dramatic, dark features, a somber but intelligent air, and a way of carrying himself that radiated authority. Though he wasn't a physically imposing man, Carlos had a way of making me feel safe, as though he had everything under control.

He waved me into the beige office chair facing his.

"Of course. What's going on?"

He looked at me for a long moment before speaking. This wasn't unusual for Carlos, who, I was almost sure, was more perceptive about people than was strictly normal. Loudly ringing telephones, the low murmur of cops chatting, and people coming and going created a wall of ambient noise that gave our conversation a semblance of privacy. Still, the setting wasn't nearly as official as I had expected it to be.

"A woman was killed yesterday."

"I'm sorry to hear that."

I volunteered nothing further. I had intended to call

Carlos today to tell him what little I knew about Griselda's death, but the fact that he'd brought me down to the
station was a sign that something big was afoot, and I
should be careful what I said.

One of Carlos's interrogation techniques was to make
a statement, then fall silent, waiting for the other person
to fill the void with whatever information he or she had.
Even when you knew it was happening it was a surprisingly hard technique to resist. But resist I did.

And so we sat in silence. After several minutes, Carlos
apparently realized I was not falling for his trick.

"It's not even my case," he said. "But I felt like I
should talk to you about it."

"Oh? Why is that?"

"The way the woman died is unusual."

He was trying again to get me talking, but I still wasn't
falling for it. I would answer his questions—as fully and
honestly as I could—but I would not take the lead.

"I remembered reading something about the method
used to kill her. So I looked it up." He leaned across his
desk, pulled a library book from beneath a stack of papers, opened it to a marked page, and read:

"Throughout the witch hunts various methods
were used with particular success by the church-led
inquisitors: there was the *strapatto*, in which the accused's hands were tied behind her back and then
lifted into the air, resulting in the dislocation of the
shoulders; and the *indicium aquae*, or ordeal of
swimming, in which drowning constituted innocence;
as well as pressing, in which the accused was sandwiched between two boards and slowly crushed by
the weight of stone upon stone."

Again with the staring. I was sure I looked white as a sheet. Even hearing the descriptions of those torments made me sick to my stomach. I caressed my medicine bag. Some things chill me to the core, which I can only assume are primordial memories or fears passed down from my witch ancestors, across the generations and through time.

"The woman who was killed yesterday," Carlos continued, "appears to have been murdered by what's called pressing, a traditional way of killing a witch."

"Actually, pressing was a method of *torturing* a witch in hope of forcing a confession. Death was a bonus, I guess."

"You want to tell me what you know about this case?"

There weren't a lot of police officers who understood, much less believed in, my powers. Carlos and I had gotten off to a somewhat rocky start, but now we were friends. Of a sort. Now that he was no longer playing games with me, I was ready to tell him what little I knew.

"I assume we're talking about the woman at the Gem Faire?"

"You were there?"

"Yes. I met the uh . . . victim, Griselda, at her stand there. We had a brief discussion about opals, and. . . ." I trailed off, deciding not to tell him about the jewelry. He would come to the store and confiscate it for evidence, and I wasn't ready to let it go; if there was anything there, I had to find it. If I turned it over to the police they would just pack it up in whatever warehouse was used to house such evidence, where it would languish alongside evidence bags containing murder weapons and bloody clothing.

"And . . . ?"

"And nothing. That was about it, as far as our interaction went."

Carlos stared at me. He knew I was lying.

I could sense his disappointment, and it pained me. I could feel our relationship shift, from wary but friendly mutual respect, back to police versus possible suspect.

"Whatever you say," he said with a shake of his head, making a note in his ever-present notebook. "You don't seem all that surprised to hear she was killed."

"I saw her body."

"You *saw* her? When was this?"

"Yesterday, when fires started in the main exhibit hall, the sprinklers were on, everyone was running . . . I saw her there. Under the board . . . the security guards were waiting for the emergency vehicles, so I . . . left."

"You just turned and left. You didn't think maybe someone might want to talk with you?"

"I didn't *see* anything, Carlos. I don't know what happened. I happened upon her body after she'd already been discovered, and had nothing to add. It seemed . . . ghoulish to hang around and gawk. Disrespectful, especially given how she suffered. I was going to call you today to tell you I was there, just in case, but you beat me to it."

He let out a sigh and pinched the bridge of his nose. "Okay. How well did you know Griselda?"

"I told you, I'd never met her before yesterday. I didn't know her at all."

"Did you see anything suspicious, anything at all? Did she say anything odd? Give any sort of warning or indication that she was worried about something?"

"Not really. But we didn't talk long."

"What did you talk about?"

"Opals, mostly."

"How did that subject come up?"

"She was selling jewelry with opals. There were two young women at the booth looking at some pieces, and one said opals are bad luck."

"And are they?"

"It depends on who's wearing the gem and how they treat it. Opals are made up partly of water, so they can shatter easily if not cared for properly. And because water is elemental, it can carry part of our warmth. Our energy. A bit of our soul, if you like."

"They're not particularly valuable, are they?"

"Not especially, no. Not like diamonds or rubies. But if they're passed down, they often hold sentimental value. It's hard to imagine someone would commit murder to retrieve something with purely sentimental value, though."

"You'd be surprised," Carlos said. "People kill for all kinds of reasons. Usually those reasons don't make much sense."

I thought of how much craziness and cruelty Carlos must have seen in his long career as an urban cop, and marveled at his ability to still care about each case.

"You meet anyone else at the victim's stand?" he asked.

"There was a young man working with Griselda—maybe her son? She called him Johannes."

"Last name?"

"I don't know."

"You say he's her son?"

"She didn't say he was; I just assumed . . ." It dawned on me that Lloyd, the owner of the Morning House, had told me Johannes was Griselda's son. I didn't want to mention that little excursion to Carlos, at least not at this moment. I thought he might take it the wrong way. "He could have been her assistant. All I really know is he's young, blond, and German. Blue eyes. He was moving some boxes for her."

"Heavy boxes? Full of jewelry?"

I nodded. When I saw him running from the Cow Palace he had seemed so frightened, so intent on escaping . . . what, exactly? He mentioned *Hexen*, but had he been running away from a witch, or simply referring to Griselda being killed like one? I just couldn't imagine him somehow taking part in such a heinous crime. As if I knew what lurked in the hearts of men.

"He say anything?"

"Something in German. I wasn't really paying attention."

"Who else?"

"Just the pair of teenagers looking at the jewelry, but they wandered off before I did and didn't seem to know Griselda. If you need to get a hold of them, I've got their number—they came by Aunt Cora's Closet afterward, looking for *quinceañera* stuff."

"Oh yeah? My niece's fifteenth is coming up this year. Costs a fortune."

I was glad to get our discussion back on friendlier ground. "Tell her parents to bring her by the store. I've got plenty of beautiful, pastel-colored flounces, and for much less than bridal or dress shops charge."

"I might just do that." He sucked on his front teeth, not meeting my eyes, and made another note on his pad. "Anyone else hanging around, seeming like they didn't fit in?"

I shook my head again. And then I thought about the man at the refreshment counter. The man in the suit, Gene, who had looked so out of place. There was something about him that seemed a little odd, but surely it wasn't worth mentioning. After all, wearing different clothes and hairstyle didn't make someone guilty of murder. The man hadn't done anything particularly suspicious. . . .

"Lily?" I looked up to find the inspector's dark eyes on me. "You sure?"

"It was probably nothing."

"What do I always say? 'Tell me everything, no matter how insignificant.' Let me be the judge of whether it's nothing or something."

Despite myself, I smiled. "Okay, but you asked for it. There was a man at the refreshment counter who seemed . . . out of place."

"How so?"

"Well, for one thing, he was wearing a suit. And he sort of stood out—a man in the Cow Palace full of mostly women."

"Man in a suit. Wool or gabardine?"

"Sharkskin, actually."

"Yikes. No wonder he stood out. Did you speak with him?"

"A little."

"About what?"

"He offered me some candy, asked how I liked the show."

"Candy. What kind?"

"Jelly beans."

"So let me sum up: a well-dressed man strikes up a conversation and offers you some of his jelly beans. Sounds to me like he was trying to pick you up."

"You said you wanted to know everything. So now you know."

"He threaten you in any way?"

"No. He really didn't do anything untoward. I think

he just struck me as odd because he was dressed so differently. Like he just flew in from Jersey for a business meeting, but wound up at the Cow Palace refreshment stand by accident. Oh, and he said his name was Gene."

"Jersey Gene with the Jelly Beans, huh?"

"I'm getting the feeling you're not taking this seriously."

"On the contrary, I take you very seriously."

As Carlos scribbled some more, I glanced around the large room full of detectives. A trio of men stood by the water cooler, talking about a contestant on *American Idol*. It struck me that while my coming here to the police station was a big deal, to these folks it was just another day at the office. Police officers were just people, like any others. Important to keep in mind.

"Tell me more about this witch-killing method."

"There's not that much to tell beyond what I'm sure you read in that book. Pressing wasn't meant to kill but to extract information. It was a kind of slow torture."

"Not all that slow in this case."

My heart lurched, my mind returning, unbidden, to the vision of Griselda dead beneath that board. . . .

"Take a look at this," he said, showing me a photograph on his iPhone. "Recognize it?"

"It's an athame. I saw it earlier at Griselda's stand. It's a ceremonial knife."

"Witches use it?"

"Along with many others. It's used for rituals, but not all worshippers are witches."

"The lab's testing it for fingerprints and DNA. I know you don't have fingerprints. Is that common among your kind?"

"Not that I know of. I told you before, I have a recognized medical condition, dermatopathia pigmentosa reticularis. It's a quirk of genetics, unrelated to my other quirks."

He nodded as a man came up and dropped off a file. Carlos looked casual, sitting back in the chair, one arm hanging over the back while his other hand played with a paper clip on the desk. But, as always, when he fixed me with a look it was challenging, intense, demanding.

I continued. "I find it hard to believe a witch would kill another witch with such a precious knife, much less by pressing her. Most of us are cognizant of the historical meaning of such things. It would be a major faux pas in the witchcraft community, to say the least."

Carlos gave an impatient twitch of his head. "Seems to me we both know witches are as capable of murder, as well as a lot of other things, as others. Just because I respect your talents doesn't mean I give you—or any other practitioner—a pass."

"I wouldn't expect you to," I said, stung.

"According to the security personnel, there was a miniature pig running around at one point."

"Oh yeah?"

"Gotta say, Lily, there aren't that many pet pigs in the city." He consulted his notepad. "Even fewer pigs belonging to, and I quote, 'A woman with dark hair and eyes, wearing an old-fashioned dress and orange tennis shoes.' Ring any bells?"

"I'd say the shoes were more saffron than orange."

His mouth turned up, just barely, on one side. "How did your pig happen to be running around the gem show? You brought him in?"

"He was supposed to stay in the van."

"Then how'd he get out?"

"I'm not sure about the details of his escape myself. But pigs are awfully smart."

He nodded thoughtfully and resumed tap-tap-tapping the paper clip on the desk blotter crowded with papers.

"The timing strikes me as interesting," he said.

"How so?"

"All the security personnel were focused on you and your pig, while back behind the curtains our victim was being pressed, as you say."

I hadn't thought about the timing. It finally dawned on me—he was implying that the ruckus stirred up by Oscar on the floor of the gem show might have served as a distraction.

"Inspector, I assure you I had nothing to do with any of this. Oscar had nothing to do with any of this. Think about it: Why would I want to draw attention away from the murder? I had met the victim only a few minutes before."

"I'm not suggesting you have any connection to the victim."

"Surely you're not suggesting I have a connection to the murd—"

As the words left my mouth, a handcuffed man in custody walked past the Inspector's desk, guided by a cop. He had a full head of snowy white hair, and wore a nice but rumpled suit. But what caught my eye were the numerous scars covering his face, his neck, his hands—every visible inch of his flesh bore the distinctive, shiny scars common to severe burn victims. He and the cop disappeared down a hall.

It had been a long time. Almost fifteen years since I'd last seen him; almost thirty since he'd abandoned me and my mother.

Declan Theodore Ivory.

My father.

Chapter 7

I tried to remain expressionless. But Carlos was no rookie. He recognized shock when he saw it.

"When I looked into your history a while back, I learned that your father left the family when you were a baby."

I nodded.

"And you were raised by your grandmother?"

"I lived with my mother until I was eight, then went to live with Graciela."

"Any idea why your father left?"

I shrugged. "I was a baby, Inspector. Remember?"

"What did your mother tell you?"

"My mother's explanation doesn't bear repeating."

"When's the last time you saw him?"

"Many years ago. After I left Jarod, when I was seventeen, I searched for him." A strange note crept into my voice, as it did anytime I spoke about my father. Even to my own ears it sounded flat, distant, as though someone else were speaking. "It took me a year to track him down to a small village in Germany."

"And how was that family reunion?"

I pulled at my lip, looked around the station. I was hoping to catch another glimpse of him.

"Lily?"

"Unpleasant." He had raged at me, demanded I leave. It had ended in an altercation, the details of which I couldn't remember.

And that was the most troubling part of the encounter. I usually remember everything—for instance, I remembered the fight between my father and Graciela the night he left us. Only a tot, I had watched it all from my playpen.

But I couldn't remember what took place between me and my father that night in Bavaria.

Graciela had warned me before I left in search of him that it was too late, that my father was already . . . lost. But I refused to believe it. I was sure I could track him down, that I could somehow save him from whatever trouble he had gotten himself into. Graciela had always told me that I was innately stronger than my father. And my powers, even at seventeen, were considerable. What I didn't know then, hadn't yet learned, was that temptation was stronger than either of us.

Power yields to corruption. So easily.

"He claims he's not your father."

"Ha!" I said, the humorless laugh wrested from me before I could stop it. "Seriously? That's a good one. But . . . how did you connect him to me?"

"Your last name is unusual. When I asked, before he could catch himself, he seemed surprised to hear your name. Though he denied it, it seemed a bit too curious. So, you're saying it's him?"

I wondered why my father would have denied our relationship. *Gee, thanks, Dad,* I thought. *As if I don't have enough abandonment issues.*

"Is he somehow connected to this crime?"

"He's a person of interest."

"Why?"

"We got a tip, and a couple of witnesses placed him at the scene. We're waiting on DNA results, so we'll see."

I thought about the cuff link I had found. If it belonged to my father that would explain why I had felt something from it, despite my typical lack of sensitivity to jewelry. Was it evidence? If it was, should I hand it over?

I was pretty sure Carlos's answer would be an emphatic yes.

But . . . I hesitated. My father may be scum, but he was kin. Even after everything that had happened, that counted for something. Perhaps it wouldn't hurt if I held on to it a little longer, tried harder to read its vibrations.

"So you're wondering if I used my pig to create a diversion while my father murdered a woman with an athame?"

"It crossed my mind."

There was a long pause

"I thought we were friends."

He leaned forward, elbows on his thighs. His dark eyes were intense and searching. "Lily, you're part of a world I can't fathom. I respect it, and I know a little more about it than my colleagues. But I also know I'll never really understand that world. Frankly, I'm okay with that. Until folks start getting hurt. Then I have to ask questions, tough questions, and sometimes I have to ask them of people I like."

"Ask away."

"Could the murder have been the result of some sort of grudge between witches, something like that?"

"I have no idea," I said. "I didn't know Griselda. Until a couple of minutes ago, I didn't know my father was in town. I don't know what his connection to Griselda may or may not have been."

"They both came from Germany."

"True. As do a lot of people. Almost all Germans come from Germany, for instance."

"But your father's not actually German." Carlos ran a hand through his close-cropped hair and let out a sigh. "Okay . . . I guess that's all I've got for now."

I waited for him to tell me to stay out of his case, like he always did. But this time he remained silent. Then again, I reminded myself, it wasn't his case. Was it possible he was thinking the inspector in charge could use a little witchy help?

"Could I . . . could I see him?"

"Not at the moment. He's here for questioning. But you might be called in for an interview with Inspector Leibowitz, who's the primary on the murder. And Lily?" Carlos said with a slight smile. "FYI, Leibowitz isn't nearly as open-minded as your old buddy Carlos."

"I wouldn't expect anything else, old buddy."

Carlos's eyes dropped to my chest. My neckline wasn't particularly low, and this wasn't the sort of behavior I associated with Carlos.

"Nice necklace. Opals, right?"

I nodded.

He pursed his lips slightly.

"You be sure to let me know if anything turns up from the gem show, or if you remember anything that might shed some light on this case. You hear?"

I nodded and stood. I peered down the hallway, where I had last seen my father.

Okay, I have a few father issues: Abandonment. Anger. Guilt. Fear. But despite it all, he was still my father.

What in tarnation was going on?

Back at Aunt Cora's Closet, Bronwyn hustled out from behind her herbal stand, beside herself with worry. Hot on her heels was Oscar, his piggy hooves clacking on the wood floor.

"Lily, oh, my *goddess*! Conrad told us you were taken away by the police! Are you all right? Did you see Carlos?"

Inspector Romero had come by the store often enough that he knew my friends well. Though I liked Carlos, it seemed sad that not only had one of my first acquaintances in San Francisco been a homicide inspector, but we'd spent enough time together to develop a relationship.

"I did," I said, stooping to give Oscar a kiss. Once more I wondered how much to tell Bronwyn and Maya about the events at the Gem Faire. Their being in the building while a murder had been committed didn't seem worth worrying them over. My father being in town . . . that might be something to be concerned about. But what would I say? *Best keep on your toes because my father's deep into magic and, oh, by the way, he's kind of nuts.* I felt protective of them, didn't want to expose them to disturbing ideas of demons and the like.

Then I reminded myself of what Bronwyn kept telling me: friendship wasn't a one-way street. True friends didn't just offer help; they also asked for and accepted help when they needed it.

Bronwyn searched my face. "You're probably getting sick of my asking this, but is everything okay, Lily? Because I can't help thinking something's bothering you."

"I've got a few things on my mind, but nothing to worry about at the moment. If something develops, I'll talk to you about it, okay? In the meantime, I've gotten way behind on my bookkeeping. But before I tackle that, I want to get changed."

"VCT?" Bronwyn asked, our code for "Vintage Clothes Therapy."

"Full-on VCT." I smiled.

After perusing the many options I found the perfect thing: a neat little '40s-era seersucker jacket and skirt, worn with a simple tank. Its vibrations were jaunty, making me feel as if I were attending the state fair back in the day, and I hoped its devil-may-care brashness would help me adjust my attitude.

Now properly attired, I sat down at the counter to start the process of adding up the store's receipts and comparing them to our overhead and inventory expenditures. I hauled out my calculator and files of financial papers, and started tallying receipts. Prior to opening Aunt Cora's Closet I had no idea how much work was involved in running one's own business. I could handle the long hours and lack of vacation and bottomless to-do lists, but the paperwork nearly drove me screaming into the street. It was even worse than the never-ending laundry.

Most frustrating of all, when it came to paperwork my witchy skills were useless.

My reward for finishing the job at hand was to go thrift-store shopping. Weekends were a prime time for folks to clean out their closets, attics, and garages, so Mondays were the best days to scope out the local Goodwill and Salvation Army stores. I always look forward to these trips: the serendipity of it; the possibility of what had been unearthed from old trunks, grandma's attic, or a fit of spring cleaning. At Aunt Cora's Closet we stock some very old items—true vintage clothing—but we also carry goods from as recently as the seventies and eighties. Polyester shirts with wild designs and candy pastels had become popular with the city's hipsters, much to my surprise. Polyester doesn't breathe the way natural fabrics, such as cotton, linen, and silk, do, and thus tends toward the . . . icky.

Happily for me, though, I wasn't required to like, much less wear, all the clothes I carry in the store. We all have our favorite styles and eras, the ones that match our figures and personalities best. Bronwyn is drawn to the clothes of the late 1960s, while I gravitate toward those from the late 1950s and early '60s.

I worked well for a while, deciding that paperwork was an effective way to get my mind off mundane concerns, such as a possible demon infestation and mysterious long-lost fathers who pop up when one is being interrogated by the police.

My father is in town. Why? And could he really be implicated in Griselda's death? I knew he was a rotten father, but this was something else entirely. What was going *on*?

My fingers hovered above the buttons on the calculator. *Dang it all.* My train of thought had jumped the rails, and I had lost my place in the long string of numbers I had been totaling. I didn't know whether to blame my lousy math skills or my father's lousy parenting skills.

Since I was already feeling bleak, I figured I might as well look up the *Malleus Maleficarum.* It turned out that the horrid tome was, indeed, available online . . . and a person could even search the document for specific types of torture and modes of execution. Unfortunately, I learned nothing new, much less anything that could help me understand what was going on. I succeeded only in making myself depressed, pondering the terrible things people do to one another.

I sat back in my chair and looked out over my shop floor. Saucy little hats with their midface veils sitting on a shelf next to the door, brightly patterned vintage scarves and the colorful strands of costume jewelry from the Gem Faire hanging from the wooden pegs that dotted the walls at convenient intervals, dozens of pairs of prim white, go-to-meeting cotton gloves buttoned at the wrists so they looked like butterflies pinned to the display table. Rack upon rack of flounces and lace, leather and cotton, evoked other eras, long-past romance and rebellion. The store was redolent of rosemary and sage sachets, and, underlying everything, the homey aroma of fresh laundry.

I felt my heart swell with pride. I had worked hard to make Aunt Cora's Closet a reality, the old-fashioned kind of sweat-and-elbow-grease hard work with scarcely any magic involved. After years of wandering from place to place, continent to continent, it had felt so good, so *right* to settle down in San Francisco's Haight-Ashbury neighborhood with its history of tolerance and openness.

The thought that my life here might be at risk somehow because of my father's arrival . . . It was too much to bear.

Plus, I might as well admit it: I was heartsick. Yearning for a man with deep brown eyes and a really bad attitude. Sailor, a powerful psychic, understood who I was and how hard it was for me to maintain the balance in my life between the normal and the supernatural. Or so it had seemed. He had rescued me on more than one occasion, and though for the longest time he insisted he didn't like anyone, including me, his kiss proved otherwise. . . .

"Stop, Lilita. That's enough." In my mind I heard Graciela taking my eight-year-old self to task. *"Stop feeling sorry for yourself. Witches don't cry. Remember?"*

"But the other kids are picking on me!" I had protested.

"What do you care? You are the granddaughter of a curandera, the descendant of generations of powerful women. It is the future that matters, m'hija, *not the present."*

I frowned. Graciela's words hadn't helped much then either. *Focus,* I scolded myself. If I started thinking like that the numbers would never add up.

My affair with Sailor had been all too brief, and I hadn't felt right since he had left, suddenly and without explanation. I was fairly certain he'd disappeared because Aidan, a powerful witch overlord and Sailor's boss, had somehow banished him from the area. But a part of me, a tiny, lingering doubt, wondered if he had gone because of me—because I was just too hard to handle. I knew it was childish and self-pitying to allow my thoughts to go there, but . . . I couldn't help it. What if Sailor had left for the same reasons everyone else in my life had? Because I wasn't worthy of love . . . ?

The tinkling of the bell above the shop's door interrupted my gloomy reverie. Maya arrived with two high priestesses from Bronwyn's Welcome coven, Wendy and Starr.

"Wow, you weren't kidding about the new jewelry. This is *awesome.* Anyway, sorry we're late," effused Starr. "Some of the coven sisters were helping with another fund-raiser for the women's shelter. Maya kindly offered to move some boxes."

"Not like I was given much choice," Maya groused, but her smile belied her true feelings. "You know, you do-gooders have an awful lot of energy."

"Damn straight," said Wendy, playing with a long strand of pearls that hung around the neck of a mannequin.

Bronwyn beamed. "Of course we do! When you put positive energy out into the world, it comes back to you threefold. You mark my words: You'll be rewarded handsomely for all the time you spend with the elderly, writing down their stories. That's important work."

"Then I'm in trouble," Maya said, "because I haven't had much time for it lately. I've got a few interviews lined up this month—on Thursday I'm going to speak with Marisela's grandmother, whom we met yesterday. But . . . my new hobby . . . well, it's not a hobby, exactly, but more of a . . ."

She blushed, a flush appearing on her high cheekbones.

"A new hobby?" I asked, amused. Maya was usually so confident, mature beyond her twenty-two years, that I was surprised to see her discomfited. "What is it?"

"Toy trains?" guessed Bronwyn, handing Starr a necklace of glittering red, yellow, and purple rhinestones.

"What? No, I—"

"I know! Burlesque," Wendy weighed in. "Or pole dancing!"

Bronwyn let out a peal of laughter, and I had to admit the idea of our serious Maya pole dancing was pretty funny.

Maya gave us all a withering look. By now Bronwyn, Starr, and Wendy were wearing multiple strands of beads and necklaces. What with their propensity for wearing gauzy tunics or, in Wendy's case, layers of negligees over leggings and leotards, the three were taking on the aura of trick-or-treaters dressed up as gypsy dancers.

"Scrapbooking?" ventured Starr. "Or stamp collecting? I heard philately is making a comeback."

"How about bonsai?" said Bronwyn.

"Ya'll are a bunch of rhymes-with-witches," said Maya, smiling wryly.

Laughter—and maybe even a witchy cackle or two—filled the shop as a half a dozen giggling young women entered the store. Oscar made a point of trotting in front of the customers, and as though on cue the women gasped and laughed, then tried to pet him as he led a merry chase through the aisles.

"Oscar, you little dickens," Bronwyn said as she went to help a woman in search of an antiacne herbal concoction. Wendy and Starr drifted over to inspect an assortment of feather boas as they debated which of the beads and pearls to use in making necklaces.

"Hey, Maya. Want to go thrift-store shopping?"

I didn't have to ask twice.

"You're on," Maya said, slinging her messenger bag over her shoulder. "Let's leave this madhouse to the witches and pigs."

"I better be the former, not the latter," Bronwyn called out as we headed for the door.

I have a Pavlovian response to the smell of thrift stores: the scent of the laundry detergent, the hundreds of items imbued with the lingering aura of their former owners. The moment I walked through the door my hands started to itch at the promise of possibilities.

"Left or right?" Maya asked as we surveyed the large, open space.

"I'll go left, you go right," I said, and Maya peeled off to search the right-hand side of the store while I began working my way through the crowded racks and shelves on the store's left-hand side. We flipped quickly through the offerings, which, as usual, were mostly cheap items a half step up from junk. But every once in a while we came across a treasure: a Dresden mesh handbag with faux sapphires found in a bin of cheap vinyl knockoffs; a delicate lace mantilla that needed only a little tatting to be good as new; a couple of old letterman's jackets from the 1960s that would clean up nicely and sell like hotcakes.

The worries of the morning slipped away as I reveled in the familiar comfort of the search for really cool old clothes.

"Check this out." Maya held up a French maid's costume with a low neckline and a short skirt. "Ooh la la."

"Oh, I think that's a definite *oui*."

"I bet it would fit you," Maya suggested.

"*I* bet you'll never find out," I replied. "But it's perfect for the costume corner. We'll have to find a feather duster to go with it. Pink, I think."

Maya laughed, and as she added the dress to the steadily growing pile in her cart I marveled, not for the first time, at how lovely she was. A natural beauty who didn't realize it, Maya had mocha skin and large, near-black eyes. She wore no makeup and refused to pluck her eyebrows, but did have one vanity: her hair, which she wore in a multitude of locks tipped with beads, the ends dyed deep colors, depending on her mood. Maya was such a funny mixture of the serious and the frivolous, and far too cynical for her age.

I wondered why. Unlike me, Maya had drawn a winning ticket in the parental lottery, and had grown up in a happy home with a mom and a dad who were still in love after decades of marriage. Then again, one's role models can only do so much to shape our individual lives. When it comes right down to it, we each walk the path of this life alone, and make our decisions based on our own distinct beliefs, desires . . . and fears.

"Score!" Maya called out, holding up a pair of what could only be described as bloomers: frilly women's undergarments from the nineteenth century. "Wait—there's a label. And get this: They're made of a poly blend."

"Who makes polyester bloomers?" I wondered.

"The real question is: who *buys* polyester bloomers?" Maya said.

"Someone, for sure. We can't pass those up, especially since they're machine washable. Into the basket."

"I'm heading for furniture real quick," Maya said. "I need a little bedside table."

"Good luck. I'm going to swing through housewares."

"Stay frosty, my friend," Maya said.

I usually avoided housewares because old kitchen gadgets are a weakness of mine, and I feared I would acquire so much inventory I would have to open a vintage kitchen annex and relocate the store. But occasionally I found something too good to pass up. This time, I was tempted only by an off-white antique tablecloth festooned with hand-embroidered sprays of leaves and flowers.

"What do you think?" I said, showing it to Maya, who had returned from the furniture section empty-handed.

"It's gorgeous. And if it doesn't sell, we can always drape it over a display table or use it in the front window."

"I like the way you think."

When we had finally mined the last nugget of gold in the store, Maya and I pushed our laden carts to the register and took our place in line behind an elderly Asian woman buying a bright yellow-and-green Oakland A's hoodie. While we waited, I perused the glass display counter. A faux tortoiseshell hair comb might be worth a closer look . . . and a woven silk medallion reminded me of Hans's description of a hair amulet.

I remembered seeing something similar at the home of a local Rom witch I knew, Renna Sandino. I wondered whether Renna could explain to me how hair amulets worked, exactly, on the off chance that it might cast some light on the crime. Could the hair I had seen in Griselda's room at the inn have been leftover from making an amulet? How could such a thing cover up a witch's powers ... and why would she want to?

I had an additional motive for wanting to speak to Renna. She was Sailor's aunt. And even though she was angry with me—and, as a matter of general knowledge, it isn't a good idea to have a powerful Rom witch holding a grudge against you—I was working up my courage to try talking my way out of that little deal gone bad, hoping Renna could tell me where Sailor might have disappeared to. After all, what's the worst she could do—hex me?

Yes, as a matter of fact, she surely could. But I doubted she would. Most witches respect their powers and do not abuse them.

"Fire dancing," Maya suddenly blurted out.

"Um ... I'm sorry?" I asked, looking up from the display case.

"I checked it out last night and I really want to do it!"

"This is the new hobby you were mentioning?"

She nodded. "It's more than a hobby, actually. It's like I'm ... obsessed. I can't stop thinking about it."

"Is this the fire dancing in the park? Conrad mentioned something about that. But ... really? You want to ... dance, with *fire*?"

Witches and fire—we have a complicated relationship. I might use fire in a very controlled setting in some of my brews and spells, but *dancing* with it? That sounded like trouble.

"It's not nearly as scary as it sounds." Maya smiled. "In fact, it's really empowering. It's ... well ... it feels sort of magical, for lack of a better word."

"How did you get into it?"

"I had seen the dancers in the park last week, but then they did a special performance at the Gem Faire, and the head guy really encouraged me to try my hand at it. I gave it a whirl last night. It was incredible."

"And how do they dance with the fire?"

"They have these pots, like, on the end of ropes? The pots contain fuel, which they light, and then they dance, spinning the pots up and around. Some use lit torches, but it's the same concept. It's ... it's hard to explain, but it's mesmerizing."

"But ... why doesn't the fuel fall out of the pots?"

"Centripetal force. If you spin the pots fast enough, the fire stays in the pot. But that's why you have to learn how to do it safely—it takes total commitment, or it's dangerous."

Like casting a spell. And like so much else in this world.

"Oh. Well, then—"

"Next!" the cashier said.

As the cashier added up our purchases Maya and I placed our items—the French maid costume, the embroidered tablecloth, some beaded pullovers from the '80s, a men's cowboy shirt, an eyelet bolero jacket, a black velvet coat with a real mink collar, and an assortment of T-shirts and cotton peasant skirts that, while not vintage, were a style my customers liked and often asked for—into the burlap sacks we had brought along. Plastic bags were no longer allowed in San Francisco, and paper bags were expensive for a shop like this one, which donated its proceeds to charity.

As I paid the bill, I marveled at the low prices. For less than one hundred dollars, I had bought three big burlap sacks of clothes. Discarded clothing was so plentiful in the United States that thrift stores at times were overwhelmed with donations and sold the overstock by the pound. The clothes were shipped overseas and sold to people in poorer nations. Maybe one day I would make a documentary on the life of an American T-shirt. Perhaps it started out as a freebie from a computer company, was worn by a college student to play intramural soccer for one season, and then ended up at the bottom of the dirty laundry bag he brought home at the end of the school year and handed to his mother to wash. The T-shirt sat for a few years in his dresser at home until he moved across country for his first job after graduating, and Mom decided to convert his old bedroom into a home gym. She gave the T-shirt to the Goodwill, where it languished on a rack among thousands of other T-shirts until culled and sent to Uganda, where it was now protecting from the blazing sun a farmer who, I imagined, had no idea what the logo on the front of the shirt meant but had chosen it because he liked the color and the look of the swoosh.

"Lily?" Maya asked, bringing me back to the present. "Penny for your thoughts?"

"You wouldn't believe it if I told you," I said. The documentary would have to wait for another day.

We lugged our heavy bags out of the store and across the parking lot, the blacktop radiating heat. The unseasonably hot spell still blanketed the city, leading to the rare sight of people sweating in San Francisco. As they'd say back home: It felt hotter than a Billy goat in a pepper patch.

"So, about fire-dancing: How are you learning to do it safely?"

"There's a man who used to work with a carnival," Maya said. "He started out as a fire eater, a long time ago, but that's too much for me. I'm just into the dancing. Anyway, he's developing a fire-spinning troupe, and he's training a bunch of us. Whoever can pass the test gets to be part of the group."

"He's training you . . . for free?" A whisper of a premonition, like the flickering of a butterfly's wing, appeared at the edges of my consciousness.

"He's sort of like a scout, looking for new dancers to join the traveling troupe. He teaches you some basics, and if you're good enough you might be chosen. He's *amazing*." The fire was dancing now in her eyes.

I unlocked and opened the rear doors of my purple van, and we plunked our heavy bags in the back, then circled around and climbed into the cab.

"Are you saying you want to join this traveling troupe? What about school? And . . . your family?"

What I was really asking was: What about *me*? But I didn't say it. Maya's life was, after all, her own. And goodness knows I should be the last one to discourage anyone from traveling and learning new things. But having made friends and decided to remain in San Francisco, it had never occurred to me that my new friends might leave, to follow their own journey. I knew as well as anybody that there are no guarantees in life, and that all is transient. But still. I liked our Aunt Cora's Closet family just as it was.

Maya laughed. "No way . . . You should see how bad I am—seriously, I'd never make the cut, even if I wanted to. But it's still fascinating. I'm telling you, you won't believe how this guy works with fire."

As I pulled out of the parking lot, a glance in the rearview mirror confirmed what I thought I'd seen right on our tail on the way over: a big old Ford Scout, dented and colored a faded minty green.

It was following us. Conrad had been right to be suspicious.

"This fellow who's teaching you to fire dance out of the goodness of his heart, you met him at the Gem Faire? What's his name?"

"We just call him Gene. You haven't seen anything until you've seen him work with fire. And in a suit, no less."

Jersey Gene with the Jelly Beans. I would bet the farm this was oh, so much more than a coincidence.

"And you say you met him at the Gem Faire? When?"

"You were rescuing Oscar from the clutches of security. The dancing troupe came in to give a little exhibit, and Gene announced they'd be meeting in Golden Gate Park and offered to train anyone who was interested."

"Could that be how the fires got started?"

"Oh no, I don't think so," Maya said. "Funny, that never occurred to me. But . . . no, now that I think about it, the fire spinners had finished their show long before anything caught fire. And no one spilled or anything. Too bad you missed it."

"Too bad I missed the fires?"

"The dancing, of course."

"Yes, too bad. Did Gene happen to ask you about jewelry?"

"Jewelry?"

I glanced at the mirror again. The truck was still there. It wasn't the first time I'd been followed, but neither was it the sort of thing a person got used to.

"Was he curious about what you'd bought at the fair—something along those lines? Or about Aunt Cora's Closet, maybe?"

Maya fixed me with an odd look. "No, nothing like that. All we've talked about so far is fire safety, and how important it is to have confidence in your moves, so you don't falter."

"Sounds more like philosophy than dancing," I muttered, hearing a cynical note in my own voice.

"Lily, what's bothering you?"

"I . . ." I trailed off as I glanced at the truck again. What I couldn't understand was why, if they were following me, would they choose such a distinctive vehicle?

Speaking of distinctive, I was driving a purple van with AUNT CORA'S CLOSET: IT'S NOT OLD; IT'S VINTAGE! emblazoned on the side. So I guessed I was a pretty easy target to follow.

There were two men in the truck, both wearing sunglasses. I didn't recognize them, at least from this distance.

I glanced at my watch. It was a little after noon. This stretch of Sacramento Street was jammed during lunchtime, and there was only one lane in each direction.

Pulling to a stop at a traffic light, I made a decision. If I was being watched and followed, it was safer to face it here, in public, than to wait until they found me somewhere alone and vulnerable.

"Don't get out of the car. I'll be right back," I said to Maya as I shifted the van into park, set the parking brake, jumped out, and headed toward the truck behind me.

Chapter 8

Horns blared as the traffic light changed to green and the cars in the lane behind us realized we weren't going anywhere.

As I approached the mint green truck, I noticed a wooden decoration in the shape of a Maltese cross had been attached to the hood. An interesting embellishment to an otherwise faded, beat-up vehicle.

The two men in the cab gaped at me, slack-jawed. Both had dishwater blond hair, long skinny necks, and unfortunate overbites. *Shared genetics,* I thought. *Brothers or cousins, most likely.* Both wore dark sunglasses, frayed baseball caps, and dirty T-shirts.

"Hey!" I rapped on the driver's window. "You two! Let's talk."

Ballcap Number One, behind the wheel, opened and shut his mouth without speaking, like a fish, while Ballcap Number Two started gesturing, apparently suggesting they go around my van.

Ballcap Number One abruptly jammed the truck into reverse and stomped on the accelerator, immediately slamming into the grille of the luxury car behind them. The molded, painted bumper of the late-model Lexus was no match for the truck's steel bumper and crumpled with a metallic crunch. The driver of the Lexus laid on the horn and started unbuckling his seat belt, but the mint green truck was already nosing into the oncoming lane in an effort to escape. I jumped aside to get out of its way, but noted the license plate number. Horns sounded as the truck darted into oncoming traffic, then swerved back into the lane in front of my purple van, raced down the street, and careened around the corner with a screech of tires.

"What the *hell*?" shouted the driver of the Lexus, a handsome, well-groomed fellow. He looked to be about twenty-five, and was dressed in a pale yellow polo shirt and madras pants. I spied golf clubs in the backseat. "You *stopped*, in the middle of the street? What kind of idiot stops like that? *Do you see what you've done*?"

"I am *really* sorry this happened, but in all fairness, *I* didn't back into you; the men in the truck did."

"This is a *Lexus*!"

"I really am sorry." My guilt at setting into motion the chain of events that had ruined this man's day waned as he continued to scream at me. Fender-benders were an inevitable part of life in a big city, like it or not. "Those men in the truck were following me, and I felt I had to confront them in public for my own safety."

"*Your* safety? What about my *car*? Look at this!"

I gave the irate driver the truck's license plate number and my business card as well. I was pretty sure it wouldn't be considered my fault—after all, cars stall at lights all the time—but, just in case, it was best to leave all those details to the insurance professionals.

When I climbed back behind the wheel of my van, Maya was gawking at me.

"Um, Lily? What was *that* all about?"

"It was either brave or kind of stupid," I said as the light turned red again. "I'm going to go with 'brave.'"

"Gotta say, I'm more inclined toward 'stupid,'" Maya said. "Why didn't you let me come with you? I could have served as backup."

"Which is why I asked you to wait here. If I'm going to do something brave"—I glanced at Maya—"or *stupid*, I don't want to drag you down with me."

"So what'd those guys do to tick you off?"

"They've been following us since we left Aunt Cora's Closet," I said as I pulled forward, putting an arm out the window and waving in apology to the traffic stacked up behind me.

"They have? You're sure?"

I nodded.

"In that old truck? Not exactly a low-profile vehicle."

"I was thinking that myself."

"Not cops, then."

"No."

A silence.

"Are we in trouble, Lily?"

My heart swelled at my friend's loyalty and generosity. I wasn't used to being a part of any sort of "we."

"You are not in trouble. Not as long as I can help it."

"Are *you* in trouble, then?"

What should I say? Why were those men following me? Could it have something to do with my father? Or did they think I was in possession of a valuable piece of jewelry from the Gem Faire?

Something else occurred to me: If they had been

watching Griselda at the Gem Faire, maybe she sold me a very obvious box in an attempt to throw them off her trail. Maybe she hoped they would follow me, as they did, and leave her alone. That would help explain why I felt nothing from the jewelry in my possession.

"I'm not sure. Maybe."

"What can I do to help?"

I reached out to squeeze Maya's arm. She was still uncomfortable with the whole witchy thing. Her mother, Lucille, was very involved in their Baptist church, and though Maya had stopped attending services she had been raised with the basic tenets of the Baptist faith and accepted them as the norm. Witchcraft didn't fit in to her worldview. Still, unlike a lot of people I could name, she wasn't hostile to the idea or to me, and had witnessed enough to understand that there were forces beyond the obvious at work in this world, even in such a beautiful city by the bay. She was a loyal, supportive friend who was willing to stand by me, whether or not it made her doubt her own sanity from time to time.

"Thank you, Maya. I have no idea what's going on at this point. But I'll be sure to let you know if you can help—I can't tell you how much I appreciate your support."

"Glad to hear it. And, by the way, the next time you decide to go *mano a mano* with a couple of yahoos, I'm helping. No ifs, ands, or buts about it."

I laughed. "Thank you, I appreciate that. Hey, when's your next fire-dancing practice?"

"Tomorrow night. Want to come?"

"I would indeed."

"Great. Everyone's welcome. But . . . something's bothering you about it, isn't it?"

Yes. I might not be able to foretell the future, but I

knew this: A woman had been killed, my father was in town, and two men were following me. The fact that Maya was suddenly all het up about fire dancing taught by a suit-clad man named Gene . . . well, I couldn't help but see trouble. With a capital "T." Still, what could I say to Maya without freaking her out? Gene . . . well, he seemed suspicious to me, but I had no proof that he'd actually done anything. As I'd said to Carlos, I was trying hard not to think of "odd" as a synonym for "wrong," because I'd been on the receiving end of more than enough of that kind of thinking.

I forced a smile. "Nah. It sounds so intriguing, dancing with fire."

"Gene says fire's like life: you can't be afraid of getting burned."

I supposed that was true. Still and all . . . this Gene character was starting to tread on my last nerve.

Back at Aunt Cora's Closet, we found Bronwyn and Lucille working on the alterations for the *quinceañera* dresses. They had draped the pink off-the-shoulder silk on the dressmaker's form and were making tucks here and there. It always amazed me how the smallest little folds in just the right places made the difference between a good fit and a great fit.

Maya and I lugged in the burlap sacks and unpacked, showing off our purchases. The French maid's outfit was the hit of the day, though after seeing Lucille's fondness for the fine lace mantilla I made a mental note to have the tatting repaired, wash it in rosewater, and let it dry in the moonlight. Thus mended and cleansed, it would be the perfect gift for Lucille's upcoming sixtieth birthday.

A few customers roamed the aisles, but all in all it was

a mellow afternoon. I was tidying up the dressing room when the phone rang.

A slight crackle as I picked it up indicated it was long-distance. Hans.

"What did you find out?"

"Nothing good, I am sorry to say. I asked around, as you requested. I learned there was a well-known witch in the county of Baden-Württemburg, near the Black Forest, named Carlotta Hummel. Very flamboyant; described as having bright orange hair and a rather big mouth. Not a favorite among the local politicos, I'll tell you that much."

"And?"

"And she was found pressed to death just last week."

I realized I was holding my breath. "That's not good."

"It gets worse, I'm afraid. Carlotta Hummel had a sister named Griselda. Last her neighbors heard, Griselda was headed to a jewelry fair in San Francisco."

I looked out over my store, at the wonderfully peaceful and domestic scene. Bronwyn and Lucille chatting as they sewed, Maya helping a young woman find a top to match a colorful peasant skirt. As usual, my shop kept me grounded whenever craziness was swirling all around.

"Lily? Are you still there?"

"Sorry, yes. I'm here. I was just wondering what this all adds up to."

"I will tell you what it adds up to: It adds up to 'Stay away from this mess.' One more thing: Carlotta had a connection to a pretty well-known witch who moved to San Francisco a decade ago. Aidan Rhodes. Have you heard of him?"

"I have, yes. What kind of connection did they have?"

"I don't have many details. But when I was asking about Carlotta's known professional contacts, his name came up. Since he's in San Francisco now, I thought there might be a link."

"Okay, thanks. Oh, Hans. What does *hexgeshad* mean?"

"*Hexgeshad*?" Hans repeated. "There's no such word. Where did you hear this?"

"Someone said it at the jewelry fair," I hedged. I'd heard Johannes mumbling something like it as he fled the Cow Palace.

Hans paused. "Could you have heard *Hexenjagd*?"

"Could be."

"*Die Hexenjagd* means 'witch hunt.' "

Of course. But was Johannes running *from* a witch hunt . . . or was he part of one? Could that have been blood I saw on his shirt, rather than ketchup, as I had assumed?

"Did you hear anything about a young man associated with Griselda named Johannes? Her son, perhaps?"

"*Nein*, no one mentioned a Johannes, or any children, for that matter. You want me to see if I can find out?"

"That would be great. Thank you for doing this, Hans."

"I told you, I'm happy to learn that you are doing well. Just let's keep it that way, all right? Be careful. Seriously."

I hung up and glanced around the store, now empty of customers. "Where's Maya?" I asked Bronwyn and Lucille.

"She's in the dressing room," Bronwyn said.

"Yes. Maya's in the dressing room," Lucille echoed.

It took me a second to realize what was bothering them. Unlike the rest of us—me included—Maya never tried on the store's clothes. She was by nature a jeans-and-T-shirts kind of gal.

"Did she find something special she liked?" I asked.

Bronwyn and Lucille exchanged glances; then Bronwyn spoke in a low voice. "She's trying on some items for a fire-dancing costume."

"Really?" I looked at Lucille, whose face was a study in how not to look worried. "I take it you don't like the fire-dancing idea?"

"It's not the dancing itself," Lucille said. "It's that Maya seems a little . . . fixated on it. She went to one session, and now can't stop talking about it. That's not like her."

"Has she been into dancing in the past?" I asked. Maya had become such an integral part of my daily life that I sometimes forgot I hadn't actually known her for very long. In many ways it felt as though I knew her well, but I was still learning about the ins and outs of her life, her passions in life.

"Maya played softball and field hockey, but she never cared for dancing," Lucille said as she snipped errant threads from a length of silk. "Any type of dancing."

"She seems to like the man who's teaching the fire dancing," I said. "Have you met him?"

"Not yet." She shook her head and scowled. "But she never stops talking about him. It's 'Gene said this' and 'Gene said that.' If I didn't know better, I'd think she had a crush on him."

The curtains of the dressing room were flung open and Maya emerged, looking like a cross between a belly dancer and a really stylish shipwreck victim.

She wore cropped pants made of a silky magenta, slung very low on her narrow hips. A revealing paisley halter top was covered by a soft yellow overshirt so sheer that it seemed to accentuate, rather than cover up, her shoulders and arms. She had tied the tails of the shirt in a knot right under her sternum, so her midriff was completely exposed. A bright patterned scarf was wrapped in her hair. Bangles covered several inches of both wrists, anklets tinkled as she walked, and a large coin necklace pointed down toward her cleavage.

"So? What do you think?" she asked, twirling to give us the full view.

We all three—Bronwyn, Lucille and I—just stared at her. Maya had a curvy, athletic figure but she'd never been the type to don a costume, much less bare her belly with skimpy clothing. She looked gorgeous and sexy; at least as good as the fire dancers I had seen pictured on the poster at the Gem Faire. But she didn't look much like herself.

"You look . . . great," I said.

"Fabulous," said Bronwyn with a surprised nod.

"You're planning to go out in *public* like that?" asked Lucille with maternal outrage. "Where's the *rest* of it?"

"What*ever*, Mom," she said with an eye roll and a snort. "How lame."

Lucille, shocked, didn't respond.

Maya's snide response to her mother was so surprising—so un-Maya-like—that we all continued to stare, speechless.

"What's wrong with trying something *new* for a change? Are you all so perfect you can't try anything different?"

"Maya, it's not like that," I began. "You look great, just really . . . different."

"And since when has 'different' meant the same thing as 'wrong'?"

"It's not," said Lucille. "But being rude, young lady, is always wrong. I'm disappointed in you, Maya."

Maya shrugged and stalked back into the dressing

room. Bronwyn put a supportive arm around Lucille and gave her a squeeze.

Our dear friend, usually so adult and reasonable, suddenly was acting like a spoiled teenager.

I was going to make darned sure I was at that fire-dancing practice tomorrow.

"Mistress, wake up!"

It took me a moment to swim to the surface through the dreamy layers of sleep. When I finally opened my eyes I saw the upside-down visage of a grimacing gobgoyle. Up close and way too personal.

Oscar had a habit of perching on my brass headboard and leaning over to peer at me, so this wasn't the first time his upside-down face was the first thing I saw when I opened my eyes. But familiarity made the sight no less unsettling. Plus, his breath was funky.

I noticed it was still dark outside. "What time is it?" I croaked.

"Three in the morning."

"Three? Why did you wake me?"

"I thought you might want to know about the two guys."

"What two guys, Oscar?"

"The two guys downstairs."

I sat bolt upright. "In the *store*? *Now*?"

"I could take care of 'em for you," he said, pounding a fisted hand into the opposite palm like a prizefighter.

I grabbed my 1950s-style pale aqua chenille robe from the hook behind the door and wrapped it around my white Victorian nightgown.

Oscar continued. "I waited 'cause I know how you hate people to see me as I really am. But the problem, mistress, is that if I go after 'em in that darned miniature potbellied pig form, well . . . you know. So, anyway, I've been thinking. I might not have thought it through when I chose the pig form. You see what I mean? Given your tendency to get in trouble, I probably should have gone with a lion. What do you think? Would a lion be too much?"

As Oscar nattered on, I flailed around, taking a step this way and that, still groggy with sleep and uncertain what to do. It didn't seem wise to confront intruders all alone. Unlike fictional witches, I had never been able to wield a wand or wiggle my nose and make things happen. When startled or extremely angry I sometimes let out a blast of energy that didn't hurt anyone, just stunned them. But I couldn't always control it, and as a matter of common sense I steered clear of potentially violent situations whenever possible.

Maybe I should barricade myself in the apartment and call the police. It's not as though there was anything of great value in the store. I emptied the cash register every night, and unless the thieves backed up a moving van and took all the clothes, I could recover from the loss. Even the jewelry . . .

Duh. My sleep-addled brain finally awoke. Griselda's jewelry. Someone was here looking for something they thought Griselda had given me. Maybe the two guys from the mint green truck.

Somehow putting faces on the presumed intruders helped. Especially since those faces were more ridiculous than scary. Not that Ballcap Number One and Ballcap Number Two couldn't cause damage, but somehow I thought my witchy mind tricks would work on those two. Rather than call the cops to deal with them, I'd handle it myself.

Oscar held his big hands up, fingers curled up like claws, and roared.

"What in tarnation are you *doing*?"

"Being a lion."

"A lion?"

He roared again.

"Why?"

"You never *listen* to me. I just told you, I think I made a mistake in choosing my 'normal' form. I shoulda chose lion so's I could protect you better."

"That's very sweet, Oscar, but ... stick with pig. It suits you."

"What do you mean by *that*?"

"Just that I love you exactly as you are."

He smiled. It looked like a grimace, but was as close as a gobgoyle could get.

If the men downstairs were the same two who had followed me earlier today, I was betting they were scared of witches. I remembered that adorning their outfit, which is what the boys back home would have called their truck, was a Maltese cross, an antiwitch mark. Back in Jarod, townspeople put them on their barns and garages to keep witches like me from curdling the cows' milk. (Not that I ever had. Well, maybe once. And it had been entirely warranted.) I wouldn't be surprised if the men had also been responsible for the hoops of rowan at the bed-and-breakfast, to lessen Griselda's power should she return while they were rifling through her room.

Time to get in touch with my inner actress. If they were expecting a witch, I would give them a witch. I gathered together a sage smudge bundle, a stick of pussy willows from a bunch I had gathered earlier this spring, a lighter, and a little club moss. I hung my head upside down and mussed up my hair even more than it already was from bed. Finally, I ran my finger across the bottom of my cauldron, then rubbed the soot around my eyes.

"What are you doing?" Oscar asked.

"Teaching some bad guys a lesson they won't soon forget," I said.

"You look scary."

"That's the point. Let's go."

"Wait. You want *me* to come?"

"What happened to the pig with a heart of a lion?"

"I'm just saying . . . as a pig I don't got a lot of defenses. Mostly pigs are a food source, as disturbing as that is to contemplate. Reason I chose that form is 'cause pigs are smart, and that's me. Oscar the smart guy, that's what they all said. If you need the brains for an operation, call Oscar, he's your go-to guy—"

"You have my permission to become your true self in situations of imminent danger," I interrupted as I headed for the door. I could hear some bumps from downstairs, and was in *no* mood. A couple of months ago vandals had broken in and trashed the place. With the help of friends and neighbors the shop was back to normal within a few days, but it had taken much longer to get past the feelings of violation. I had no intention of going through that again. Besides, I reckoned I was just about angry enough to do some magical damage.

"Really?" Oscar asked, loping behind me. "I can be myself if I need to?"

"Not like you've waited for my permission in the past. Seems to me that when the chips are down, you've done what's necessary."

"That's me: Oscar the down-chip guy."

Since my familiar mimicked accents flawlessly, I sometimes forgot that he wasn't a native English speaker.

"Come with me," I said. "I have a task for you. And don't worry. It doesn't involve hand-to-hand combat. In fact, you'll be out of sight the whole time."

We crept quietly down the stairs and into the store's back room, past the washer and dryer and the kitchenette on the first floor. We paused at the velvet curtains that separated the workroom from the shop floor. I lit the sage bundle and handed it to Oscar—now in pig form—to carry in his mouth.

"Ready?" I asked.

Oscar nodded.

I took a deep breath, let it out slowly, stroked my medicine bag, and peeked through the curtains.

Chapter 9

Sure enough, it was the two guys from the truck. Ballcap Number Two was holding a flashlight, while Ballcap Number One was attempting to jimmy open the locked jewelry display counter.

"You put nigh there, Zeke?" said the one with the flashlight.

His accent was so strong that if I hadn't been from the South I doubted I would have understood. He was asking Ballcamp Number One, whose name was apparently Zeke, if he was "pretty near there," or almost done.

"Near 'bout. Jest hang on, now, Clem. I'm a-fixin' to take care of it."

I made a mental note: Ballcap Number One was Zeke, and Ballcap Number Two was Clem. The more I knew about someone, the more effective my magic was.

"I don't like bein' here," Clem whined. "Lookit them pentagrams! Lookit!"

"I seen 'em, I seen 'em." Zeke sounded annoyed. "What you want me to do 'bout 'em?"

"Tol' you she was a witch."

"Pentagrams don't mean she's a real witch, nec'sarily. Half the people in this town wear pentagrams. Hell, some of 'em even have 'em tattooed on their bodies." He shook his head and blew out a disgusted breath. "This is one crazy-ass town."

"I tell you what: That man has a thumpin' gizzard for a heart sendin' us here, an' that's the truth."

"Clem, I been tellin' ya and tellin' ya, you cain't be sayin' things like that about him. He find out, he'll cancel your birth certificate."

"He can kiss my go-to-hell. He's jest as reg'lar as you an' me. He don't have magic ears."

"That may be so, but you an' me both know he's got the big guy in his corner, and that's good enough for me." Zeke swore as the screwdriver slipped.

"Why don't you just smash hit?" Clem suggested.

"Boy, I swear, if you had a good idea it would die of loneliness. If I just smash hit, that witch be comin' right on down in here. Now shine that light in closer. Ya hear?"

"You even see any fire opal rings in there? It's supposed to be kind of a yellow-orange stone. Maybe a little red and brown. I don't see nothing looks like that . . ."

Clem moved the flashlight to illuminate whatever he was looking at.

Zeke's screwdriver slipped again and he stood, waving his hand in the air.

"*Oooow*. See what you did? Took the light away, and now I done hurt my gol-danged finger. This is stupid. I'm jest gonna smash it."

"Wait. You said it'd wake her up!"

"Too late," I said, stepping out from behind the curtains with a flourish. I lit the club moss and tossed it in the air. It sparked brightly and cascaded like miniature fireworks.

Oscar, meanwhile, trotted through the aisles with his smoldering bundle so that smoke arose over the racks of clothes. Since he was too short to be seen, I hoped the haze would seem mysterious and sinister.

I pointed the pussy willow stick in their direction. Zeke and Clem gasped and held up their hands as though I were holding a shotgun.

"What in the *Sam Hill* you two doin' in my place?" I demanded, letting my own Texas twang fly.

Sandy hair, skinny necks, bad skin and teeth: my perfunctory assessment of the pair from earlier today was confirmed. They reminded me of some of the men I knew in Jarod: the sad ones, social losers who wound up doing someone else's bidding, whether it meant working for the grouchy old guy at the ARCO station, or running meth for someone smarter, more ambitious, and far more violent than they. Like me, they were rural Southerners. Raised in a god-fearing church that had taught them to believe in, and to fear, a witch.

And just as I recognized them, they had recognized me.

Their Adam's apples bobbed up and down, and they were so scared their eyes looked like four buckeyes in a barrel of buttermilk.

Clem was whispering something. I finally realized he was intoning: *"Kiss my ass kiss my ass kiss my ass."*

"If you think that incantation is gonna hold me off, you got another thing coming," I said, cocking my head. Though it sounded like something from a recent Hollywood movie, chanting "kiss my ass" three times is actually an ancient admonition against witches. It wasn't effective, as far as I could tell, but the fact that Clem knew enough to try was telling.

"Hey," said Clem, glancing nervously at Zeke. "We

didn't mean no harm. We're . . . we're hungry, is all. We lost our jobs in this, on account o' the bad, *uh* . . ."

"The economic downturn, is what he's trying to say," Zeke interjected. "And with, the, er, state of the economy we couldn't get no jobs. So we're hungry."

"Somethin' 'bout that explanation sounds a mite feeble to me," I said. "Matter of fact, sounds to me like someone told you to say that if you got caught."

"How'd she *know*?" Clem whispered, a note of awe in his voice. Zeke hushed him.

"And I don't suppose you two had anything to do with hoops of rowan scattered around the bed-and-breakfast where Griselda was staying?"

"*Zeke!*" Clem exclaimed, looking at me with mouth agape. "How'd she know *that*?"

"*Clem!* You're not supposed to use names. 'Member?" Zeke barked. "I swear, you put nigh as feeble-minded as they come."

"Don't call *me* feeble-minded jest 'cause you're older. Why, Mama always said—"

"Hear me good, Zeke and Cle-em," I pronounced the second name as though it were two syllables. "It's three in the morning. That's the witchin' hour, for sure. Now y'all are gonna tell me what in the Sam Hill you're doin' here and what you're after, or I'm gonna use this here wand to make both of ya'll into my pet zombies."

Two Adam's apples started bobbing some more.

"D-don't, please, ma'am witch," said Clem. "We . . ."

"Keep your big trap shut, boy," said his brother in a harsh whisper.

Just then, Oscar tripped on the lace train of a wedding dress, and the dressmaker's mannequin teetered then fell to the floor with a resounding crash. Startled, Oscar dropped the smudge bundle on the ivory satin. I lunged to grab it, but Oscar managed to pick it up and stomp the sparks out with his piggy hooves. Taking advantage of the distraction, the men started backing toward the shop door, Clem holding a carved wooden Maltese cross at arm's length in front of him.

"I'm not a vampire," I scoffed. "That won't work."

"Don't need to," Zeke replied, and held up a gun, its dull black muzzle pointed straight at me.

"Now, we don't want no trouble, ma'am," said Zeke. "We're gonna walk on outta here, and you gonna keep that wand down by your side. Ya hear?"

I may be a powerful witch, but I'm as mortal as the next person, and I don't go up against firearms. Even when armed with pussy willow sticks.

Clem and Zeke slipped through the door and slammed it behind them, the little bell pealing forlornly in the silent night.

The next morning I got up early to cast one whopper of a protection spell over the store.

Under the circumstances, the spell was necessary for my safety and peace of mind but, as with all magic, there was a cost. A spell strong enough to discourage intruders would also mute the creativity and independent thought of all within the shop. I would remain largely unaffected by it since I was the witch casting the spell, but it seemed unethical to subject my friends to it without their knowledge or permission. I soothed my conscience by telling myself it was just temporary and, considering how things might have turned out last night, it was warranted.

And I felt thoroughly justified later that morning.

"Where did this bag of clothes come from?" I asked Bronwyn.

"Maya brought it in yesterday, right before we closed. Someone left it on the stoop."

This wasn't all that unusual. Though we purchased most of our vintage clothing, many people wanted their discarded clothes to go to a good home and used Aunt Cora's Closet rather like the Salvation Army donation center.

What was unusual was that the knotted neck of the bag was ringed by a twist of rowan.

Carefully avoiding the rowan, I dragged the bag outside by one corner. On the sidewalk, the early-morning sun was already blazing hot.

Bronwyn followed me, and Conrad got up from the curb and joined us, watching as I tore a hole in the side of the plastic bag.

Clothes. I half expected something ghastly, like evidence of a spell done with blood sacrifice. But the bag appeared to be full of vintage clothes: even without looking closely I could see a men's antique flax linen shirt and Victorian-style white undergarments trimmed with hand-tatted lace—the kind Lucille would be able to salvage for her new dresses, even if the garments were stained beyond repair.

"Dudette, you should go work for Homeland Security. I thought you were totally gonna blow the bag up!" said Conrad, a gleeful tone in his voice.

"Everything okay, Lily?" Bronwyn asked. She was clearly worried about me lately, and I didn't blame her. "Maya will be here within the hour. We can ask her if she knows anything more about the bag or who dropped it."

"No worries. Conrad's right; I was overreacting." *Not every piece of rowan is meant to quell the powers of witches,* I reminded myself. Whole rowan trees were lovely, and they never bothered me at all unless they were imbued with the power of a well-cast spell. On the other hand, I didn't want to take any chances. Ignoring Bronwyn's questioning look, I asked Conrad to take the bag around to the trash bin in back of the store.

"I need to run out for a bit, Bronwyn. Will you watch the store?"

"Of course."

It was high time to try to find Aidan Rhodes, the self-appointed godfather of Bay Area witches. If he knew Carlotta Hummel in Germany, it was certainly possible this was why her sister Griselda had come to San Francisco. Perhaps before Carlotta was killed, she gave her sister something—a powerful ring, for instance—that Griselda smuggled in under the guise of the Gem Faire, and perhaps she got it to Aidan before she was killed. Somehow.

At the very least, it was worth hearing what Aidan had to say for himself. It was becoming clear to me that I needed some supernatural help with this situation. Sailor was AWOL, and this wasn't my voodoo friend Herve's kind of magic. And though I didn't exactly trust him, Aidan had helped me in the past.

Unfortunately, despite my prodding Oscar had been close-muzzled about Aidan's whereabouts. I could usually count on him to know where Aidan could be found, but Oscar had been so silent I was beginning to think he really *didn't* know where Aidan was. Oscar was reasonably good at keeping mum in the short run, but was terrible at keeping secrets over the long haul—he usually slipped up and mentioned something. Not this time.

Still, it was worth a visit to his office. So I headed to the Fisherman's Wharf Wax Museum.

I zipped down the Embarcadero, past the Ferry Building farmer's market and the old port buildings, most of which were now in the process of being converted into restaurants and tourist destinations. Some time ago San Francisco—like so many other port cities—realized that giving over prime waterfront spots to working people was a waste as far as tourism was concerned. Much of the city's actual shipping business had shifted to China Basin, or across the bay to the port of Oakland.

I waited at an intersection to let a streetcar pass before I turned left, then took a right to sneak up on the Wax Museum on Jefferson, the street that ran in front of Fisherman's Wharf and was always chock-full of happy tourists stuffed with crab, clam chowder, and sourdough bread.

Parking in this area was a real bear, and while I generally take my chances and wait my turn like everybody else, last night's encounter had left me with a sense of urgency. When I spied a gas-guzzling SUV hogging two parking spaces I used my parking charm to convince its owner to abandon his crab feast and move his vehicle. I slipped into the first space, and a Johnny-on-the-spot Honda grabbed the spot behind me.

When I breezed past the young woman at the Wax Museum's ticket booth without pausing, she put her battered romance novel facedown on the counter and yelled, "*Hey*!"

I ignored her. Clarinda didn't like me, and kept trying to get me to pay the admission fee even though she knew darned well I wasn't there to ooh and aah over the wax figures.

"I said, '*Hey*'!" Clarinda said, chasing after me.

I stopped. Clarinda *never* left the ticket booth. "What's up?"

"He's not here."

"Where is he, then?"

Clarinda shrugged, conveying so much more than uncertainty or lack of knowledge. Together with her Queen of the Dead goth outfit, pale skin, black hair and eye makeup, multiple piercings, and "I don't know you but I know I hate you" gaze, the shrug suggested I should not only get the hell out of her space, but also put my head where the sun doesn't shine.

"Are you sure about that?"

Her lip curled.

"Fine. When will he be back?"

Another shrug, this one saying "Even if I knew, I wouldn't tell you."

"I'm going to check his office, in any case."

"It's your funeral," she said to my back as I turned and started up the stairs. I'm pretty sure she mumbled something under her breath, but I didn't strain to hear. I got the gist.

Upstairs, I hurried past the Chamber of Horrors—though I knew it was all fun and games, it still made me nervous—and through the exhibit of European explorers to the walnut door to Aidan's office. When he wasn't there—or didn't want to be disturbed—the door was hidden by a glamour that made it invisible to those with normal sight. Even to me it was almost invisible, but since I knew it was there I approached and rapped on it loudly.

A loud, scratchy meow was the only reply, and I spotted a pure white, long-haired cat atop the ledge over the door. This was Noctemus, Aidan's familiar. We did not get along. She had, however, helped me to discover part of Aidan's secret: that he bore burn scars on half of his face. Similar to my father.

Looking into the cat's periwinkle eyes—so reminiscent of her master's—I said, "I need to speak with him. It's very important."

The cat meowed again. Not being an animal whisperer or a mind reader, I had no idea if this meant Noctemus would communicate to Aidan that I needed him, if she was telling me to go wherever a cat familiar might send someone if she could, or if it was just a random feline response to being spoken to.

Frustrated, I tried the door handle just in case. It was locked. I wondered whether I should try to break in. I was in the habit of taking liberties with Aidan, but he was a powerful witch, and one of these days I just might end up getting burned.

Speaking of getting burned ... Aidan had told me himself that he used to work with my father, and had hinted at some kind of spell gone wrong. It made sense that they had both been burned in the same incident years ago. But that was all I knew about any shared past between them.

Frustrated, I kicked the door. The cat meowed in reproach.

"Well, that's what he gets for not keeping in touch."

Noctemus hissed at me and strolled away, her upright tail twitching.

I sighed and threaded my way back through the museum.

A crowd of children with matching yellow summer camp T-shirts were darting about, shrieking and tittering nervously in the Chamber of Horrors, which I studiously avoided. Personally, I much preferred the exhibit called the Palace of Living Art, which featured wax portrayals of famous paintings like the *Mona Lisa*, but also slightly more obscure works such as *American Gothic, Whistler's Mother*, and the *Laughing Cavalier*. The figures of movie stars were pretty fun, and even the Wicked Witch of the West from The Wizard of Oz wasn't so bad ... though frankly all of these wax figures, fictional or not, gave me the willies.

Not far from Aidan's apparently abandoned office was a new addition to the museum's collection: Mary Ellen Pleasant. The plaque described her as THE MOTHER OF CIVIL RIGHTS IN SAN FRANCISCO. Not so long ago I had agreed to have this sculpture made as payment to a voodoo priestess who had helped me out.

As I looked into the figure's dark eyes I found it unsettling . . . but, then, I found all the wax figures disquieting. We people are so much more than our human form; I know that better than most. Nonetheless it is our living tissue that allows us to remain on this plane, to vibrate in such a way that we maintain our physical presence in this world. This is why so many magical systems use poppets as stand-ins for people, and even the pentagram features a star in the shape of a human: arms, legs, head.

Like all the wax figures, Mary Ellen Pleasant was dressed in authentic clothing. I wondered if the museum's artists had selected items in the proper style for the period, or if Herve, voodoo priest and a party to the deal I had brokered to create Pleasant's wax representation, had given the museum some of Pleasant's real clothes. I tried to sense any vibrations from the clothing, but the figure was too far away and the room was too crowded with random vibrations from the museum's visitors.

After glancing around to see if anyone was watching, I ducked under the velvet ropes meant to keep visitors at bay and felt the figure's watered silk gown.

The dress was authentic, not a reproduction. This explained the fine, hand-tatted lace, which was unusual in even the most authentically re-created ensemble. The gown's vibrations were brilliant, much stronger than normal in historic fibers; I picked up fierce determination, a pride mixed with fear and hate. I wasn't surprised by the complexity of the vibrations. Pleasant had led a difficult but important life—born a slave before the Civil War, she had worked with the Underground Railroad, had for a time passed as white, was married several times, and had repeatedly challenged civic authorities and the courts over civil rights issues.

Hers was the sort of dress that, were it in my store, could be worn only by a select few. It would overwhelm most people.

"Hey, lady!" said a girl of about eight. She wore a yellow camp T-shirt, jeans, and a pink headband. "You're not s'posed to go past the ropes! Not s'posed to touch the clothes. You could get it dirty!"

I blushed as other children ringed Mary Ellen Pleasant's sculpture, watching me in disapproval. How embarrassing.

"You're right," I said, stepping behind the rope. "That was wrong of me. I apologize."

The outrage on the little faces suggested my apology wasn't enough. "I'm a, um . . . I'm a consultant for the museum. A fashion specialist."

"Where's your badge?" she asked.

"My what?"

"Your badge," she explained impatiently. "All the museum workers have badges. That's how you know they're okay to talk to if you get lost."

Busted. The other children looked equally unconvinced. I stared at them, unsure what to do. Fortunately a teenage girl—one of the camp counselors, judging by her yellow T-shirt and jeans—appeared and announced it was time for lunch. I breathed a sigh of relief as they marched off.

Over the years I had gone up against all sorts of challenges, but the scathing disapproval of children? That, apparently, never got easier.

As I turned to leave, Mary Ellen Pleasant's jewelry caught my eye. Around the sculpture's neck hung strands of Mardi Gras beads and a near-black medallion that appeared to be made of twine. After confirming the children had indeed left the area, I reached out and made a discovery as I touched it: the medallion was made of hair, plaited and twisted so tightly that it resembled braided silk.

I looked longingly at Aidan's nearly invisible door. I would bet my cauldron he knew whether the hair amulets were significant and why, or what the Ballcap boys were after. How ironic. Angry with him for banishing Sailor, I had been giving Aidan the cold shoulder for the past several weeks. Now that I needed him, he was nowhere to be found.

Feeling frustrated, I left the museum—calling out cheerfully to Clarinda as I passed the ticket booth—and drove back to the store. Bronwyn was helping a customer at the register, so I headed to the workroom to call Renna, the one Rom witch I knew. Her phone rang and rang until finally bumping me to voice mail. I left a message asking if I could stop by for a visit, and gave her my number so she could call me back.

As I sat with my hand on the telephone, pondering my next move, it dawned on me that Maya was hanging up clothes I hadn't seen before.

"Are those from our thrift-store outing?" I asked, though I doubted they were. I almost always remember the clothing that has passed through my hands.

"No, they were left by the front door yesterday."

"In the black plastic bag? I threw those away."

An odd expression on her face, Maya continued to

hang up piece after piece, smoothing their wrinkles with her hands. "Is that why they were out in the alley? I wondered."

"You brought them back in?"

"They're perfectly decent. And look: several are men's, and we don't have much of that."

It was true that women's fashions make up the bulk of vintage clothing. But as a norm, we draw the line at picking up clothes from the trash. And we certainly never put out clothing that hasn't been laundered and mended.

"Why don't you let me take care of those, Maya? You could start sorting through the clothes we bought yesterday at the thrift store."

She shrugged and allowed herself to be led into the main shop floor of Aunt Cora's Closet, where Bronwyn needed help at the register.

"Don't forget, Lily," Maya said. "The fire dance is tonight in Golden Gate Park, and all are welcome."

"Oh, I haven't forgotten," I said as I ducked back into the workroom.

In fact, Maya's involvement in the fire dancing was very much at the forefront of my mind.

Chapter 10

I tried to assess the dubious clothes, but found nothing untoward—in fact, the most suspicious thing about them was their lack of vibrations. This wasn't unknown for clothes of their age, however. If the vibrations of former owners weren't that strong to begin with and then the items were tucked away in a drafty attic for several decades, they were sometimes devoid of all but the most subtle sensations.

Or . . . was it possible that the rowan really was working at damping down my sensations? I noted loops of rowan on two of the hangers. Maya probably found them in the bag, thought they were pretty, and used them to adorn the clothing. It was the sort of thing I did all the time—and these loops looked like something I would have made, like my sachets of rosemary and sage. She wouldn't have known any better.

But it chilled me to think that Aunt Cora's Closet could be accessed so easily by those with mal intent. Had Clem and Zeke left the bag in an attempt to dilute my powers?

I blew out a frustrated breath, shoved all of the clothes—and the rowan—into a new Hefty bag, and hauled it back out to the trash—*inside* the Dumpster. Surely Maya wouldn't cross that line.

That evening I filled a backpack with precautionary supplies: herbs, a candle, amulets, a small jar of protective brew. Then I added a few more pedestrian items: a flashlight, a warm sweater. Even on the warmest San Francisco nights, a wall of fog could quickly engulf the city, causing the temperature to plummet within minutes.

When Maya and I arrived at the designated clearing in Golden Gate Park, the sun still hovered in the sky and soaring eucalyptus trees cast thick, stark shadows in the orangey light, their fragrant leaves pungent in the balmy summer air.

It was another unusually warm evening, and a damp but pleasant breeze from the ocean blew in. Locals called it earthquake weather and muttered about omens. I suspected it had more to do with the unfamiliarity than any geological phenomenon; typically San Francisco evenings were cool, no matter how hot the day might be. When people got too accustomed to predictable, pleasant weather, it didn't take much to throw them off their game. Everyone seemed to be waiting for the sun to set, and the excitement was palpable. Tonight's fire dancing might have been one of a thousand events held in this park: music festivals, potlucks, rallies for a variety of political and social causes. I spotted the fire dancers gathered on a slight knoll in the middle of a meadow. They were painting one another's faces as people milled around greeting one another. A couple of men and women sat cross-legged on the grass, beating drums in an uncoordinated fashion as though they were still learning.

Everywhere tanned and healthy young bodies were on
display: many of the women wore halter or swimsuit
tops, while the men were bare-chested. One pale red-
head seemed determined to learn how to drum. Another
girl was dressed in steampunk-goth clothing, and yet another was clad in purple, from her hair to her clothes. In
addition to the face paint—and arm paint and chest
paint—the women wore flowers and lots of jewelry. They
looked like hip, modern versions of belly dancers,
crossed with the street-kid chic that predominated in the
Haight neighborhood.

"Isn't this great?" asked Maya. "Wait until you see
them dance. It's spectacular."

"Is your teacher here? The one you told me about?"

She shook her head. Her eyes scanned the crowd, as
did mine. Though I'd seen plenty of young people, as
well as a handful of tourists, nearby residents, and local
merchants like me, I'd not seen a man in a suit, sharkskin
or otherwise.

As the last orange rays of the sun faded, someone
cried out "La, la, la," in a loud, ululating cry that reminded me of the few weeks I spent in Morocco, years
ago. The mournful call seemed to announce the disappearance of the sun.

A strange silence and calm descended as the fire
dancers took their places on the grassy knoll. Their de-
meanor was surprisingly solemn; they seemed transformed from slightly goofy hippie kids to serious
acolytes.

The drummers began a steady rhythm, as though re-
sponding to the first calls of the crickets and tree frogs.

And then in the dark I heard the click of a lighter. A
flame shot up, illuminating a single face.

Gene. The man I had met at the Gem Faire's refreshment counter. Once again dressed in his sharkskin suit and polished wingtips, he stuck out like a sore thumb.

"Thank you all for coming." His deep voice carried easily in the still evening as he waved the lighter in an arc in front of him. "Tonight you will see an astonishing performance, demonstrating the play of life ... with fire."

He suddenly looked straight at me, over the heads of the crowd, and smiled.

I returned his gaze, unflinching. There was something about this guy, but I couldn't get a fix on him. Was he a witch? Some other kind of practitioner? Something ... more?

Demons did occasionally take human form, though usually for short periods of time. To possess a human continually, a demon would have to be incredibly powerful.

Much more powerful than I was.

But when I suggested the demon might have taken human form, Oscar had laughed at the idea. I certainly hoped that meant Gene was just as human as I was. I had gone up against a demon once before, at the San Francisco School of Fine Arts, and in the end had vanquished it. But that demon hadn't been at full strength, and I had had a lot of help. As Graciela had drummed into me, *"You have supernatural powers, m'hija. But you are not superhuman."*

I heard the crowd laughing and tuned back in to what Gene was saying. "... help us keep the fire in the pots! So please remain still, and do not take pictures. Distractions might cause the dancers to stumble ... and it's dangerous to play with fire. And please, when the hat comes around, won't you give, and give generously?"

One by one, with great drama and flourish, he held his lighter to the dancers' pots and torches.

The drumbeats swelled, louder and more insistent, and the dancing began. The drummers were wholly focused on their drums, and for a moment I watched the frenetic movement of hands fluttering on taut skins stretched over the gourds.

One beautiful young woman with long blond hair and a lithe, half-dressed body wore a belt with spokes that looked like torches sticking out. Gene lit each one in turn, and she started spinning so fast it looked as though she was surrounded by a hoop of fire. Another young woman held what looked like the head of a rake in each hand. When these were lit, she waved her arms and the rakes turned into flaming butterfly wings. A bare-chested young man bounded across the knoll and knelt as Gene lit a series of pots on strings, then did the same for several other women and a few men. Each of them started swinging their pots, this way and that, appearing to be calm and in control though surrounded by arcs and circles of fire. The speed of the dancers' movements against the dark night air gave the fire the appearance of moving of its own accord, forming shapes and arches, sweeps and bends with the sinewy nature of a serpent.

The woman with the butterfly wings lowered herself to the ground in a backbend, bringing the flames high above her head. The blonde with the hoop of fire danced around her, hopping over her, all the while spinning the pots of fire.

I tore my eyes away and scanned the crowd standing mesmerized in the darkness. The park's street lamps were not shining, and a sliver of a crescent moon cast a weak light over the scene.

"Maya," I whispered so as not to distract the dancers. "Do you know any of the troupe personally? I'd like to speak to them."

She didn't answer, watching the dancers without blinking.

"Maya?"

She moved not at all, her eyes wide and her mouth agape, while the fire pots spun. The performance was hypnotic, and I realized the crowd, like Maya, was going into something akin to a trance.

I looked around, scanning the crowd. It was dark now. The sun was fully set, only the sliver of the moon shone, and the park lamps remained out.

All around us faces were eager yet placid. The red-haired guy, the steampunk girl, the one in purple. All of them enthralled, unreachable now by words or touch. A few had started twirling their bodies in a frenzied whirl.

I wasn't overly alarmed or even surprised. Spinning was a traditional method for entering a trance, the centerpiece of numerous religious ceremonies. Whirling helped to separate thought from mind and achieve an altered state.

The purple girl, spinning wildly, lost control and stumbled into the woman with the fiery butterfly wings, who lay outstretched on the ground, undulating. The spinning girl's purple yoga pants caught on fire.

The onlookers started to laugh and cheer.

For a moment I couldn't believe what I was seeing—no one moved to help the girl whose clothes were now on fire, and she didn't stop dancing.

I had to act. Grabbing the sweater from my backpack, I ran to her, wrestling her to the grass and smothering the flames with the sweater.

"Somebody call 9-1-1!" I shouted, but no one, not even Maya, responded.

As I searched the crowd for help, my eyes lit on Gene,

lurking in the shadows. Not panicking, not even moving. Just smiling and staring. At me.

I scowled at him and turned my attention back to the young woman. Gingerly, I checked her leg for injury; the fire had scorched the outermost layer of cloth, but hadn't reached her skin.

"Are you all right?" I asked, and she nodded, a beatific but vacant expression on her face. "Want me to call 9-1-1?"

She looked at me blankly. *Guess not,* I thought. As I looked closer at her shin, I realized it was covered in some sort of waxy substance. Was that some kind of fire protectant, the kind Hollywood stuntmen used? Maybe Maya was right. Maybe Gene really was a safety-first kind of guy.

So how come I didn't believe it?

I left the young woman writhing happily on the ground and headed for the nearest lamppost. I chanted a spell, focused, then touched the lamppost and watched it spark to life, illuminating the knoll. I'm good with electricity. I don't really understand it, but I'm good with it. Without the contrast of light against dark, the fire dancing was much less hypnotic.

Then I began to dance myself, spinning, chanting, throwing my powers up against whatever spell had been cast over the crowd. I felt something push back, a palpable sensation of magic, and focused harder. I know my witchy limitations—but I also know my supernatural strengths. Whoever was fighting me was no match for my magic.

One by one, the spectators seemed to awaken. They began milling about, murmuring excitedly, many rushing to speak with the dancers who now stood around, relaxing and breathing deeply. I pushed my way through the throng, heading for Gene, but he had disappeared. The people in the crowd jostled one another, laughing and dancing, apparently without a care in the world. Not appearing to realize they'd just been manipulated.

I needed to find out what Gene was doing and why. Especially if Maya was serious about pursuing her new hobby.

As if my current to-do list wasn't long enough—what with worrying about finding a piece of jewelry worth killing for, the two yahoos following me and breaking into my store, and working out what my father was up to—I now added figuring out the machinations of a well-dressed man who loved jelly beans and, in his spare time, quite literally played with fire and mesmerized crowds in Golden Gate Park.

"Maya!" I called out, then spotted her chatting with a drummer. She was excited, and had I not known better I would have assumed she was drunk or high on something. Her eyes shone and her mien was unfocused, a state not at all characteristic for her.

"Let's go," I said firmly, and she obediently turned and followed me. I escorted her the several blocks to her home, a Victorian typical of the neighborhood. The house had some historic charm but was rather run-down, with peeling paint, a few broken windows, and a weed-choked yard. Maya's four housemates were students, very sweet and fun but chronically short on cash and time—and space. The house had only three bedrooms. Two shared the largest room, Maya and another girl had their own small bedrooms, and the fifth slept in what used to be the dining room, which the students had roped off with a couple of Indian blankets.

"Thank you for walking me home," Maya said as she

unlocked the Victorian's front door. "Wasn't that *amazing*?"

"It was . . . something," I said.

"You didn't like it?"

"It wasn't that. It's just . . ." I didn't know what to say. "Something was . . . wrong."

Maya looked surprised. "What are you talking about? It was incredible, just like last time. Just like it always is."

"There was something unnatural about the dancing, Maya. Didn't you feel it?"

"I didn't feel anything but joy and unity—and your cynicism, frankly. Lily . . . the last thing I want to do is to hurt your feelings . . ."

"But . . . ?"

"You need to be more trusting. You know, let your hair down. Go with the flow."

Uptight, serious Maya was telling me to let my hair down? Go with the flow? I could scarcely believe my ears.

"Please don't go back to the fire dances, Maya. Not just yet, anyway." I needed time to figure out what had transpired tonight, and to find out more about whom—or what—Gene was.

Maya laughed. "Don't be silly."

"Maya . . . could you just trust me on this? As someone who's older and who wants the best for you?"

Maya rolled her eyes like a teenager listening to a thoroughly unhip parent.

"At least promise me you won't go back without me. Will you do that much?"

"Lily. . . ."

"Please?"

"I . . . sure. Okay, you can come. But I *am* going. The next one's on Saturday, I think."

"Okay, I'll be there. Oh, and Maya—what's Gene last name?"

"Gene doesn't have a last name, silly," Maya said wit a laugh. "He doesn't need one."

After letting myself in to Aunt Cora's Closet, I turne on an Edith Piaf CD and took yet another look at all th jewelry that might have been in the box Griselda ha sold me. Feeling like a pirate looting my own store, gathered up the rings, necklaces, and other assorte items. I held the medallion with the fire opal and cor centrated on the sound of Edith's crooning filling th store, but try as I might I felt nothing. There were sever; more lapis pieces, and a few beltlike items that looke North African. I looked through all the rings, trying t sense anything suspicious. The rings, as before, include two school rings, a silver band, a cameo, and a big fak engagement ring diamond in a gold leaf setting. Sever; pendants were Southwestern-style turquoise in pounde silver settings, which seemed funny, since they cam from Germany. But a collection of "junk" like this coul have accumulated over the years and might hav originated from anywhere.

I felt no vibrations, no history, nothing. But that wa no surprise.

Once again, I studied the fire opal in the medallion I taken to wearing. It was surrounded by blue-green opal and it was a pretty setting, so it might sell for up to couple hundred dollars. There was nothing about it tha would be worth killing over, unless it had awesome mag ical powers. But if so, it sure was good at playing possun

Marisela's mother and grandmother had mentione fire opals were found in Mexico, while most opals com from Australia. The native peoples of Mexico had mine or gold and silver; it was no stretch that they would have mined for precious stones as well. The Maya were ancient and had resided in the area long before the Aztecs, who were an invading tribe of nomads from the north.

Could the Aztecs have gathered fire opals from the Maya, and their conjurers used them for spells or incantations over human sacrifices that imbued them with power . . . for what purpose? And how would this connect to me in any way? Watching Maya dancing with fire tonight . . . it all seemed too coincidental. The fires at the Cow Palace. The discussion of fire opals. The fire dancing, and seeing Gene there.

Clem and Zeke had been looking for a fire opal ring. Hans had mentioned sensing a ring as well, and that special amulet rings could be used to exorcise demons. I had been through every piece of new jewelry from the Gem Faire and hadn't found any suspicious rings, though. It was very possible I had no such item in my possession. Clem and Zeke were probably tracking down multiple leads, and could have seen me interacting with Griselda at the fair.

Could those two have been responsible for her death? They seemed more wretched than calculating, but Zeke appeared to have a bit of a mean streak. And if someone had ordered them to press Griselda, for example, they might well have done it wrong, adding too much weight and killing her without actually intending to. And before she had told them about the location of the ring.

But then . . . why would someone have stabbed her with the athame? Had she told her interrogators where the ring was, so they simply stabbed her? And yet Clem and Zeke were still searching for it.

Most important: Who were the Ballcap boys working for?

The Piaf CD came to an end. Suddenly I realized how shadowy the shop floor was. I was sitting in a pool of light in an otherwise dark shop, examining jewelry and so absorbed in my thoughts that I was oblivious to anything else. If someone were watching me with evil intent, I could hardly be an easier target. The memory of Zeke and Clem's visit last night put me on edge.

I double-checked all the locks, turned off the lights, and climbed the back stairs to my apartment.

Where a garrulous, grumbling gobgoyle awaited me.

Chapter 11

Oscar and I sat on opposite ends of the couch, our feet on the steamer trunk–turned–coffee table and books in our laps. On top of the steamer trunk sat a late-night snack of toast with butter and homemade raspberry preserves, and a pot of honey-sweetened peppermint tea. My familiar crunched his toast loudly, spewing crumbs this way and that and cackling as he read.

I swear, we were becoming like an old married couple.

Since Oscar was often home alone while I ran around town on business, witchy and retail, I had taught him how to use the DVD player. I hated the idea of him getting bored and lonely—for his sake, as well as mine. A gobgoyle with too much time on his hands is a recipe for trouble. What I hadn't anticipated was Oscar becoming such a movie fan—especially a *scary* movie fan—that before long he'd seen everything worth watching, plus a whole lot that wasn't. The films' gruesomeness factor kept ratcheting up, and after a weekend-long *I Know What You Did Last Summer* film festival in my living room, I snapped.

"No more screaming," I had announced. *"No more shrieking, no more knives, no more bloodbaths."* From here on out, we would spend our free time reading.

Oscar had acquiesced, reluctantly, and although he liked *Little Women* well enough, he soon insisted on something more thrilling. And so I brought home a stack of classic mystery novels from the San Francisco Public Library, hoping they would satisfy his strange bloodlust while teaching him a thing or two. On the whole, the experiment had been a huge success.

At the moment my familiar was working his way through Agatha Christie's finest. Oscar read with his mouth agape, eyes wide, and insisted on sharing the juiciest parts. "Mistress! Just listen to *this* . . ." was now a regular refrain of my evening.

For my part, I was currently doing a little light reading, too, but in my case the topic was demonology. I was disconcerted to learn that not only were there more demons than I had ever imagined, but there were all manner of fire demons, each more terrifying than the one before.

Some of the lesser demons, I read, could be harnessed and their powers put to the benefit of those seeking knowledge and pursuing the arts. Artists, for example, were often said to be inspired by muses, which were demons by another name. The trick was to keep these lesser demons under control, because when they took over trouble ensued.

Dealing with a demon was *always* dangerous, however. Exorcising a demon bound his powers and stopped him from using his portal to plague humans, but he would never go away entirely. Demons were as ancient as the Earth—some said much older—and they weren't about to be defeated by a mere human witch, no matter how talented she might be at brewing.

A lot of people were bound to demons by choice. Greed, ambition, and a lust for power were the usual reasons, and a combination of all three was not uncommon. Such fools typically made a pact with a demon, thinking they would be able to keep the upper hand. It almost always turned out badly.

Elemental demons were particularly interesting, and were defined as "spirits embodying one of the elements of antiquity." The earth elemental was a gnome, water was a nymph, air was a sylph, and fire elemental was represented by a salamander.

A fire elemental's minions, I read, were known to have a sweet tooth and, like the salamander, to shun the light.

A fondness for sweets—like jelly beans?

I had just opened a chapter on amulets of control and exorcism—with an emphasis on magical rings—when Oscar leaped up as though he'd found the Holy Grail.

"Mistress! I have it!"

"Have what?"

"The answer!"

I closed my book, glad to take a break from my grim studies. "What was the question?"

"The solution to your search!"

"I'm all ears."

"We hire Miss Marple!"

"Miss Marple?"

He held up Agatha Christie's *The Mirror Crack'd*.

"She doesn't miss a trick, this lady. No offense, mistress, but she could give you a serious run for your money, and she's just a *cowan*."

"Hate to break it to you, little guy," I grumbled as I got up to put on the kettle for more tea. "But Miss Marple is fictional."

"Come again?" Oscar said, suddenly standing right behind me.

"She's not real, Oscar. She's a fictional character." The expression on his face was blank, as though what I was saying did not register. "She was invented by the book's author, Agatha Christie. That's what writers do."

"They *lie*? Agatha Christie *lied*?"

"Well, it's not a lie, exactly. It's pretend. Make-believe."

He looked skeptical. "What about this French guy, then? Hercules somethin'-or-other? He was on the Orient Express train and figured out a real humdinger of a mystery. Boy, that was a *tough* one. We can hire him!"

"Hercule Poirot? He's like Miss Marple; he's a made-up person. It's all pretend." I shredded dried peppermint leaves and crushed cloves and a few rose hips harvested from my garden, mixed them together, and put them into a metal tea bob.

"You're saying these are all a bunch of ... false-hoods?" His jaw dropped. "Why would Agatha Christie *do* something like that?"

"Because they're stories, meant to entertain. Just like movies."

He gave me a skeptical side eye. "That can't be true, mistress."

"And why is that?" I asked, amused at his refusal to accept the existence of narrative fiction.

"Because the Maltese Falcon is real. I saw it myself, downtown at John's Grill on Ellis Street."

"When were you at John's Grill?"

His muzzle clamped shut. In theory, a witch's familiar doesn't have its own, individual existence; it's more an extension of its mistress's. My familiar is different. Oscar had lived for centuries before I was ever born. At some point he had become indebted to Aidan, who gave him to me. Or perhaps Oscar still worked for Aidan. In any event, Oscar's loyalty was not exclusively to me. From time to time he would disappear for a day, driving me insane with worry.

For all I knew he regularly met with a bunch of other magical creatures at John's Grill, where they groused about their current mistresses and masters over a two-martini lunch. As was so often the case with my familiar, I decided to let it go.

"Sometimes authors use real settings," I tried to explain. "But that doesn't mean the stories are real, much less the people described in them."

"That Anna Karenina was a real person. And what about Abraham Lincoln! He was in that book about zombies you wouldn't get for me."

"Yes, sometimes authors use real people in books, too."

"And then lie about them?" Oscar shook his head and tapped his taloned foot. "What a bunch of lowlifes."

When the kettle whistled I poured the steaming water into the old chipped teapot and enjoyed the fragrance wafting up. I pondered how to explain the difference between fiction and a lie, then wondered whether it was even worth a try. But before I could decide, Oscar continued.

"I still don't buy it. I mean, a lot of this stuff is way too crazy not to be real."

"You've got me there."

"Tell you what: I'm gonna see if I can get in touch with Sam Spade. He's a local boy, from right here in San Francisco. If I track him down, will you hire him?"

"Yes, Oscar," I said with a little laugh while I carried the teapot to the living room. "I guarantee you, if you find Sam Spade, I will gladly let *him* track down killers and demons and whatnot. I will pay any fee he asks."

I saw a gleam enter Oscar's bottle glass green eyes. Since my familiar has no need of money, I have never understood his greedy streak.

"*Any* fee?"

"Any reasonable fee. If you find Sam Spade, I'll cover the expenses."

"And what about my finder's fee?

"You're going to charge me, your mistress, a finder's fee?"

"I didn't say I wanted money," Oscar said self-righteously.

"I'm afraid to ask."

"Mashed taters and homemade mac and cheese and Tater Tots for dinner?"

Oscar was perpetually hungry and resolutely fought my attempts to get him to eat much of anything other than fat, sugar, and carbs. Vegetables rarely entered that scaly muzzle. What really surprised me was that a creature as fearsome-looking as a gobgoyle wasn't all that interested in red meat. Whenever I asked Oscar about his taste in food he would claim it was a goblin thing that I couldn't possibly understand, and for all I knew, he was telling the truth. It's not as though I had much experience cooking for goblins. In any case, I let that one go, too.

I smiled. "Mashed potatoes and homemade mac and cheese and Tater Tots. It's a deal."

"Pinkie swear?" He held out a scaly greenish gray oversized pinkie.

I hooked my own around it and squeezed. "Pinkie swear."

*   *   *

The next morning I opened my shop as usual and went down to the café. Conrad informed me that the men in the truck weren't there today, though it would have been pretty obvious to me if I'd cared to look. Their big, gas-guzzling, mint green outfit stuck out in San Francisco like Gene in his suit.

Coffee and assorted bagels purchased, I strolled back to Aunt Cora's Closet, enjoying the early-morning sunshine and wondering about another player in the drama surrounding Griselda's death: Johannes. Lloyd, the proprietor of the Morning House inn, seemed to think Johannes was her son. Did he know that, or had he just assumed? The strapping young man's interactions with Griselda hadn't emitted a filial vibe to me, but what did I know about parent-child interactions? I was the original poster child for screwed up families.

An image popped into my mind: Johannes running out of the Cow Palace, his white T-shirt wet and sticking to his skin, covered in ketchup. But what if it wasn't ketchup?

My thoughts were interrupted as I handed Conrad his breakfast. "Eat hearty," I said.

"Yes, ma'am," he replied and saluted, then added, "Duuuude."

Bronwyn arrived just after I finished my coffee, so I turned the store over to her and walked to the Morning House. *With any luck,* I thought, *Johannes will be there and willing to speak to me, and perhaps reveal something that will make all that has happened make sense.*

Unless . . . perhaps he had returned from the Gem Faire, found his room had been ransacked, and, assuming he had some inkling about who Griselda was and what she might have been hiding, caught the first Lufthansa flight back to Germany. Or the police had already picked him up for questioning. If so, what were the chances Carlos would inform me? Not good, I imagined.

But Johannes was the only lead I could think of. His last known residence was the Morning House inn, and it was just a few blocks away. It couldn't hurt to try, right?

As I walked up to the front gate I noticed the hoops of rowan still adorned the fence. Lloyd had said he thought they were pretty, so presumably that was why he left them up. Unless he had lied to me, a total stranger, and was actually trying to ward off witches. One way to find out.

The garden was lush and inviting yet overgrown in a zest-for-life kind of way. It beckoned. I climbed the broad wooden steps.

The sign on the door said COME ON INN!

I hesitated, then knocked on the tall, narrow double doors. While I waited, I studied the frosted glass pattern of the rising sun and tried to ignore the trepidation I felt when waiting to be admitted to a private home. As a child I had been rejected and shunned so often that I reflexively adopted a defensive stance. I'd been trying to fight it, but changing was harder than I'd anticipated.

I knocked again, thought I heard someone call out "*Just a minute!*" and relaxed. As I waited, I began to ponder what Maya had said last night, that I needed to be less cynical. I was slow to trust—it's true—and it was often hard for me to relax and enjoy the moment. When you're surrounded by people who hate and revile you for being the way you were born, cynicism isn't just smart, it's necessary for survival.

And speaking of reviled witches, maybe what I really needed to do was talk with my father. I couldn't believe he had caused Griselda's death, but I'd wager my cauldron he had played some role. If he was in town while something unscrupulous was afoot, more than likely he was part of it. I should call Carlos and ask him if there had been any progress on the case, and whether there was any way I could come down to the jail and speak with Declan Ivory.

Lloyd opened the door, interrupting my thoughts. "Come in, come in! I got a late start this morning; sorry I kept you waiting. You're welcome to walk on in anytime."

"Thank you. You remember me?"

"Of course. Lily, wasn't it? With the vintage-clothing store and the miniature potbellied pig. I've been meaning to drop by."

"That would be lovely. Anything specific you had in mind?"

"No, no. Just to say hello to a neighbor. And to meet your pig. I must confess I'm curious."

"He's a friendly fellow. I'm sure he'd love to meet you." That was an understatement. In his own mind, Oscar was a celebrity. He received his supplicants with a kind of strutting porcine dignity that had only been enhanced when, a few months ago, his picture had run in the newspaper. Somehow he'd managed to acquire several copies of the *Chronicle*, and had hung up three pictures of himself: one in the kitchen, one in the living room, and one behind the store counter. I was still trying to figure out how he'd managed to get the photos professionally matted and framed.

"Lloyd," I said. "Might I ask you a few more questions? I assume the police have spoken with you about Griselda?"

Flames of red entered his cheeks at the mention of the police.

Two guests came down the carpeted stairs at that moment, cameras around their necks. I was impressed when he spoke to them briefly in Japanese before handing them brochures on Coit Tower, Ghirardelli Square, and Fisherman's Wharf; calling them a cab; and inviting them to wait outside on the porch swing until it pulled up. He had barely set the receiver down when it rang again, and he took a reservation for later in the month.

"You seem busy," I commented unnecessarily.

"Hardly ever a vacancy," he said, and I sensed the pride in his answer. "We're really catching on, and I love it. Must have been born to be an innkeeper. I just get a kick out of making people happy. And in a city like San Francisco, that's easy. There's so much to see and do."

So I was learning. My first few months here had been spent in a kind of fog as I got my business off the ground. Before I could relax and really take notice of my surroundings, I had become embroiled in supernatural murder investigations. Only recently had I found the time to get out and about, and had been delighted to find the city as charming and interesting as did the thousands of tourists who flocked here every year.

My eyes alit on a bowl full of Mardi Gras beads, which reminded me of the Gem Faire and the reason for my visit.

"Carnaval," said Lloyd. He pronounced it the Brazilian way, *car-nah-VAL*.

"I'm sorry?"

"The beads, they're from the Carnaval parade. If you've never been, you should make a point to go next spring. Brazilians, costumes, and music. So much fun."

"I'll be sure to go. People came to the shop looking for costumes—I sold a lot of boas that week."

"I'll bet. But, anyway . . ." He cocked his head and fixed me with a curious look. "You're here . . . why? I get the sense you're not looking for a room, much less to chat about Carnaval."

"No," I said, choosing my words carefully. "I was wondering, did anything happen in the aftermath of the police visit? You heard about Griselda?"

"Oh!" He clapped his hand over his mouth. "I really could *not* believe that. Hey, you didn't know anything about any of that when you came here, did you? I had to tell the authorities you came by, and that we looked in the room."

"It's no problem. I've spoken to them as well."

"Shocking, I must say. They went through her room, even fingerprinted the furniture. You know how hard that stuff is to clean up? Took me *hours* to put the room right."

"I can imagine." I clucked sympathetically. "What about her son, Johannes? Do you have any idea where he might have gone?"

"Well, for one thing, he's not her son."

"He's not?"

He looked at me curiously. "I thought you said you were family friends. How come you didn't know that already?"

"I'm as flummoxed as you, Lloyd," I said truthfully.

He shook his head but seemed more perplexed than upset. "They led me to believe they were mother and son. But apparently it was nothing of the sort. Still, she looked decades older than him. Could have been his mother easily."

"Indeed. Any idea where he is now? I'd like to talk with him."

"Said he was moving to the youth hostel over on Ellis. I already told the police."

The phone started ringing again.

"Would you happen to have the address?"

"I wrote it down somewhere.... Listen, why don't you take a seat, let me attend to this call, and then I'll find where I wrote down the forwarding information for him?"

I wandered through a set of double doors off the foyer into the library, a pleasant, sunny room lined with shelves filled with handsome, leather-bound volumes. In one corner a ladder had been set upon a drop cloth, and someone had been painting a traditional border with stylized ginkgo leaves and lizards. It must be a huge job to bring a place like this back to life, but it was clearly a labor of love.

At first glance I suspected the books had been chosen as part of the room's design scheme. But as I skimmed the titles I realized the library housed an extensive collection focused on spirituality. There were also the collected writings of Sir Thomas More as well as Thomas Aquinas, and scholarly histories of the persecution of Jews through the ages. There was even a New Agey section on the healing properties of crystals. I took a peek at one.

I snapped the book shut with a little poof of dust when Lloyd walked into the room.

"Fascinating collection, isn't it?" he said, nodding at the walls of books. "Found them boxed up in the attic when I inherited the place. Love books; couldn't bear to throw 'em out, though I must say they make me a bit uneasy. Somebody in the past was big into spirituality and philosophy. Not surprising, though, since it used to be that spiritualism was as legitimate as any other type of scientific inquiry. I'm guessing dear old Grandpapa was the collector. On the other hand, he had quite an assortment of books about Egypt and the pyramids and the Solomon Islands. So perhaps he just had eclectic interests."

I smiled. "I love libraries. And you're right: You almost feel like you know someone, in a way, when you look at what's on their bookshelves. Right? What a precious thing to have handed to you through the generations—along with the house, of course."

"I'm a lucky guy." Lloyd nodded. "Inherited the whole place, intact with everything from furniture to kitchen paraphernalia. Hey, I'm cleaning some things out of the attic. Do you deal with kitchen stuff at your store? I'd love to unload it somewhere fitting."

"I'm afraid I don't have room," I said. "I'm sticking to clothes, unless I manage to open an annex somewhere."

"Not easy to run your own business, is it? I'm doing all the decorative painting myself, and it's taking me *forever*. Here's the address for the youth hostel. It's not in a very good neighborhood, I'm sorry to say, so if you go be careful. Still not sure why I seem to know more about these folks than you, given they're old family friends."

"They were more friends of my father's than friends of mine," I improvised. Who knows? Maybe it was even true. "I'm just trying to track Johannes down . . . as a favor."

"None of my business either way," Lloyd said. "You learn that as an innkeeper. Seriously, though, be careful. Johannes seemed a little, I don't know . . . tightly wound, I guess I would say. I don't suppose it's possible he's the one that, you know, *did* it?"

"Could be. I really don't know him. We're . . . connected, but, as I said, we're far from close."

The phone started ringing again, and I said my goodbyes and left Lloyd to run his busy bed-and-breakfast.

Chapter 12

I lingered for a moment in the Morning House's beautiful garden, enjoying the flowers, whose fragrance had been intensified by the warm sunshine, and trying to decide my next move. A big part of me wanted to just go back to Aunt Cora's Closet and fold scarves, chat with Maya and Bronwyn, and hang out with my pig.

But the rowan loops reminded me of Clem holding up the witch's mark as though he could banish me with it; the memory gave me a sense of urgency.

First I stopped by Aunt Cora's Closet, saw that everything was under control, and consulted a city map. Then I headed downtown to the youth hostel.

The address on Ellis Street was written in bold, black letters on a glass transom above the scarred wooden entrance. The door opened onto a long flight of stairs, its treads splintered and worn from the thousands of young travelers who had stayed here through the years. At the top of the stairs was a small foyer, with the obligatory rack of travel brochures along one wall and a conversation area formed by three mismatched armchairs and a sagging couch. A young man with a scraggly goatee sat behind a tall counter to the right, and behind him was a wooden hutch with dozens of tiny pigeonholes, some holding keys and others messages. Very old school. I liked it.

I started to ask for Johannes, then realized I didn't know his last name.

"I'm sorry," said the clerk, looking through an old fashioned visitors' log. "I can't see anyone by that name registered."

Had Johannes used a pseudonym? "Do you ask for ID when people check in?"

"Yup. Usually a passport. We get a lot of foreign students."

"And you don't remember a young German man, a little over six feet, blond, good-looking? He speaks English with a heavy accent."

The clerk shook his head. "Haven't seen anyone like that, at least not during my shift. Doesn't mean there couldn't have been someone here that I didn't see, but there's nobody in the book under the name Johannes."

I must have looked disappointed, because he glanced around the empty foyer, then added: "Dwight's been working a lot of shifts lately; maybe he knows something. He went up on the roof for a smoke before heading home. Want me to see if I can catch him before he leaves?"

"I would be so grateful. Thank you."

"Keep an eye on things for me for a second. Will ya?"

I couldn't say much for the hostel's security, but I was happy to slip behind the counter and play hotelier for a few moments. There was no piped-in music, only the sound of far-off voices and someone playing a harmonica. The ceilings were tall and the windows were large and multipaned, bathing the reception room in sunlight. Despite the worn furnishings and generally shabby ambience, the hostel was appealing. It had the strong, energetic vibrations of youth mixed with the wide-open, eager pulsations common to tourists exposing themselves to new worlds.

In fact, I thought as I helped a young couple from India locate Chinatown on a city map and then sent them off happily in search of dim sum, *if I needed a place to stay in San Francisco I might well enjoy this hostel more than the Morning House inn, despite the obvious disparity in luxury.* When it came right down to it, I was more about vibrations than comfort.

The young clerk returned, trailed by a pale, oversized, middle-aged man who smelled strongly of cigarettes. Dwight, I presumed.

"Yeah, I remember that guy," Dwight said without prelude. "Johannes Herzberg, right? The cops were already here asking about him. Big blond, looked like he could be a model. I thought he might be looking for work down at the strip club, till he started talking and it was obvious he wasn't from here."

"What strip club?" I had to ask.

"All-male revue, right down the street. Some of the kids land here when they first arrive from Missouri or wherever, and the strip club's some easy money for those good-looking country boys."

"Oh. Anyway, about Johannes . . . any idea where he went?"

"Nope. Didn't even sign out. Left his passport here; we require it in exchange for a room key. Like I got any use for a passport. Right?"

"So you think he'll be back?"

He shrugged. "He's out of luck on the room. It's already been cleaned and rented."

Darn. I had hoped to see his room in case there were signs of . . . what, exactly, I wasn't sure. A demon's sigil, indicating he was beholden? Evidence of having murdered Griselda? The ring everyone was searching for?

"Could I see his passport?"

"Gave it to the cops . . . Gotta say, *you* don't look like a cop." The look in Dwight's eyes told me I had pushed too far, which was frustrating but almost comforting at the same time; I'm always surprised how much information most people will tell you simply for the asking. Since I hadn't cast any sort of spell to make him trust me, why should he be telling strangers about his clients? I was already keeping him from leaving work, and now I was asking for more.

"I'm a friend of the family," I added. "Johannes dropped out of sight, and I wanted to touch base with him, make sure he's all right."

Dwight nodded. "He didn't look so hot, I gotta say."

"How do you mean?"

"I mean, he was good-looking, but not looking good. Know what I mean? Like, green around the gills a little. Real tired, like. Some of these kids, they get off the plane and run right out and tie one on, don't figure in time to get over jet lag. When I saw your guy Monday morning, I thought to myself, *If he doesn't take it easy I'll be callin' an ambulance for him pretty soon*. Wouldn't be the first time the paramedics had to pump a kid full of fluids and stick 'em in bed for a few days."

"Did he leave anything in his room?"

Dwight shook his head.

"Did you two talk about anything?" I continued "Anything at all?"

"Nothing. Look, lady, if he's got a cell phone maybe you could track him down through GPS or something. I don't know what else to tell you. The extent of our conversation was the cost of the room, how to get in after hours, and where to buy a CityPASS. That's it."

"What's a CityPASS?"

"It's this doohickey that gets you into the museums and on public transportation for a day or two, all for one price. The European kids always ask about it. They're smart travelers. Costs a lot more to pay for everything separate, plus it's a pain. CityPASS gets you everywhere you need to go."

He plucked a slick brochure extolling the benefits of the CityPASS from the display and handed it to me. I wondered, *If Johannes checked into to the hostel Sunday night and wasn't feeling well Monday morning when he spoke with Dwight, why would he buy a CityPASS—to go sightseeing on a queasy stomach?*

"Thanks. Listen, could I leave you my contact information, just in case he comes back looking for his passport?"

"Okay by me." Dwight shrugged. "You know, I hate to say it, but it's possible he disappeared into the streets. This city eats people up sometimes." He shook his big head. "Damned shame."

I handed Dwight and the other clerk a business card and gave them each a tip for their trouble and to help them remember me. Back out on the street, I paused and blew out a breath. I wasn't surprised Dwight was concerned about what might happen to a confused young man on the city's streets. Even though it wasn't far from the tony Union Square shopping district, this stretch of

Ellis was run-down and seedy. The grimy historic buildings were crumbling, and just about every crevice was filled with trash. A few folks stood clustered together, smoking and drinking out of paper bags. A cyclone fence sported a dozen articles of clothing; I couldn't tell if they were someone's possessions hung out to dry or if it was an informal a tag sale.

Dozens of men stood in a line nearly a block long, waiting stoically to enter Glide Memorial Church, which offered shelter, hot meals, job-placement assistance, and, most important, hope to those in need. Other men and women shuffled along the sidewalk, appearing aimless and defeated. Many gave off the bitter stench common to addicts.

The scene reminded me of Conrad, whom I wanted so much to help. It was so sweet the way he looked out for me as best he could, how he had been suspicious of the men in the truck ... strangers who had, indeed, turned out to be following me.

The nape of my neck tingled.

Footsteps rang out behind me.

I started to turn around when I felt something poke me in the back—the muzzle of a gun.

"*Look straight ahead, and put your hands up,*" a voice hissed in my ear.

I put my hands up, though I wasn't scared as much as astonished. I am as mortal as the next person, but my psychic guard and protection spells kept most folks at bay. Besides, it was broad daylight and there were dozens of potential witnesses waiting in front of the church.

"Check her pockets," a man said.

"*You* check her pockets," a second man replied.

"Now you listen to me," the first man said. "*I'm* the

one holdin' the gun, so that means *you're* the one doin' the friskin', remember?"

"Zeke? Clem? Are you *kidding* me?" I said, letting my hands fall to my sides and turning around to face them. They both wore dark glasses so I couldn't see their eyes, but Clem stepped back nervously. Zeke, unfortunately, just gestured with the gun.

"Don't try any funny stuff," he said. "We're fixin' to git that ring one way or t'other."

"She's not wearing it," Clem said in a low voice.

"I can see that. I'm not blind," said Zeke.

"I have this one," I said, holding up the hand still adorned with the resin ring with a picture of a raven against a bright yellow background. "You might want to look deep into it, see what you see . . ."

As was the case last night, Clem seemed put off by my spooky witch routine; his brother less so.

"Check her pockets," said Zeke.

"You really don't want to do that," I warned. "I'm a pretty awesome witch, if I do say so myself."

"Ze-e-eke," whined Clem, his Adam's apple bobbing crazily. "I think she's telling the truth."

"You bet I am, Clem. I would never fool around with something like this. You can feel it, can't you?"

"Just go ahead and find the thing so we can get out of here," said Zeke.

Clem reached out again, putting one hand on my hip pocket. As he moved in close, I concentrated on his energy. Scattered, frenetic, unsure.

"Seriously, Clem," I whispered. "You ever seen what a witch can do to a person?"

He backed away. I could hear Zeke swearing at my back. And finally the muzzle was gone and I felt his much rougher hands on me instead.

He went through my purse, emptying it on the sidewalk.

"You want this, maybe?" I held out the necklace I was wearing. It was the one with the fire opal, and as much as anything else I wanted to see how they would react to it. "It has a fire opal in it. The orange one."

Zeke was cleverer than his brother, it was clear. Still, that wasn't saying much. His hands skimmed my waist and felt the medicine bag at my waist.

"Zeke, you ever seen what a powerful witch's medicine bag does to a person if you open it up?"

I felt him rear back a tad.

"Look, you two. Why don't we make a deal? I'll give you what you want if . . ."

"If what?" Zeke asked.

". . . if you give me what I want."

Zeke and Clem exchanged a glance.

"And what might that be?" Zeke asked.

"A lock of your hair." I stared at them, unblinking, and saw fear. "Come on, what harm could it do? Just a simple lock of hair."

Clem started backing away, shaking his head so fast his mop of sandy hair seemed to blur.

"You think we're skeered o' you, lady witch? You don't know what 'scared' means until you go up against something like—"

"Zeke! No!" cried Clem. "Don't say it!"

Zeke fell silent, swore, then pulled out a pocket knife, and with a twist of his wrist my medicine bag was in his grimy hand.

I fought a wave of anger and sadness, and reminded myself that it was *my* medicine bag; one way or another it would make its way back to me. I didn't have to wear it at all times and had even loaned it out to

protect others a few times in my life. It always returne
to me.

"Do yourself a favor, ma'am," Zeke sneered. "Git ou
of town."

He swung around and dashed into the street, righ
into the path of a speeding black Escalade.

Chapter 13

The impact sent Zeke cartwheeling into the air, his limbs as limp as a ragdoll's. It felt as though I were watching everything unfold in slow motion; then reality came rushing back when Zeke landed on the pavement with a sickening thud.

"*Zeke!*" cried Clem.

The Escalade slowed momentarily, then sped up and disappeared around the corner with a squeal of tires.

Clem and I ran to kneel beside Zeke. Blood was flowing from a wound to his head, and one leg was twisted beneath him at an unnatural angle. He was breathing, still alive and conscious, but just barely.

A crowd surrounded us, offering help. One woman had scooped up the contents of my purse and handed it to me; another stood in the middle of the street, directing traffic around us. One man offered his grimy shirt to stanch the flow of blood, but I already had applied my handkerchief, very gently, to the wound on Zeke's brow.

One of the men from Glide Memorial Church had

raced to summon a pair of beat cops, who hurried toward us. Panic in his eyes, Clem looked at the police, then back down at his brother, and finally at me.

"Don't run, Clem," I said. "We have to talk. I can help you, if—"

"*Please*, don't let him die. I'm sorry we took your medicine bag, but you shouldn'a kilt him! Keep him alive, and I can pay you. I got lots to pay you."

"I'll do my best," I said.

After casting one last desperate look at his brother, Clem jumped up and disappeared down a narrow alley, his footsteps ringing out in the empty space. As I watched him go, I saw a man in a dark gray suit pass by the end of the alley, holding a newspaper up as though to shield his face from the strong sun—or could he be hiding his face from witnesses?

I cradled Zeke's head in my lap. He was a scumbag and a lowlife, but there is something so . . . pathetic and simple about us humans when we are hurt. I wished I could lay my hands on him and understand what was wrong, how serious his injuries were, and perhaps help him . . . but my curative powers weren't that strong. Blood trickled from the corner of Zeke's mouth, and I knew enough to know that was not good.

"Zeke, can you speak to me?" I lowered my head to his and whispered, watching as one of the approaching cops spoke into his radio. "Who sent you? Tell me, and promise to help your brother, Clem."

"I . . ." He shook his head, then gave what was either a cough or a weak laugh.

I noticed my medicine bag lying on the pavement next to Zeke and tucked it into my pocket just as the cops arrived.

"What happened?" asked the first officer.

"Hit and run," I said. "Late-model Escalade, black. I didn't catch the plates."

I did notice, however, that there didn't appear to be anyone driving the vehicle.

I had seen such a thing once before, and it turned out a witch had been controlling the runaway car. But not a regular witch. More like a demonic witch.

Either someone very powerful was trying to shut up Clem and Zeke, or my medicine bag had gotten its revenge.

As the ambulance rushed Zeke to San Francisco Medical Center, I gave a witness statement to one of the officers. Finally free to go, I dragged my sorry and tired self back to my apartment over Aunt Cora's Closet, stripped off my blood-soaked dress, and took a very long, very hot shower. I washed three times with lemon verbena–olive oil soap, then slipped into a snuggly pink cotton jumper from the 1960s. The outfit made me look and feel about twelve years old, but at the moment it suited my mood.

I felt as if I had been chewed up and spat out.

I made myself a cup of peppermint tea and stood in the corner of my kitchen, studying the dress I had laid out on the counter. It was stained with Zeke's blood. Oscar watched me from his cubby over the fridge, uncharacteristically silent. He knew what I was thinking.

Blood is life. Blood is powerful. I could use Zeke's blood to brew and discover at least some of what was going on. At the very least I would learn to whom Zeke—and Clem, by association—were beholden.

But if my suspicions were correct and we really were dealing with a demon of some sort, brewing could be dangerous. Tapping into my powers opened a portal to the supernatural. I would have to be very, very careful not to accidentally invite an entity into my home.

"*Lily?*" Bronwyn called up the stairs.

Darn it all. I needed to concentrate.

I went to the door and found her nearly at the top of the steps. "Your friend Carlos is here."

I let out a frustrated sound akin to "*Unnrrggghhh.*"

"He's such a lovely man. He mentioned his niece has a *quinceañera* coming up . . ." Bronwyn liked Carlos. But, then, Bronwyn liked almost everybody.

"He's here looking for dresses? Would you mind help—"

Carlos appeared in the doorway at the bottom of the stairs. "Sorry, Lily. We need to talk. It's important."

Reluctantly I closed the apartment door and went downstairs to join Carlos in the workroom. Zeke's bloody clothing would keep, and, to be honest, it wasn't such a bad idea for me to take a little time to regroup before casting. What with Griselda's murder, my father's unexpected arrival in town, and the gruesome sight of a human being bouncing off the shiny chrome grille of an Escalade, I was feeling off balance.

Carlos took a seat at the green linoleum early-'60s table in the back room of my store. We had sat here together before, many times. Usually we were discussing murder, which, considering I hadn't been in town all that long, was starting to feel more than a little strange. How had Carlos handled supernatural deaths before I came to town? Or . . . was my presence somehow stirring up such paranormal crime?

"Your name keeps popping up in the oddest of places," said Carlos.

"Is that so?" I said noncommittally.

"What is your connection to Zeke Jones?"

"How did you hear about— Wait. Did he . . . die?" Carlos was a homicide inspector, after all. Still, I hadn't been in the shower *that* long. Surely he would still be working the scene. Wouldn't he?

"As far as I know he's still alive. It's not my case; I just happened to hear. And I noticed your name came up. Again. Got me curious. So, what was your connection to him?"

"He tried to mug me. I guess you could call that a connection."

"In broad daylight?"

"You ever been to that part of town?"

"And then he was hit by a car."

"Yes."

Long silence.

"There were plenty of witnesses," I continued. "Including two cops who arrived almost immediately."

"You didn't see who was driving?"

I shook my head. Then I decided to come clean. "I don't think anyone was driving, actually."

"You think it was a runaway?" With the steep hills in this town, runaway cars were about as frequent as their owner's failure to curb their wheels. "It turned the corner."

"I just think maybe it was being manipulated by someone. I . . . saw someone in a suit."

"Again with the suits?"

"It seemed rather unusual in that part of town."

"Was it the guy you saw at the Gem Faire?"

"Could be. Hard to tell. He was a ways away and shielding his face from view."

"Your father was wearing a nice suit when he was picked up."

I shrugged. "I guess the entire financial district could be suspect, if that's the only clue I've got. Right?"

Carlos nodded thoughtfully. "And you had no connection to the hit-and-run victim prior to the mugging?"

"He and his brother, Clem, had been following me."

"Following you? How long has this been going on?"

"Not long."

"Ever since you were at the Gem Faire?"

"Yes."

"And you didn't think I would be interested to hear about this?"

"They started following me Monday, but I had no way of knowing why or who or what they might be connected to. Do you think it might have something to do with Griselda's death? How is the investigation going?"

"It's not going well, as a matter of fact. Funny thing, though. Your name came up there as well. The owner of the bed-and-breakfast where Griselda was staying mentioned you dropped by to get something from her room."

I started pulling on my lip then stopped, worried I was developing a new tic. "I thought I might see something the police wouldn't recognize. Given the way she was killed . . . I was looking for anything that might help with the whole witch angle."

"And did you see anything?"

"No. Someone had ransacked the room, or so it seemed. I didn't see anything that seemed significant."

"Did you touch anything?"

"I touched the sheets on the bed, just to see if I could feel anything out of the ordinary." I let out a sigh.

"You okay?" Carlos asked.

"Sure. Why?"

"You look a little . . . off-kilter."

"It's been a tough couple of days."

He studied me. "I guess it has, at that. Did you feel anything significant from her sheets?"

I shook my head. "Nothing. I didn't take anything, didn't even touch anything else. I know I shouldn't have gone there . . . I really did think I might be able to help. I thought there might be some sort of connection between us and I was trying to figure out what, exactly."

Carlos nodded. "Well, I told Inspector Leibowitz I would take your statement about your visit to the bed-and-breakfast, so at least you don't have to worry about yet another SFPD inspector breathing down your neck. For the moment."

I managed an appreciative smile. "Thanks, Carlos. You're the best."

"Better not forget it."

"Oh, in the interest of full disclosure, I should mention that when Zeke mugged me, I was right outside the hostel where Johannes, Griselda's assistant, was staying. They said the cops had already been there; I just wanted to mention it."

"Anything else you want to mention?"

"That's all I can think of."

"Okay." He paused as though choosing his words carefully. "I wanted to tell you your father was released."

I felt an unexpected wave of relief wash over me. Good to know my father wasn't a murderer. At the very least, not Griselda's murderer. I opened my mouth to ask for more details, but quelled my curiosity. When it came right down to it, I didn't really want to know.

"Watch your back, Lily," Carlos said.

"You mean with regards to my father?"

"Yes. You say you barely know him?"

I nodded.

"My cop's intuition tells me he's bad news. So, back to this character hit by a car . . . his name also came up in the Gem Faire murder investigation. You have any idea why these guys were following you? Did he say any-thing? You two talk at all?"

I thought for a moment. I didn't want to go into all the demon stuff, but I could tell Carlos an edited version.

"I think they were after something Griselda might have had."

"Like what?"

"A ring. A . . . special ring."

"Special. As in witchcraft?"

"Yes."

"You have this ring?" He fixed me with his patented Inspector Carlos Truth-Laser Gaze.

I shook my head. "I sure don't think so. Griselda sold me a box of junk jewelry, but I've been through every-thing several times, and I can't find a durned thing. There were only five rings, and none of them fit the bill."

"Thought you told me she didn't give you anything."

"I was afraid you'd confiscate things before I could study them. I wasn't trying to hide anything, exactly . . ."

Carlos snorted.

"If I had figured anything out, I would have told you."

"Do you know what you're looking for?"

"Not really. But from what I've learned the ring is a fire opal, like this one but of better quality." I showed him my medallion, and he reached out to cradle it in his hand, studying it.

"You're positive this isn't what they're after? Maybe the ring was made into a necklace."

"I thought of that, too, but when I offered them the necklace they didn't react. Then again, they're both a cob or two short of a bushel, so maybe they just got it wrong. Still, I've been wearing the medallion since Sunday and haven't felt anything at all unusual."

"Doesn't feel magical or special in any way?"

"Afraid not. Carlos, I imagine y'all looked carefully through Griselda's things at the fair, but would it be possible for me to look? I might recognize something y'all wouldn't."

"You're asking me to allow a witch—a *civilian* witch—to look through the evidence in a murder investigation?"

"You could stay there with me. I won't hurt anything."

He studied me for a moment, then blew out a long breath and got to his feet. "I'll see what I can do. And don't forget what I told you: be careful of dear old Dad if he comes a-calling."

I nodded and stood to see him out. Just as we reached the velvet curtains that cordoned off the work room from the shop floor, something occurred to me.

"Carlos, have you heard about the fire dancing in Golden Gate Park?"

"What's fire dancing?"

"I take it that's a no?"

He shook his head.

"Could you ask around, maybe let me know if you hear anything?"

"Like what?"

"I don't know . . . injuries, kids going missing . . ." I shrugged. "Probably nothing. Witch's intuition."

"Anything else I can do for you?" Carlos asked.

"Nope, that'll do. For now. Thank you so much, Inspector."

"You're very welcome, Ms. Ivory."

I meant to go back upstairs to brew, but the store got busy and my presence was needed. Usually Maya could handle the store by herself, but today things weren't going well. Customers were acting stupid: misplacing items, popping buttons, ripping out hems, breaking down in tears in the dressing room when a dress designed for a 1950s teenager didn't fit a twenty-first-century matron.

It's this darned protection spell, I thought as I went about putting out emotional fires. It suppresses creativity and, after all, smarts and rolling with the punches use up a lot of creativity.

With Zeke and, I presumed, Clem out of commission, maybe I could dial back the protection. But I hesitated. There were too many variables in play, not the least of which was when—and if—my father decided to make an appearance.

By the time I went back upstairs it was late afternoon. I did a purification spell, looked at the bloodied clothing, and suppressed a bubble of fear. I wasn't usually afraid when I was brewing in the safety of my own home, a carefully guarded environment full of herbs and charms. But maybe there really was something to this witchy pre-monition thing. . . . If Zeke was beholden to a demon, I had to be dead certain to attend to every detail in the spell so as not to invite anyone in, much less allow them to exert power over me. I had faced a demon, a fellow named Sitri, only once and frankly it had scared the pants off me.

And there was always a tiny flicker of doubt that since our interaction meant Sitri and I were now bound together, that he was wise to my tricks and if I had to go up against him again I might not triumph.

Not that I had any reason to think Sitri had anything to do with what was going on now. After all, demons didn't all know one another any more than we humans all knew one another. It was a big, wide, terrible demonic world out there.

And here and now, Zeke was my only tangible connection to what was going on.

I made myself another cup of tea to calm my nerves, then focused once again on the bloody garments. Blood is special. It shimmers with our energy. The Aztecs knew this, along with so many other cultures that sacrificed life—sometimes even human life—as a vital offering to the gods. Practitioners know this. too, and some use sacrifice to contact their ancestors and invoke their abilities to alter reality. As a matter of principle I avoided blood sacrifice, but this time it had quite literally dropped into my lap. I would be foolish to ignore this boon.

I set a clean white cloth on the kitchen counter and laid out my jewel-encrusted athame, trying not to think of the one that had killed Griselda. Had she refused to talk? Had her torturers gotten what they came for and decided to silence her for good?

I shook off such thoughts. One of the most salient aspects of spell casting is concentration. I chanted and stroked my medicine bag to achieve the right frame of mind. I consulted my Book of Shadows, an old red leather-bound volume handed down to me by my grandmother. A piece of sacred rope; herbs such as sorcerer's violet and magical vinca. As I brewed, I dropped small squares of the bloodied clothing into the bubbling cauldron. Then cemetery dust and marsh weeds, spider silk, and a sharp rock. Red dirt from home. Fresh and dried herbs.

I stirred deosil, or clockwise, and chanted steadily, until the concoction started swirling on its own. I allowed it to boil for about ten minutes, when a distinctive, rank odor signaled the brew was ready. I cut a tiny "x" in my palm with my athame and added two drops of my blood. Then I called upon my helping spirit to guide me ... and to protect me while the connections were made.

The spell was cast well, and I could feel the portals

opening, the power slipping through. Oscar watched silently from his perch atop the refrigerator, his mere presence making my casting easier, smoother.

Try as I might I couldn't read the steam and divine who Zeke was, who he worked for, or what he wanted. What I *could* read was another's influence over him. Since nothing in the world of magic was ever simple, it wasn't as though I perceived a name or a face. But if I met the person, I would know him or her. I would recognize his or her vibrations just as one might recognize a distinctive face in a crowd, just as I might recognize the owner from feeling the clothes he or she had worn.

Zeke was held in sway by someone. Not just influenced by that person, but . . . held. As though a prisoner, Zeke didn't have any choice in the matter.

And those vibrations reminded me of something else I had sensed recently. What was it? I thought of all the jewelry I had been studying or any recent acquisitions for the store. Finally I recognized it. I pulled out the little drawer by the sink, where I had placed the gold cuff link I found at Griselda's stand.

It felt as though it were burning in my palm—it hummed with the same vibrations I had read from the brew using Zeke's blood. But I couldn't imagine Zeke, or Clem, for that matter, wearing a solid gold cuff link. Besides the fact that they didn't appear to have much money, they had been wearing dirty T-shirts both times I had seen them. They didn't appear to be the types to don cuffs, much less cuff links.

It was much more likely that the cuff link belonged to my father, Declan Ivory. Which would mean . . . could my father be the one holding Zeke in sway? And since there were some definite demonic overtones to this vibration, could my father be more than a simple witch? That

would help explain the memory loss when I met him—
demon encounters were known for such a thing.

Like I didn't have enough issues. A rogue witch for a
father was one thing, but a demonic dad? Quite another.

I wondered what the paramedics had determined
about Zeke, whether he was going to make it. He wasn't
far from a good hospital, the San Francisco Medical Center. I hoped for his sake he had gotten help in time.
Would he be conscious and able to talk to me?

And then I wondered whether his little brother would
be showing up for visiting hours. Clem was scared, but
kin was kin. He'd probably visit sooner or later. And I
was willing to bet that with a little effort, I could get at
least one of the Ballcap boys to speak to me.

Chapter 14

The next morning I embraced my familiar, comforting routine of casting a protective spell over the store, going down to Coffee to the People, and eating breakfast with Conrad and Oscar—in his piggy form, of course.

When Maya came in for her shift that morning, she reminded me that she was interviewing Marisela's *abuelita* today.

Carmen seemed to know a lot about legends of fire opals, I thought to myself.

"Would you mind if I join you?"

Maya was gathering her things from her leather backpack. "Of course not. That would be great. You might well come in handy with the Spanish—Marisela agreed to translate, but just in case. I feel like such an idiot not knowing Spanish. I should take a class."

"In all your spare time, between art school and working here and running the Web site and doing oral histories . . . and now fire dancing?"

She smiled. "What can I say? When it comes to life I have ADHD."

"I'd say it's more like a passion to live life to the full-est," said Bronwyn. "Never apologize for that. And yes, Lily, I'm happy to watch over the store in the meantime."

"I see you've anticipated me. Becoming a mind reader?"

"Oh, good goddess, I *hope* so," said Bronwyn, who was cradling piggy Oscar in her arms. "Wouldn't *that* be something?"

"Sounds a little scary to me," I said.

"Ditto," said Maya.

"Oh, by the way, if I'm going to work the afternoon shift, would you mind if the coven meets here? Just a partial meeting; we won't be forming a circle or calling upon the Lord and Lady. Just a few bureaucratic issues we need to discuss."

"Not at all," I said, grateful I wouldn't be here for such a meeting. I had witnessed one once . . . it dragged on for *hours*. Bronwyn's coven was committed to a nonhierar-chical, communal decision-making process. In theory I applauded their efforts; in reality, it meant even the smallest decision was subject to endless debate and ceaseless tinkering. Yet another reason I was a solo act. I didn't have the patience for group process.

On the way over to Marisela's house that afternoon, I asked Maya to be sure to ask Carmen about the legend of the fire opals that she had alluded to on her trip to Aunt Cora's Closet.

"Sure . . . are you looking for any information in par-ticular?"

"Just anything she might know," I said. "I think those guys who were following me were looking for a fire opal ring they thought I might have gotten at the gem show."

"I don't remember seeing a ring like that."

"No, I don't have it, at least nowhere I know about. But that's why I was hoping you could talk to Carmen and see ... Maybe she could shed a little light on the subject."

"With an old legend?"

"Hate to break it to you, my friend, but old made-up legends often have a grain or two of truth. It's worth a shot."

Marisela lived in a house in the Sunset, a part of San Francisco that looks out over the Pacific Ocean and, ironically, rarely saw the sun setting because it was so often beset by thick banks of fog off the sea. The area was developed later than much of the city, in the 1940s, and featured long rows of stucco homes built for working-class families.

Maya and I were buzzed through an iron gate, then entered into a little courtyard to the right of the garage, then up a full staircase to the living area, which was located on the second floor.

Marisela and Metzli, Rosa, and Carmen were joined by another half dozen young women and one adolescent boy. They were all sitting around the living room, on couches and chairs and the floor, making party favors out of little squares of pink tulle wrapped around chocolates and key chains marked with the date, and tied off with wire twists decorated with tiny silk flowers. Two fans hummed while they kept the air circulating, a radio played Motown oldies in the background, and the sounds of children playing outside drifted in through the open window.

"Sorry about all this," Rosa said as she stood to greet us. "I thought we'd be done by now, but ... it's getting a little down to the wire."

"No problem," said Maya. "I really appreciate your mother's willingness to talk to me, and Marisela's offer to translate."

"My daughter speaks better Spanish than I do—she studied it in school. Terrible, isn't it? I mostly know how to talk about food."

"I feel like that with a lot of languages," I said with a smile. Food brought people together and linked the generations; cuisine-based traditions were almost always among the most persistent. "I'd be happy to help with making favors while Maya conducts the interview."

"Really? I won't say no—we could use all the help we can get."

I plopped myself down on the floor next to the boy—overcoming the family's protests that I should be given a chair—and he patiently explained to me how to make the little purses, including tucking in Hershey's Kisses. They reminded me of witch's charm bags, and in a way they were: small tokens made with love, meant to imbue their new owners with memories and connection to the energy of the event.

Maya, meanwhile, set up her tiny recorder, took out her notebook, and sat near Carmen, with Marisela in between. She started off with lots of factual information about where and when the older woman was born and raised, when she came to the United States and why. How long she'd lived in San Francisco—almost sixty years now. And, very delicately, Maya asked Carmen why she'd never learned to speak English.

Rosa broke in to say that though *Abuelita* first came to this country decades ago, she often returned to Mexico and stayed for years at a time. She was from a small village in the state of Jalisco, where she enjoyed her little home as well as the admiration of her neighbors. She was the source, apparently, of all sorts of local history and lore. When she was in the United States, she rarely ventured outside of her home for fear of violence in the streets.

"She doesn't live here with us," said Rosa. "She insists on staying in her own place in the Bayview, and it's not a great neighborhood."

Just then a knock sounded at the door. The boy jumped up and buzzed the person in; a few moments later Shawnelle appeared at the top of the stairs. We all said our hellos like it was old-home week.

"Wow. They've got you making favors? How's that working out for you?" Shawnelle asked me.

I smiled. "Joel and I are racing to see who can make them fastest." I nudged the boy, who had returned to sit next to me, with my elbow. "Care to join the competition?"

"I don't suppose I have much choice," she said, taking a seat and picking up scissors and a length of cloth.

At a significant glance from me, Maya asked if Carmen could expound on the subject of the fire opal, or *Ojo del Fuego*, that she had mentioned the other day at Aunt Cora's Closet. Carmen smiled and started speaking. I understood most of it, but was glad for Marisela's translation, just in case I missed anything.

Marisela began, "This character Xolotl, like I was saying before, was the god of disease and bad luck . . ."

"And fire," said Shawnelle with a smile. "Mustn't forget the fire."

"Right. Disease, bad luck, and fire. *Anyway*, Xolotl was twin brother of Quetzalcoatl. You must've heard of him."

Shawnelle shook her head.

"Quetzalcoatl was the feathered serpent," I answered. "Most revered god of the Aztecs."

"Right," said Marisela. "He was the head honcho, the one they made human sacrifices for. In fact, when Cortés arrived, a blond on horseback—they had never seen horses before, much less light hair—the Aztecs thought maybe he was the embodiment of Quetzalcoatl, so they didn't realize what a danger he was. Oops, sorry. That was *me* talking, not *Abuelita*."

The grandmother, meanwhile, had paused in her story and was waiting patiently, accustomed to the translation drill. At a nod from Marisela she started telling her story once again.

"But, anyway, long before that, Xolotl and Quetzalcoatl were twin brothers who stole fire from the underworld and brought it to the human world. So, *Abuelita* says the *Ojo del Fuego* stone was unearthed from the very heart of the Earth, and right away the priests knew it was special, so they made a special silver setting to hold it. At dawn and midnight, the opal shows its color best. Any *curandero* who wore it could use it for miraculous healing, even regenerating limbs—like the salamander I was telling you about, the axolotl."

In European folklore, the fire elemental was associated with salamanders as well. I remembered how my grandmother laughed and said maybe they got it wrong, that in the old days when people threw logs on the fire they often saw salamanders emerge, shiny and wet, almost glowing, appearing as though sparks were coming off their skin. This led to the belief they were impervious to the fire, a living creature containing the energy of an elemental being.

"But then Xolotl arose, bringing disease and bad luck with him. The people tried to placate him with fire dances and sacrifices, but nothing worked. Then a powerful *curandera* wore the ring; when she performed the proper ceremony and twisted the ring so the stone faced her palm, it emitted lights and a kind of magical fire, and she was able to send him back to the underworld."

"So the *Ojo del Fuego* was the only thing that worked against Xolotl?" asked Shawnelle, apparently interested in spite of herself.

Marisela asked Carmen the question in Spanish, then translated her answer with a nod.

"Yes, ever since then not just Xolotl per se, but any of his minions that are occasionally unleashed, the ones that arise from the elements, from the earth and air and fire itself."

"Way cool," said Shawnelle. Then she held up her small pile of favors. "And look. I'm totally beating you guys."

The conversation moved on. Maya clarified a few points with Carmen and Marisela, and Rosa discussed a cousin's new baby with a couple of the other women in the circle. The murmur of voices, the circle of women and one boy made me think of sewing circles, quilting circles, scrapbooking circles ... all those moments throughout history when women and children come together to share tasks, making of them opportunities for socializing and community building.

Joel sneezed. "*Salud*," sounded a chorus of voices.

"Gesundheit," I said, using the German word without thinking. Then something dawned on me.

"Shawnelle, I don't suppose you have any way of getting in touch with Johannes, that guy from the Gem Faire?"

"The cute German guy?"

I nodded.

Shawnelle and Marisela locked eyes and giggled.

"Yeah, we had sort of, like, a date the other night."

"When was this?"

"Tuesday, I guess. He was kind of sick, though. But he was still cute."

"What did you do on your date?"

"We went and did touristy things. He's never been here before, so he was totally into it. It was actually kind of awesome. I've lived here my whole life, but the only time we do stuff like the cable cars is when people are visiting from out of town. Ya know? So it was kind of cool. Why? What's up?"

"I've been looking for him, that's all. I think he might have . . ." *the sacred ring called* Ojo del Fuego, *meant to combat a fierce elemental demon.* "I'd just like to talk with him. Any idea where he's staying?"

She shook her head. "He was at a youth hostel for a night or two, but I guess he found another place. He doesn't, like, have much money, I guess. Besides, he says he doesn't like to stay put."

That was interesting. Trying to keep one step ahead of the police or a demon or . . . ?

"Does he have a cell phone? Do you have any way of getting ahold of him?"

"No, he doesn't have an international phone. But he'll probably be in touch. . . . He's supposed to be my escort to the *quinceañera* next Saturday. Are you coming?"

I hated these awkward moments. I hadn't been invited, and it seemed a little much to presume, since the extent of our interactions so far were me selling them clothes and listening to a legend about a fire opal.

Besides, I was a creature of my childhood—I remembered too well the crushing feeling of not being invited to the party that all the other kids in town were going to.

Drinking tea with Graciela in her hut on the outskirts of town, acting like nothing was wrong.

But this wasn't Jarod, Texas. And I wasn't a kid. And if Johannes was going to show up, I'd love to have a little chat with him.

"Oh, yes! You should both come!" said Marisela. "Right, Mom?"

"Of course! The more the merrier. And you're altering those dresses in such a hurry for us, we really appreciate it."

"I can't take any credit for the alterations on the dresses—that's all on Maya's mom, Lucille. But . . . if you really don't mind, I would love to come. I wouldn't ruin your seating for the dinner, but I'd love to drop by and see the decorations and the dresses, and, of course, the full court." Metzli beamed. "Maya, shall we go?"

"I'd love to," she said, gathering up her recording equipment and loading her backpack. "I've only been to one a long time ago. A friend from high school."

"That's settled, then," said Rosa. "Wonderful. Joel, stop eating all the kisses."

As Maya and I drove home I pondered what I'd learned.

If Johannes was involved in the murder and/or the hiding of the ring, why would he agree to show up to a *quinceañera*? For that matter, why was he hanging around Shawnelle at all? She couldn't be more than seventeen, eighteen at the most, and he looked like he was in his twenties. Alone in a strange country, his boss killed . . . wouldn't he have more pressing concerns?

And that story of the *Ojo del Fuego* was still ringing in my ears. What was I thinking—that Griselda had arrived in town with a ring with which to face down a demon? And, if so, why hadn't the demon shown itself?

What was the connection to the legendary Xolotl in San Francisco? Gene was hanging around at the Gem Faire and then at the dancing in the park ... when fires broke out on both occasions. Could he be Xolotl's human underling?

Carmen had also mentioned performing fire dances to placate the demon. So maybe Gene was doing what he could to appease Xolotl. And Clem and Zeke, presumably, were searching for the ring so they could destroy the magical stone so no one would be able to control Xolotl. And if I was correct when I felt their vibrations connected to those of my father's, that would mean he was doing the same.

And, quite frankly, I thought San Francisco already had its fair share of disease and bad luck. I couldn't imagine what it would mean if Xolotl were allowed to act freely.

If the ring really had been passed down through the ages, it held not only its own power but a little of each practitioner that had worn it.

It was unique; irreplaceable.

It was up to me to find it. I refused to give over my adopted city to a fire demon and his sharp-dressed underling.

I dropped Maya off at her house, then returned to Aunt Cora's Closet to find Bronwyn's granddaughter, Imogen, was visiting with Beowulf the cat. In the beginning Oscar hated Beowulf, so the black cat would follow him around. Once Oscar decided he liked the feline, though, she disdained him and would walk away, tail held high and twitching. At the moment in his piggy guise, Oscar was trotting after her like a lovesick, well ... piglet.

I said hello to the pure black, silky cat by petting her,

then sneezed. I'm allergic. Which, I supposed, was part of the reason I got stuck with a miniature potbellied pig in the first place.

Imogen was putting together a project for the science fair, with Bronwyn's help, about herbal medicines. She was working on a big poster board to set behind the actual samples of herbs and plants. After telling me all about it and asking me a few detailed questions, she got back to work. Lying on her stomach in a quiet corner of the store, markers scattered around her, she drew while Beowulf and Oscar vied for her attention.

Bronwyn went to check on Imogen's progress, and I helped a young woman looking for a dress for a swing-dancing competition. As I was ringing her up, I looked up to see a well-groomed, nice-looking man in his twenties walk into the store. He was carrying a briefcase and wore a gray suit and red tie. Alarm bells went off.

A suit and tie in this part of the city? Could he be working with Gene?

I kept an eye on him while I wrapped the full-skirted dress in tissue paper and put it in a recycled paper bag with AUNT CORA'S CLOSET written on the side along with our slogan: IT'S NOT OLD; IT'S VINTAGE!

As the customer turned to leave, the man approached the counter.

"Hi. I'm Spade." He handed me his card. "Sam Spade."

"I'm sorry?"

"I received a note saying you wanted to speak with me? I'm a private detective, er, investigator. I'm a private investigator."

"You *guys* . . ." I smiled and glanced over at Bronwyn and Imogen. Bronwyn was now lying on the floor next to her granddaughter, kicking her feet in the air. She was the best grandma ever. "Very funny. You called *Sam Spade* to consult with me about a case?"

They looked puzzled, and it dawned on me: Oscar never transformed in front of Bronwyn and Maya. They couldn't have spoken about it and worked out the gag.

"You mean this isn't a joke?"

Bronwyn shook her head. "Not that I know of."

Oscar. How had he managed to track down a man named Sam Spade? I was going to kill me one gobgoyle pig.

The man looked pained. "It's that movie, right? *The Maltese* whatever?"

"*The Maltese Falcon*, based on the novel by Dashiell Hammett. Featuring Sam Spade."

"Hardly anybody remembers that film anymore."

I couldn't have been more than five years this guy's senior. But, then, I'd always been out of step when it came to popular culture. Or any culture, for that matter.

"Anyway, my father named me Sam. Not even Samuel or Samson . . . just Sam."

"So you grew up as Sam Spade, and then you decided to become a private investigator?"

"Actually . . ." A pretty blush came over his face, staining his cheeks and making him look like he was still in high school. "I'm a stockbroker. I got laid off. I figured, how hard could it be?"

He reached into his suit breast pocket and brought out his wallet, then flipped it open to show me his private-investigation license.

"I didn't even realize you needed certification."

"Oh, sure. You have to pass a test. There's even a handbook. And if you want to carry a gun, that's a whole other process. Anyway, I'm good with computers, and I figure there's always the advanced-search button on Google."

I was embarrassed to admit it, but he was probably right; even with such rudimentary investigative skills, he could probably find out more than I did without ever leaving his office. After all, all I accomplished by running around, trying to talk to people, was to stumble into dangerous situations without preparation.

"I received a message that you're looking for help," Sam said.

"I . . ." This poor man was here under false pretenses. *Unless* . . . "How much would it cost me to have you track someone down?"

"It's . . . just one second." He put his briefcase on the counter, opened it, pulled out a book, flipped through a few pages, ran his finger along one entry, then finally nodded and snapped the book closed.

"Two hundred a day, plus expenses."

"Two hundred? Gee . . . that sounds like a lot. Especially since I'm your first case and all."

"How did you know that?"

"Wild guess. Anyway, seems a little high to me."

"Does it?" He seemed to be calculating something in his head. "How about one-fifty?"

What could it hurt?

Besides, I thought as Oscar started trotting in circles around my legs . . . *I promised my pet pig.*

I agreed to two days of looking for the young Johannes—I figured that was plenty of time to figure out whether he'd already fled the country or, heaven forbid, been killed in some sort of witchy pogrom.

"So," said Sam. "This Johannes character—is he your philandering husband?"

"What? No. Of course not."

"Boyfriend gone astray? He owe you money?"

"No, nothing like that."

There was a pause. I got the sense that Sam Spade was mentally going through his handbook. Perhaps there was a List of Reasons for Pursuit noted on page 7.

"Did he get your daughter pregnant?"

"Just how old do you think I am?" I demanded. I wasn't all that much older than he was. But maybe my lifestyle—lack of sleep, too much worry—was beginning to show on my face.

"Sorry. Just a guess."

"Is it part of your professional code that you have to know why I'm looking for someone? Or could I just hire you without a reason?"

"I suppose." He shuffled around in his briefcase for a moment and pulled out a contract.

"Seriously? In *The Maltese Falcon* it was more of a handshake-type deal."

"I'm more a paperwork guy."

"You really should check out the movie. It could give you some ideas. For instance, you should get yourself a fedora. We have several, right over on the hat rack."

"Thanks. Maybe I'll do that," he said, as I signed the agreement.

Two days, three hundred dollars. If this character actually tracked down Johannes, and Johannes could shed light on what was going on—or even had the ring—it would be money well spent.

After he left, I gave Bronwyn a very abbreviated rundown of what was going on, and in order not to out her "Oscaroo," I suggested perhaps Carlos, knowing I was looking for Johannes, had sent the note to Sam Spade. Which didn't make much sense, but Bronwyn wasn't pushy that way.

And then I excused myself to go grocery shopping
That night, as per my agreement with Oscar, I would be
called upon to make mashed potatoes, Tater Tots, and
mac and cheese for dinner. I hadn't been specific enough
about which Sam Spade we were talking about, after all

And I should know to mind my p's and q's when strik-
ing deals with a smarty-pants gobgoyle familiar.

Chapter 15

The next morning I decided I should go to see Zeke while he was still in really bad shape. I might be able to learn more from him in his prone position, and if I were lucky I would run into Clem at the same time.

As I was approaching the main entrance for the San Francisco Medical Center I realized that for the life of me I could not remember Zeke's last name. Carlos had used it when he asked me about my connection to him after the mugging, but I couldn't remember. Which was odd for me; usually I had a very good memory. I imagined that my protection spells on the shop and my apartment were tamping down on my natural abilities, too.

It turned out to be a moot point: Zeke had been checked in as a John Doe. The details of the accident and a chatty nurse were enough to discover that he was in serious condition and in room 312.

To my surprise, 312 was a private room. That was good; we could speak without being overheard.

Zeke was asleep. The curtains were drawn and the lights were off, making it dim inside the room, lit only by the lights on the beeping machines and the little sunlight that managed to squeeze through the borders of the blackout shades.

I started snooping.

In the bedside table I found a ziplock bag containing a plastic card key from the Hyatt, a cell phone, and a tiny notebook. I had just started to look through it when I heard Zeke stir.

Upon seeing me, he pulled back in fear and I could see his Adam's apple bobbing up and down.

"I'm not here to hurt you. I want to help you, Zeke."

"You don't care about me."

"You're right about that."

He stilled and studied me, as though surprised at my frankness.

"You broke into my shop and then attacked me," I said. "Don't expect a lot of sympathy from the likes of me. But I can still help you."

He looked away, toward the window. "Cain't see anything here . . . there's always lights, even at night. Cain't hardly see the stars, even."

I opened the curtains, but he squinted and turned away.

"I like 'em closed. The light hurts my eyes."

I drew the curtains back over the window, leaving the room shrouded in dark.

"Where you from?" I asked in a soft voice, pulling the room's single chair over to the side of the bed and taking a seat.

"Gunston, West Virginia. Little town no one's ever heared of."

"I'm from a small town in West Texas, myself. I like it here, but sometimes . . ." I let my voice take on a wistful note, confessing something to this near stranger that I'd

ot told anyone. "Sometimes I miss things. Like the
irt—it was red. It would sink into your fingers, under
our nails. . . . I don't know why, but I think a lot about
hat dirt. Also, the dust made for the prettiest sunsets
ou'd ever like to see."

"We're from hill country. I don't much like the flats."

"I reckon whatever we're raised with feels like home."

"I reckon," he agreed with a nod.

I let silence reign for several minutes. The only sounds
vere muted *boops* and *bleeps*, and occasional calls over
he loudspeakers out in the hall. I let myself think about
arod, Texas. My grandmother Graciela was still there,
nd my mother. Sometimes I missed them with a bone-
eep sense of loss. But as for the town. . . . usually I
hought of Jarod with dread, as it was all mixed up with
ain and fear and memories I'd rather erase from my
nind. But it was my hometown, after all, and I wasn't
ying: There were parts of it that were sunk so deep in my
onsciousness that I would always miss them. Not that I
vould ever consider moving back; far from it. I loved my
dopted city for a great many reasons, not least of which
vas that I was much less likely to be exorcised and killed
y my neighbors.

"Why can't you go back home?" I asked Zeke.

He shook his head.

"Who are you beholden to?"

Silence.

"I'm not kidding you, Zeke. I'm pretty powerful my-
elf. I can help you." I leaned forward and put my hand
n his arm and looked into his eyes. I could feel weedy
ibrations of healing . . . subtle but present. But he was
veak. The more vulnerable we are, the easier to influ-
nce. In his condition, Zeke would be pretty easy to ma-
euver. Besides, he wasn't the sharpest tool in the shed

to begin with. I concentrated on helping him to trust my words.

"Do you believe me?"

He nodded. "I ... I don't think you can help me But ... please, if you can, please help my little brother Clem don't know no better. It's all my fault he got caught up in this mess. ... I got too big for my britches and got us into trouble. He just followed me is all. Clem's got a sweetheart back home in Gunston. He should go back there, set up a family. He's a good boy."

"I will, Zeke. I promise I'll do whatever's in my power to help him. Tell me how to find him. Does he come here to visit you?"

"No. We mostly go out at night; stay in during the day The light hurts our eyes ..." He coughed, wincing in pain. He glanced toward the window again.

"You're staying at the Hyatt?" I asked, thinking of the card in his possession. I would have expected them to be in a flophouse somewhere. I guess that would teach me to make assumptions.

"How'd you know that?" he asked, his eyes fearful again.

"I know things. Is it the one over near the Embarcadero? That's a mite pricey."

"Gene likes room service."

"Ah, that makes sense, then. Tell me about Gene. Is he a witch?"

" 'Course not! You think I'd be workin' for a witch?" Zeke cast a look over at me, as though he'd forgotten exactly who he was talking to. "Don't mean nothin' by that. I'm jest sayin' ..."

Gene was his boss? Did that mean Zeke wasn't working for my father after all? I felt a brief second of relief until I realized that the only thing that would explain their shared vibrations with the cuff link, then, was that they were held in sway by the same demon. That was bad.

Though, admittedly, thinking of my father *working* for a demon seemed slightly better than him actually being a demon himself.

But, boy, my standards were low.

"Tell me about Gene."

"Look, lady. I know you think you're 'bout as fancy as they come, but Gene . . . his boss is more powerful than you can imagine. He don't need to be no witch; he can make things happen."

"Who's Gene's boss, then?"

Zeke coughed again, raised his hand, and wagged his pointer finger in the universal sign for "no." I decided to take another tack.

"Tell me about the ring you're looking for."

"Some kind o' ring with a fire opal." His eyes widened as though staring at something invisible and fearsome. "*Whosoever holds the ring, shall exercise dominion over . . .*"

I sat forward, eager to know, but he trailed off.

"Over who . . . or what?" I urged.

Zeke started coughing again. But this time it didn't seem he could stop. In the dark, it took me a moment to realize that what looked like ink spots on the sheets were blood—he was coughing and spewing droplets of blood.

"Zeke?" I leaned forward, put my hand on his arm. Gone were the healing vibrations . . . suddenly I feared he was dying.

I hit the nurses' call button repeatedly, then jumped up and ran out into the brightly lit hallway.

"*Help!* We need help!"

A nurse came running. I stood back, lingering in the doorway and feeling helpless while she worked on Zeke.

Other staff arrived and surrounded his bed. I slipped out to give them room; a nurse was running down the hall toward us, pushing a crash cart. I wished there was something I could do ... but this was best left in the hands of medical science. As I stood waiting for the elevator, I caught of whiff of smoke. I looked back to see a nurse running out of Zeke's room, and the fire alarm screamed. The sprinklers were triggered.

Overhead I heard "Code blue" and a call for fire. Several hospital personnel ran past me, toward the ward.

I stood for a moment, indecisive and overwhelmed with guilt. Should I go back? Was there any way to help? Could it be ... demon's fire? I couldn't shake the nagging sensation that all of these recent fires must be tied to a fire demon in San Francisco. And if Zeke was beholden to a demon powerful enough to know from afar that an underling was speaking to me and to punish him for it, there was no way I could help Zeke. He was already too vulnerable, too sick.

But maybe I could save his brother. I had made Zeke a promise, and I intended to keep it.

Besides ... it was the only lead I had.

I hurried down the stairs and out of the hospital, dodging the hustling staff and near-panicked visitors.

Back at my Mustang, I flipped through Zeke's notebook until I came across a sigil, a demon's sign. A complicated one. Part of it almost looked like Aztec glyphs. I was going to make the assumption this was Xolotl's sigil.

Also in the notebook was a tiny piece of paper with a list of names written in a pretty handwriting that looked both feminine and foreign—it had the distinctive slant and lettering I remembered from my time in Europe. It was hard to imagine either of the Ballcap boys writing like this. Of all the names I recognized only three: Aidan Rhodes, Renna Sandino, and Lily Ivory. Three powerful Bay Area practitioners.

If the ring could only be carried safely by someone powerful, it would make sense we were all on that list. Those looking for the ring must have assumed Griselda had passed it to one of us.

I thought again about my encounter with Griselda at the Gem Faire. She mentioned wanting to meet me later, but kept looking over my shoulder at someone—or some*thing*—behind me. And then she sold me the opal pendant and the box of junk jewelry. Could that have been a decoy? Perhaps she was making sure they saw that I was taking something from her, sending them on a goose chase after me?

Which didn't seem particularly sisterly of a fellow witch, but if this ring really enabled a sorcerer to control something demonic, it was worth putting a few of us at risk.

Perhaps this was the real reason Aidan was nowhere to be found—maybe he was keeping himself safe somewhere. And if the likes of Clem and Zeke paid Renna a visit, I didn't suppose they'd get very far. She was talented and could take care of herself. Still, just in case, I should warn her, at the very least.

After all, I couldn't forget poor Griselda. As I thought back on the sight of her body pressed between boards . . . it seemed too vicious to be Clem and Zeke. Not that I knew for sure, and of course they could have made a mistake; the pressing might have been their boss Gene's idea and it got out of hand. Still . . . I wish I had thought to ask Zeke about it before . . .

A wave of sadness and guilt came over me. I had en-ticed Zeke into talking and then abandoned him to his fate.

I used Zeke's cell phone to call Renna, but once again got voice mail. I left a vague warning. That would have to do for now. I would go talk to her in person, but first I would tackle Clem and Gene.

The Hyatt sat at the bottom of Market Street, not far from the Ferry Building. Its central downtown location made it attractive to tourists and business travelers alike. It had been built sometime in the seventies and featured a central atrium that soared seventeen stories high, a huge water feature that reminded me of a dandelion puff, and glass elevators that whooshed patrons up to their rooms at a steady clip.

I had a key card but didn't know the room number or even a last name. *Dang it all.*

I watched the man behind the reception counter for a moment. Young, friendly. His gaze lingered a little too long on the low-cut dress of the pretty woman he was checking in. I could probably finagle a way to shake his hand, and if I concentrated enough I might be able to convince him to trust me. People in the hospitality industry were usually open and happy to please.

However, though I hated to admit it, last night's brewing and spell casting—and then the interview with Zeke and its traumatic aftermath—had left me drained. I wasn't sure what I would find upstairs, and I really didn't want to spend any more of my magical energy on convincing the desk clerk to give me information.

Instead I fixed on a decidedly nonmagical way of getting what I wanted.

I slipped into the women's room, stuffed my bra with tissue, and pulled down the neckline of today's teal cot-

on sundress. Taking my hair out of its customary ponytail, I flipped my head and combed it upside down.
Practicing my come-hither look in the mirror, I dabbed
on a little frosted lip gloss and applied extra mascara.

As Maya had pointed out, I sort of sucked at flirting.
But what the heck? Time to stretch a little.

When it was my turn at the counter, I leaned forward
a little.

"I am *so* sorry, but my little old card's not working . . .
I think it got too close to my cell phone." I forced a
breathy quality into my voice and let my accent fly. "And
you're not going to believe this, but I can't remember my
own room number. This hotel is so bi-ig!"

"No problem, ma'am," he said, glancing at the view I
was affording him. "Last name?"

"Here's another problem. I don't know if it was under
my name or my *boss's* name or my first *husband's* name."
I leaned even farther over the counter to give him a really good peek down my shirt. He glanced up at my face
and I held his gaze, half closing my eyes "Or maybe my
second husband's . . ."

He looked back at his monitor and frowned slightly.
"Looks like the information is still on the card . . . maybe
you swiped it too fast?"

"You know, I might have. I just lose patience sometimes. It's a fault. Like being . . . impulsive."

He glanced down again, first at my chest, then at his
monitor.

"Jones?"

"I'm sorry?"

"Is one of your names Jones?"

Jones. Of course. It was either that or Smith.

"Why, of course it is! Aren't you just the smartest
thing!"

"Room 1102?"

"Oh, that's it! Thanks *ever* so much! Y'all San Franciscans are just *peaches*, that's what you are."

I headed for the bank of elevators, swinging my hips exaggeratedly just for effect. I felt a little surge of triumph; I wasn't without feminine wiles.

On the eleventh floor I found the room not far from the elevator. A PLEASE DO NOT DISTURB sign hung on the doorknob. I slipped my card into the slot, and the light turned green.

Slowly, carefully, I pushed in the door. To my surprise the dead bolt wasn't latched.

The room was dark, the blackout shades drawn over the window, which, I felt sure, must offer a stunning view of the Ferry Building, the Bay Bridge, and the San Francisco Bay. But Clem and Zeke weren't here for the view, obviously.

It took a moment for my eyes to adjust to the dark. I made out the form of a man sleeping in the closer of two double beds.

I crept in. My heart pounded in my chest; my stomach clenched. I stroked my medicine bag for luck and calm. I wasn't afraid of Clem Jones, per se, but sneaking up on a man sleeping in a hotel room . . . well, this was a first for me.

Suddenly he jumped up.

"*Ah*!"

I leaped back and echoed him, "*Aaah*!"

It wasn't Clem Jones.

Instead I stood face-to-face with an old man with a shock of white hair . . . and terrible scars distorting his face.

Chapter 16

My father.

"*Wha . . . ?*"

He was a powerfully built man, but he looked oddly defenseless with his hair sticking out from his head at all angles and wearing only a white T-shirt and cotton pajama bottoms.

I had imagined this day from time to time. I had dreams wherein my father would take me in his arms and explain everything—why he left. And nightmares wherein I relived what had happened when I found him in Germany and offered to help him and spend time with him, and he reviled me and threw me out.

He flicked on the lights and grabbed for a white terry cloth hotel robe.

"What the hell are you doing in my room?"

Of all the things I expected to hear from my father when I finally encountered him again, this sentence would not have made it into the top ten.

"Hello, *Dad*." I said "Dad" with the kind of sarcasm

reserved for spoiled teenagers. It felt childish but somehow right. "Imagine meeting you here."

"Answer my question. How did you get in here?" His eyes were nervous, flickering behind me to see if I was accompanied by anyone.

"You should have bolted the door."

"Just tell me: Are you acting alone?"

"Yes."

"You wouldn't lie to your father, would you?"

"Sure I would. But I'm not lying now."

He visibly relaxed and sank down on the side of the bed, his elbows on his knees, head in his hands.

I waited. For some reason I kept hoping he'd say my name. I wanted to hear it from him in his distinctive voice, which I remembered so well. Sonorous and lush. Deep. I realized with a start that Max Carmichael, a journalist with whom I'd had a brief fling, had a similar voice. Perhaps that was why I had been so attracted to Max—a man who remained distant and disapproving. Don't they say we're attracted to people that remind us of our parents? That we seek the approval we were denied in childhood? What a depressing thought.

I tried to center myself as best I could, but as I reached for the desk chair I realized my hand was shaking. I took a seat. Scattered on the desk and nightstands were candy bar wrappers, Coca Cola cans, and a large bag of Jelly Belly candies.

"I have a few questions," I said. "What are you doing in town?"

He rubbed his hands together, as though gathering his thoughts.

"Aidan Rhodes."

"What about him?"

"I need to see him."

"You're not here for me, then?"

"I didn't even know you were in San Francisco. I thought you were in Hong Kong."

My heart sped up a little at the idea that he had been keeping track of me, that he knew I had been in Hong Kong. I was acutely aware that the emotions of childhood still held mastery over a part of me, my heart still wanted this man to care, to act like a real father. The feelings of betrayal and abandonment were still as tender—or more so—than the day he left.

"I moved here a few months ago. This is my town now. I think you should move on."

"I can't. I'm here looking for . . . something."

He reached over and opened a Mars bar. Without offering me any, he bit into it.

"What's with the candy?"

He shrugged and took another bite. I couldn't get over how old he seemed. The burns gave his face a ravaged look, but they didn't put me off nearly as much as the age evident in the careful way he held himself, his bloodshot eyes.

"What about Aidan Rhodes?" he asked.

"What about him?"

"Surely you know *of* him, at least. How long did you say you've lived here?"

"A few months. Yes, I know Aidan."

"Listen to me," he said as he sat up, suddenly animated. "I have to find something . . . It's something only a very strong practitioner could hold on to. A piece of jewelry. This piece . . . anyone else . . . it drains their power. I need it. My very salvation is at stake. I think . . . I think Aidan must have it."

He paused. It didn't take a mind reader to figure out what was coming next; he wanted me to get it for him.

After all this time, no apology, no loving words of regret, no hug. He wanted me to do something for him. Rather than tell him I knew about the ring, I decided to play along, just to see how far he would go.

"*I* have no power over Aidan."

"I wouldn't be so sure. You've grown up to be a very attractive woman." His mouth kicked up on one side. "No shock there—you take after my side of the family."

Given that my mother had once been declared Miss Tecla County, and my father was—at least these days— irreparably scarred and hard to look at, it seemed rather bold to take credit for whatever good looks I might possess.

But what really bothered me was my reaction to his words; I was pathetically pleased to hear that he thought I was attractive. I felt like a mongrel yearning for scraps of affection. My own weakness made me angry.

"You're suggesting I—what? Seduce him?"

"Whatever it takes. This is important."

My father was happy to pimp me out to get a magic ring from Aidan. Gee, was it any wonder that we didn't swap birthday cards?

"Let's back up here one *gol-danged* second," I fumed. "You pop back into my life for all of five minutes, after abandoning me as a baby and then tossing me out on my ear when I came to look for you in Germany, and now you expect me to *help* you?"

"I need you. I need your help."

"Tell me why this piece is the key to your salvation, and maybe I'll consider it."

"It's a ring, an ancient ring imbued with power. It's called *Ojo del Fuego*, and in the hand of a powerful witch it can be used to exorcise . . . a spirit. A powerful evil spirit."

"And why go up against this spirit?"

A long pause. "I'm beholden to him. In fact, I'm here at his command."

"Along with Clem and Zeke?"

"They're working for Gene, and I'm ... I guess I'm supposed to be working with them as well. But I intend to find it first and win my freedom. If Gene finds it, he might be strong enough to use it to control the spirit, and I'll be in thrall to *him*. Don't you see? Whosoever commands the demon, commands me. The only way I can break free is to find it before anyone else uses it to exorcise the demon, or before Clem or Zeke or Gene finds it and destroys it according to the demon's bidding."

"Did you go after Carlotta?"

He shook his head. "That was Gene's doing, I'm sure. He's been searching for the ring for years. When I heard Carlotta had been killed and then her sister took off to San Francisco, I figured she was bringing the ring back to Aidan. He's strong enough to keep it, and he has ... history with it."

"So you tortured Griselda to death, hoping she would tell you where it was?"

"*No.* That wasn't me, I swear, Lily." He finally used my name. So glad he remembered what it was. "I don't know anything about it. Ask the police—they let me go; they couldn't place me at the scene."

"Why were you a suspect in the first place?"

"Zeke was angry at me. He was suspicious about me—rightly so. Tell the truth, I think he had his own plans for breaking free, for him and his brother."

"This Gene character sure knows how to pick 'em. Does he realize you're all working independently?"

"Not exactly independently. Once you're beholden ... well, nothing's that simple anymore."

"If this character is so powerful, how can you be talking to me about this?" I asked, thinking of what happened with Zeke. Angry as I was, I couldn't bear a repeat performance with my father as star.

He shook his head and one hand went up to his chest, where there was a slight bulge under his T-shirt. "It's taking a great deal of power to cloak myself."

I noted the grayish white twine around his neck, a perfect match to his hair. I presumed he was wearing a protective talisman of some sort. Perhaps his own hair amulet?

"Listen," he continued. "I knew Carlotta in Germany and tried to strike a deal with her there, but she refused. In fact, I'm afraid I inadvertently led Gene to her. Then Zeke called in an anonymous phone tip telling the police that I had a connection with Griselda and had threatened her. So they brought me in for questioning. That's all."

"You were in handcuffs."

"You saw me?" His eyes held mine for a long moment. "You were there?"

"I was suspected of causing a ruckus to distract the security guards from her death."

"You were at the Gem Faire, too?" He sat up once more, eager. "Did you speak to Griselda? Did she give you anything—anything at all?"

I shook my head. "But I found a gold cuff link at her stand. Your gold cuff link. Wonder what the police would make of that."

There was a long pause. He searched my face, assessing. After a moment he smiled. "It's rather sweet, really, that they would think you'd do something like that for your dear old dad. And now you've withheld evidence just for me?"

"I wasn't completely sure it was yours until right this moment."

"Anyway, the only reason they cuffed me ... I may have lost my temper when they came to talk to me. But I swear, I had nothing to do with her death." He finished the candy bar and sat hunched over on the edge of the bed. When he looked back up at me, it surprised me to see he had tears in his eyes. How come he could cry, when I couldn't?

He spoke in a whisper. "Lily, I have to find it."

"I thought you just said Aidan Rhodes had it. You two know each other. Why don't you go talk with him?"

A flush crept up his neck and into his cheeks. "I can't go out in the light, and I've been weakened by having to keep my guard up around Gene. But *Aidan's* the one responsible for all of this." He passed a hand over his face. "He and I ... we were supposed to go up against the spirit, the demon, together. We had a pact, but he betrayed me."

"He was burned, too. Yet he's not beholden?"

"He betrayed me to save himself."

I didn't know what to think about that. I certainly took my father's words with a grain of salt, but while Aidan had helped me on more than one occasion, there was something about him I still didn't trust. And frankly ... from what I'd seen of demons, I could imagine doing a lot of things—even, perhaps, betraying someone—in the panic of trying to escape their clutches.

"You're sure Aidan has this ring?"

"Not entirely. I assumed he was the only local practitioner with sufficient power to hold the piece. There are only so many candidates with that kind of muscle. Unless ..."

He fixed me with an odd look, frightening in its intensity.

"Unless what?"

"Your powers have grown," he said. "I can tell. You weren't anywhere near this able when I saw you last."

"I was a teenager when you saw me last. I've grown up. I've worked at it, learned a lot."

"Without Graciela?"

"I had to leave Jarod. I told you that when I came to Germany."

"But your grandmother . . ." He faded off, then gave me an odd look. Then nodded, as though he'd made a decision. "You're positive no one's given you anything? Griselda didn't pass anything to you?"

I shook my head, suddenly very sure I didn't want my father to know I might well have possession of something I had yet to find among my new jewelry. I felt another wave of anger surge within me; after everything that had happened between us—or *hadn't* happened between us—this is what my father concentrated on? All he wanted from me was information and help, no matter the risk to me?

He stared at me, assessing.

"No, you're right. You aren't strong enough. I need to find Aidan."

"Have you tried his office?"

"He has an office?"

"At the Wax Museum, down on Fisherman's Wharf." It wasn't as though I was giving away a confidence; the man was listed online and in the yellow pages as the go-to guy for curses and spells.

"The Wax Museum? Really? Doesn't that seem a bit . . . macabre?"

"That's exactly what I said." I felt absurdly pleased at his reaction as confirmation that there was, in fact, a link between us.

"Do not trust him, Lily. He's not to be trusted."

"Yeah, well . . . there's a lot of that going around."

Another long pause as he studied me.

"You know, before this all happened, before Aidan betrayed me . . . I was coming back for you. I had always planned to come back for you. I never stopped thinking about you, Lily, never stopped loving you. You're my baby girl."

The tears I couldn't shed stung the back of my eyes. Those were the words I had longed to hear for so long.

"I need you to do this for me, Lily. Find the ring; help me break free. You have no idea what it's like to be under a demon's control. I'm your father, Lily. Help me, I'm begging you."

I was shaking my head, not refusing him so much as overcome by emotions too long suppressed.

"Please, Lily. We can be a family again. "

Chapter 17

I left the Hyatt and walked down hectic Market Stree[feeling battered, as though all those sore spots that hac long since scarred over had been scraped raw again.

There was a tiny sneaking hope, a slight whisper, tha perhaps my father was telling the truth, that if I foun(the fire opal ring and helped him escape from the de mon, we could be a family again.

I'm not naive; I knew that it wouldn't be all sweet ness and light. But still . . . for the first time in so lon(there was the slightest hope. Just to have communica tion with my father, an attachment to a blood relativ(that went beyond the unanswered phone calls and let ters and checks I sent to my mother, beyond the awk ward annual Mother's Day phone call, during whicl she mostly wept on the other end of the line while told her I loved her. Graciela still cared for me, and treasured our connection. But what if I could hav(more?

Probably he would ride right off into the sunset if managed to free him, but it was still worth a try. I couldn'

stand to think of anyone under a demon's thumb, much
less blood kin.

So I was back where I started: How did I get my hands
on the elusive *Ojo del Fuego*, presuming Griselda really
had brought it with her to San Francisco? My father said
it could only be held by a very powerful person, which in
his mind meant Aidan.

Could that be why he was nowhere to be found?
Might he have the ring, and if so . . . could I talk him into
helping me free my father? After what had happened
between them . . . maybe if Aidan had, indeed, betrayed
my father, he would help him out of guilt.

Aidan had never shown a whole lot of guilt about
anything, but it was possible. If not, perhaps I could
promise him something in exchange for it. Which would
mean that I would be beholden to Aidan, which seemed
only slightly less awkward than being held in thrall to a
demon.

These thoughts filled my mind as I drove back to Aunt
Cora's Closet, where I went straight into one of Bronwyn's famous hugs. She was a little taken aback—usually
I wasn't much of a hugger. But then she slowly stroked
my hair.

"Lily, what's wrong?"

I gave her a brief rundown about encountering my
father—leaving out all the demon stuff and the witch
stuff and the manipulation stuff. I offered only the broadest outlines of his abandonment and the fact that he was
now in San Francisco, and I wasn't sure how I felt about
seeing him, much less whether I should try to work on
any sort of relationship between us.

"I myself am always an advocate of doing whatever
you can for peace and reconciliation. Look how it
worked for me and Rebecca!"

Bronwyn had been rather estranged from her very respectable daughter, who didn't care for her mother's involvement in Wiccan activities, among other things. But after Rebecca's husband was caught up in a nasty murder investigation, the two had become much closer. Now Rebecca's daughter, Imogen, was allowed to come hang out with us at Aunt Cora's Closet, which she did with frequency.

"I know," I said, and tried to think whether I could put into words why my relationship with my father was, perhaps, more convoluted than most. Why our estrangement might have to do with issues of demons and loyalty and fate. "It's just . . . I guess I'm afraid, when it comes right down to it."

"We're all afraid of being hurt," said Bronwyn, her voice as gentle as a dove's coo. "But as you know, there's no way to embrace change without allowing oneself to be vulnerable. That's why you have good friends at your back, so even if things go terribly wrong, you can rely on them for strength."

And then, as was her wont, she enveloped me in yet another long, vanilla-scented bear hug.

"Were you baking today, by any chance?" I asked as I finally pulled away.

"How did you know? Imogen and I had a kitchen project this morning."

Bronwyn brought out a plate of fresh-baked snicker-doodles from behind her herbal stand. That would explain the crumbs I had noticed on Oscar's snout—he had no doubt begged a few from her.

I smiled and bit into one. "Mmm . . . scrumptious."

"Homemade cookies make everything better, I always say."

My mouth full of cookie, I turned as the bell over the

ront door failed to tinkle when someone walked in. I
idn't have to rely on any extrasensory perception to
now who it was.

As my own *abuelita* Graciela used to say: *Cuando
parezca el diablo, estará vestido de caballero.* When the
evil shows up, he'll be dressed as a gentleman.

"*Lily*," said the hard-to-find Aidan Rhodes in a silky
oice. "How wonderful to see you. It's been so long. *Too
ong.*"

Oscar, in his piggy form, did his obsequious bit, run-
ing circles around Aidan's legs, begging for attention.
idan gave him a twitch of the head, and Oscar scooted
ack over to the purple silk pillow Bronwyn had bought
im. Recently she'd had it monogrammed, with OSCAR
vory embroidered in giant florid letters, the "O" and "I"
rominent. Maya called it his OI pillow and suggested
e come up with two more names starting with "N" and
K," so it would spell "oink."

"Aidan, we haven't seen you in ages!" gushed Bron-
yn as she ran across the shop to give him a big hug. I
magined not many people dared to hug Aidan, but he
miled and returned the embrace.

"I swear you are looking more gorgeous with every
irthday, Bronwyn. That shade of lilac is exquisite with
our coloring." Bronwyn had just turned fifty-three and
elebrated with a party that would make any coven
roud.

How Aidan knew this was anyone's guess . . . but
idan always knew things. It was the way of it, just as
atural as the sun rising in the east.

The handful of women in the aisles of Aunt Cora's
loset glanced over at Aidan and sighed. It was a typical
esponse of women, and most men.

Not long ago Bronwyn had referred to Aidan as a

golden-haired god, which wasn't all that far from the truth. Not that the man was a god—far from it. But there was no denying that his sparkling aura cast a magical demigodlike spell over just about anyone he walked by. His eyes were a deep, captivating shade of periwinkle blue and seemed to hold secrets you were just dying to know. Tall and broad shouldered, he cut a fine figure and was always impeccably dressed.

His beauty seemed unreal, and part of it was. But love him or hate him, Aidan was a force to be reckoned with.

Lately my own feelings for him had been closer to hate than to love. Though he wouldn't admit it, I was pretty sure Aidan had run Sailor out of town. In fact there was part of me that was hoping this was so, because if it was true, I didn't have to consider the painful possibilities that Sailor had fled because he was either afraid of me or didn't want to be with me. It was one thing to be a disaster in the romance department, and quite another to make men flee.

"Where's Sailor?" I demanded of him, as I had every time we had met since Sailor's disappearance.

Aidan cocked his head and gave a tiny frown as he looked at me quizzically. "How would I know?"

"Because you ran him out of town once you learned we were dating."

"Personally," he said as his long, graceful fingers played with a strand of Venetian glass beads, "I'd ask his relations. Perhaps he left a forwarding address."

I pursed my lips to avoid saying anything more damaging. Besides, we had more immediate concerns at the moment than my love life, such as demons and magic amulets.

Witchy politics, and witchy feuds, made strange bedfellows.

"It looks like *some*body had fun at the Gem Faire," he said as he admired a long string of dark purple-gray misshapen pearls that adorned a nearby mannequin. He smiled. "Either that or a magpie's been busily decorating."

"If you're not going to tell me about Sailor, what are you doing here?" I asked. I had no desire to swap small talk with this powerful mage, but I wanted *him* to bring up the business with Gene and the ring and my father. Even though I'd been trying to get in touch with him, I was certain he had shown up here for his own reasons. That was how it was with Aidan.

"Seriously?" Aidan said, his eyebrows raised, a half smile on his lips. He glanced over at Bronwyn, who was now showing an elderly woman her new salve to fade age spots. They seemed engrossed in the discussion, and within moments all the other women in the store joined them, crowding Bronwyn's herbal stand. They were mesmerized suddenly with whatever concoction Bronwyn was mixing up.

It took me a moment to realize Aidan must have cast a cocooning spell so they wouldn't overhear our conversation.

"Perhaps we could go upstairs and speak in private?" he suggested.

Aidan had never been to my apartment. I planned to keep it that way. I wasn't sure why, exactly, except that my place was my inner sanctum.

"Let's go for a walk instead. It's so sunny out."

"Hot, even," Aidan said with a smile, fixing me with an intense look from those sparkly blue eyes. I wasn't fooling him. "Of course, whatever you'd like."

Aidan released Bronwyn from the spell, and I left the store in her more than capable hands. As Aidan opened

the door for me, the bell again failed to make any noise.
I lifted an eyebrow.

Aidan paused and glanced overhead. The bell rang
obligingly.

"Why do you *do* that?" I asked as he closed the door
behind us.

"You don't find that incessant ringing a bit annoying?
Reminds me of the faerie court—those little guys do
adore their chimes. Anyway, I don't like to give you any
warning of my arrival." He grinned. "You might escape."

"This is all a joke to you, isn't it?" I demanded. I was
on edge, not feeling like myself. I had no idea how
Aidan was involved with any of this, or even whether
he *was* actually involved, although when something
magical was going haywire, it seemed he was *always*
involved.

He laughed outright. "*Someone* woke up on the
wrong side of the bed this morning. 'Mares bothering
you again?"

I just shook my head as we walked past a street vendor selling earrings, and another with a display of tiny
handmade clay flutes.

"I told you," he said in a quiet, seductive voice, "it's
not natural for a witch to sleep alone. You're inviting all
sorts of nocturnal trouble. There's no reason to be by
yourself; you could enamor any man you like."

"You're giving me *romantic* advice now? Seems to me
you've done your level best to run off any such possibilities in my life."

He scoffed. "Any man worth his salt wouldn't be that
easily run off. Besides, that journalist you liked—what
was his name? Max?—was a train wreck."

"And Sailor?"

"Sailor is . . ." He suppressed it quickly, but I knew the

hought of Sailor and me together still stuck in his craw.
Sailor is trouble, no two ways about it."

We paused for the light at Cole Street. Aidan reached
ut to tuck a strand of my dark hair behind my ear.

"Besides ..." he said in a low voice. "We both know
here's someone else so much better suited to you. One
f these days, maybe you'll stop fighting it."

The mere touch of his fingers caused a searing tingle
f heat to race through me, but I had already braced my-
elf for it. There was no denying there was chemistry be-
ween us. The only question was what to do about it. We
ad kissed once, and our combined magic spun out of
ontrol. I had the feeling that Aidan's romantic track re-
ord wasn't much better than mine; we both seemed to
eave a trail of battered lives in our wake.

But for the moment, at least, I was putting that at the
ery top of the list of things I didn't want to think, much
ess talk, about.

We crossed Stanyon to enter Golden Gate Park.

"What has your father said to you?"

I studied the side of his face as he looked straight
head at a group of children playing hide-and-seek in a
ucalyptus grove. I wasn't going to bother to ask how he
new my father was back in town—Aidan had more
couts and spies than I could fathom.

"Nothing."

"He hasn't asked you for anything?"

I shook my head.

We walked farther into the park in silence. Aidan
vasn't one prone to fabricating long pauses for dramatic
ffect. He was choosing his words carefully.

"You haven't been contacted in any way?" He
earched my face. "No unusual characters in your life
ately—anything like that?"

"Someone was sent to follow me."

"Who? How?"

"Couple of look-alike guys in a big mint green Ford Scout. Not exactly subtle. Named Zeke and Clem. They're pretty incompetent—came into the store, then tried to mug me."

"*Mugged* you?" Alarm in those beautiful blue eyes. Maybe he really did care about me. "Did they take any thing from you, a piece of jewelry?"

Or . . . maybe not. He was worried about them finding the ring, not the health and welfare of yours truly.

I shook my head.

"This is very important, Lily: Was anything given to you? A gift or present of some kind?"

"What kind of present?" I played ignorant, seeing what he'd say.

"A ring."

"No," I said, relieved not to have to lie to Aidan. Though we couldn't read each other's thoughts, it was usually pretty evident when the other was lying.

As we followed a bend in the path to a small meadow, we saw a couple of young women in halter tops and cut offs, swinging pots on ropes, dancing and swaying.

"Are they practicing fire dancing?" Aidan asked with a frown.

"I think so, yes."

He swore under his breath. "Since when has this been going on?"

"First time I heard about it was Sunday. You've been out of touch. Shouldn't you be on top of this sort of thing?"

"Fire dancing is a great art, actually, but in this case . . . it's not good. Not good at all. Listen. With regards to your father: Don't trust him."

I snorted. "Like I need you to tell me that?"

Again with the searching of my face. It was starting to make me nervous. Aidan was clearly trying to figure out how much information to share with me and how much to hold back. It was rare for him. I almost never saw him unsure.

"I was once entrusted with a very important magical thing. Because of something that happened with your father, I wasn't able to keep it. I wasn't strong enough at the time. So I gave it for safekeeping to a powerful witch I knew."

"Carlotta Hummel?"

He looked at me, startled. "How did you know?"

"I have my sources," I said, feeling inordinately proud of myself for getting the jump on him for once. It was the sort of thing he was always doing to me.

He nodded thoughtfully. "Yes. Carlotta. I had to get the ring to someone powerful enough and who had no obvious connection to me. She was able to hide it for many years, but recently she was forced to forfeit it."

"Along with her life."

"Yes."

"And you don't know where it is now?" I wasn't ready to tell him the truth about how much I knew. I still didn't trust him.

He shook his head. "Part of the ability of the ring is to keep itself hidden. There is no feeling its hum, its vibrations, unless it wants you to. In a very real sense, it is alive. Too many practitioners have poured in a bit of their abilities for it to be otherwise. And if Carlotta gave up her life keeping it secret, it very likely holds a good deal of her powers as well now. It grows stronger, which is a very good thing. Because the ... entity that it controls does as well."

We were talking about demons. A lot of us powerfu
folk can't speak the names for fear of invoking them
particularly if we share a bond. Demons are diabolicall
clever and have wicked good memories. Once you use
spells and incantations to control them or escape from
their clutches, they remembered. The next time you me
up, if you were so unfortunate as to see them again, yo
had to have a whole new arsenal of tricks.

"And what makes you think this ring is here in Sa
Francisco?"

"Carlotta's sister, Griselda, arrived a few days ago. A
did your father."

"And you think he's looking for it?"

"I would assume so. I believe Carlotta must have trie
to send the ring to me. I am not sure how, or who sh
might have trusted for the job besides her sister. Unfor
tunately, my own investigation has been stymied by m
need to go underground."

"Why are you so sure my father's looking for th
ring? Maybe he came here to visit his daughter. Yo
never know."

His blue eyes sparkled as they looked into mine. I re
membered only too well, however, the time I had walke
in on him unexpectedly and seen him without the glam
our he used to hide his scars. I wondered if he still ha
nightmares about the flames of that demon's fire.

"You went up against this demon together. Didn'
you? Is it . . ." I hesitated to say the name Xolotl, just i
case. "The X-man, the Aztec fellow?"

"Sounds like you know plenty."

"Not enough. Tell me what happened. You told m
you and my father used to work together."

He nodded. "We did, some time ago. But then . . . w

ent up against a powerful foe. Everything went wrong.
. . your father . . ."

"He betrayed you?"

"It wasn't that. Declan thought he could gain con-
ol . . . that he could utilize the entity. And then I . . ." He
ailed off, shaking his head. "I made a mistake. A crucial
istake."

"You're saying he's beholden to a demon and it's
mehow your fault?"

Aidan looked back at the children playing among the
ees, their high-pitched young voices reminding us of
y and life. Dwelling on demons tended to suck that
nd of thing out of a person.

"I owe him; let's leave it at that. I think he's here in
rsuit of the ring."

"To use it to free himself?"

"That's the most benign explanation. It's possible,
ough, he's intent on destroying it *for* the demon."

"Why would he willingly stay beholden?"

"He would gain great powers, beyond anything a reg-
ar human could ever hope to attain. And your father is
very ambitious man."

Food for thought. "So where do we go from here?"

"We find the ring first. Besides stopping a good deal
carnage, we could use it to free your father from the
ntity's clutches."

"Easier said than done. I've been looking for it since
e Gem Faire."

"You're very sure Griselda didn't give you anything?"

"I bought a box of junk jewelry from her, but it was
ng before anything happened, and it seemed so ran-
om . . ."

"It's probably with her other things. I had people

search her inventory and her room, but we weren't the first ones there. They'd already been gone through."

I nodded. "I asked Carlos Romero about looking through whatever evidence they gathered from her stand."

"Good. I had my man on the inside check it out, but it couldn't hurt to have you look as well. Still, it's more likely she hid it somewhere . . . or got it to an accomplice. Which brings me to my main reason for coming to see you: I'd like you to go speak with Renna Sandino."

"I was already planning to. But . . . I have the feeling she's angry with me."

"I have the feeling she's *furious* with you, but I guarantee you she's even less pleased with *me*. Just be careful—a Rom witch is not a good person to cross."

I glared at him. "I had no intention of crossing her. It's all your fault."

He gave me a sad smile. "You'll work it out. Anyway, I want you to find out if Griselda made contact with her before . . . before her unfortunate demise. Meanwhile, I'm touching base with a few other local practitioners whom she might have reached out to."

"Zeke had a notebook with a list of names. You, Renna, and I were on that list, along with several others I didn't recognize."

"I believe I'm aware of all the possible candidates, but show me the names just in case. Wouldn't want to miss anyone."

I nodded and we headed back to Aunt Cora's Closet.

"Lily, I shouldn't have to remind you that this is a very delicate affair. When you speak to Renna, don't volunteer any information. Wait for her to give you a sign of how much she knows."

Witchy politics were intricate, the traditions an

sleights and requirements labyrinthine and largely beyond my ken. I would imagine with a powerful ring like
this at stake, it was even worse than normal.

"And think of it this way," Aidan said as we turned
and started meandering back to the shop. "You can always ask her if she's heard from Sailor. Perhaps he really
did leave a forwarding address."

Chapter 18

Renna Sandino lived in a bubblegum-pink house in the Oakland hills with her husband, Eric, who had charmed me when we met by playing the accordion and singing a flamenco song.

Over the front door a sign read FORTUNES TOLD; LOVE LIVES SET RIGHT. The pink house put all the staid beige and putty-colored houses on the street to shame, at least in my mind. I guess the neighbors weren't fond of the place, but that was their problem.

The man next door had been trimming his hedges, but he shook his head in disgust when he saw me turn into the drive, and ostentatiously went into his house and slammed the door. Across the street a woman was playing in her front yard with two children; she looked away when I glanced in her direction.

The big black wrought-iron gate was open, so I drove on through, grateful I could try to explain myself and my reason for coming in person, rather than having to deal with the static-prone intercom. Pulling around the circular driveway to the front yard, I started to note disturb-

ng details: a charm of animal fur and flowers was nailed
o the wooden post of the mailbox, there were rowan
hoops on the rail leading up the front steps, and the front
door was ajar. Plus, the neat line of salt Renna always
kept on her threshold was scattered.

Carefully I climbed out of my car, looking and listening. No barking dog greeted me, no sounds of flamenco
music, no welcome, but, thankfully, also no screams.

Then I smelled . . . fire?

I watched the house for a moment, and sure enough . . .
smoke floated out of the kitchen window.

I don't carry a cell phone, so I shouted to the neighbor, "Call 911!"

I ran in carefully, mindful of smoke and fire.

"Renna?" I shouted "*Renna!*"

Symbols of protection were smoldering on the tile in
the foyer, and the living room rug was afire. As I watched,
flames started to march up the floor-length paisley curtains that covered large windows.

And through the opening to the kitchen, on the floor,
a pair of shoes peeked out from behind the counter.

No, not shoes. *Feet.* Men's feet. I ran into the kitchen
to find Eric sprawled on the kitchen floor. His shirt was
open, and on his bare chest, as though burned into flesh
with hot metal, was a sigil. Xolotl's sign.

I knelt beside him, put my hand to the side of his
neck. The vibrations were still strong. He was still alive.

I grabbed his arms and used all my strength to pull
him out the front door, where I left him on the stoop,
praying emergency workers would arrive any moment.
But for now I had to find Renna. I prayed she wasn't
here, but if she was . . .

Wetting a dish towel under the faucet, I wrapped it
around my nose and mouth to shield my lungs from

some of the smoke. The house was filling with the acrid scent as the small flames grew. In the living room the curtains burst into flame, and a pile of newspapers blazed in one corner. Large black pieces of ash, lined in burning red, floated on air and landed around the room, spreading the sparks.

"*Renna*! Can you hear me? Are you here?" I yelled. Fire was louder than I had ever expected. The whooshing sound of flames and the crackle of whatever burned resounded through the house. "*Renna*?"

I ran down the hall to Renna's bedroom, where she had once read her tarot cards for me, back when we worked together to cast a spell that defeated a powerful witch. Though strangers to each other's methods and magic, we had felt a sense of mutual respect, if not kinship.

The bedroom had been destroyed, the drawers emptied and clothes strewn everywhere. Lamps lay broken on the floor, the bookshelf was turned over, and the mattress upended. Her tiger-striped bedspread lay in a heap with her tarot cards scattered over it, but the Queen of Swords was pinned to the wall with Renna's jeweled athame.

The flames hadn't reached the bedroom yet, but the smoke was thickening. I was about to search the rest of the house when I decided to check the bathroom and closet, just in case.

I opened what I thought was a closet door, but it led instead to a small writing nook that Renna apparently had used as her private altar.

And hanging from the ceiling was Renna, her arms tied and yanked up behind her. Her shoulders were probably dislocated. I recognized the torturous method as *strapatto*. Yet another traditional technique for extracting information from witches.

"Renna! Can you speak to me?"

She made a raspy, croaking sound deep in her throat; her eyes rolled back in their sockets. She seemed barely alive.

I yanked the athame from the wall. Holding Renna up as best I could with my left arm to relieve the tension, I started sawing through the rough rope tethering her to the beam. She was deadweight, too weak and injured to help me. I heard the faint sound of sirens approaching, and thanked the goddesses that the neighbor must have called 911, as I'd asked.

The cutting seemed to take forever. One strand snapped at a time, with hundreds to go. My muscles burned with the strain of holding Renna in my left arm and with the staccato motion of the sawing back and forth with my right. The stench of smoke assailed my nostrils, despite the wet rag that was still over the lower half of my face.

Finally the rope snapped. We both fell onto the floor, our combined weight hitting with a solid *thud*. The fire was growing quickly in the outside bedroom; already in one corner of the room smoke was filling the chamber and moving our way. I climbed out from under Renna and threw a small stool to break the glass of the window, which led to a narrow side yard. To avoid pulling on her injured arms, I grabbed her by her waist and dragged her, but she had a good twenty or so pounds on me. After much heaving and tugging we were finally next to the window. I took the dishcloth from my face, wound it around my hand for protection, and cleaned the glass shards off the windowsill. Thrusting my head out, I could see emergency vehicles in front of the house and fire-fighters running to connect their hose. I tried to call to them, but no one heard me over the noise of the truck, the fire, and the shouting.

Renna's candles, amulets, and small prayer tokens scattered around the room like confetti as I grabbed the heavy cloth off the altar and threw it over the shards of glass on the sill. I used my last reserves of strength to hoist Renna up, draping her body facedown over the sill. I then climbed out around her, and while breathing in great breaths of blessed fresh air, pulled her the rest of the way out of the building, trying to break her fall with my own body.

I laid her down as gently as I could on the sparse, crackly yellow-brown grass of the yard, and ran for the emergency workers in front of the house.

"*This way*! An injured woman. Quickly, please," I said as I found a uniformed EMT and grabbed him by the hand. He gestured to a few others and they all ran down the side yard toward Renna.

Then I stood, gulping fresh air, indecisive and stunned. Paramedics were loading Eric onto a stretcher, his sooty face obscured by an oxygen mask. It took three men to control a strong blast of water from a huge hose they had aimed at the upstairs windows.

Just then a hand touched my shoulder from behind. I whirled and let out a blast of energy that threw the poor emergency worker down on her butt.

"Oh, I'm so sorry!" I exclaimed. "Let me help you up."

The woman looked confused, as did most people who received a blast from me. They didn't usually connect it with me; they simply didn't understand what had just happened.

She got up, still looking perplexed, and I let her lead me to the open back doors of an ambulance. She wrapped a blanket around my shoulders and started asking me a number of questions. Only then did I realize

at my arms and hands were wounded, covered in soot
nd small scratches, and some bigger, from the glass.

She started cleaning me up, wiping off the soot and
lood, then applying antibiotic cream and wrapping my
ounds in gauze. Vaguely I thought it was a shame I
idn't have any mugwort salve handy, as it was good for
urns. But then I saw the stretcher coming. They had
ooked Renna up to an IV and oxygen and were rushing
er into the back of an ambulance. The doors were
ammed shut behind her, and it sped down the street. As
watched its flashing lights grow smaller in the distance
nd the siren came on when they neared the intersec-
on, I thought to myself, *Someone has to tell Sailor*. He
asn't close to his aunt and butted heads with her. But it
as a family tragedy. Surely it would draw him home?

I felt a surge of sick pain in my gut. Nausea swept over
e as I thought of Eric lying there on the floor, and
enna hanging from her arms in *strapatto*.

I lost my lunch, right there on the neighbor's nicely
immed hedge.

he acrid scent of smoke does not wash out of hair
asily. This I know from experience, unfortunately. I
aped myself up twice with lemon verbena soap and
ashed my hair three times, but it still lingered.

Despite my own sooty stench I had fallen into a fitful
eep just after one in the morning, but awoke, groggily,
while later. Visions of fire and smoke, Eric lying prone;
enna hanging . . . They attacked my senses so I felt like
castle under siege.

I heard the cuckoo clock in the hall sound: *cuckoo,
uckoo, cuckoo*. Three in the morning. Renna had been
ken to Summit Medical Center and, when I had called
st night, was said to be in serious but stable condition.

They wouldn't give me more details over the phon
even though I immediately lied and said I was her siste

In a way it was true. All of us witches are sisters und
the skin.

Now I struggled with what to do next. Should I ca
the hospital and try for an update? Would they talk
me at three in the morning? I let out a little sigh upo
the realization that I spent way too much of my time an
energy trying to get hospital personnel to share priva
medical information with me. How was it that I knew
many people who ended up hurt and hospitalized? W
it me?

But finally I realized something else had awaken
me. Not my cuckoo clock—I was used to its chiming an
found it comforting. No, there was something more. . .

Slowly, carefully, I pushed myself up on my elbo
and looked around.

Sailor.

I smiled, reveling in the dream. I had had similar on
before. Repeatedly since Sailor had left town. Dreams
which Sailor came back to me.

He was sitting in the armchair by my bed. Strong arr
crossed over his broad chest. Unshaven, unkempt; ey
as dark and intense as always. Brooding. Sexy. Deliciou

"What the hell happened?" he growled.

Well, *that* was new.

"Lily?"

And just that fast, the scene went from dreamy fa
tasy to cold reality.

"Sailor?"

"I haven't been gone *that* long. You don't recogni
me?"

Chapter 19

He was here. He was *real*.

I let out a ridiculous squeak as I flung myself at him, wrapping my arms around his neck.

But rather than returning my embrace, Sailor remained rigid. I pulled back and tried to study his face in the dark. I have excellent night vision, but all I read in his countenance was barely repressed fury.

"I *said*, what the hell happened to Renna and Eric?"

"I don't know."

"You were there; I could feel it."

I let my arms drop, sitting back on the bed and pulling the old hand-sewn quilt over me. My snowy white Victorian nightgown covered me from neck to ankle, but somehow I still felt exposed.

"How are they?" I asked.

"They'll both survive. It'll be a long recovery, the psychic scars worse than the physical ones."

"Sailor, I am so very sorry. I—"

"Just tell me what happened."

"I don't know much," I said, swallowing hard. His

chilly disposition was difficult to reconcile with the mo
ments of closeness we had shared not so very long ago
"I really don't know anything about what happened wit
Renna and Eric, but strange things have been occurrin
since a few days ago, at a big jewelry expo at the Co
Palace. I bought some jewelry from a woman name
Griselda, who was later killed there. She was pressec
And I think someone's been after me ever since."

"Pressed? As in pressing a witch?"

I nodded. "And my father's back in town, and wa
briefly held on suspicion of her murder. And a couple o
thugs have been trailing me, but I obviously got off a lo
easier than Griselda or your aunt and uncle."

He went still. "You're saying your father's involved?

"No. I mean . . . I guess I don't really know." Could h
have done such a thing? He seemed so old when I sav
him, somehow, though he'd always been strong. And ac
companied by Clem and Gene, who knows what the
might have done in their quest for the ring? Now th
question was, How much should I share with Sailor? H
was known to fly off the handle with the proper motiva
tion.

"Here's the thing: I think Griselda had in her posses
sion a ring that could be used by a strong practitioner t
exorcise an elemental demon. The ring has a fire opal i
it and I think it's connected to a Mexican fire demon.
think my father and others are in town looking for i
We're having an unusual heat wave, and I think it's con
nected to the fire demon coming to town."

He swore under his breath. "Okay. What's the connec
tion to Renna and Eric?"

"It might just be that Renna is known to be powerfu
She was on a list, as was I. One of the screwups who wa
following me is in the hospital"—*If he survives,* I though

myself—"but the other one could have gotten to Renna."
r Gene—he seemed more likely to be that vicious.

"You put one of them in the hospital? Good for you."

"No, it wasn't me. I think someone was trying to keep
m quiet, maybe. I don't know, actually." Now that I
ought about it, it wasn't as though he was about to tell
e anything. Why would anyone want to keep him from
nning away with my medicine bag . . . ? Or was it sim-
y about the ring?

"You think someone followed you to Renna's and
ought you gave her something or told her something?"

"I wasn't followed—I arrived on the scene after
ey'd been there. But it's possible Griselda sent the opal
ng to Renna, or they thought she did."

"So whoever killed Griselda went after Renna and
ric. It would make sense."

He fell silent for a moment. Silvery moonlight slid in
rough the sash, highlighting the strong planes of his
ce. I could see his jaw clenching.

Finally he blew out a loud breath, sat back in the
air, and ran his hands through his hair.

"What are we going to do about it?" I asked.

"*We*?" he said with the sardonic tone I knew so well.
There is no 'we.' I will track these folks down and make
em tell me what's going on. How can I find your father?"

"Last time I saw him was at the police station," I lied.
Sailor went to the Hyatt and confronted him, I was
raid he would run into Gene. He wouldn't be able to
andle the situation without me. Heck, he might not be
le to handle it *with* me.

"Where is he now?"

"I don't know."

I felt it then, the fingers of Sailor's psychic ability
aching out to me, trying to read my aura, my thoughts.

Sailor had never been able to read my mind, for which
remained profoundly grateful. But that didn't mean h
wouldn't try. Still, I had never felt him try so hard, tryin
to force me. It ticked me off.

"*Enough*," I said. "You're giving me a headache."

"Worth a shot," he said with a casual shrug. "You sai
you bought some jewelry from Griselda at the Ger
Faire. Let me see it."

We spent most of the rest of the night with him fee
ing the jewelry. Unlike me, Sailor had a gift for psychom
etry. He bent his head low over the jewelry as h
inspected the pile, piece by piece. It took a long tim
with me simply watching as he methodically eliminate
one item after another.

There was no small talk, no discussion of where h
had gone and why. I supposed now was not the tim
Still, it was hard to act as though we were strangers.
found myself wondering how close to stand to him, nc
sure where to put my hands. Accustomed as I am to fee
ing awkward, this really took the cake.

Finally he reared back and blew out a loud, frustrate
breath.

"Not a damned thing. It's a bunch of junk."

"Aidan mentioned the ring would be good at hidin
its powers."

"Aidan," he sneered. "Where does he fit into all this?

"He possessed the ring once, years ago, in German
He passed it off to a witch for safekeeping, but he think
she might have been sending it back to him. I guess th
demon's henchmen tracked her down. She was killed, a
was her sister who came to San Francisco, possibly t
bring the ring back to him."

"What's he done to find the ring, and the killers?"

"He's been keeping a low profile."

"He's hiding out while witches are being maimed and killed?" Outrage sparked in his eyes.

"I'm sure he's doing what he can. You know how he is: He must have dozens of people working for him, trying to figure this all out. It wouldn't do any good if he put himself in danger, much less let himself be killed."

He stuck out his chin and gave a little shrug. "It might do *some* good."

I wasn't sure whether to smile in response. I opened my mouth to say something, anything, about us. To talk about what had happened, ask him where he had gone. But I couldn't find the words.

Suddenly Sailor stood and reached out for me. I remained stock-still, not knowing what to do, but knowing I wanted him to touch me.

He laid his large, warm hand over the medallion on my chest.

"What about this? Aren't these opals?"

"I wondered about it, too," I said, shaking my head. "But I'm looking for some kind of ring. And when I offered this to Clem and Zeke, they weren't interested."

I looked down at it. His hand still lay on it, and I was hyperaware of his fingers touching my chest.

"D-do you, uh, feel anything from it?"

At first I thought the medallion had started madly humming with vibrations, but then I realized it was the energy transferring from Sailor's hand to my bare skin.

I looked up into his dark eyes.

A long moment of silence passed. My breathing came faster. He leaned toward me, just a tad, and I did the same . . . and then, as though in unspoken agreement, we both pulled back.

Sailor turned to look out the window, his hands riding low on his narrow hips.

He cleared his throat. "So, where do we go from here?"

"Carlos Romero was going to arrange for me to examine the jewelry from Griselda's stand. It's a long shot to think the item's still there, since everything's been gone through already, but it might be worth a look, just in case it's managed to go undetected. The thing is . . ."

"I'm afraid to ask, but what?"

"As you just witnessed, I really suck at psychometrics."

"I don't understand why you're so good at reading textiles."

I just shrugged and shook my head.

"I'll go with you, then."

"Yeah. That might be a problem. I'm not sure Carlos is all that fond of you."

"You mean he hates me."

"That's a little strong. I'd say he doesn't trust you."

"He'll have to get in line."

"My point is that it might be difficult to convince him to let you study the evidence with me. I'll call and see Are you . . . are you free today? Any plans?"

"Well I was planning on having my nails done, but I'll put that on hold if you get us into the evidence locker."

"There's no need for sarcasm. I'm really. . . . so sorry about Renna and Eric, Sailor."

"I want to look at Griselda's things, but you know as well as I do we won't find the ring there. She must have gotten it to safety somehow. So, you were saying there were two guys following you, and your father's in town. Anyone else involved?"

I nodded. "There's a man named Gene. He's organizing fire dances in the park, and I think he's after the ring as well."

"Is he working with your father?"

"It's a little hard to say. I think all of them—Zeke and Clem and my father and Gene—are beholden to the demon. Whether they're looking for the amulet to do the demon's bidding and destroy it or to try to use it to free themselves . . . that's another question."

"How can I get in touch with your father?"

I nodded and chose my words carefully. "I'm not so sure it's a great idea to go up against these guys alone. I think we need Aidan."

"I *know* we need Aidan, but there's no way in hell he'll work with me on this. Don't be naive."

"Gene is frightening, Sailor. I don't know exactly what his story is, but I think he's able to channel the demon at times. During the fire dance, for example. He might be more than beholden; he might be a voluntary minion."

"So when's the next fire dance?"

"Listen to me a second. I'm not sure you're strong enough."

"Excuse me?"

How do you tell a man who prides himself on his self-sufficiency and independence that he's not strong enough? This was not something Sailor wanted to hear.

"You tune into people's vibrations, right? So if you connect with Gene's mind at the time the demon's channeling, what's to keep you from being possessed by him as well?"

"I'll keep my guard up."

"That might not be enough. Before you talk with Gene—or my father, for that matter—I think the weak link here is Clem. If we can track him down, you might be able to get information from him."

"You didn't get much from him, and it sounds like you've spent a fair amount of time together."

"I'm not psychic," I said, feeling vaguely insulted "And despite what you think, I've only been dealing with this whole thing for a few days, and I think I've done a pretty good job figuring things out so far."

He inclined his head slightly. I supposed that was a close as I was going to get to an apology.

I couldn't tell if he was just enraged by the attack on his aunt and uncle and was taking it out on me, or whether he thought I hadn't done enough for him when he was banished by Aidan, or whether he was angry at me for some other reason. I was mad, too, and couldn' exactly say why. Obviously we needed to talk about our relationship. But this wasn't the best time.

My cuckoo clock tweeted five times. We had been up all night. I didn't need much sleep to function . . . but nei ther was I superhuman.

"I have to get some rest, Sailor. Why don't we . . . mean, if you want you could . . ."

"I'm going to go check a few things out. I'll check back in later today. Arrange that thing with your cop friend, will you?"

"How can I get in touch?"

With a funny twist of his mouth, he wrote down a number on a scrap of paper. "My cell phone."

Sailor didn't give his cell phone number to *anyone*.

And without so much as a peck on the cheek or a lingering look, he was gone.

The next day I was matching gloves from a great trove Maya had acquired from an elderly woman, when the phone rang. The man on the other end introduced himself as SFPD Inspector Carlos Romero.

"We're being very formal today, Inspector Romero."

"Calling from the office," he said, still in his official op voice. "I've arranged for the visit we spoke about. onight, six p.m."

"About that..." I began. "I really want to look hrough the things, just in case. But the truth is I'm not ll that great divining things from jewelry. In fact, I sort f suck at it."

Silence on the other end of the line. I could just see arlos pinching the bridge of his nose in frustration, sti-ing whatever invectives were springing to mind.

"So what I'd like to do is bring a friend along, some-ne much better at it than I. You would be there with us he whole time, and we'll share any information we can lean from the stuff."

"Who is this friend?"

"Sailor."

Again he failed to respond. I could hear voices in the ackground, the ringing of phones, some radio chatter. It eminded me of sitting with Carlos at the police station nd looking up to see my father.

My stomach clenched at the thought.

"Maybe Neil could take us?" I suggested. Neil was arlos's partner. He liked me better than Carlos did, nuch of the time.

"No, Neil cannot take you." I heard some shuffling on he line and his voice dropped. "I refuse to be laughed ut of the department if it gets out that I'm letting the ocal witch battalion march through the evidence room."

"I'm hardly a battalion. And, anyway, a group of vitches is typically known as a coven."

"I know what it's known as. I'm already suspect round here because I recognized the manner of death s a witch thing."

"Have they made any progress on the investigation?"

"Nothing. Total dead end. Sounds like it was pande
monium, no one saw a thing."

"So, it sounds like you might need me and Sailor t
come in and take a look at the evidence, just in case."

"Tonight. Meet me at the Heart and Dagger at th
corner of Harrison and Ninth. I'll lead you over fron
there."

"Okay."

"And, Lily? Try to be discreet, if you possibly can."

"Aren't I always?"

"In other words, leave your pig at home."

I agreed and hung up. What now? I hate the phone
But while I was at it, I placed a call to Germany. Han
answered, his voice sounding as formal as Carlos's had a
moment before.

"I'm about to meet with a client, so I have to make
this brief. The young man you asked about was a neigh
bor who was orphaned in a house fire some years ago
Griselda took him in, raised him as her own. That's al
I've got."

I thanked him, hung up, and placed one more phone
call. After all, I had hired Sam Spade to do some investi
gating for me. He answered the phone like a stockbro
ker. "This is Sam Spade. How may I help you?"

"Hi, Sam. It's Lily. Just thought I'd check in to see i
you'd made any progress with Johannes."

"One Johannes Herzberg recently checked into th
Hyatt."

"Seriously? The Hyatt on the Embarcadero?"

"Unfortunately, I staked the place out all last night
but he never left his room." I heard the pages of a book
flipping, and could have sworn he was looking something

). No doubt reading out of his handbook. "Yeah, here is. . . . Overnights are extra."

"You didn't mention that in our fee negotiation."

"True. But I figured you wouldn't want to miss the ance to catch him once I had him in my sights."

"Fine, keep on it. And hey, while you're there, keep an e out for a man named Sailor, dark eyes and hair, gen- ally bad attitude. Last seen in jeans and a black T-shirt." wouldn't put it past Sailor to use his contacts to track em or my father down to the Hyatt.

"It's . . ." More pages flipping. "Um . . . If I'm looking r more than one missing person, the rate increases."

"Why am I not surprised?" I shook my head and oked down at my watch. "Tell you what. I'm on my way ver to you."

am looked much less out of place here in the Hyatt's and lobby, filled with businesspeople and upscale avelers. His suit and tie and briefcase fit right in, as a atter of fact, not to mention his expensive haircut and ean-shaven, healthy, all-American good looks.

When he spotted me, he practically ran across the wide bby to greet me. He was excited, flush with success.

"He's up on the sixth floor. You can see him from ere," he said, gesturing overhead.

The Hyatt was built with a massive central atrium, so e rooms were accessed by catwalks overlooking the ar and lobby.

I looked up, and, indeed, there was young Johannes, aning over the railing, looking down.

"What's he doing?" I asked.

"That's an excellent question. Pondering his fate, per- aps? You never told me why you were looking for him."

"Good point. Okay, I'm going to go talk to him. Yo
stay here and watch the elevators in case he comes dow
in the interim, all right?"

"Whatever you say, boss."

It was shocking to see how much Johannes had change
since I had seen him at the Gem Faire. The onc
strapping young man hunched over the railing, eye
twitching and vacant. He swayed slightly, as thoug
barely able to support his own weight.

It took a great deal of energy to hold the ring. I wa
betting that Johannes was loyal enough to Griselda t
try to get the ring someplace secure after she gave up he
life trying to keep it safe.

"Johannes?" He looked up as I approached him o
the catwalk. "What are you doing here?"

"Someone, they rent a room for me. Sent me a note t
say it was paid . . . I don't know who. Was it you?"

I shook my head. My money was on Gene.

"Johannes, tell me: What did you do with the ring?"

"I couldn't hold it any longer; it was making me sic
Still my hands shake. See?" He held out one tremblin
hand. "So I got it to a powerful *Hexe*. She can hold it, bu
she can't do what's necessary. I feel a little better nov
but still not well."

"You can trust me, Johannes." I concentrated, hopin
he would understand that I truly wanted to help hin
"Tell me where the ring is. Who has it?"

He studied me for a moment. "Griselda had a list c
names of people who might be trusted. You were on th
list. But then . . . after what your father did . . ."

"What did he do?"

"I saw him with the athame. Standing over Griselda
A sudden chill passed through me, like I had bee

used with cold water. Then something else occurred to
e. "Are you sure it was my father? How would you
ow that?"

"Carlotta told us the story, that your father lost his
ttle with the demon. She told us he was badly scarred
m the fire. But she said he had a daughter who came
Germany once, a witch powerful enough to take care
the ring. That is why you were on the list."

"But what—"

Johannes's eyes grew huge.

A *tsk* sound came from behind us.

I swung around. Gene was strolling casually toward

"Leave him alone, Gene," I said, placing myself be-
een the two men. I was acutely aware that I had noth-
g particularly useful with me: no brew, no charms or
otection other than my medicine bag. "He doesn't
ve it."

"Oh, but he knows where it is. And you'll tell me,
n't you, young Johannes?"

Suddenly Gene's eyes shifted over my shoulder, and
grinned.

I swung around. Johannes was climbing over the rail-
g.

"Johannes, *don't*!" I cried.

Chapter 20

"*Bitte* . . . please forgive me."

He tumbled over the side.

I lurched for him, grabbing one arm just as he we
over the rail. I braced against the half wall, feeling
though my arms were being pulled out of their sockets
wouldn't be able to hold him for more than a few secon

Onlookers from below screamed as they watched hi
dangle six stories up.

"*Tsk, tsk, tsk*. The folly of youth, am I right?" sa
Gene as he looked at Johannes with greedy ey
"They're so impulsive, so emotional. That's what's gre
about young people, though, don't you think?"

There were shouts from below, and I heard a far-c
alarm.

"Help me," I implored. I knew Gene was evil, but I
wanted information from Johannes. In the heat of th
moment, I hoped he would want to keep the young m
alive for the sake of finding out the ring's location.

I could feel Johannes slipping from my grasp. I
wasn't hanging on to me; he dangled like deadweight.

And then with a sudden wrench, my fingers gave out. Our contact was broken as he slipped from my grasp. ...aned over the railing but squeezed my eyes shut. Un...tunately I couldn't close my ears; I heard more ...eams.

Arms wrapped around me from behind. Thinking it ...s Gene, I tried to twist free, but it was Sam Spade. My ...y own private investigator. He eased me down to the ...or. I felt the blood rush from my face and was en...fed by nausea.

...I couldn't think. All I knew was that I had to find a ...y to stop Gene from the havoc he was wreaking ...und town, but the regular police would be no help at ...What would I accuse him of? Being at the Gem Faire ...d teaching kids to fire dance for free, and then being ...arby when Johannes ... jumped? *I am here, too,* I ...ought. But I wasn't strong enough to hold him, to stop ...n before ...

Another wave of nausea hit me, and I saw black spots. ...ut my head between my knees and concentrated on ...athing.

"Lily? *Lily!*" Sam was saying. "Listen to me. They put ...t a net below him. Lily, do you hear me? Apparently ...s isn't the first time they've dealt with a jumper. He's ...ng to be okay. Let me see your arm."

"He's not ... dead?"

"No, but unconscious, apparently. They're working on ...n now. Let me see your arm."

...Until that moment I hadn't realized I couldn't move ...I looked at it as though it didn't belong to me.

"I was an Eagle Scout," he said. "Trained in first aid. ...nt me to pop it back in?"

"What?" I still wasn't thinking straight. But without ...ing again, Sam positioned himself in front of me, one

hand on my shoulder and the other holding my forea[r]
He pulled and twisted. I felt a stab of pain and a tingl[i]
sensation, and still felt that strange sense that it v[?]
someone else's arm. But I was able to wiggle my finge[r]

I looked around the hallway. Gene was long gone. [?]
he had left his card, marked with an invitation to the [?]
dance that night at the setting of the sun.

Before that, I was supposed to meet Carlos at six o'clo[ck]
to look through Griselda's things. I showed up at [?]
Heart and Dagger before the appointed time. Sailor v[?]
already there, already imbibing. I strode up to the b[ar]
didn't say a word, and ordered a shot of Jameson.

Sailor raised his eyebrows and looked at me askan[ce]
"You've become a drinker in my absence?"

"I'm working on it," I quipped, intending to down [the]
whole shot but managing just a single throat-burni[ng]
swig. Nonetheless, the heat felt good. I still hadn't rec[on]
ciled what I had just witnessed: the visual of Johann[es]
going over that railing would, I feared, remain vivid [in]
my mind until the day I died. I felt sick to my stoma[ch]
every time it came back to me.

Apparently, the net had saved his life. However, [he]
was unresponsive and was taken to the hospital, whe[re]
he would remain on a close suicide watch. Sam Spa[de]
promised me he would stay with Johannes and rais[e a]
huge stink if anyone tried to come near him. Gene was[n't]
all-powerful, after all, and since Johannes wasn't [be]
holden to the demon, they wouldn't be able to read [his]
mind or hurt him from afar.

I believed Johannes had carried his burden with h[im]
as best he could, forfeiting his own health for it. And h[e'd]
been about to tell me where I could find it until Ge[ne]
showed up. I imagined Johannes knew Gene would [?]

e information out of him, one way or another, and
ed to put an end to it before he could say. He had been
lling to sacrifice himself to keep the ring safe.

Somehow the idea that Griselda, and Carlotta, for
at matter, had done the same didn't seem as bad. They
ere mature witches, aware of what they were doing and
e dangers they played with every day. Like me. Jo-
nnes seemed like . . . an innocent.

I hoped to blazes I could stop Gene and his hench-
en before they got to Johannes or found the *Ojo del
iego*.

I downed the rest of my drink. The tightness in my gut
coiled slightly, and the ache in my shoulder receded a
t.

Sailor gestured to the bartender to refill my shot glass,
it kept his puzzled gaze on me.

"You okay there, tiger?"

"I've been better."

"Listen, Lily—"

Just then Carlos arrived and interrupted him. "So re-
suring to see my supernatural crime-fighting crew get-
g snockered right before I take them into the evidence
om."

"Sorry, Inspector," I said, erring on the side of polite-
ss. "It's been one hell of a day."

His eyes rested on Sailor. Sailor returned the look,
e of pure male challenge and recognition of the rival.
ival for what, I wasn't sure. But it was clear the men
dn't care for each other. So what else was new?

"Let's get going while you're still sober. This bar is
pen till two in the morning, so you could come by after-
ard and tie one on."

As Carlos led us both back to the Hall of Justice, I
ve him a brief outline of what had happened with Jo-

hannes, who was an official person of interest in the Ger
Faire murder. He asked a number of pointed question
but agreed to send over police protection.

Carlos brought us into a small, enclosed room. On
table sat several boxes full of jewelry and a few othe
small items. On a second table were items from Grise
da's room at the Morning House B and B.

I didn't expect we'd find anything and wanted to mak
short work of it. Johannes told me he had gotten th
amulet ring into the hands of a *Hexe*, a witch, and I be
lieved him. If only he'd told me who before flinging hin
self over the railing.

While Sailor concentrated on reading the jewelry, I
rummaged rather dispiritedly through stacks of misce
laneous items. There was paperwork for the fair and re
ceipts from shipping. But then I unearthed a number o
letters, like the ones I had seen on Griselda's desk at th
inn. The handwriting looked the same as in the list o
witches' names I had taken from Zeke.

I picked up a letter I had seen before; it wasn't writte
by Griselda, and was instead from her sister, Carlotta.

"Can you read this?" I asked Sailor, handing him th
note.

"I don't read German," he said, handing it back.

"I thought you understood all languages? You sai
something about understanding your landlord's Cantor
ese . . . ?"

"That's if someone's speaking and I can read thei
thoughts. Written language is a whole different ba
game. Only thing I can tell you about German is the
capitalize just about all the nouns."

I looked over at Carlos, who shrugged and shook hi
head. "Took enough French in high school to order
café au lait, but that's about it."

The only part written in English was the last sentence:
If All Else fails, remember to have a Pleasant Day."

"Why would the last sentence be written in English?"
wondered aloud. Both sisters were native German
speakers. Neither man ventured a theory.

"Carlos, I meant to ask you: Was Griselda wearing
jewelry when she was found?"

"In that bag there."

Sailor had just emptied an evidence bag chock-full of
tarnished silver jewelry—along with one yolk-yellow
woven hair amulet. *That must be the charm she had been
using to mask her supernatural abilities,* I thought.

Sailor hunched over the pieces, concentrating. After
several moments of watching for a reaction, I realized I
was just gazing at the way his lashes swept down over
dark eyes and how his large hands fondled one item after another with long, graceful fingers.

Concentrate, Lily.

Also among Griselda's papers was a CityPASS and a
tourist map of San Francisco stamped with *Compliments
of Morning House*. Written in red pen were directions on
how to get to the Cow Palace by public transit. There
were several red circles around various locales in the city,
including the corner of Haight and Ashbury—where my
shop was—and a location near Fisherman's Wharf that
might have been the Wax Museum. Finally, a red arrow
indicated the Bay Bridge, which led to the East Bay and
Oakland. Renna lived in Oakland.

According to the shipping receipts, Griselda had sent
the heavy boxes of jewelry directly to the Cow Palace. So
she and Johannes bought CityPASSes to get around the
city on public transportation. Nothing suspicious about
that.

Except that Johannes didn't have a pass until Monday.

Or, more likely, he'd simply lost his at some point in all the confusion.

There seemed so much I didn't know about all of this. I decided to turn it around and try to specify what I *did* know. Griselda was killed Sunday during the jewelry show. Someone ransacked her room. Johannes moved to the youth hostel on Ellis. Already he wasn't looking well, according to Dwight at the front desk. Tuesday Johannes met up with Shawnelle and they went sight-seeing.

That was four days ago. He could have gone to meet anyone, hidden the ring anywhere since then. He had referred to the powerful practitioner as a "she." It wasn't much, but I should check in with Aidan and check on the list Zeke had, to see how many women were on his list of practitioners who might be strong enough to hold the ring.

I looked up to find Sailor's gaze on me. I lifted my eyebrows in silent question. He shook his head.

Nothing. No fire opals, no magical rings. I had expected a bust, but it was no less disappointing for having been anticipated.

Before we left, I turned to Carlos.

"The man I mentioned seeing at the Gem Faire, Jersey Gene with the Jelly Beans? He was at the Hyatt today when Johannes jumped over the railing. He threatened him."

"Threatened him how?"

Good question. I tried to remember exactly what he said. The thing about Gene was that it was clear he was up to no good, but it was hard to pinpoint anything. Had he even spoken to Johannes, or just looked at him with that creepy smile?

"It was . . . an implied threat. Gene also teaches kids

to fire dance in Golden Gate Park—in fact, I'm headed over there right now. This guy's bad news."

"You don't like fire dancing, I take it?"

"Trust me on this one: I imagine most fire dancing would be beautiful, but this isn't like regular old dancing. I don't know what he's doing, but it's not normal. And it's not good."

"You have anything on him other than being in the wrong place at the wrong time?"

"Not really."

"A last name, maybe?"

I shook my head. "But I think he'll be in the park in an hour with the fire dancers."

"Tell you what. I'll speak with Inspector Leibowitz and see if it rings any bells. And if I get a chance, I'll stop by the park, or at least send over a couple of uniforms, see if anything's up."

"Thank you."

"SFPD, here to serve."

I couldn't talk Sailor out of going with me to the fire dance, but at least he conceded to let me cast over him, to keep him free of the demon's thoughts.

Oscar lurked silently on my kitchen counter while I looked up a spell in my old leather-bound Book of Shadows and brewed.

Once the concoction had boiled and concentrated, I had Sailor drink a thimbleful and then instructed him to wash his hands, face, and hair with the brew.

Afterward, Sailor stood in the middle of my kitchen, arms outstretched on either side, while I chanted.

Unfortunately for me, he was supposed to be barechested for this part.

"Could you take off your shirt, please?"

"With pleasure," he said with a sardonic smile as he started to unbutton his blue chambray work shirt. "You sure this is part of the spell?"

"Just do it."

He handed me the shirt and I placed it on the counter, trying my best to ignore the way it was warm from his skin and carried his scent. If I'd been alone I would have held it up to my nose and cheek to revel in it. And then I probably would have slept in it.

I was one pathetic excuse for a witch.

His chest was well muscled. His skin had a natural olive tint. Black hair grew across the width of it, tapering down to his stomach. I was in the middle of spell casting and concentration was crucial, but there was no way I could look at that chest and not remember the one hot, steamy, glorious night we had shared.

I blew out a breath.

"Everything okay?"

I nodded, swallowed hard, and closed my eyes, forcing my thoughts back to the task of opening and maintaining my magical portals. Once I focused, the energy slid through, like sinewy snakes passing from me to my ancestors and back.

I jabbed the tip of my finger with a needle and drew an X over his heart with my blood. Sailor's heart thudded reassuringly under my hand; I could feel it resound through me, its movement pulsing for a brief moment through my own veins.

He would be protected as well as I was from the demon's thoughts. He wouldn't be able to read Gene's mind, which was too bad, but it just plain wasn't worth the risk.

Once Sailor was taken care of, I turned my attention to Maya.

After much begging, cajoling, and something akin to ubtle threatening, Maya finally agreed to stay with her other and Bronwyn. Ostensibly they needed her to elp them with the *quinceañera* alterations, but in reality had recruited them to help me keep Maya from Golden ate Park and the fire dancing. Without going into de- il, I told Lucille that I thought Gene was some kind of ult leader and that he did not have his followers' best terests at heart. That was enough for her.

Everything was much as before when we arrived at e park: the informal gathering of mostly young people, ainting one another's skin, banging on drums, chatting d laughing. One woman had made fairy chains of tiny aisies and was distributing her garlands to the crowd. he placed one on my head and I was about to take it off hen I noticed Sailor looking at me, a half smile on his ice.

"Looks good. You would have been an adorable hip- ie, back in the day."

I left it on.

And just as last time, a ululating woman welcomed e setting of the sun. The lampposts remained dark. ometime later, as true dark overcame us, Gene ap- eared to greet the crowd and lit the pots and torches of e dancers.

They whirled and danced, hopped and rolled, their re making crazy designs in the air.

"This doesn't feel good," said Sailor quietly as we atched the action.

"They're just getting started," I replied. Sure enough, ist as they had last time, the crowd seemed to slip into sort of trance, mesmerized by the fire.

"Can you get a handle on what he's after?" I asked ailor.

He shook his head, frowning. "Not really. He's .
There's something going on. The dancing energy is buil
ing, and I think your pal Gene over there is trying
piggyback on it."

"Like the power of a circle?" Covens relied on th
power of forming a circle and focusing their intent
create enough energy to manifest magic.

"Something like that. But with one serious differenc
this is not chosen by the participants. They're being m
nipulated, not exactly against their will, but without fu
knowledge of what they're agreeing to."

I nodded. That made sense.

As the frenetic movement ratcheted up, I looked ov
to see Gene staring at me and smiling.

"There," I said to Sailor, nodding in Gene's directio
"That's what he does. I think he's using the energy
channel something . . . maybe the demon?"

"I think you're right."

"Since he hasn't found the ring yet, maybe he's ju
entertaining his master or adding to his energy som
how?"

Silence. I turned around to see Sailor had alrea
taken off and was striding over to where Gene w
standing. I hurried to catch up. Gene just smiled serene
as we approached.

"I see you've become quite the devotee," Gene sai
Gone was the Jersey accent. Instead his voice had a di
ferent inflection; something foreign I couldn't quite p
my finger on. "I saw you here last time. You fought n
spell. *Tsk, tsk, tsk.*"

"Are you responsible for what happened to Ren
Sandino?" Sailor asked, his voice low and threatening
looked at him askance, wondering whether he rea

ought he could just haul off and punch a demon's hu-
an minion.

Gene barely even noticed Sailor was speaking. His
yes were for me alone. As was his message.

"You think to go after *me*? What about your friend
ver there?" He gestured over near the edge of the eu-
alyptus grove.

And there stood Maya, smiling and staring at the fire
ancers. What in the world was she *doing* here? When I
rned back to Sailor, he appeared to be just as en-
ralled with the dancers as everyone else.

"Your young friend is just about mine now," Gene
ontinued with a shrug. "These kids, they're seeking di-
ection in life, and I give it to them. They become mine
use. Your sweet little Maya there, she'll do as *I* say
ow. I got her to come here tonight against your wishes.
id I not?"

"You leave her be. I command you."

"You and what supernatural army? I command le-
ions." His voice changed, grew deeper. "'*I flamed amaze-
ent; sometimes I'd divide. And burn in many places.*'"

I recognized that quote from somewhere. Then it
awned on me . . . Shakespeare's *The Tempest*. It was
poken by Ariel, the fire elemental. One of the discon-
erting things about demons is that they are often well
ead, and have a wicked sense of humor.

"Listen. Leave her alone, and I'll work with you on
nding the ring. That's what you're really after, right?
ow about I find the ring, and you release her and my
ther? And Clem."

His smile grew. He threw his head back and started to
ugh, a kind of deep, frightening sound that dipped be-
w the range of normal hearing, stinging my ears, mak-

ing my head ache and my heart pound. I slapped m
hands over my ears, but not before I heard the cloppin
of horse hooves on pavement and looked around to se
two uniformed officers on horseback come down th
pathway into the clearing.

They looked at the half-clad young people dancin
and spinning and drumming, and shook their heads in
"young people today" sort of attitude.

Until clothes started to catch fire. A few screams ran
out, but the dancers mostly laughed, seemingly uncon
˷erned by the flames. The police officers jumped off thei
mounts and ran to assist them.

Sailor, having suddenly snapped out of his stupor, ra
to help as well.

When I turned back, Gene was gone.

Chapter 21

nce I had taken Maya back home to Bronwyn and Lu-
le with strict instructions to keep her in their sight at
times, I strode off toward my car with great purpose.

White-hot anger flowed through my veins when I
ought of Gene—or Xolotl, really—threatening Maya.
y father and Clem and Zeke, for that matter, had made
eir own deals with the demon Xolotl, had entered into
reements based on their own greed or stupidity, but
ey were grown men. Maya was grown, too, but she
emed more vulnerable somehow. And besides all that,
e was my friend and therefore under my protection.

And then there was Johannes . . . that poor young
an's fate was in my hands as well. And Renna and Eric
served vengeance.

"Lily?" I heard Sailor's voice behind me. "Where are
u going?"

"To meet up with an old friend of mine."

"You don't have any old friends."

"Maybe 'friend' isn't the right word. I'm headed to the
n Francisco School of Fine Arts. You coming?"

Sailor reared back slightly. "Woah, hold on there. [
don't think that's a good idea."

"Will you help me?"

"If you're signing up for a painting class, sure thin[
But why do I have the sense you're thinking about wak[
ing up a certain demon you once bound and banished?

Arriving at my vintage Mustang, I put the keys in th[
door lock and looked at him over the roof of the car.

"Are you coming or not?"

"Will that spell you cast earlier keep me from bein[
susceptible? Since I fell into the trance, I assumed it ha[
worn off."

"Fine. Don't help. I'll do it myself."

"Stop it, Lily. You said yourself that if my though[
meld with a demon's . . . I have no way of protecting my[
self, of keeping him from riding on whatever abilities [
have. I could end up hurting you."

"You saw him, Sailor. You felt him. I can't stop tha[
thing by myself. Not without that ring, anyway."

"I agree he's bad news," said Sailor. "Although an[
demon who quotes Shakespeare can't be all bad."

I didn't laugh at his feeble joke.

"I could feel the surge of power through Gene," I con[
tinued. "I can*not* go up against him by myself. But I'll b[
damned if I'll let him take Maya."

"He's trying to trap you. Can't you see that?"

"Maybe so. But the demon at the School of Fine Art[
Sitri, he's bound to me. If I call him correctly, he has t[
bend to my will and assist me. I'd be powerful enoug[
with him in my corner. I've got plenty of supplies in th[
trunk, and if I keep focus . . ."

I climbed in behind the wheel.

"Lily, *stop* it. You can't control Sitri alone."

He came around to the driver's side as though to stop me, but I gunned the engine and sped down the street.

I found a parking space on Chestnut Street and started climbing the hill toward the San Francisco School of Fine Arts. I was scared but determined, driven by anger.

Aidan Rhodes was standing in front of the main set of double doors.

Dammit.

"Sailor called you?"

"Imagine my surprise," Aidan said. His voice, though smooth as always, radiated annoyance. He was dressed in a tuxedo, as though Sailor had interrupted him during the opera or some fabulous dinner. Aidan liked to hobnob with the city's upper crust. "I thought Sailor wasn't speaking to you. I'm not sure how he knew what you were up to, since he claims to still be in New Mexico, as per our agreement. But I guess you called him . . . ?"

"Yes."

"May I ask why you didn't call *me*?"

"Because I don't trust you."

For a brief moment I thought I saw hurt in his sparkling blue eyes. But then he gave me a sad smile and responded, "Well, relationships are tough. Sometimes you wind up trusting the wrong person. Anyway, you don't have to trust me to ask me to help you."

I didn't answer.

"Here's the thing," Aidan continued. "I'm not going to let you contact Sitri."

"I think I can handle it. I can't find the ring and Maya's in trouble. This is the only way. Unless *you* have the ring?"

"I've already told you I don't. You don't think if I did, I might have mentioned it?"

I shrugged.

"Think about what you're doing. You share more with your father than you know. You are both arrogant enough to think you can control a demon."

"Sitri isn't elemental. I can do it."

"It isn't worth the risk."

"We could do it together. You and me."

"I tried something similar once with your father. Remember? It's an unholy alliance. I repeat: It's not worth the risk. I guarantee you."

Had I been able to cry, I believe I would have shed tears of pure frustration. I was at my wit's end. I didn't know what else to do, was afraid for Maya, and even of losing my father again.

Then Aidan did the most amazing thing. He hugged me. He didn't try to kiss me or read my mind or do anything untoward. He simply held me for a moment and stroked my hair.

Then he held me at arm's length and gazed at me. "Come on, Lily. Pull yourself together. We still have a real chance against this character. We simply need to locate that ring."

Yes, that's all, I thought to myself. *How hard could that be?*

"In the meantime, I suggest you save your energy for the inevitable showdown. Trust me," Aidan said. "We'll find the ring. Just trust me."

The next morning Shawnelle, Marisela, and Metzli came back to Aunt Cora's Closet to try on their dresses and make sure the alterations were done perfectly.

At the moment Metzli stood on a short platform by the dressing room while Lucille made some last-minute adjustments. The birthday girl kept twisting this way and

hat, trying to see herself in all angles in the three-way
iirror. Marisela was helping by holding the pins for Lu-
ille.

Last night I had placed a protective spell on Bron-
yn's apartment and asked her to keep Maya home with
er for a day or two, until I could figure this thing out.
3ronwyn agreed; she had gotten a stack of DVDs, and
his morning they were all involved in a baking project
vith Imogen. I shared a little of what was happening
vith Bronwyn; enough, I hoped, to make her cautious
vithout scaring her too badly. Above all, I tried to con-
ey that it was crucial she keep Maya from fire dancing
n the park.

Lucille would go join them once she was through with
he alterations. I didn't want Maya going to her mother's
ouse, just in case Gene knew Maya's last name and
ooked her up.

While Marisela and Metzli were busy, Shawnelle was
hecking out my display of jewelry. She tried on a big
methyst ring and held her hand out in front of her. It
eminded me of the first time we'd met, at the gem show,
vhen she was trying on rings at Griselda's stand.

"Cool ring," she said.

"It looks good on you."

She smiled. "Nice hands; 'men like that.' Isn't that
vhat the funny old woman at the fair said? What was her
ame?"

"Griselda."

"Right. Griselda. What kind of name is that, d'you
uppose?"

"I think she was from Germany. Like Johannes." Just
he thought of him made my stomach clench. I squeezed
ny eyes closed and tried to avoid the thought of him
oing over the railing.

"Oh, right."

"Speaking of whom ... what did you two do when you got together on Tuesday? Did you do anything at all unusual?"

"Not really." She tried on another ring, this one a bright orange glass ring from the late 1960s. "I told you we did a whole tourist thing."

"I thought you said he wasn't feeling well."

"Yeah, that's what he said, but he really wanted to go."

"Which sights did you see?"

Her eyes lit up and a faint smile played on her full lips. "We took a cable car, then walked around Fisherman's Wharf and got some chocolate at Ghirardelli Square. We tried to get an Irish coffee at the Buena Vista, but we didn't have ID."

Nothing suspicious about that. Unless ... "What did you do at Fisherman's Wharf?"

"I already told you, we just walked around and then we had dinner—Johannes got a real kick out of the clam chowder in a bowl made of bread. Have you seen that? You eat the soup, then the bowl. He said they didn't have anything like that where he was from. And then he was pretty excited about the oyster crackers, until I told him they weren't actually made of oysters."

"Is that all? Did you see any attractions, by any chance?"

"He wanted to go to Alcatraz, but we didn't have time. So instead, before dinner we went to the Wax Museum."

"Really ... what did you do there?"

Shawnelle appeared to tire of trying on rings, as well as of answering my questions. Marisela and Metzli laughed about something, and Shawnelle looked over at

e try-on session as though that was the fun table, but
e was stuck with me.

"I dunno. Just looked at the lame statues." She
rugged. "It's cheesy, but it's still sort of fun. Johannes
lled it the false museum, where the people are false."

"Shawnelle, I have to ask you something very impor-
nt. Did he leave you at any point? Did he do anything
nusual while you were there?"

"Yeah, that was the only kind of weird thing. I mean,
e coolest part of the whole museum is the Chamber of
orrors, right? But he told me he'd be right back at one
oint, and when I found him he was hanging out at the
uropean Explorers exhibit. I mean, *snore*. Who cares
out a bunch of old dead white guys you've never even
eard of?"

"Did Johannes seem to feel better after you left the
useum, by any chance?"

"A little bit, yeah. How'd you know that?"

"Just a hunch." So Johannes felt better after visiting
e European Explorers exhibit. The exhibit I had
alked through when in pursuit of Aidan how many
mes?

Johannes witnessed his boss being killed and wasn't
eling well, but he made sure he got to the Wax Mu-
eum. Where the people are false.

ater that night, outside the Wax Museum, Sailor was
ousing.

"This makes me nervous as hell."

"Told you to stay in the car."

He snorted, "Yeah, right."

I cast my spell over the door and then brought out the
and of Glory. I had picked up this gruesome little item,
candleholder made from the mummified hand of a

hanged man, from a bizarre murder scene some tim
ago. As long as I didn't think about what it actually wa
it was one of my favorite magical tools. It opened an
lock, and then lit up the room as though it were daytim

"I thought you lost that thing last time we broke int
a building after hours."

"Max got it back for me."

Sailor snorted again, more loudly this time. "Ma
Great. I gotta say, Lily, you do seem to get men to d
your bidding for you."

I stopped in my preparations and glared at hin
"What do you mean by *that*?"

"I'm just saying ... Seems like maybe you're castin
your spell over the menfolk in your life, one way or ar
other."

"Oh, so you're saying the only reason a man woul
want to do me a favor is if I *enchanted* him? Is that wh;
you're saying?"

"Simmer down, now. I said no such thing. The mer
tion of Max just...." He shrugged in a gesture that w;
more akin to shaking off an annoying gnat than an apo
ogy. "What can I say? He brings out the worst in me."

"I thought Aidan brought out the worst in you."

"Him too. You've got rotten taste in men."

"No argument there."

He gave me a long look.

"Let's just get this over with and get out of here be
fore Aidan gets wind of what's going on."

Breaking into the actual Wax Museum had been sin
ple, but breaking into Aidan's office was another thin
altogether. I had to get past his protection spells an
undo any number of magical warning devices. It was e
hausting.

One thing worried me: Noctemus, Aidan's familia

as nowhere to be seen. That could be a problem. She
might have run off to find Aidan and tattle on us.

But I wanted that ring. From what Shawnelle had told
me, I was now certain Johannes had brought it to Aidan
two days after Griselda had been killed. Why Aidan
would have kept it a secret from me I wasn't sure, but
neither was I all that surprised. Aidan doled out information on a need-to-know basis, with him, of course, the
sole arbiter of who needed to know.

What I *did* know was that he had not yet used the ring
to banish the demon or his minions. I was sure Aidan
thought he had reasons for hesitating . . . or perhaps he
was just scared, knowing what the fire demon had done
to him last time Aidan tried to go up against him. But I
wasn't willing to wait around. I wanted to make sure
Maya didn't fall any further under Gene's influence, and
wanted to free my father. And I had made a promise to
Zeke to help Clem.

Most of all, I just wanted to banish that overblown
Aztec critter before he unleashed disease and bad luck
upon this city of which I had grown so fond.

I looked through Aidan's desk while Sailor concentrated on trying to intuit something or feel magical vibrations. Though the ring was said to be able to hide
itself, Sailor was awfully good at this sort of thing.

I was hoping the ring might not be too hard to find.
Aidan would want it to be easily accessible in case the
demon showed, and, besides, he would think he was
thoroughly protected from just about anybody . . . anybody but a witch like me.

I started rifling through Aidan's collection of witch-
craft-related tomes on the wall-to-wall bookshelves, trying not to grow frustrated. If only a ring weren't so small;
it could be anywhere. I looked in the little chamber,

Aidan's cloister, off the main office. It was a tiny, five
sided room studded with magnetic stones, mirrors, and
charms set up to encourage fields sympathetic to scrying

There were amulets and talismans and crystal
aplenty, but nary a single ring.

I emerged from the cloister to find Sailor sitting in
Aidan's big leather chair, his feet up on the desk, Nocte
mus sitting on his shoulders the way she often did with
her master.

"Hey, check me out," said Sailor. "Now I know what
it feels like to be Aidan. I guess I should start issuing
proclamations or ruining someone's life."

I had to laugh. But then . . . "Hey, where did the cat
come from?"

Realization sank in just a little too late. Sailor and
watched as Noctemus bounded toward the open door
leaping into Aidan's arms. His blue eyes were icy with
anger.

"Well, isn't *this* charming?"

Chapter 22

If I'm not mistaken, *you*, sir, were banished from this town. And you"—he gestured toward me—"should have known better than to try a stunt like this."

"Give me the ring, Aidan. We can do this together. You and I would be strong enough."

"I told you I don't have the infernal ring!" Aidan yelled. I tried to remember if I'd ever heard him raise his voice before. "Do you honestly think that if I did, I'd hold out on you and let the demon's strength grow? What kind of witch do you think I am?"

"A scared one," I said. "Aidan, I know how hard it is to go up against a demon, especially one you've met before. And I know what you must have gone through in . . . the fire."

"You will never know what your father and I went through," he said in a quiet, intense whisper. He stroked Noctemus, and regained his carefully casual air. "So, what gives you the sudden impression that I have the ring?"

"Johannes, Griselda's assistant, came here two days after she died."

He looked genuinely surprised. "Here, as in, to m
office?"

"Yes."

"But that's . . ." He trailed off, his eyes meeting thos
of his familiar. Noctemus had leaped onto the bool
shelves and now loomed over us, silent and disapprovin
as was her way.

Aidan shook his head. "He never entered my chan
ber."

"Then what was he doing here?"

"Good question. Perhaps he was looking for me, bu
I haven't been around much lately."

"I noticed." I blew out a loud breath in frustratio
When Shawnelle talked about the Wax Museum and e
pecially the European Explorers exhibit, I had been s
sure. "All right. Aidan, I apologize for breaking into you
office. It was wrong of me. I'm sure you'll think of som
way I can make it up to you, and I'll be happy to, but I
appreciate it if it could wait until this whole demon thir
is wrapped up."

Aidan gave me an almost imperceptible nod. I turne
toward the door but realized I was alone.

"Sailor, aren't you coming?" I asked.

"Aidan and I have a few things to discuss. We need t
have this out, once and for all."

"*Now*? We have a lot to do . . ." I looked to Aida
hoping for a little coolheaded rationality. Given th
heated, angry look in his eyes, I was going to have t
keep on looking.

Great. I was trying to save my friend, my father, an
my city, and the boys had chosen this moment to do the
top-dog macho thing.

I stormed out, casting my thoughts about for an ide
Where to now? I paused and studied the wax statue

oking into the faces of John Cabot and Ponce de León.
either of them were talking. They might not have any-
ing to say, even if they could. Johannes might have hid-
n that ring anywhere in this city, could have dropped
in a gutter for all I knew at this point. If the *Ojo del*
uego wasn't going to assist us by sending out a signal,
ere was no way to . . .

My eyes alit on the sculpture of Mary Ellen Pleasant.
Did she just wink at me?

I circled her. One reason reproductions like this worry
e is that they can serve as poppets for skilled practitio-
rs. But . . . could they serve as conduits for powerful
irits as well? Giving them a way to exist on this plane,
well as in the next?

Though Pleasant had been accused of practicing voo-
oo magic and persecuted for it, there didn't appear to
any actual evidence that she'd ever practiced. But
adame Decotier, a powerful—*deceased*—voodoo priest-
s who had once helped me in exchange for this very
ax statue as a tribute to a largely maligned and forgot-
n champion of civil rights . . . well, Decotier might well
powerful enough to inhabit this poppet. And to keep
e ring safe.

I remembered the note from Carlotta to her sister,
riselda: *If All Else fails, have a Pleasant Day.* Germans
pitalize nouns, but "pleasant" is an adjective. And I
d wondered why that last sentence was in English. Did
e English make it stand out, so Griselda wouldn't miss
e instruction? Or was it that she wanted to use the
ord "pleasant" as in Mary Ellen Pleasant? Perhaps
easant's wax figure was the backup plan, and when Jo-
nnes couldn't find Aidan to pass off the ring, he left it
her custody for safekeeping?

I checked Pleasant's hands. No rings.

Darn. Maybe I was stretching, making things up
this point, seeing significance where there was none.

From the vicinity of Aidan's office, I could hear de
voices raised in anger. I rolled my eyes. Soon they'd
having a fistfight. What were they, fifteen?

But then I noticed the pendant Mary Ellen Pleasa
wore. The one made of human hair. But this time it w
bright orange, in place of the black one she wore l
time I saw her. Didn't Hans say Carlotta's hair was dy
a bright carrot orange?

The necklace was bulky, as though woven arou
something. I flipped it over. There was an Aztec glyph
the back, with a stylized lizard—or could it be a salama
der? As in a fire elemental? Pleasant was from Louisi
originally, then New York, then California. An Azt
symbol seemed like an odd choice.

I laid my hand over the medallion. While my ha
rested on her chest, I could have sworn I felt her breatl
Her glass eyes reflected the lights; they seemed genui
real, alive.

Next I examined the medallion around her neck mo
closely. The hair was plaited intricately into a cord, w
a fastener at the back. I undid it and slipped it over
head. At first the vibrations were absent, then dissona
almost painful. Finally, they seemed to fall in step w
my own vibrations, following along with me so as not
be detected. It hummed between my breasts, warm a
evocative. This was different from the sensations I pick
up from clothing. These were almost alive, as thou
Carlotta—and others before her—had imbued the m
dallion with parts of themselves.

I took it off to study it.

Carefully, I pulled strands of hair from the wov
cord. They put up resistance; the weaving was so fine a

ricate that they did not release easily. I hated to take
apart. Aside from not wanting to destroy a work of art,
ither did I want to deal inappropriately with an obvi-
s charm of a powerful witch, dead or alive. I could feel
umming now, and emotions streamed through me.

But when I cupped it in my palm, the hair began to
plait itself, lock by lock. Finally it revealed a massive
e opal cabochon in a tarnished silver setting. The trans-
cent stone was a vivid yellow-orange with green, red,
d yellow flashes within. It gleamed as though reflect-
g the sun.

At dawn and midnight, the opal shows its color best.
fore I fully processed the fact that I had finally found
e coveted *Ojo del Fuego*, colors began flowing over the
lls and ceiling, falling like stars.

"It's like a disco ball!" said Oscar.

His voice, so unexpected, pulled my attention away
m the powerful fire opal, from the treasure so many
d sought for so long.

"Oscar? What are *you* doing here?"

"Aidan sent for me. What are *you* doing here?"

"I . . ." I trailed off while I watched Oscar spin around,
en put one hand up pointing to the ceiling while an-
her was pointing down and slightly behind him, à la
hn Travolta in the iconic posters for *Saturday Night
ver*. He started crooning "Stayin' Alive" in his gravelly
ice, which sounded surprisingly good in a Tom Waits,
ck-and-roll kind of way.

I smiled but tried to filter out his antics, concentrating
stead on the colors whirling around the room. How
ey moved as I did, yet also fell of their own accord.
d, orange, yellow, green. Were they trying to tell me
mething? Or were they just a beautiful phenomenon?

I tried to decide what to do next. The *Ojo del Fuego*

had been safe here in the museum, with Mary Elle
Pleasant. I wondered whether there was a way to lur
Gene here, on Aidan's turf, and to have a showdown.

I felt something I could only describe as a strong pre
monition, an urging to put the medallion back arour
Pleasant's wax neck. Whether Madame Decotier's spir
was directing the medallion or it was compelling me i
self was hard to say. But I obeyed and slipped the necl
lace over her head for safekeeping.

Perhaps it knew I wasn't strong enough to use the *O*
del Fuego by myself. Once things calmed down, I wou
have to confer with Aidan as to what to do with the piec

But first . . . I thought I might know who had kille
Griselda and who hurt Renna and Eric. Zeke was a
ready in the hospital by the time Renna and Eric we
attacked, and I couldn't imagine Clem carrying out tho
tortures by himself. Gene, a demon's devoted minio
would likely have someone else do his dirty work. B
there was someone who had access to Griselda's thing
including, very possibly, the notes she kept about Renr
and me and Aidan. Someone whose own place was su
rounded by rowan loops, and whose grandfather had le
him old clothes in the attic, like the bag of clothes left o
the stoop in front of Aunt Cora's Closet. Someone wh
was painting a border that looked like lizards—or sal
manders.

Someone entirely human, who might well be in th
process of throwing in his lot with the demon in order
secure success for his inn, and whatever else it was th
demons offered.

I hurried down the stairs. If Lloyd was trying to pledg
himself to Xolotl, was there a way to stop him befo
he'd done even more harm? I needed to speak with m
father. He would know.

As I reached the bottom of the stairs, I slowed.

It looked like one of the wax figures was lying on the
ound. But no—it wasn't wax. It was breathing.

"*Clarinda*?" I said, kneeling by her side. "Are you
ay?"

There was a sudden rush of blinding pain, and then all
nt black.

Chapter 23

When I came to, a gun was being held to my temple an
I was in a headlock that choked off most of the oxyg
to my lungs. I clutched at the arm wrapped around m
neck, trying to loosen it not so much to escape as fo
more immediate need: to breathe.

"Lloyd . . ." I managed, a whispery croak.

"Oh, you're awake. Good. You can walk on your ow
then. You're heavier than you look." He released the ar
but kept the gun trained on me and wound his hand in m
hair, urging me along painfully. My head ached from t
earlier blow, and my scalp stung where he pulled my ha
Still, it was better than being choked. I swallowed conv
sively, trying to ease the crushed feeling in my throat.

The scene was nightmarish. We were in a windowle
dank room—I was guessing the basement of the m
seum. The ticket taker, Clarinda, lay on the floor, looki
as broken as the misshapen wax figures surrounding h
Rows of heads, a table full of boxes labeled REAL H
MAN HAIR, containers of fingernails, and medical-gra
glass eyes. Dismembered arms and legs.

"Woah, check this out!" Lloyd said, awe in his voice.
Gene told me how to get down here. Isn't it awesome?
us, no cameras, which is helpful."

"Lloyd, please listen to me," I said. "Try to understand
hat I'm saying. Gene isn't . . . he isn't a normal man.
e's working for a . . . demon, for lack of a better word."

"You think I don't know this? 'Demon' makes him
und like a bad thing, but demons can be helpful as
ell. Gene explained it all to me when I first met him. It
as on that trip to Europe, five countries in as many
ys, but I really loved Germany, so I stayed on for an
tra week. That's where I bought the cuckoo clock you
ed so much. Remember?"

He started to drag me by my hair across the room. My
ead pounded and my scalp ached; I held on to his wrist
lessen the pain.

I was racking my brain, hoping Lloyd would keep
lking. In my experience, this sort of person usually en-
yed the sound of his own voice and relished the op-
rtunity to vent his frustrations. If I could buy time,
idan or Sailor might be able to find me. I used my mind
call out as loud as I could, hoping someone, some-
here, might sense my need. I'm not psychic, but as a
ained witch my powers of concentration are highly de-
loped. Empaths could pick up on my calls, if I tried
rd enough. I hoped.

"I came back from that trip and I finally understood
y place in the world, what I had been lacking. The lack
respect . . . no one showed me enough respect. I
arted to study, just as Gene had told me to. It turned
t there was lots of information about demons in those
d books Grandfather left me. Years passed, and I won-
red whether I'd ever be called, but finally Gene con-
cted me and asked for my help with Griselda. I had to

pretend to meet her by chance when she arrived at SF
but I pulled it off. And now, if I find the talisman, I wo
ever have to work another day in my life. But Gene's g
other people looking for it, like those two backwoo
brothers. Those guys are like all those damned imn
grants, coming into this country and stealing jobs."

Sailor had always heard me in the past. But I wo
dered whether we still had that connection. It did
seem like anyone was going to burst in and save me.
sudden shaky sigh of fear and regret surged up in me.

"Lloyd, is Clarinda . . . dead?"

"Nah, she'll be fine. She's still breathing and ever
thing. No one dies from a simple tap on the head."

"Why are you doing this?"

"I need that talisman, Lily. It's as simple as that. I w
be rewarded greatly for its return. And I deserve a lit
reward in my life. Why should I have to work my butt
and pay all those taxes to the goddamned governme
have other people living as 'guests' in my family hom
How is that fair? I could sit around and enjoy myse
waiting for government handouts. But instead, *I* have
do it the hard way. I guess it's like my father always sa
Nice guys finish last."

Anger edged out the fear. *As though his life is all th
hard,* I thought to myself with disdain. Why is it that
often, it's the most fortunate of the world who feel sor
for themselves? This man lived in the Bay Area, inh
ited a beautiful old house, and seemed to be educat
and healthy. And yet somehow he was the victim he
because he had to work for a living?

I welcomed the anger. It was clarifying, helped
concentrate. I could use it to—

Lloyd suddenly picked me up as though to cradle
in his arms, then dropped me unceremoniously on t

oor. The wind was knocked out of me and I lay there, unned. Before I could push myself up he set a heavy ank of wood on top of me.

Lloyd sat on the board for a second, making me grunt om the pressure.

"Oh, look. It's a sandwich. Get it? A sand-witch?" He ood, releasing the compression momentarily, but then aced two heavy supply boxes right on top, over my idsection. The board pressed on my chest and abdo-en.

It wasn't bad at first. The board on top of me was eavy, but it didn't hurt.

"You can put a stop to this anytime," Lloyd said. "Just ll me where you've hidden the talisman, and it's over. imple as that."

"It's in Coit Tower," I lied. "Behind a heating grate on e third floor. I'll take you there."

"Gene told me it had to be in someone's possession. ike, with a witch. I detest liars." Lloyd gave me a pained xpression and put another box on the board. "Mendac-y of any kind, really. And yet it's all around me. I'm a re honest man in a deeply dishonest world."

I took another breath just as deep as I could, savoring e air and desperately trying to concentrate, and it awned on me whom I should call: Oscar. He was my miliar. Could he hear me? Could he help me?

Lloyd crouched down, putting his mouth very close to y ear. When he spoke his voice was very soft and gen-e, seductive, like the whisper of a lover.

"Tell me where to find the talisman."

My concentration wandered, interrupted by my body's gnals of distress. Lloyd placed yet another huge box on e, and my breaths became shallow and strained. Never efore had I realized how much movement was involved

in breathing, the up and down of the chest, however in
perceptible in daily life. Just a fraction of an inch to e
pand and draw in sweet oxygen.

"Tell me, Lily . . ." Lloyd's voice was a singsong no
as though we were playing a game and he had all th
time in the world.

He might have time on his side, but clearly *I* didn
Nausea swept over me, and I fought down panic an
concentrated simply on breathing. The pressure on m
body was immense, and I felt tingling in my arms an
legs. But that was nothing next to the desperate, sicken
ing need for more air. I started to twitch frantically, m
eyes darting around the room.

Lloyd reached out toward the pile of boxes again.

"No!" I called out in panic. There was a note of plea
ing in my voice, a whimpering that would have emba
rassed me, had I had my wits about me. Though I didn
make it a habit to envision my own death, I never wou
have imagined facing it with cowardice. But it wasn't th
pain that bothered me; it was the hideous sensation
one's body being slowly starved of oxygen that w
pushing me beyond reason to one sole thought: *N
Please, please,* no.

"No, what?" said Lloyd.

"Not another box, I beg you."

"Would you prefer the *strapatto*?" His tone sounde
disinterested, as though he were happy to proceed wi
whichever torture method I wanted. "That's what I use
on that gypsy witch, though I hear she lived. It's not r
ally meant to kill, you know. Neither is pressing. It's r
ally a way to extract information, not to kill anyone."

"You killed Griselda."

"I didn't! I pressed her, that much is true. And som
times a person can miscalculate, apparently, so she w

aving a very hard time telling me what she needed to.
he passed out, I went to get some water to revive her,
nd by the time I came back someone had stabbed her
ith an antique knife. That's sort of ... hitting someone
hen they're down. Right? What the heck was that
bout?"

He put a stone atop me.

"Please ..." was all I could manage, but then realized
shouldn't waste my breath. Quite literally. It wasn't as
ough begging would change the mind of this madman.

My vision started to narrow, the peripheral vision
arkening. All I could think about now was breathing.

Lloyd started to whistle, and then began prancing
round the room, as if preparing for the next fire dance.
s I panted my shallow, quick breaths, I watched him
wirl and fling his imaginary pots of fire.

"Gene says I'm a natural. A little more practice, and
'll be invited to join the troupe if I want. I know I'm a
it older than the others, but I'll be the best fire dancer
here."

I felt a wave of calm come over me. The tingling in my
xtremities stopped ... but now they were numb. The
ounding of my heart sounded in my ears. And I heard
thrumming, so low it wasn't perceivable to the human
ar. But I could feel it.

As could Lloyd. He stopped his dance steps and
oked at me with a frown.

"What is that?"

I just stared at him, panting.

"Can't you speak?" He lifted one of the boxes off of
e. "Better?"

Like a fish dying on the pier, I opened and closed my
outh uselessly. Then I shook my head slightly, as though
couldn't speak.

"*Dammit.* Too much weight again." He took off th
stone. "You know, I read those witch-hunting manual
looked them up on the Internet. I did my damned re
search. But they weren't really clear on how much weigh
is too much or how long to leave it on. How's that?"

Lloyd looked at me with concern, as though he wer
some sort of twisted therapist worried about my welfare

"Like I said," he continued, "I'm not trying to *kill* any
one, just get some information. And if there's one thin
I've learned in the past few days, it's that you witches ar
stubborn creatures. Also, you die a lot easier than a per
son would think."

He crouched down and put his hand to my neck. I fel
the rough calluses of his finger as he pressed, hard, t
feel my pulse.

Behind him, I saw a slight movement behind a broke
wax sculpture of Genghis Khan.

Oscar. He had come for me. With the *Ojo del Fueg*
pendant around his neck.

My head lolled to the side, and I tried to telegraph m
thoughts to him: *He's got a gun.* But truth was, Osca
wasn't paying attention to me. Everything in his gnarle
adorable little face was concentrated on my attacke
Lloyd. I had seen my familiar in action before—othe
times when he had come to my assistance—and when h
was in his natural form he was surprisingly strong.

Lloyd has a gun. I tried to shake my head at Osca
suddenly frantic at the thought that he would be sho
Could gobgoyles stand such an injury? I had no idea, bu
I knew they were mortal. Naturally long-lived, but just a
mortal as the next person if they were shot at close rang

As I watched, the strands of hair began to unwra
themselves, revealing the *Ojo del Fuego.* And it was, in
deed, afire, blazing with its own light.

Still staring at Lloyd, Oscar closed his large, humanlike hand around the fire opal, facing the gem into his
palm.

The lights began twirling around the room, like colored reflections off a disco ball. At first I thought I was
seeing things as a result of the lack of oxygen, but then I
realized Lloyd saw them, too.

"What the—" he exclaimed, looking around, spinning
to try to focus on the lights, which sped up, weaving
among themselves. They rotated faster and faster, growing in size until everything was a blur of pure white light.
Lloyd spun so fast he was whipping around, out of control, spinning to keep up with the lights.

He cried out, then fell to the floor, his eyes still spinning, unfocused.

The lights subsided.

Oscar ran to me and threw the boxes off, then the
board. Without a word he grabbed one of the heavy boxes,
lifted it high over his head and turned to loom over Lloyd.
He held the box right over the prone man's head.

Still unable to sit up, I drew in a ragged breath and
croaked out: "*Oscar*! No!"

"I'll smash his head!"

"No. Put the box down, Oscar. *Now*. *Listen* to me."
My hands and feet were overwhelmed with tingles as I
regained sensation in my limbs. "You're my familiar; you
have to do what I say."

He stood there with the box raised overhead for several more beats, breathing hard. He was facing away
from me so I couldn't see his expression, but after another moment his shoulders relaxed slightly and he
tossed the box as hard as he could toward poor Genghis
Khan, whose head split off with the force, falling to the
floor with a thud and rolling into the corner.

Shaky, I sat up and started to rub my hands vigor ously, trying to get rid of the painful tingles.

"*Oscar*. Thank you. You saved my life. Did you hea me calling?"

He nodded and pulled the talisman over his head. Th *Ojo del Fuego* was once again wrapped up in its hai cocoon, hidden. Oscar walked up to me and slipped th pendant over my head.

The talisman thrummed that strange bass tone, meld ing with my energy. I felt my breathing normalize, an the awkward pain from the pressing subsided, the tin gling dissipating.

Finally, it quieted, matching its rhythm with mine, s we were indistinguishable.

"You keep that, mistress. It is too powerful for me. almost couldn't make it here. It took my energy fror me."

"How did you find it?"

"It called to me. I don't understand how. I've neve seen that kind of behavior in a necklace before."

"Thanks, Oscar. Come on. Let's tie this guy up befor he comes round. I'll call Carlos and tell him what hap pened. Let's let the justice system deal with him."

"I'd like to serve him a little justice, goblin style."

"I know. Me, too. But we have to rise above, let hir be judged by a jury of his peers."

"They won't know everything, though. They won't un derstand that he wanted to help a . . ." He looked aroun as though we might be overheard, then leaned towar me and whispered. "A *demon*."

"I know. But he's an attempted murderer. The inspec tors have DNA evidence from the scene, and I'll testif about what happened here tonight. He'll be punishe Now let's get out of here."

Physically, I felt remarkably chipper, given my ordeal. The talisman had lent me its energy. Mentally, though, I couldn't deny I was shaken. Right now all I wanted was to get the hell out of this basement, call the paramedics for Clarinda, and go hide somewhere.

Just then, Sailor raced down the basement stairs, with Aidan right on his heels. At the sight of me and Oscar, Sailor stopped short and Aidan plowed right into the back of him, giving rise to a rather slapstick moment of floundering on the steep wooden stairs. Both men wound up grabbing on to each other to maintain their footing.

"You two make a cute couple."

Scowling, they distanced themselves from each other.

"You're all right?" Sailor asked, his dark-eyed gaze shifting over my shoulder to the man lying on the floor, trussed up like a Christmas goose.

"Just dandy," I said, still not over my snit. I realized at some deep level that these two had worked together, somehow, to come to my rescue. I'm sure once I calmed down I would be grateful—touched, even—for them working out their differences in order to help me. But at the moment I still had my mad on.

"What happened to Clarinda?" Aidan demanded, picking her up in his arms and starting back up the stairs. Sailor and I followed, and Oscar brought up the rear. The stairs creaked loudly under our feet, and we all seemed to pause and take a deep breath when we passed through the door to the main floor.

"I don't know," I said. "If it was the same as he did to me, it was a blow to the back of the head."

Sailor lifted her lids to check her pupils, then put his hands on her head, closing his eyes and letting out a long breath, his head cocked slightly. After a moment he straightened and nodded.

"She'll be okay," he said.

Aidan just nodded and resumed his hurried stride.

"And you?" Sailor asked in a low tone, putting hi
hand on my arm to stop me.

"I'm fine," I lied, avoiding his eyes. Normally Sailo
couldn't read my thoughts, but at the moment I was s
weakened I didn't trust my own guard to be stron
enough against this man, who still held such a huge par
of my heart. The truth was, my head was pounding, an
the nausea, after subsiding earlier, was back with a ven
geance. But right now all I wanted was to get out of thi
house of horrors and get back home, where I could hea
myself. I would call Graciela . . . she would know how t
cure this ill . . . which went way beyond the physical mal
aise.

*I had almost been pressed, just like witches through th
ages.* I still couldn't process it.

Rather than head for the exit, Aidan started up th
main stairs to the second floor.

"Aidan? Where are you going? We need to call a
ambulance, get her some help."

"We don't have time for that," Aidan said, his breath
ing becoming labored with the effort of carrying Clar
inda, who wasn't a large woman but, after all, he was o
his second set of stairs.

"Here, let me carry her the rest of the way," Sailo
offered, taking pity on the man.

"I'm fine," Aidan snapped, shrugging him off. "Bu
explain to Lily, if you will, what's going on."

"What is it?" I asked as we reached the second floo
and Aidan strode toward his office.

"I'm afraid this thing isn't over."

"Lloyd's the one who killed Griselda, and who wen
after Renna and Eric."

"Yes, but the others are still on the loose. Including our father. They're headed here."

"*Here*?" I had to jog to keep up with the men, and Oscar trotted along as fast as his little piggy legs would carry him. "Maybe I'm a little slow on the uptake, but if they're headed *here*, shouldn't we go, you know, *not* here?"

"Can't run from this sort of thing. Too much is already in motion," Aidan said as the door to his office opened of its own accord and we all slipped through.

Noctemus hissed at me, as was her wont. The feeling was mutual. Give me my pig over that cranky feline any day. Speaking of pigs, Oscar immediately scooted over to hide in the footwell of the desk.

Aidan laid Clarinda gently on his red velvet love seat, cradling her head on a down pillow. She moaned a bit, frowned, opened her eyes.

"Go back to sleep," he said in a quiet, gentle tone, waving his hand very close in front of her face, casting a cocooning spell so she wouldn't hear what we were talking about. She fell asleep.

Aidan glanced at Sailor. "You're sure?"

"As sure as I can be."

"And how sure is that?" Aidan snapped.

"As sure as any doctor would be, Aidan. You know as well as I do there are no guarantees, even with my sight. But she wouldn't be any better off at the hospital than she is here, and if that demon gets hold of the *Ojo del Fuego* we'll all be in a world of hurt."

With a curt nod of his golden head, Aidan ceded the point.

I looked at both men, who seemed now to be avoiding my eyes. They were waiting for something. Apparently, this was the Lily show.

"What do you need me to do?"

"You don't have the time or the resources to brew ä home, Lily. I know you're not as confident in other area but I'll be here to help you."

"As will I," put in Sailor.

"As will Sailor," Aidan said with an inclination of h head. Then under his breath he added, "For what that worth."

Sailor's eyes rolled to the ceiling.

"Could we please concentrate on what's going on?" said.

"When the others get here, they'll call on . . . yo know who. In order to have the strength to fight hir we'll need our own demon to help."

He was talking about Sitri, the demon I had bound ä the San Francisco School of Fine Arts. For the first tim since I had escaped being pressed, I lost my breath.

"You said that would be *bad*," I said, shaking my hea vehemently. "*You* said I wasn't strong enough to contro him. You *said* I would wind up like my father, bound t the whims of a demon. And you were right."

"I know what I said."

Chapter 24

esperate, I looked toward Sailor, hoping for an ally.
"here's got to be another way."

Sailor held my gaze with his, looking at me intently,
it didn't say anything.

Aidan continued to try to convince me. "You think if
ere was, I would be suggesting this? The fact is, you
ve the *Ojo del Fuego*—" I opened my mouth to deny
but he held out his hand, palm out, to stop me. "Please,
ly, don't bother to deny it. You have the *Ojo*, and don't
u dare tell me—or anyone else—where it is. I don't
nt to know. But this guy will *not* stop in his quest. We
uld kill the Jones brothers and your father and the
an in charge, and he will send more now that he knows
10 you are."

"I'll leave town."

Sailor and I could run away together, use our com-
ned talents to skate under the radar. And . . . we could
together. I would have to give up my friends and life
re in San Francisco, but it would be better than risking
bmitting to a demon's control.

"You can't run from this. He commands legions, an
he's elemental. He will never cease to exist. He w
never cease looking for you. You have to face him."

Sailor stood, leaning back against the bookshelf, arn
crossed over his chest. He held my eyes for a long m
ment, fingers of his intuition reaching out for n
thoughts. He wasn't so much reading my mind as readi
me, as a man might read a woman, or vice versa.

A look of deep disappointment came over his fac
and he shook his head. "You know how much I hate
admit it, but Aidan's right. We have to do this here an
now."

I could feel the pendant between my breasts, und
my shirt, starting to thrum. It seemed to be siding wi
the men. Traitor.

It seemed I had no alternative. I gave in to the inev
table. I had hoped to live the rest of my life without ta
ing on another demon, but I would do it for my frien
and for my town.

"How do I start?"

Working with Aidan's things was like an avid b
humble cook being invited to whip up a meal in a fan
chef's kitchen. I missed the familiarity of my own plac
but I had to admit that the man had an excellent
stocked magical arsenal.

"You'll need to do a Lesser Banishing ritual of th
Pentagram, obviously," said Aidan. "As well as the Mi
dle Pillar Ritual, just to prepare."

I nodded. His reminder was unnecessary; the rit
were second nature to me. But, I realized, Aidan w
nervous. Going over the rote stuff was a way to find ca
and center ourselves.

If I was the cook of this magical brew, Aidan was n

us-chef. He brought me herbs, his athame, white can-
es; then he set out incense, the triangle of Solomon,
d a black mirror for the altar.

"Black mirror?" I asked. These were used in a way
milar to that of crystal balls, as a method for scrying, or
eing, the beyond. "You, of all people, should know that
n no good at scrying."

"We're going to try to keep Sitri on the astral plane,
ther than the physical. He'll appear through the mir-
r."

"Okey dokey. If you say so, chief."

I knew that since I had bound him, Sitri and I were
nnected by threads that formed channels, through
hich our energies radiated back to each other. The
oblem is these threads are a two-way street; what we
st can be used against us.

"They're coming," said Sailor. "Ten minutes, fifteen,
ps."

"Okay," said Aidan. "Let's get this started."

Aidan had Sailor draw Sitri's sigil on a piece of parch-
ent. Aidan and I were both too powerful to do so—we
ight inadvertently call on the demon before we were
ady, which would be disastrous.

I drew the magic circle carefully with the brew, plac-
g a white candle at each of the four directions, east,
uth, north, west. Within this I sketched the pentagram
ith the five points marking the elements: earth, wind,
e, water, spirit. At the top I drew a triangle, within
hich was placed the black mirror.

Using the athame, I performed the cleansing rituals to
tablish the sacred circle, then began the evoking ritual
hile I was safely ensconced within the circle.

Holding the athame in both my hands, I pointed it at
e parchment with Sitri's sigil.

"I call upon the strength of my ancestors. I am th
power. I command you to show yourself. I evoke thee an
conjure thee, O Sitri, to appear before me in a fair an
comely shape. With the strength of my ancestors, with th
ties that bind, I command thee."

The pendant thrummed steadily now, and I could fe
it lending me its power. Suddenly I felt sure, confident
used the athame to cut a tiny "x" in the palms of both
my hands, then lifted the athame over my head an
channeled the strength of all those witches that ha
come before me. They were part of me; their bloc
coursed through my veins. My helping spirit appeare
before me as the conduit, the holder of the threads.

The stench of sulfur burned my nose, swirling aroun
me. And just that easily, Sitri appeared. Not as a visic
in the mirror, but as though emerging from it, confine
to the small triangle and yet seemingly huge, a griff
with the body of a leopard and wings. The sound
those wings was terrible somehow, and had haunted n
dreams.

"Liiiiiily," he said. His voice was seductive; mere
hearing it was a temptation. "I have miiiiiissed you. . .

"You are here at my command, to do my will." Th
pendant thrummed as he looked at Aidan and Sailc
both of whom were in trances, lending me whatever ps
chic strength they could.

"You will look at *me*, Sitri. I call you by name, I ho
you within the triangle. I *command* you."

He laughed, trying to look beyond me as though fo
someone else to enchant. He was a wily, clever one.

The door flung open, and in walked Gene, backed k
Clem and Zeke. Zeke seemed fully recovered. The Jon
brothers gawked and trembled in the face of the hug
demon standing in the center of the room.

Gene, for his part, scoffed loudly.

"What's this? You've got what—a pet demon? He's
t what? A few hundred legions? My master's got ten
es that number, and gaining more all the time. That
-dancing gig is bringing people in like moths to a
me. *I flamed amazement; sometimes I'd divide. And
n in many places.*"

A small fire broke out atop the broad walnut desk,
t Aidan and Sailor remained in their trances. They
sted me; their lives were in my hands.

"Poor old Lloyd," said Gene with a smile. "Guess he's
ing to prison, eh? Too bad. I liked that guy. Turned out
be quite brutal; no training at all. Just channeled his
neral bitterness and dissatisfaction with life and *boom*,
ruly violent man was born."

"So, the promise of the good life stops when some-
e's arrested, does it? That hardly seems fair."

Another small fire began in the corner of one book-
se.

He shrugged, pushing out his chin as though ponder-
; my words. "Truth is, I've never understood why peo-
 sell out so easily. They do so much and ask for so
le in return."

"How about you? What do you receive for being a
mon's lackey?"

Anger flared, bright and fierce, but passed through
n quickly. "I serve my lord with loyalty. I love him.
at's enough."

The fires blazed hotter.

"Is it enough? Maybe I should be talking with your
ster, Xolotl."

"Dare ye not invoke his name!"

I wrapped my hand around the pendant. The hair un-
und itself, showing the *Ojo del Fuego*. I slid the ring

onto my finger, then turned the stone to my palm a
closed my hand to make a fist.

"*Xolotl*, I call on thee and command thee to manif
here and now."

"No!"

"*With the strength of my ancestors, I am the power.*
could feel the huge power surge afforded me by Sitr
whether he wanted to or not, he was acting as my ass
tant on the astral plane. "*I call you by name, Xolot
know you. I command you. I exorcise you.*"

Holding up my fisted hand, pointing the athame at t
pentacle point for the element of fire, I barely notic
that Gene had fallen to his knees at the edge of the cir
where I was pointing, hands cast to the side, crying o

Zeke and Clem were both on the floor, cringing a
covering their heads as though the building were goi
to cave in.

It was only then that I realized things were shaki
books were tumbling from shelves, falling papers stoki
the fires that were already burning.

And the lights began flickering. Whirling overhe
and all around us, the *Ojo del Fuego* spun a web of li
and magic around the room, then shrunk and pass
through everyone in the room until it spun around o
Gene, like a cocoon.

Despite the strength of my ancestors, the borrow
power from Sailor and Aidan and Oscar, and the astral
sistance of Sitri, I could still feel myself losing strength. T
pendant was draining me, taking the energy I had built

I couldn't hold it.

The room still shook and the smoke from the fi
began to gather, choking us all. Sailor and Aidan ca
out of their trances.

Suddenly my father showed up at the door.

He was chanting. At first I thought he was going up
inst me, but as my strain eased, as I regained my psy-
: footing, I realized he was helping me. His energy
boosting mine.

And fire burst out upon his suit jacket. But he didn't
itate or pause in his chanting. Our eyes locked.

took a deep breath and repeated loudly, *"I call you
name, Xolotl. I know you. I command you. I exorcise
. I call you by name, Xolotl. I know you. I command
. I exorcise you!"*

And suddenly, all was quiet. Sitri's terrible flapping
gs, the roar of the fires, the whooshing of the lights
e silenced. The cocoon of light was extinguished, and
ne lay still on the pentacle, his eyes open and terrified.
was dead.

Aidan rushed over to my father and threw his own
t over the burning jacket, smothering the flames. Af-
a stunned moment, we all seemed to realize at the
ne time that while Xolotl had been expelled, Aidan's
ce was now beginning to blaze out of control. We ran
as fast as we could. Aidan carried Clarinda, Sailor
ried Oscar in his pig form, and I had Noctemus
pped around my neck, her claws gone clear through
cotton of the shirt and sunk into my shoulders, mak-
me sneeze. Zeke and Clem led the way, and my fa-
r took up the rear.

A deafening clanging noise indicated the fire alarm
l been tripped, and it was clear to see why: Disparate
s had begun all over the building. Worse, they were
ning so hot that the sculptures were melting like
thday candles: Juan Ponce de León keeled over, de-
ted by the heat; Sir Francis Drake and John Cabot
owed. The Chamber of Horrors was ablaze, its figures
pearing even more gruesome than usual.

Mary Ellen Pleasant's sculpture, I noticed, was
softening. On the contrary, I could have sworn she
smiling.

But she was the exception. Colored wax pud
started to run together, making the floor slick and
with the burning. It seared through the canvas of
shoes.

It felt like an eternity before we made it to the fl
ing metal-and-glass stairs, where a small river of wax
already dripping down. We made our way down ni
marishly slowly, hanging on to the railing to keep f
slipping. Clem offered to help Aidan with Clarinda,
my father helped Sailor with Oscar.

In the foyer, other than the wax dripping down
stairs, everything was clear. There was no fire here. At
insistence, Aidan and Sailor went down to the s
smoke-and-flame-free basement and managed to h
out the tied-up Lloyd, dumping him outside the f
door.

Our group of six, plus two familiars, stumbled out
a miraculously cool, foggy night. It appeared that
heat wave had finally broken.

Chapter 25

at's worse than being menaced by a demon's num-
-one flunky? Being followed around by sullen min-
. Luckily, it wasn't Xolotl's gang, but a few of Sitri's
ons had decided I was the one in charge for the mo-
at, and trailed me, waiting for orders.
o the first order of business, just as soon as I regained
strength, was to cast another circle, carefully evoke
i once again, and cast him and all of his legions back
he astral plane. I was plumb worn out lately, though,
had asked Bronwyn's coven for a little backup.
A few days after the fire at the Wax Museum I re-
ved a postcard from a little town in West Virginia, in
ch Zeke thanked me, told me his mother was praying
me, and informed me that Clem and his sweetheart
already set a date. The brothers had taken off on the
ht of the fire without telling me how they'd become
olden to Xolotl. Though I was curious, I supposed
e things were better left unsaid. The important thing
that they were freed from Xolotl's clutches and had
rned to their hometown. I noted the return address

on the postcard, and decided to send the vintage wh
embroidered tablecloth I'd gotten at the thrift store a
wedding present. Let bygones be bygones, and all tha

Eric was recovering from a concussion and smoke
halation, and though he would carry the scars on
chest for the rest of his life, he was already in his typ
high spirits. Renna's condition had been upgraded fr
serious to stable; she had even accepted my heal
salves and brews to speed up the recovery process. Br
wyn and Maya had gone with me to comb through
charred wreckage of their Oakland home, but her la
extended Rom family had beat us to it. They would s
port Renna and Eric through this difficult time and h
get them back on their feet.

After a short stint in the psychiatric ward, Johan
finally convinced his doctors he hadn't intended to
himself, but he remained hospitalized for the exhaust
and dehydration he suffered from holding the ring.
was hoping to be released in time to accompany Shawn
to the *quinceañera*, as he'd promised, before returning
Germany.

My father . . . well, what could I say about my fath
When I confronted him with what Johannes had sa
that he had witnessed my father kill Griselda with
athame, my father told me that he had left the knife
her hand so she could kill herself. It was horrific, bu
least she had been able to choose her own death. Sti
wasn't entirely sure I could believe him. He also den
sending the Escalade in an attempt to take Zeke ou
the equation, but this time he wouldn't meet my e
and I was sure he was lying. He was a ruthless man.

Then again, I had to remind myself that in the conf
ing showdown at the Wax Museum, he had worked w
me to defeat Xolotl. He had ignored the flames a

ked his energy with mine at the final, crucial moment.

I couldn't condemn him out of hand, even though
erward, as was his wont, he had disappeared just as
t as Clem and Zeke.

I couldn't help but wonder: *Did he do it for me, or to
e himself?* Probably a little of both.

As far as family reunions go, it was less than satisfy-
. But at least I knew a little more about him than I
d before, and I had been instrumental in freeing him
m Xolotl. And I decided I believed him when he said
sent me away that time in Germany to keep me safe
m the powers of Xolotl.

All in all, I was glad he'd come to town.

I wasn't so sure Aidan would agree. His office had gone
in smoke, but then he'd helped to defeat the demon
t had injured him so badly, once upon a time. Last I
ard he was shopping around for new office space until
e museum was repaired, but despite several obvious
ts for an invitation, I wasn't offering him any of my
or space. Things were way too crowded in Aunt Cora's
oset as it was. I did, however, agree to go real estate
pping with him, just because it sounded like fun.

In the meantime, there were clothes to wash, custom-
to fit, and books to be tallied. As usual, the busy days
re in my shop helped me to find my balance, to re-
ver my equilibrium.

And today, during a momentary lull in customers,
aya and I were trying on dresses for the *quinceañera*
risela's family had invited us to. Maya was herself
ain, saying she looked back on the last few fire-dancing
hts through a dreamlike haze. But she had taken one
bit from the experience: She had started playing with
e store merchandise, trying on dresses like never be-
e.

At the moment, we were cracking each other up, tr
ing on one tulle-laden, crinoline-stiff, frothy number
ter another.

"I swear, you two are worse than Metzli and h
gang!" said Bronwyn, laughing at us as she pushed t
rack of prom dresses into the large communal dressi
room.

I blew at the bright pink netting sticking up from t
bodice of the gown I had on; hiked up the many layers
voluminous, crinkly skirts; and shambled out to adm
myself in the three-way mirror. The puffy sleeves, lo
scoop neck adorned with netting, and satin roses at t
ruched waist appeared to have been inspired by a Barb
fashion design circa 1986. I had no doubt that if I'd be
allowed to have a *quinceañera*, my fifteen-year-old s
would have chosen something exactly like this hideo
concoction.

"You're just being cynical, Bronwyn," I teased. "I lo
it. I think I look just like a—"

"—princess." A deep voice finished my sentence.

I spun around.

Sailor.

He stood in the doorway. Though the look on his fa
was brooding and intense—as per usual—he nodd
hello to Bronwyn and Maya before returning his sca
ing gaze to me.

My heart thudded and my palms started to sweat
hadn't set eyes on Sailor since the night we escaped t
burning museum, when Aidan had insisted *he* wou
make sure I got home safely. Before I'd had a chance
talk with Sailor, he had slipped away into a sudden w
of fog.

"Sailor, how lovely to see you," Bronwyn said. "Ma
could I ask you about something in the back room?"

Subtlety wasn't Bronwyn's strong suit.

"Of course! Hi, Sailor. We've missed you," said Maya. Wearing rhinestone-covered high heels and a butter-yellow princess-style gown, Maya hiked her skirts up and tottered after Bronwyn. "Excuse us while we go talk bout important things in the back room, with the radio n *really* loud."

Maya wasn't exactly Ms. Subtle herself.

Moments after both women disappeared through the curtains, lilting 1920s-era music came floating toward Sailor and me, not only giving us some privacy but also making the scene eerily reminiscent of another time, with me in my formal gown and the violins swelling.

"You're still here." My voice sounded calm, not matching my inner turmoil. "I . . . I thought you'd left own again."

"Apparently I'm welcome back in San Francisco," Sailor said as he slowly strolled across the shop floor toward me, one outstretched hand passing over the silks nd satins hanging on the racks, leaving the garments waying slightly in his wake. "Even got my old apartment back, the one in Hang Ah Alley. Seems no one wanted to nt it."

"I guess a lot of tenants are put off by haunted murder scenes."

"Cowards," Sailor said with a shrug, coming to stand very close to me. Too close. "Luckily, a simple haunting doesn't faze a manly man like me."

"Oh, right. I forgot. Nothing scares you."

"Nothing at all." His smile faded as he reached up and traced the line of my jaw with one finger. His voice dropped, quiet but gruff. "Nothing, except seeing you in danger. The thought of something happening to you . . ." He shook his head. "That scares the hell out of me."

"Sailor . . ." I began, but didn't know what else to sa
I moved toward him ever so slightly. His arms wrappe
around me.

I tilted my face to his, and his mouth came down o
mine. I tingled from my head to my toes, passion and jo
coursing through my veins. Though I couldn't cry, I fe
the sting of tears behind my eyes; it was so good, so ve
right to be with him again.

After a long moment he lifted his head and whi
pered, "Promise me you'll stop scaring me."

"I can't do that." By now it was clear my life in Sa
Francisco would never be without excitement—som
times dangerous excitement—and I refused to make
vow I couldn't keep. "But I can promise to keep kissin
you."

"You drive a hard bargain, woman," he chuckled, the
sighed, eyes searching my face. "But since I'm new
town, and currently unemployed, I guess I'm no pri
myself. So I'll take what I can get. Unlimited kisses. I
a deal."

We embraced again, locked together for several mi
utes until a pair of customers walked in; and Oscar ra
in to greet them; and the music was lowered; and Bro
wyn, Maya, and I got back to work. Sailor took a seat o
the velvet bench near the dressing rooms, watching ov
me—and the suddenly busy shop—with a slight, relu
tant smile.

As far as I was concerned, banishing minions cou
wait. Sailor was back, my friends were safe, Aunt Cor
Closet was bustling . . . and at the moment, that was
that mattered.

ou know your job sucks when you find yourself escap-
g into a Port a Potty for a minute alone.

The blue outhouses are indispensable on a jobsite,
nd, like the old joke about growing old, are a darned
te better than the alternative. But they're not normally
place I choose to spend much time.

Today, however, I found myself lingering in the bright
lue toilet. Warmed by the early-spring sunshine, it
eeked of hot plastic and a sickly-sweet air freshener, but
ffered me a few minutes' respite from the steady bar-
ge of questions and demands from the dozens of eager
ut singularly unqualified volunteers I was directing.

*"Mel, was I supposed to apply a coat of primer before
ainting?"*

"I think I stepped on a rusty nail. Is that bad?"

*"Mel, there's this thing inside that's marked 'Biohaz-
rd.' What should I do with it?"*

*"Where's the dust mask/safety glasses/respirator/firs-
d kit?"*

"Is this mold toxic? Do I need a lawyer?"

"Um . . . Mel? You should probably come see this."

Running a renovation project involves answering
lot of questions, and since I renovate houses for a livin
I've grown accustomed to fielding rapid-fire inquirie
about building details, design issues, and bureaucrat
snafus. Usually, though, I work with professionals wh
know which end of a miter saw is up.

This current project, I had come to realize, was
much about wrangling well-intentioned volunteers as
was about home repair.

A few months ago, in a burst of charity inspired by
champagne-induced New Year's resolution, I had volur
teered to help a local organization that renovated th
homes of the elderly and the disabled. It was a wonde
ful cause, seemingly tailor-made for me, the general d
rector of Turner Construction. I figured I would show u
a few weekends a year, tools in hand, go where I wa
pointed, and do as I was told. By the end of the projec
my conscience, and someone's house, would be ship
shape, and I could relax for another six months or s
until the next project came along.

As with so many of my life plans, it hadn't exactl
worked out as I'd anticipated. Ashley, the perky and de
ceptively shrewd Neighbors Together recruiter, ha
taken one glance at my business card and appealed t
my vanity. Merely volunteering my labor was a waste c
valuable and *rare* expertise, she had suggested. Wouldn
it be a far better use of my talents if I agreed to be
"House Captain"? That way, Ashley insisted, I woul
*"more fully experience the joy and unique sense of ac
complishment that comes from giving of one's self, work
ing with a homeowner in need, overseeing the proje
from beginning to end, and supervising the eager volur
teers."* I think she probably knew she had me there, b

t willing to leave anything to chance, she finished with, *magine turning a loving grandmother's house from a ily nightmare into a warm and safe home sweet home, only someone with your skills can do."*

I'm such a patsy. I fell for it.

I spent the next several months inspecting the project use, prioritizing repairs and improvements, and gathing materials preparatory to this project weekend, 1en a horde of volunteers descended upon a modest t charming two-bedroom cottage on a quiet street in n Francisco's Bernal Heights. The scene was reminisnt of an old-fashioned barn raising: folks swarming er the place like ants as neighbors dropped by to 1tch and kibitz. The untrained volunteers would be ıle to accomplish an astonishing transformation in one ort weekend because even though most had never ·ld so much as a paintbrush, many pairs of hands could turned to good effect when directed by a House Capin who knew what she was doing.

And this House Captain had been up since four a.m., ganizing food for the volunteers, gathering tools and e blueprints for the wheelchair ramp, checking on the rival of the Dumpster and the Port a Potty, and runng around picking up supplies.

And if all that weren't enough to occupy my mind, I as also focused on ignoring the big abandoned house xt door to the sweet stucco cottage ... where flickerg pale faces kept appearing in the windows.

Ghosts.

Why does every interesting building in San Francisco em to be infested with ghosts?

Ignore them, Mel.

I knew they weren't figments of my imagination. I em to have a knack for attracting souls from beyond

the veil, whether I like it or not. Besides, Dog also ke[
looking at the house, barking up a storm.

I had found Dog, abandoned and starving, on a cor
struction site some months ago. Despite my initial rese
vations, we wound up adopting each other. It wouldn
be so bad, I thought: He could ride around with me du
ing the day, come to sites and hang around, be my co
stant companion. Mel's best friend, and all that. But the
it turned out Dog got carsick, and had a tendency t
wander off when I wasn't watching. He didn't play bal
catch Frisbees, or fetch sticks. He wasn't much of a do
really, as dogs go. We adored him.

But, like me, he appeared able to see—or hear c
smell—ghosts.

This morning Dog's barking got so bad, I had to cor
fine him to the car. The canine lovers in the crowd ke[
visiting with him through the half-opened windo
sneaking him snacks, and glaring at me for being mea
Luckily, as a general contractor, I wasn't particularl
fazed by dirty looks.

But the neighbor's ghosts were *not* my problem—n
today, anyway. Today I had seventy-two volunteers t
coordinate and put to work before their enthusias
flagged, plus a house with peeling paint, a warped roc
line, and a sagging porch to repair and spruce up,
wheelchair ramp to build so the disabled homeown
would no longer be a virtual shut-in, and one weeken
to do it all.

Which is why I was hiding in a plastic outhouse.
needed a moment to steel myself to ignore the ghos
next door.

"Sooo," my friend Luz said, catching me as I emerge
from my ignominious Port a Potty break. She was clad i
the bright yellow T-shirt of the "Tool Czar" because, b

gosh, if I'm going to sink into the quicksand of do-good volunteerism, I'm taking my friends and family down with me. In fact, after my father had razzed me about "giving away" my services one time too many, I had goaded him into joining himself. As the (unofficially) retired founder of Turner Construction, Dad offered a wealth of construction know-how to Neighbors Together, and Ashley had swiftly appointed him House Captain for the renovations on the rose-covered bungalow across the street—a project that appeared to be humming along quite nicely, darn it all.

We had a friendly rivalry going: Team Mel vs. Team Bill, Turner vs. Turner. Whoever finished first got control of the television remote for one full week. If Dad won, he was going to watch repeats of *NCIS* from dawn to dusk. If I won, I intended to keep the television turned off.

The stakes were high.

I had also strong-armed my friend Claire, a landscape architect, into running a yard crew. She was gleefully barking orders to a group of New Age Berkeley types planting a drought-friendly garden of native California grasses and flowering bushes. My buddy Stephen, a clothing designer and barista, was the project's health and safety coordinator. It was perfect casting: Stephen was a world-class hypochondriac who fussed over the smallest splinter with a wad of gauze and Neosporin. He also roamed the jobsite, slapping gobs of sunscreen—donated by a civic-minded local drugstore—on necks and noses. Although it was only April, the sun shone fiercely on the jobsite, which meant reminding everyone to keep hydrated, as well.

"The frat boys have arrived," Luz said, nodding toward the street, where half a dozen young men in UC

Berkeley T-shirts and Bermuda shorts leaned against a huge SUV. Others had stretched out on the dry brown sorry excuse for a lawn, apparently napping.

"Oh, good. They were supposed to be here two hours ago."

"Yeah, well . . . ," continued Luz, "I hate to be the one to tell you this, but half of them appear to be hungover. Drunk frat boys—what're the odds?"

"Isn't the fraternity here to do community service because of an alcohol infraction?"

She grinned. "Gotta love college students."

"If half are hungover, what about the other half?"

"Still drunk."

"Let me get this straight: You're saying my dad gets assigned the engineering students, the Eagle Scouts, *and* Turner Construction's best, while *I* end up with drunken frat boys and a sorority of girls more interested in fashion than construction?" I washed my hands with water from the hose in the jerry-rigged stand on the lawn and clamped my mouth shut to keep from repeating one of my father's favorite sayings: *No good deed goes unpunished.*

"And this surprises you—how, exactly?" asked Luz, lifting one eyebrow. "He's a crafty old coot, your dad."

She was right about that. While I was busy wasting time working for a living, Dad had cozied up to Ashley, the Neighbors Together point person, and nabbed the most skilled volunteers. I'd also been so consumed bringing to conclusion several paying Turner Construction projects that I hadn't noticed when Dad convinced our best construction workers, and even my stepson, Caleb, to join his team.

I'd been lucky to get Luz. She was my best friend, but she and my dad adored each other. Sometimes I thought

liked her better than me. Fortunately, my semi-sort-of
yfriend, Graham, was out of town. I'm not sure I
uld have liked the outcome had his loyalty been
ted.

"Hey, Mel?" Monty Parker, the homeowner, rolled
to the front door, two large, scroungy-looking dogs
dubious ancestry attached by leashes to his wheel-
air. After a motorcycle accident had paralyzed the
rty-one-year-old a few years ago, he had lost his job
d couldn't afford to maintain his home, much less to
ild an access ramp or other modifications that would
ke his life easier. That was where Neighbors Together
me in.

I felt for the man, but my stomach clenched at those
o little words: "Hey, Mel?" I'd heard them so often the
t few months. *"Hey, Mel? What do you think about
ilding a small deck out back when we make the ramp
I could sit outside and watch the world go by?" "Hey,
el? I hate to ask, but would you change these
htbulbs?" "Hey, Mel? I heard maybe some of the other
nilies are getting new linoleum for their kitchens?" "Hey,
el? My dogs could really use a flea bath; think you
uld put a new tub in the bathroom?"*

Today Monty was trying to be helpful by relaying
estions from the volunteers. But he was driving me
azy. Not for the first time, I wondered why my father
t sweet Ms. Etta Lee, who appeared accommodating
d grateful and had baked him fresh cinnamon cookies,
ile I was stuck with the needy, grasping Monty.

"Hey, Mel? The folks fixing the kitchen sink found a
oblem," he said. "Maybe dry rot? Hey . . . Are those
ys taking a nap on the lawn?"

"Not for long they aren't," answered Luz.

"Tell the kitchen crew I'll be right there," I said to

Monty, then spoke to Luz in a low voice. "Whatever y
do, don't let those frat boys near the power tools."

"They're on the schedule as the painting crew," sa
Luz, flipping through the sheaf of papers on her ove
stuffed but organized clipboard. "We're slated to get t
place painted today. Not sure the boys are really up f
that. How about we leave today's painting to the soror
girls—they're not quick, but at least they're sober
while I find something else for the boys?"

"Any ideas?"

"Well, I was thinking . . . Monty has those two t
dogs. Before we can do any work out back, somebo
needs to clean things up. What say I put the frat
pooper-scooper duty? Make them the Kaopecta
Krew."

"You, madam, have a mind of rare and infin
beauty."

"So true. You should tell the promotion and tenu
committee."

"How's that going?"

The committee was ruminating on Luz's promotion
Professor of Social Work at San Francisco State Unive
sity. Luz was a dedicated teacher, a brilliant scholar, a
an astute judge of human nature . . . but her interpe
sonal skills could stand some adjustment. Simply state
when it came to tolerating fools, Luz had about as mu
finesse as a demo crew.

"Let's just say I'm considering applying to be a soro
ity mother. According to the girls, there's an openi
Anyway, after the fraternity finishes doggie-doody du
I thought I'd get them to clean out the old shed."

"Sounds perfect. Keep an eye out—Monty says
has no idea what's in there, so there may be somethi
we can repurpose for the renovation. Could be a re

reasure trove. But be sure to explain to them what con-
titutes hazardous waste, since they're likely to find some
ld paint or gasoline cans."

"Will do," Liz said, then turned toward the fraternity
members. "Yo, boys!" she bellowed, and I saw more than
few wince. "On your feet and follow me! Fall in!"

If the gig as a sorority mother didn't work out, I
aused, Luz could always join the army. She was a natu-
al drill sergeant.

But just before I turned away . . . I heard Dog barking
gain. Before I could stop myself, I looked at the house
ext door. There, in the window, was a ghost, its pale
ountenance as clear as you pleased. Looking straight at
e, as though yearning, seeking . . . something.

Ignore it, Mel. You've got dry rot to deal with.

What does it say about my life when *rot* was a pleas-
t alternative?

ABOUT THE AUTHOR

Juliet Blackwell is the pseudonym for a mystery author who also writes the Haunted Home Renovation series and, together with her sister, wrote the Art Lover's Mystery series. The first in that series, *Feint of Art*, was nominated for an Agatha Award for Best First Novel. She also writes the Haunted Home Renovation mystery series. Juliet's lifelong interest in the paranormal world was triggered when her favorite aunt visited and read her fortune—with startling results. As an anthropologist, the author studied systems of spirituality, magic, and health across cultures and throughout history. She currently resides in a happily haunted house in Oakland, California.

CONNECT ONLINE

www.julietblackwell.net
facebook.com/julietblackwellauthor
twitter.com/julietblackwell